#4

MY BOYFRIEND IS A MONSTER

Under His Spell

OR

ELF POSSESSED

OR

LOVE AND DUST

OR

MY BOYFRIEND IS A FAERIE

MARIE P. CROALL

Illustrated by HYEONDO PARK

GRAPHIC UNIVERSE™ · MINNEAPOLIS · NEW YORK

STORY BY
MARIE P. CROALL

ILLUSTRATIONS BY
HYEONDO PARK

LETTERING BY
ZACK GIACCONGO

Graphic Universe™
A division of Lerner Publishing Group, Inc.
241 First Avenue North
Minneapolis, MN 55401 U.S.A.

Website address: www.lernerbooks.com

Main body text set in GFY Jeanna. Typeface provided by The Chank Company.

Library of Congress Cataloging-in-Publication Data

Croall, Marie P.
     Under his spell / by Marie P. Croall ; illustrated by Hyeondo Park.
        p.   cm. — (My boyfriend is a monster ; #4)
     Summary: Bethany Farmer cares more about soccer than romance until transfer student Allein shows up, but after joining him in his battle to maintain control of the throne of Faerie, she must decide to give up the mortal world for him or ask him to give up his immortality.
     ISBN: 978–0–7613–5602–8 (lib. bdg. : alk. paper)
     1. Graphic novels. [1. Graphic novels. 2. Fairies—Fiction. 3. Dating (Social customs)—Fiction. 4. High schools—Fiction. 5. Schools—Fiction. 6. Soccer—Fiction.] I. Park, Hyeondo, ill. II. Title.
PZ7.7.C76Und 2011
741.5'973—dc22   2010035201

Manufactured in the United States of America
1 – BC – 7/15/11

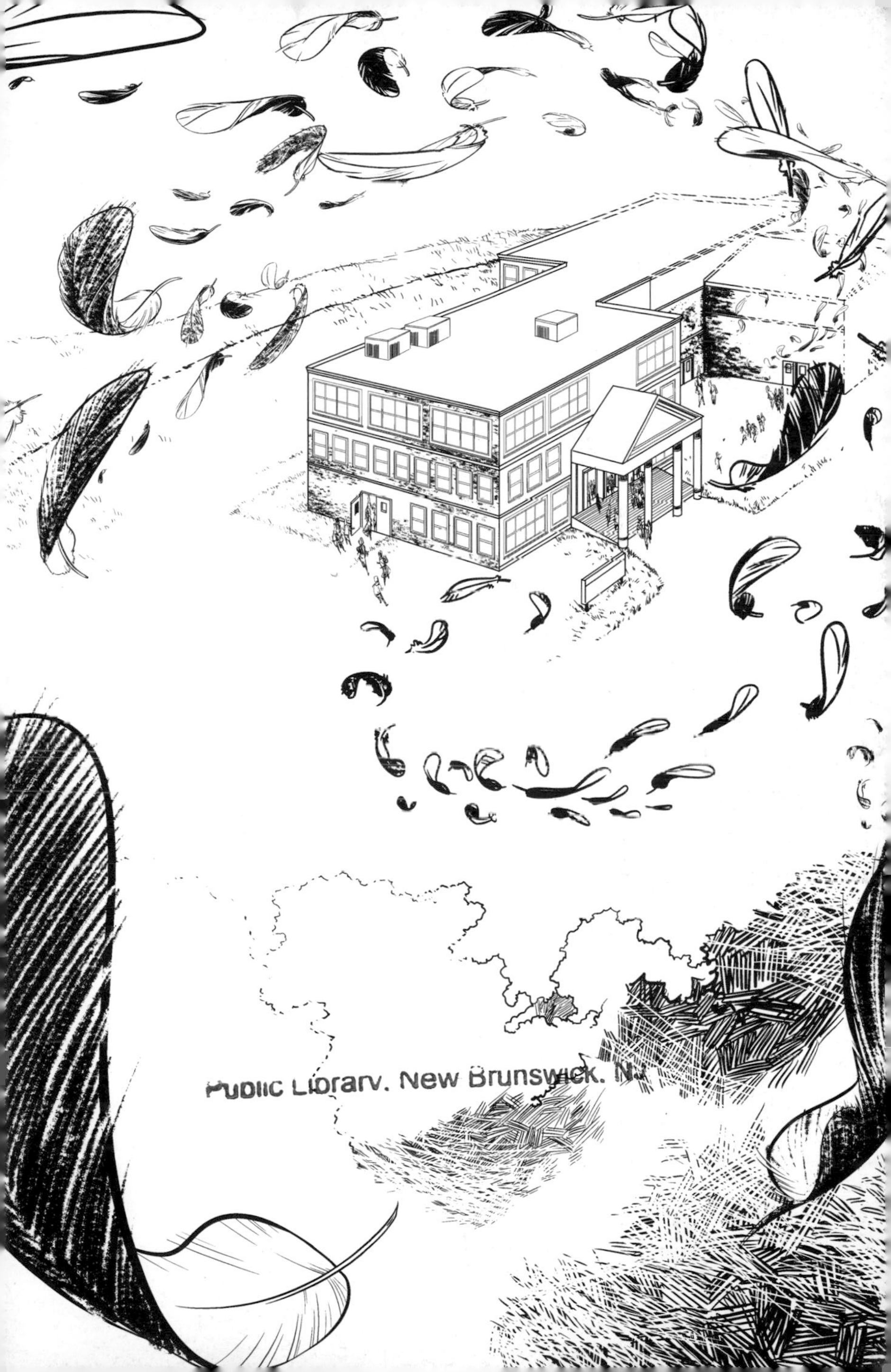

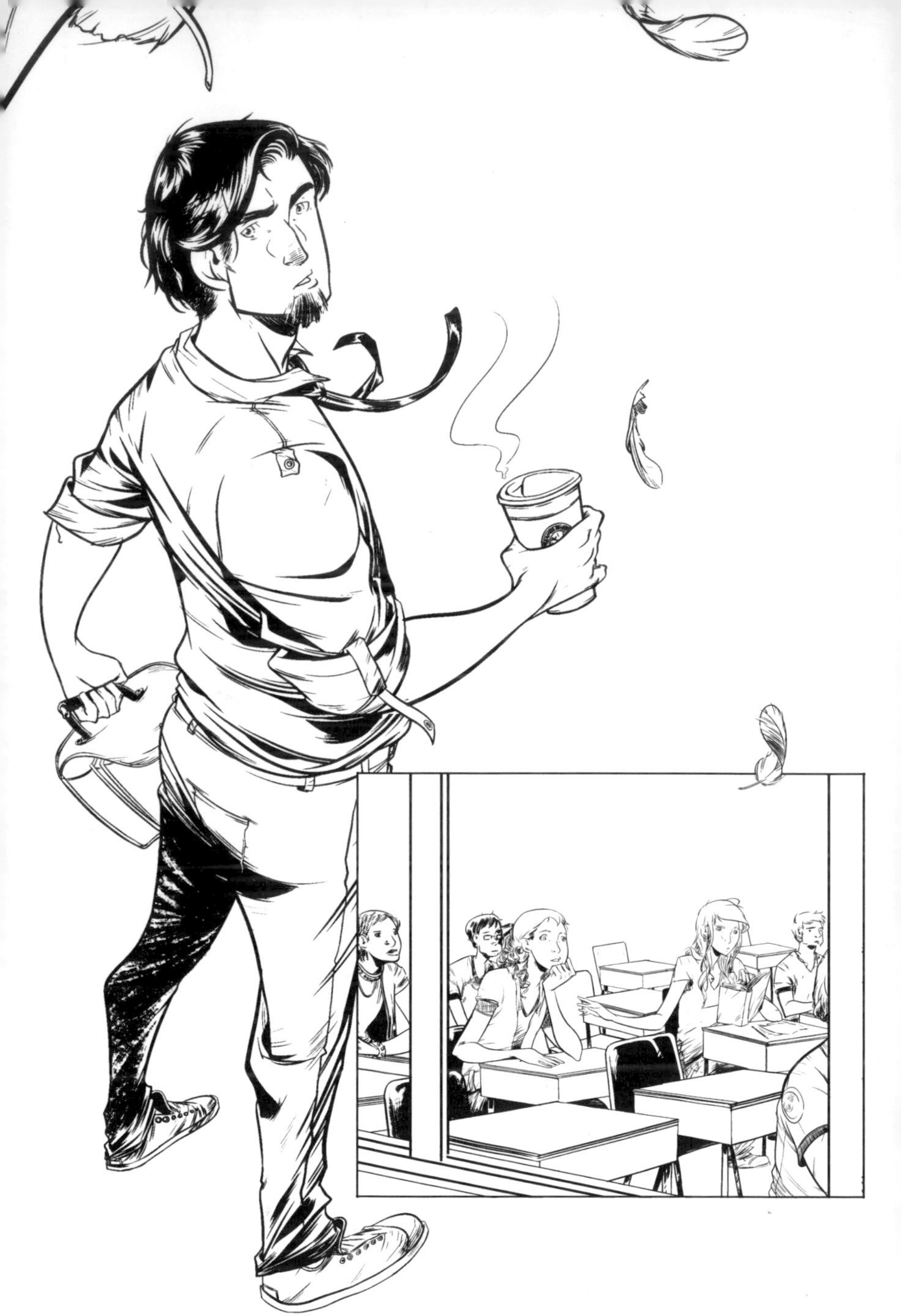

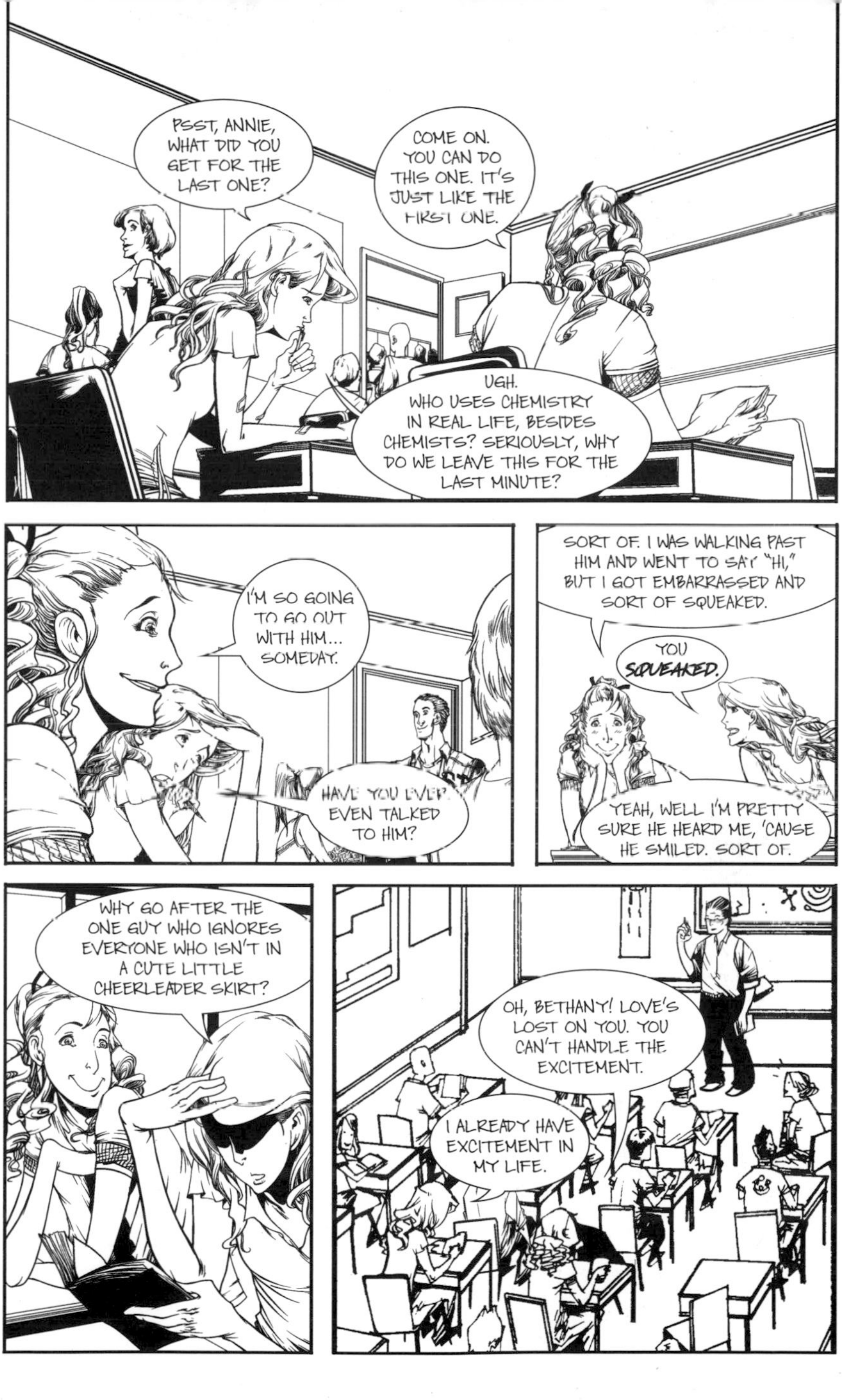
PSST, ANNIE, WHAT DID YOU GET FOR THE LAST ONE?
COME ON. YOU CAN DO THIS ONE. IT'S JUST LIKE THE FIRST ONE.
UGH. WHO USES CHEMISTRY IN REAL LIFE, BESIDES CHEMISTS? SERIOUSLY, WHY DO WE LEAVE THIS FOR THE LAST MINUTE?
I'M SO GOING TO GO OUT WITH HIM... SOMEDAY.
HAVE YOU EVER EVEN TALKED TO HIM?
SORT OF. I WAS WALKING PAST HIM AND WENT TO SAY "HI," BUT I GOT EMBARRASSED AND SORT OF SQUEAKED.
YOU SQUEAKED.
YEAH, WELL I'M PRETTY SURE HE HEARD ME, 'CAUSE HE SMILED. SORT OF.
WHY GO AFTER THE ONE GUY WHO IGNORES EVERYONE WHO ISN'T IN A CUTE LITTLE CHEERLEADER SKIRT?
OH, BETHANY! LOVE'S LOST ON YOU. YOU CAN'T HANDLE THE EXCITEMENT.
I ALREADY HAVE EXCITEMENT IN MY LIFE.

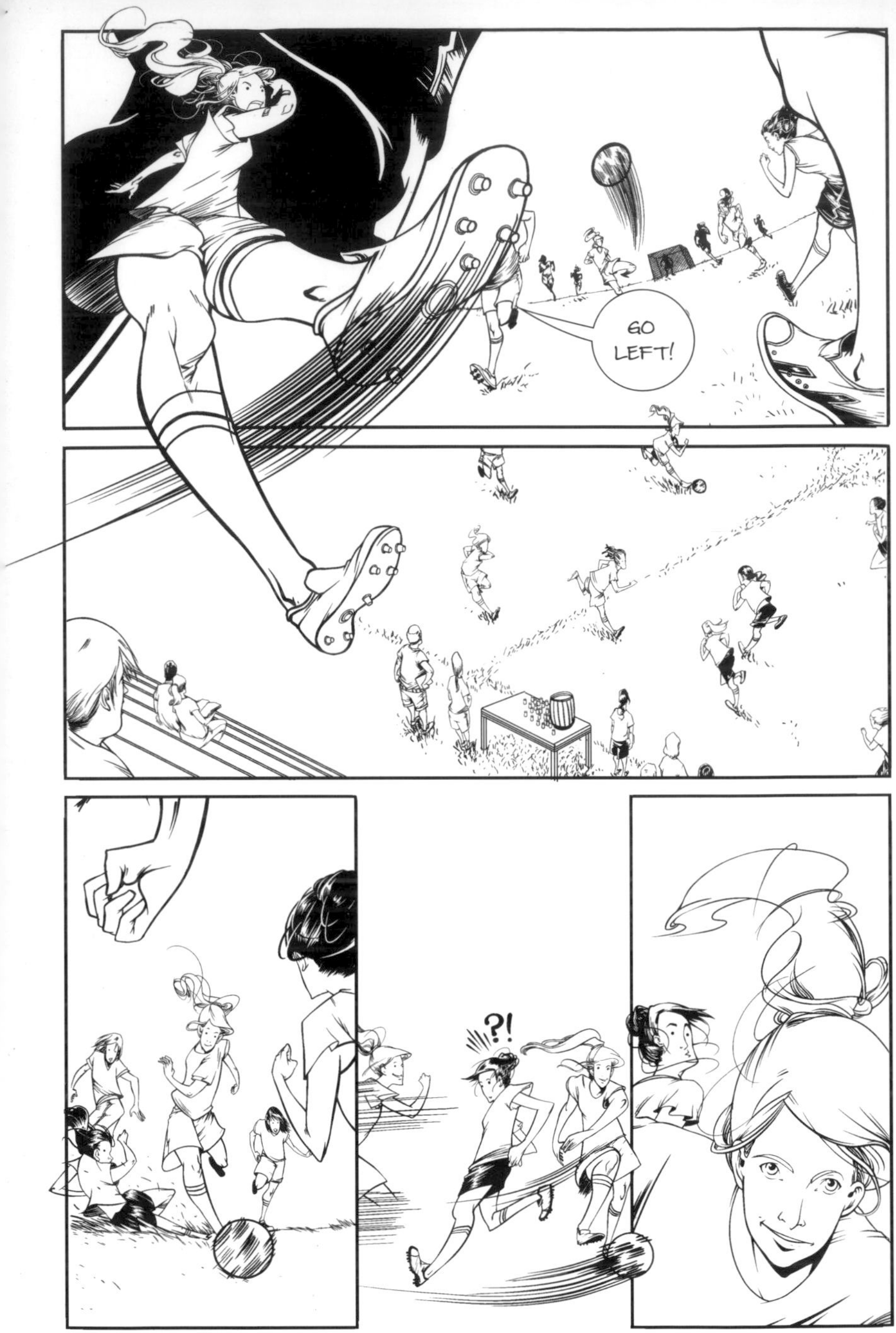
GO LEFT!
?!

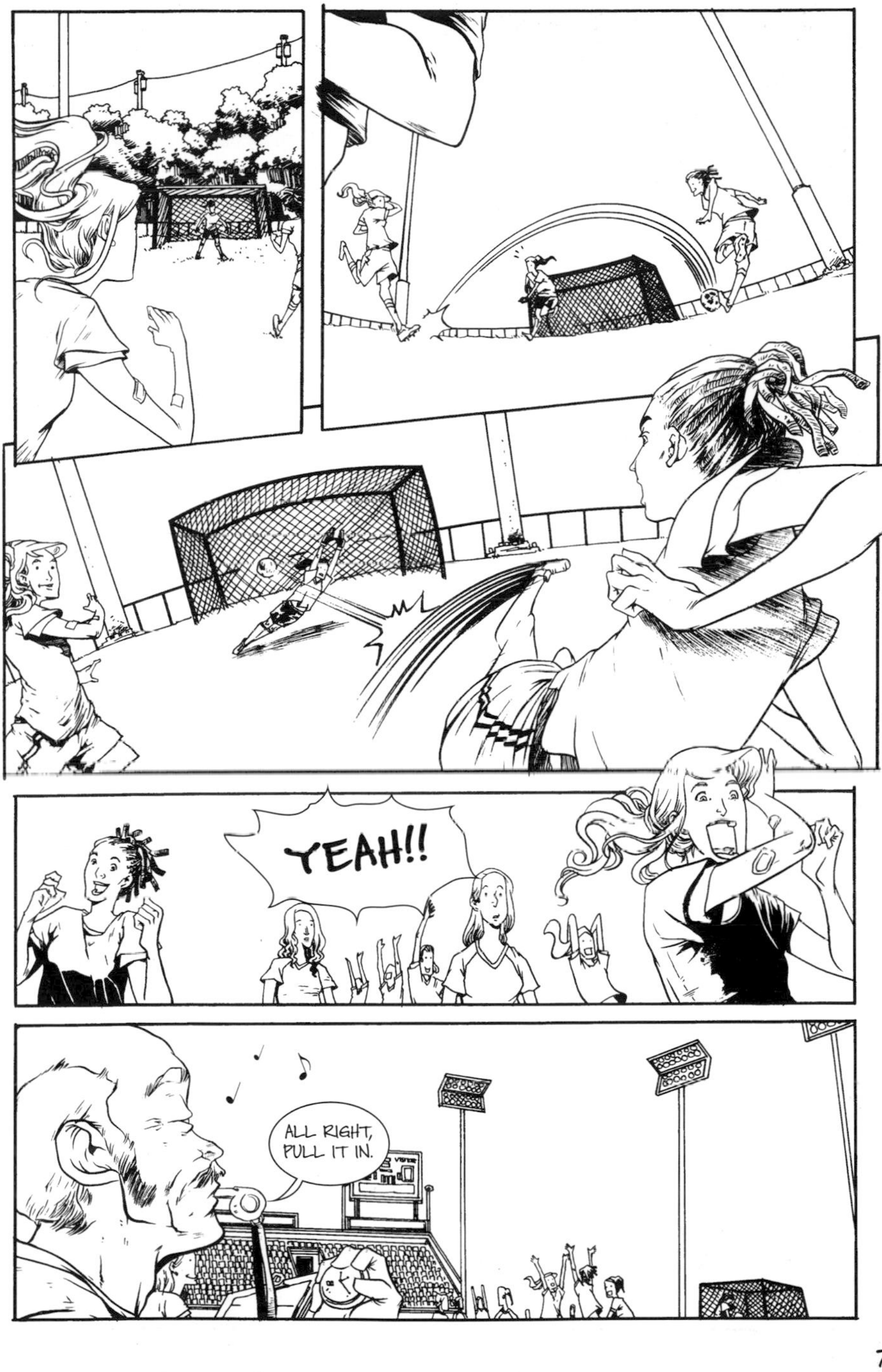
YEAH!!
ALL RIGHT, PULL IT IN.

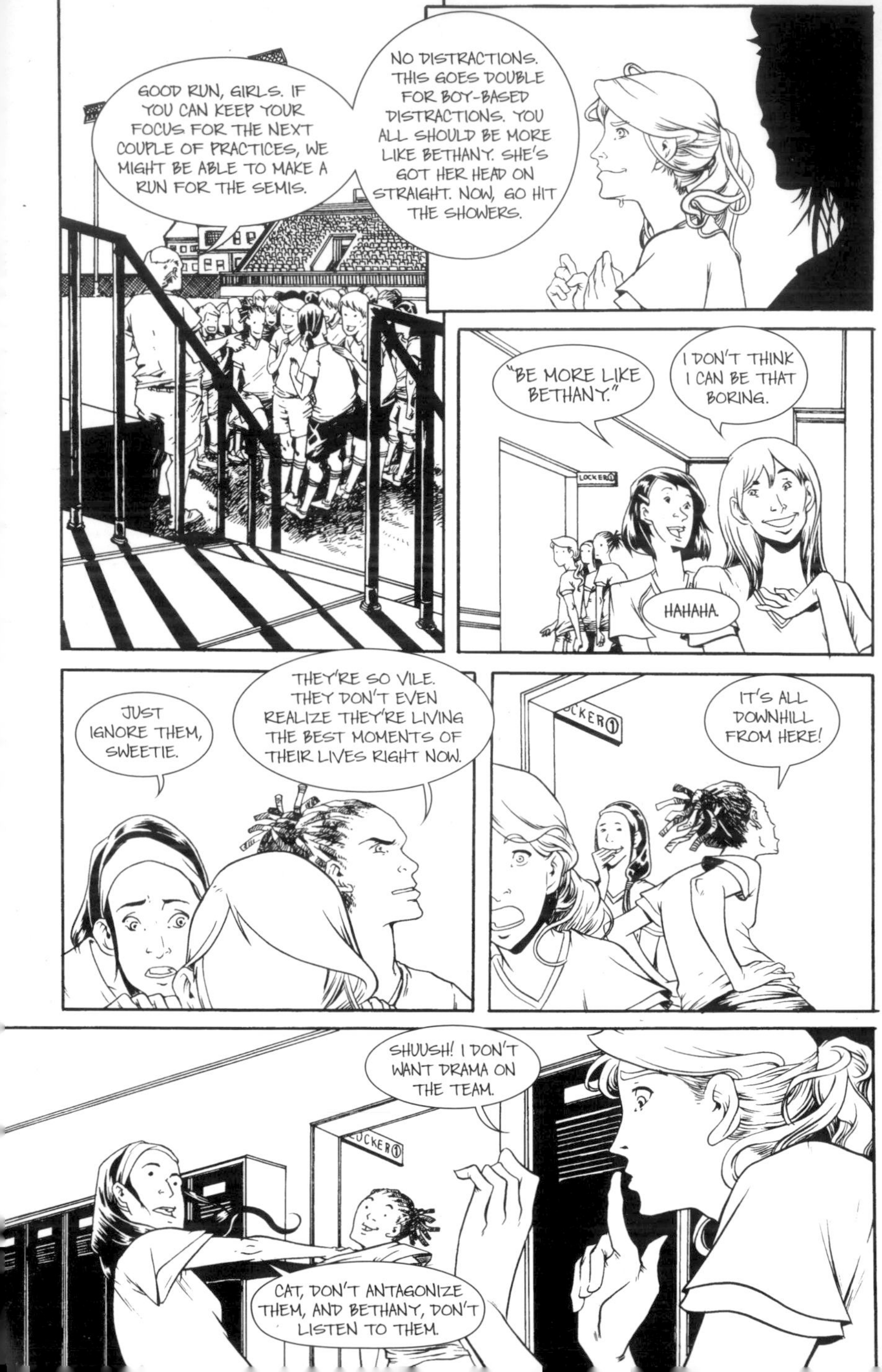
GOOD RUN, GIRLS. IF YOU CAN KEEP YOUR FOCUS FOR THE NEXT COUPLE OF PRACTICES, WE MIGHT BE ABLE TO MAKE A RUN FOR THE SEMIS.
NO DISTRACTIONS. THIS GOES DOUBLE FOR BOY-BASED DISTRACTIONS. YOU ALL SHOULD BE MORE LIKE BETHANY. SHE'S GOT HER HEAD ON STRAIGHT. NOW, GO HIT THE SHOWERS.
"BE MORE LIKE BETHANY."
I DON'T THINK I CAN BE THAT BORING.
LOCKER①
HAHAHA.
JUST IGNORE THEM, SWEETIE.
THEY'RE SO VILE. THEY DON'T EVEN REALIZE THEY'RE LIVING THE BEST MOMENTS OF THEIR LIVES RIGHT NOW.
LOCKER①
IT'S ALL DOWNHILL FROM HERE!
SHUUSH! I DON'T WANT DRAMA ON THE TEAM.
LOCKER①
CAT, DON'T ANTAGONIZE THEM, AND BETHANY, DON'T LISTEN TO THEM.

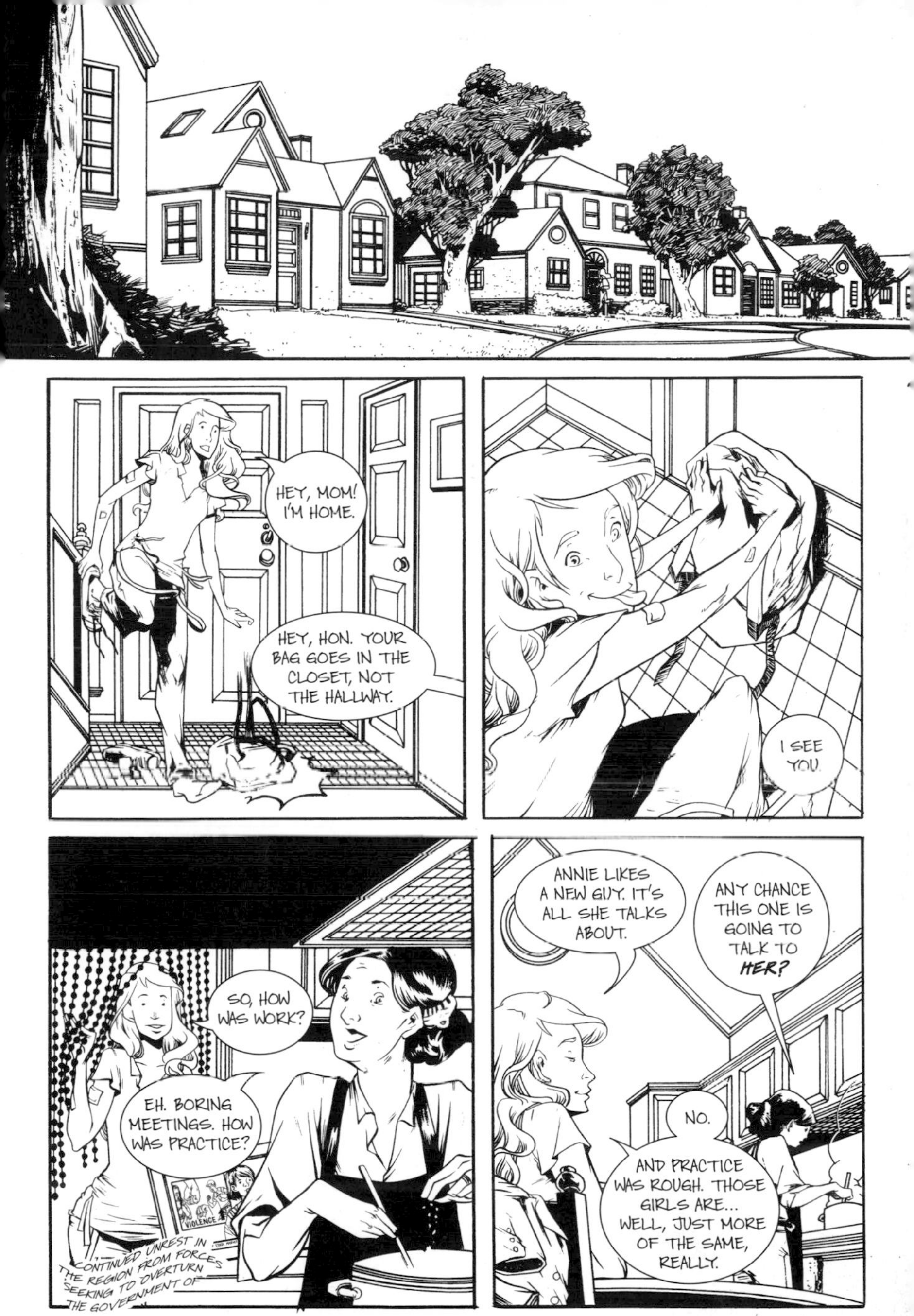
HEY, MOM! I'M HOME.
HEY, HON. YOUR BAG GOES IN THE CLOSET, NOT THE HALLWAY.
I SEE YOU.
SO, HOW WAS WORK?
EH. BORING MEETINGS. HOW WAS PRACTICE?
VIOLENCE
CONTINUED UNREST IN THE REGION FROM FORCES SEEKING TO OVERTURN THE GOVERNMENT OF
ANNIE LIKES A NEW GUY. IT'S ALL SHE TALKS ABOUT.
ANY CHANCE THIS ONE IS GOING TO TALK TO HER?
NO.
AND PRACTICE WAS ROUGH. THOSE GIRLS ARE... WELL, JUST MORE OF THE SAME, REALLY.

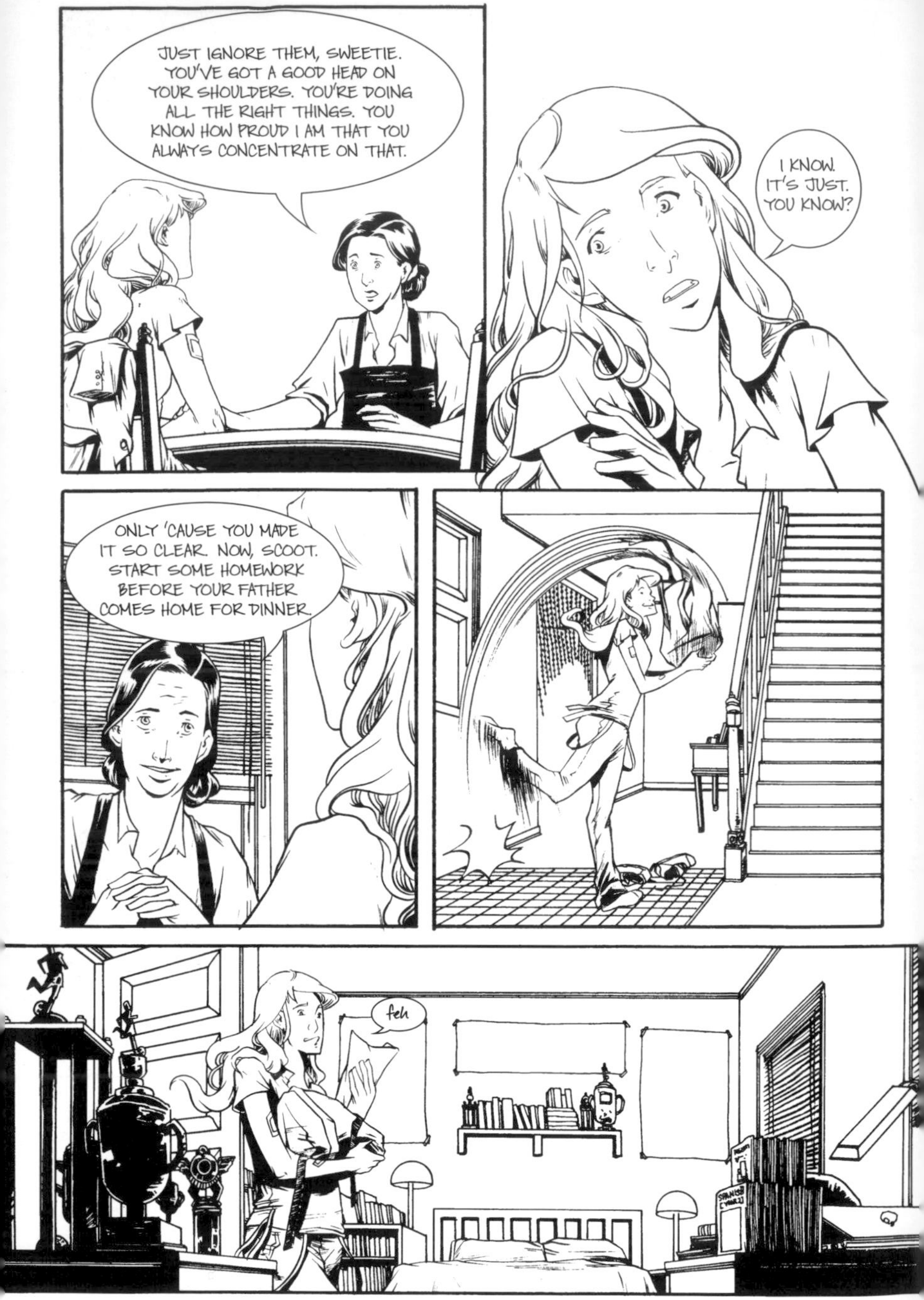
JUST IGNORE THEM, SWEETIE. YOU'VE GOT A GOOD HEAD ON YOUR SHOULDERS. YOU'RE DOING ALL THE RIGHT THINGS. YOU KNOW HOW PROUD I AM THAT YOU ALWAYS CONCENTRATE ON THAT.
I KNOW. IT'S JUST. YOU KNOW?
ONLY 'CAUSE YOU MADE IT SO CLEAR. NOW, SCOOT. START SOME HOMEWORK BEFORE YOUR FATHER COMES HOME FOR DINNER.
feh

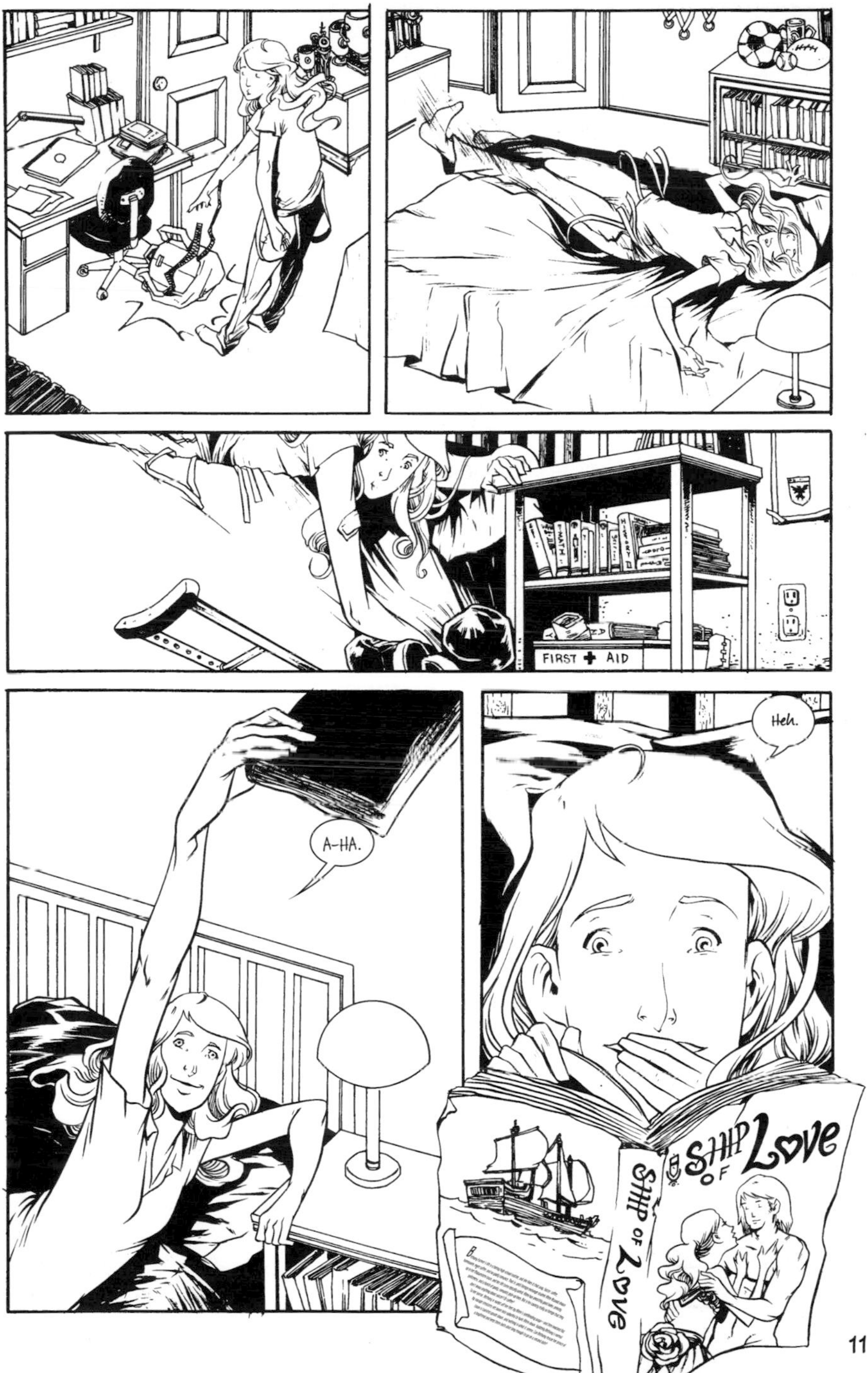

FIRST + AID
A-HA.
Heh.
SHIP OF LOVE
SHIP OF LOVE

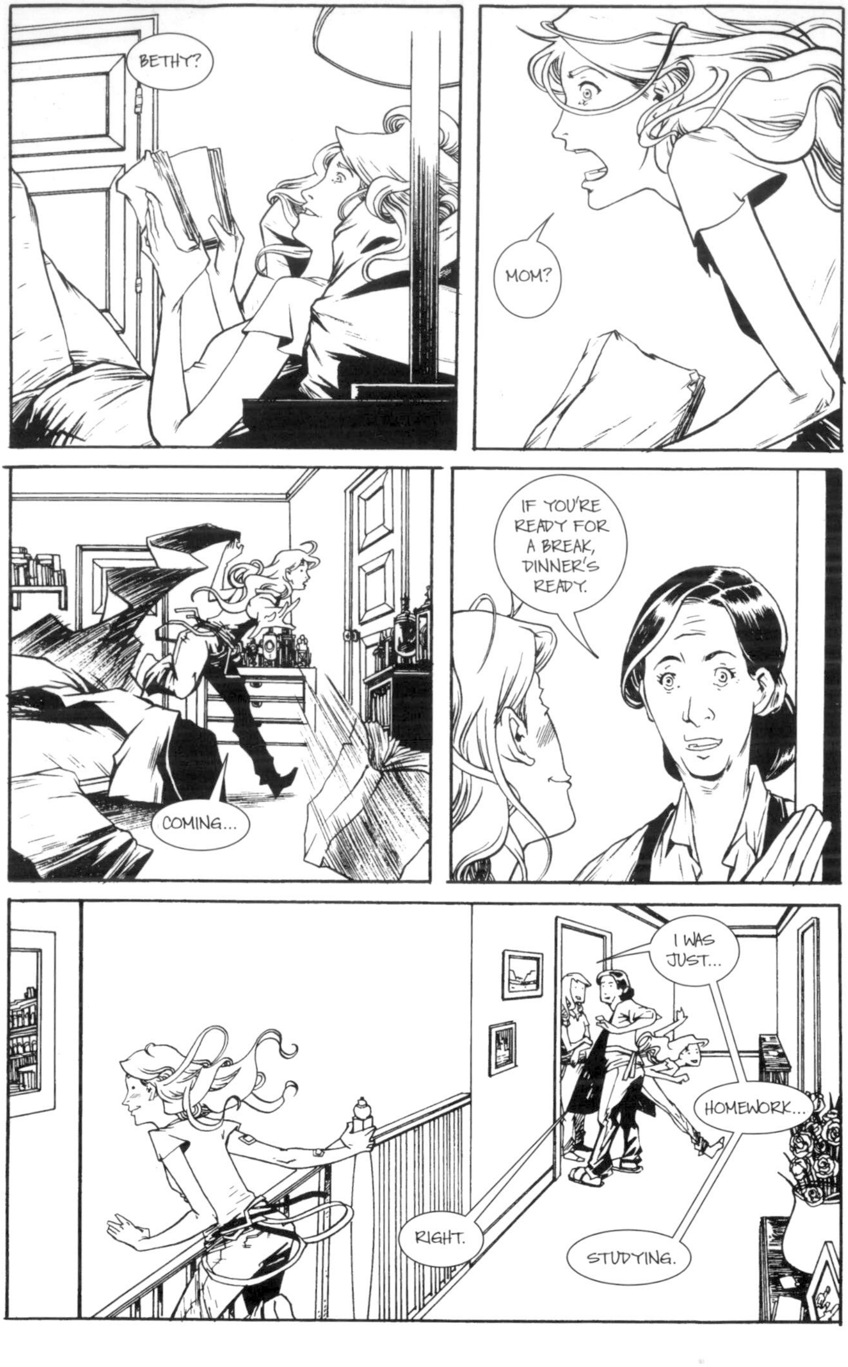
BETHY?
MOM?
COMING...
IF YOU'RE READY FOR A BREAK, DINNER'S READY.
I WAS JUST...
HOMEWORK...
STUDYING.
RIGHT.

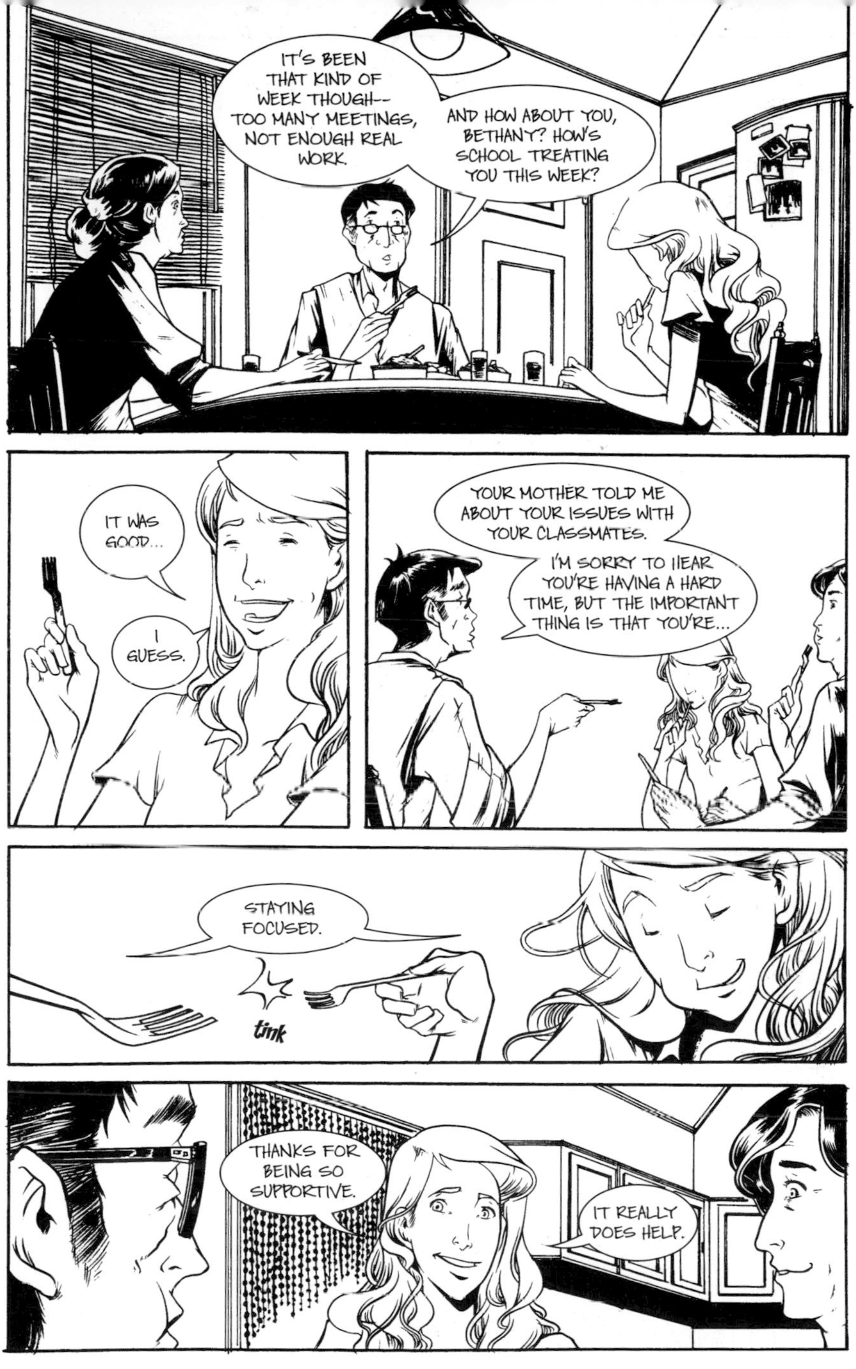
IT'S BEEN THAT KIND OF WEEK THOUGH-- TOO MANY MEETINGS, NOT ENOUGH REAL WORK.
AND HOW ABOUT YOU, BETHANY? HOW'S SCHOOL TREATING YOU THIS WEEK?
IT WAS GOOD...
I GUESS.
YOUR MOTHER TOLD ME ABOUT YOUR ISSUES WITH YOUR CLASSMATES.
I'M SORRY TO HEAR YOU'RE HAVING A HARD TIME, BUT THE IMPORTANT THING IS THAT YOU'RE...
STAYING FOCUSED.
tink
THANKS FOR BEING SO SUPPORTIVE.
IT REALLY DOES HELP.

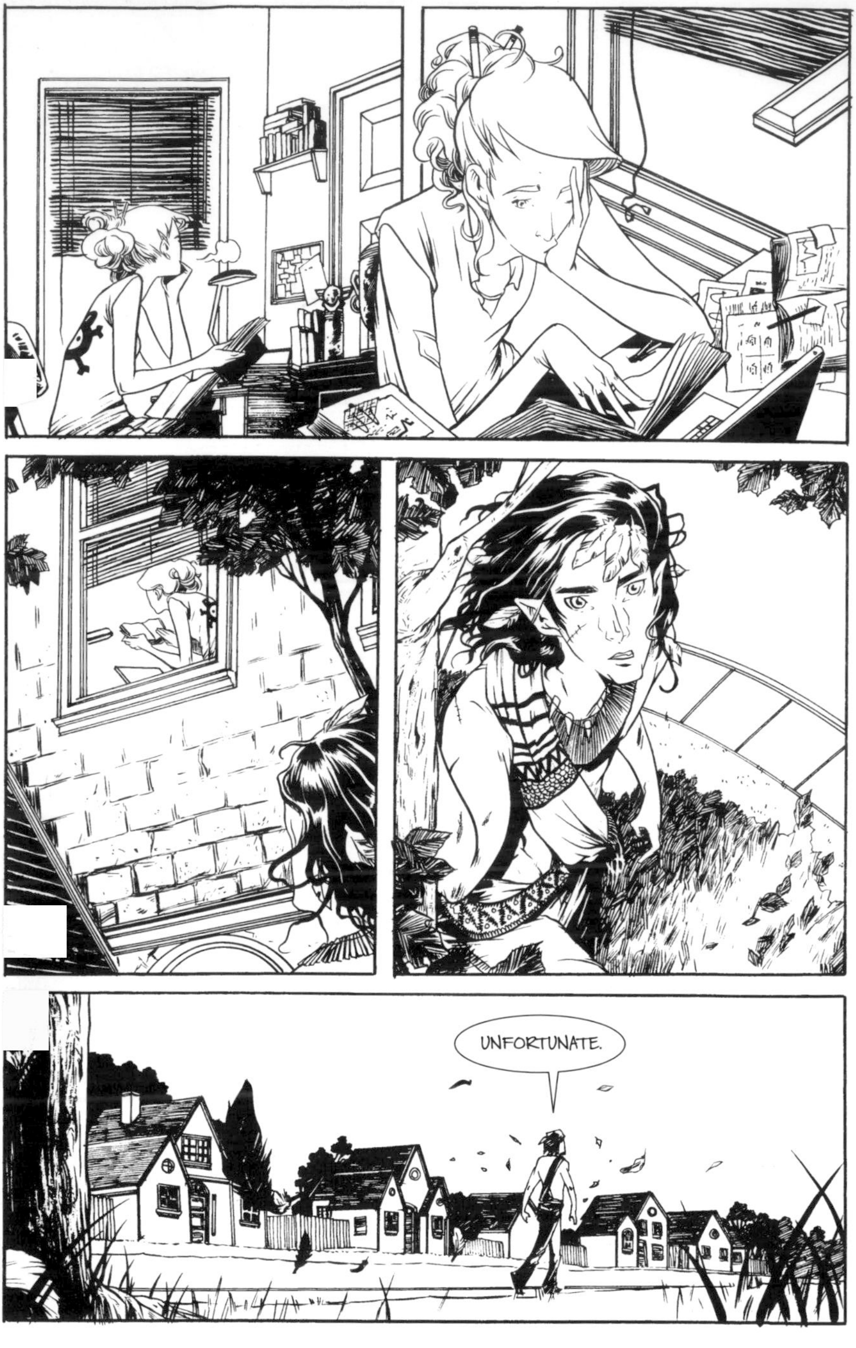
UNFORTUNATE.

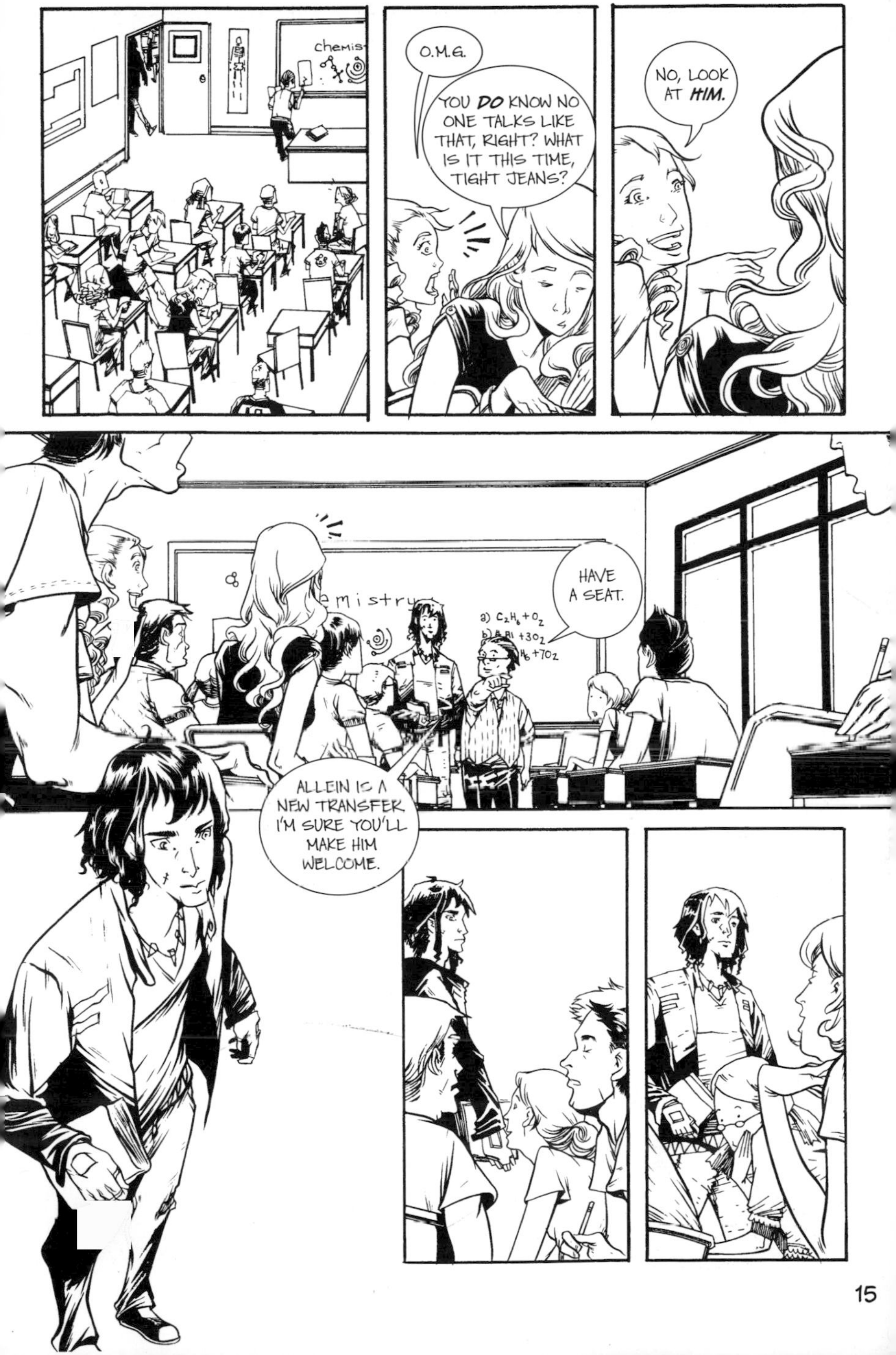
chemis
O.M.G.
YOU DO KNOW NO ONE TALKS LIKE THAT, RIGHT? WHAT IS IT THIS TIME, TIGHT JEANS?
NO, LOOK AT HIM.
emistry
HAVE A SEAT.
ALLEIN IS A NEW TRANSFER. I'M SURE YOU'LL MAKE HIM WELCOME.

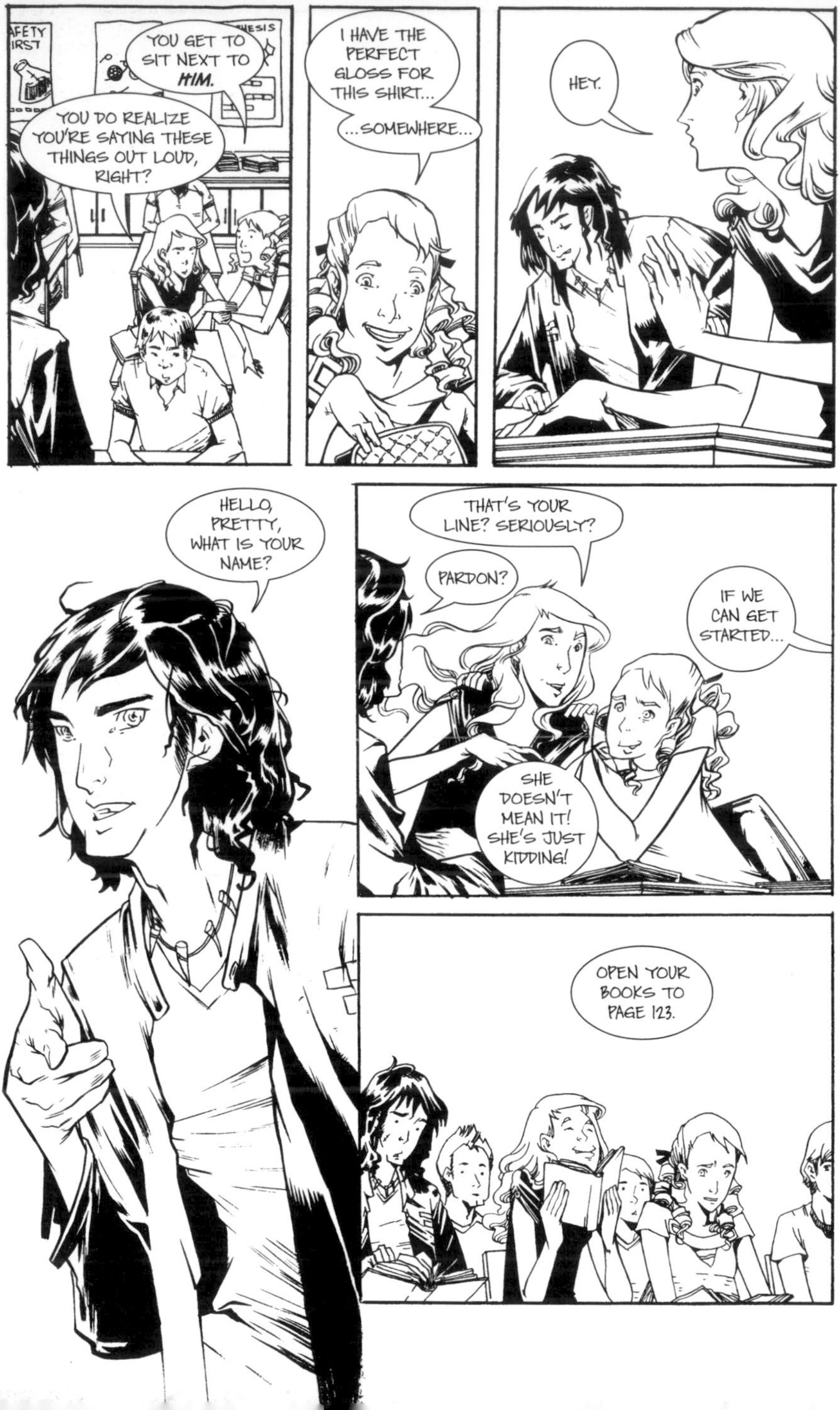
AFETY IRST
YOU GET TO SIT NEXT TO HIM.
YOU DO REALIZE YOU'RE SAYING THESE THINGS OUT LOUD, RIGHT?
I HAVE THE PERFECT GLOSS FOR THIS SHIRT...
...SOMEWHERE...
HEY.
HELLO, PRETTY, WHAT IS YOUR NAME?
THAT'S YOUR LINE? SERIOUSLY?
PARDON?
IF WE CAN GET STARTED...
SHE DOESN'T MEAN IT! SHE'S JUST KIDDING!
OPEN YOUR BOOKS TO PAGE 123.

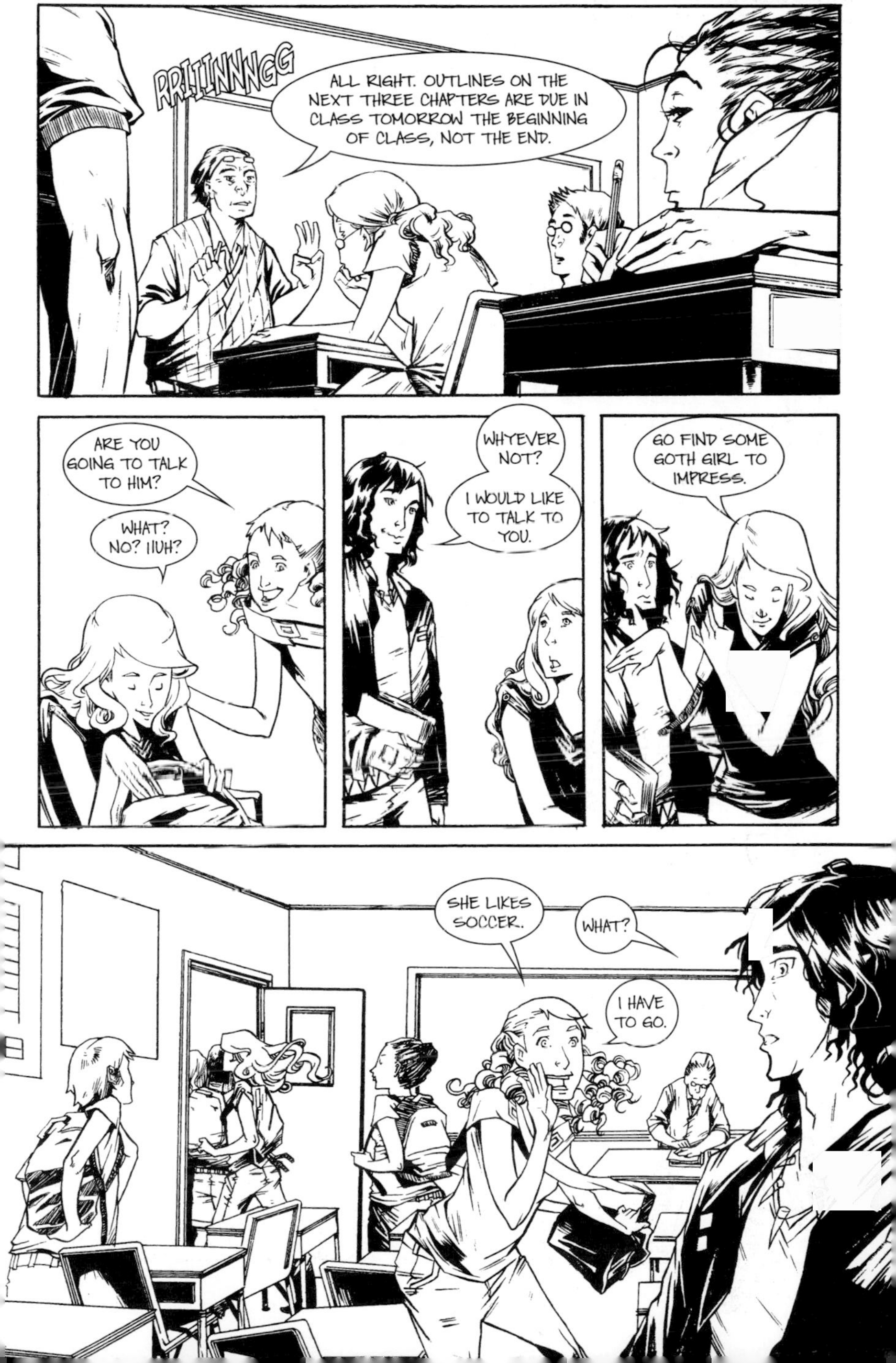
RRIIINNNGG
ALL RIGHT. OUTLINES ON THE NEXT THREE CHAPTERS ARE DUE IN CLASS TOMORROW THE BEGINNING OF CLASS, NOT THE END.
ARE YOU GOING TO TALK TO HIM?
WHAT? NO? HUH?
WHYEVER NOT?
I WOULD LIKE TO TALK TO YOU.
GO FIND SOME GOTH GIRL TO IMPRESS.
SHE LIKES SOCCER.
WHAT?
I HAVE TO GO.

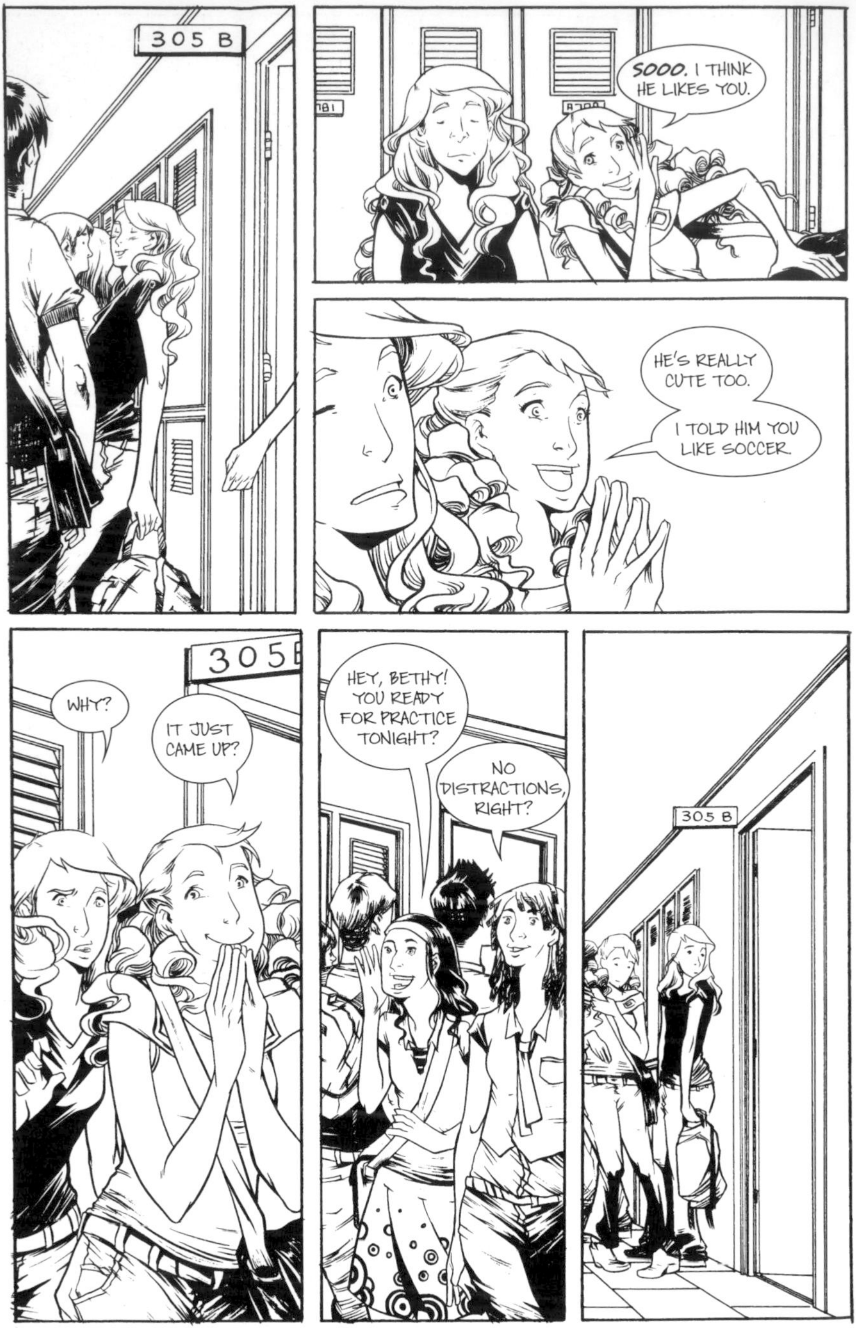
305 B
SOOO. I THINK HE LIKES YOU.
HE'S REALLY CUTE TOO.
I TOLD HIM YOU LIKE SOCCER.
305 B
WHY?
IT JUST CAME UP?
HEY, BETHY! YOU READY FOR PRACTICE TONIGHT?
NO DISTRACTIONS, RIGHT?
305 B

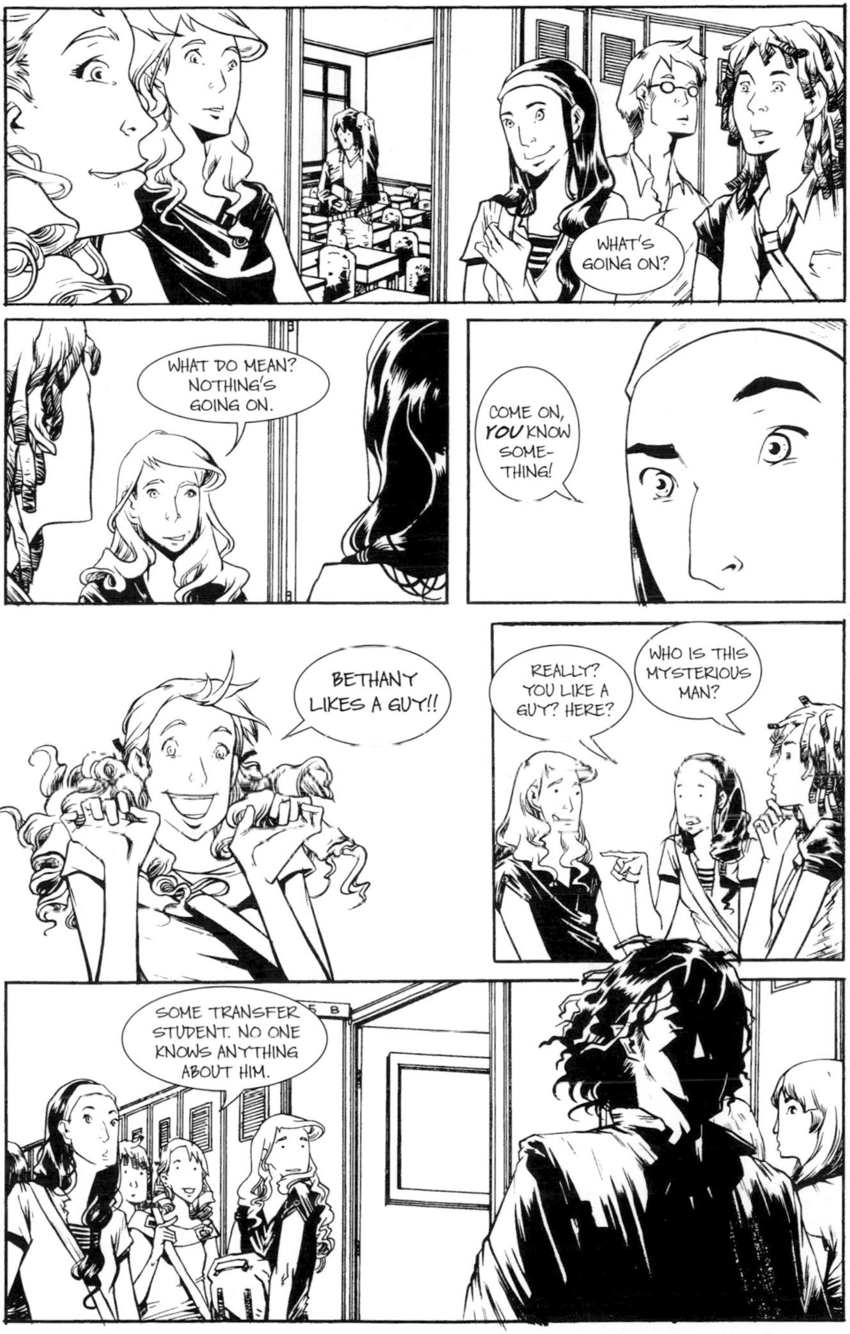
WHAT'S GOING ON?
WHAT DO MEAN? NOTHING'S GOING ON.
COME ON, YOU KNOW SOME-THING!
BETHANY LIKES A GUY!!
REALLY? YOU LIKE A GUY? HERE?
WHO IS THIS MYSTERIOUS MAN?
SOME TRANSFER STUDENT. NO ONE KNOWS ANYTHING ABOUT HIM.

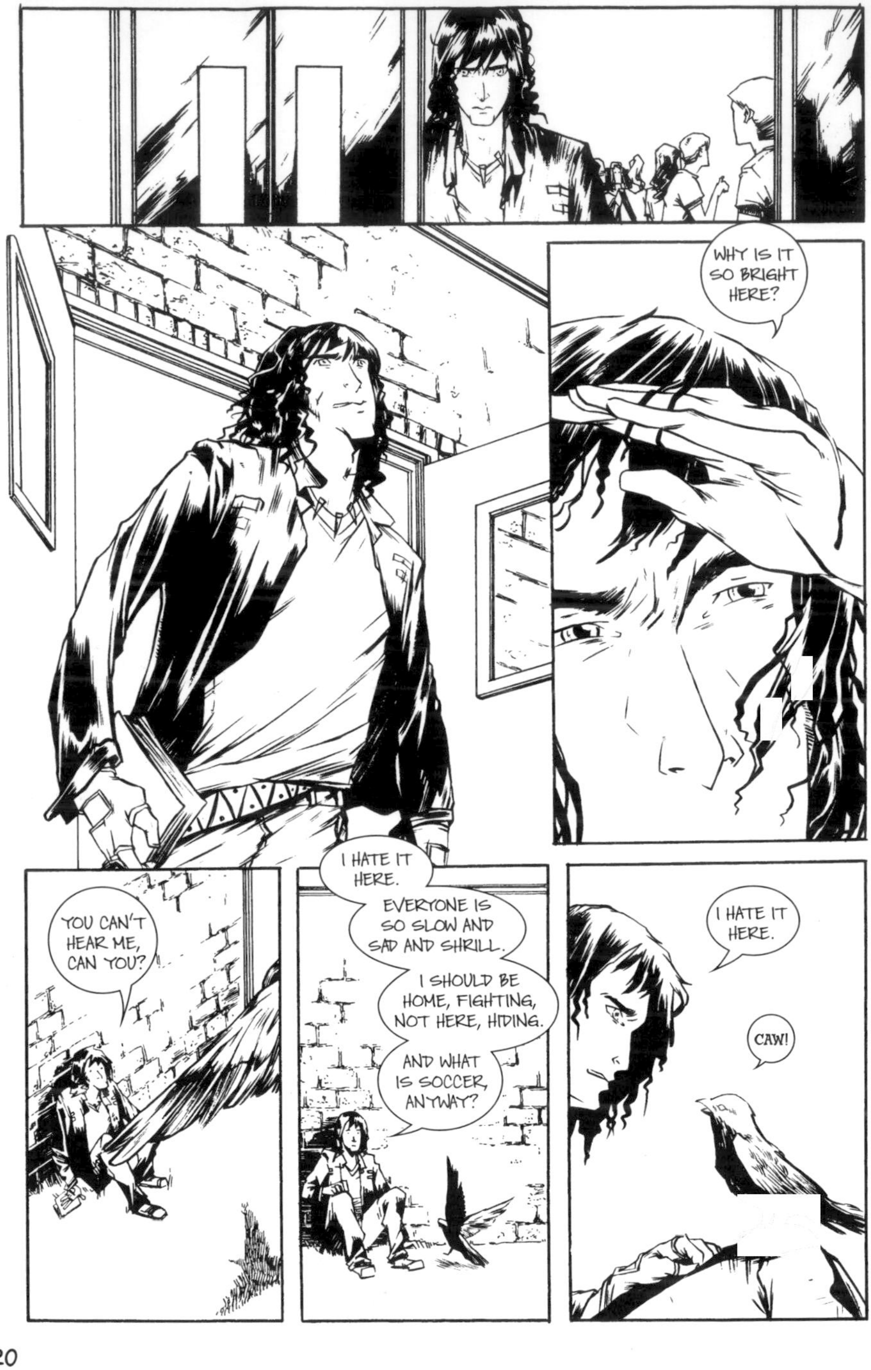
WHY IS IT SO BRIGHT HERE?
YOU CAN'T HEAR ME, CAN YOU?
I HATE IT HERE.
EVERYONE IS SO SLOW AND SAD AND SHRILL.
I SHOULD BE HOME, FIGHTING, NOT HERE, HIDING.
AND WHAT IS SOCCER, ANYWAY?
I HATE IT HERE.
CAW!

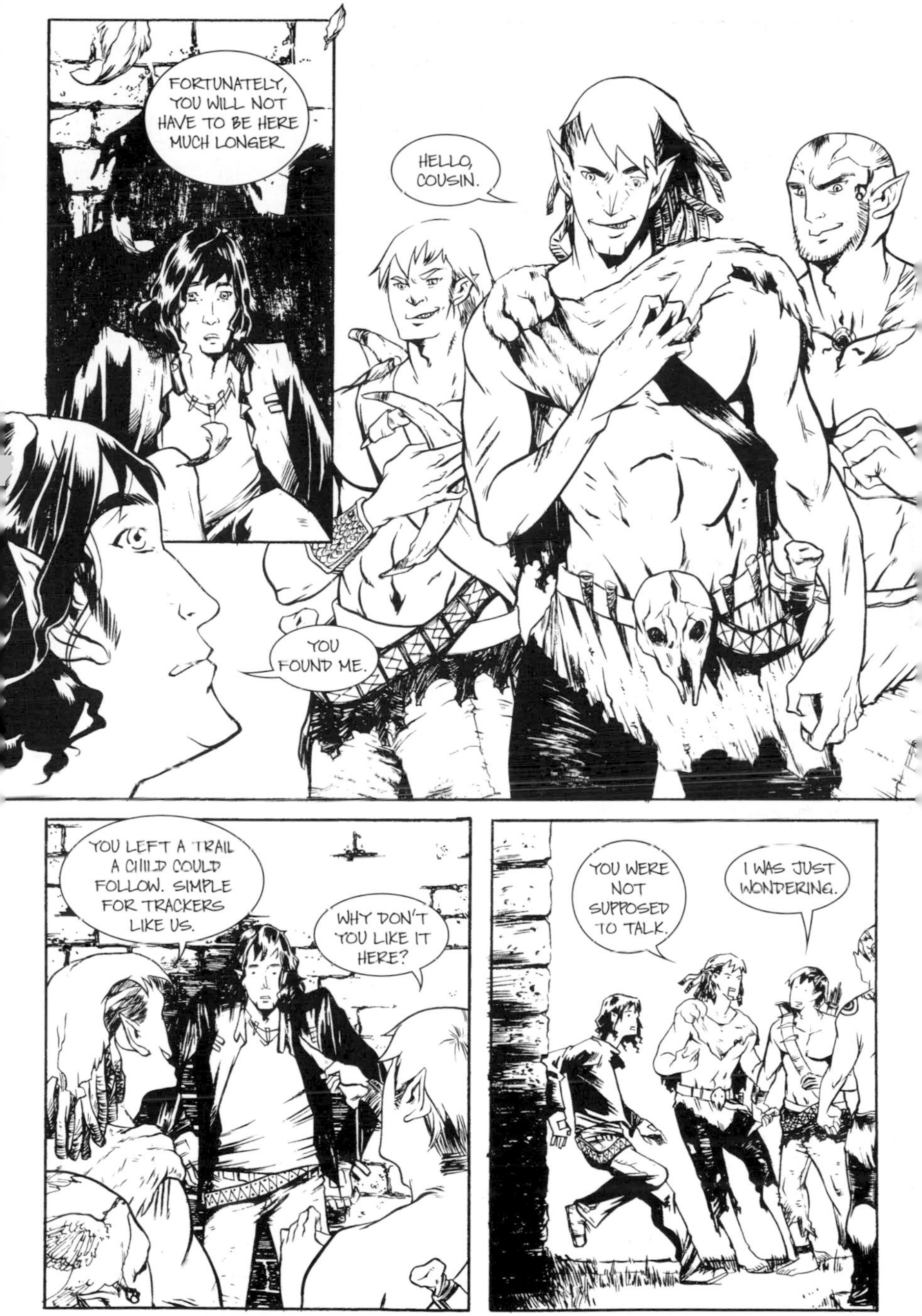
FORTUNATELY, YOU WILL NOT HAVE TO BE HERE MUCH LONGER.
HELLO, COUSIN.
YOU FOUND ME.
YOU LEFT A TRAIL A CHILD COULD FOLLOW. SIMPLE FOR TRACKERS LIKE US.
WHY DON'T YOU LIKE IT HERE?
YOU WERE NOT SUPPOSED TO TALK.
I WAS JUST WONDERING.

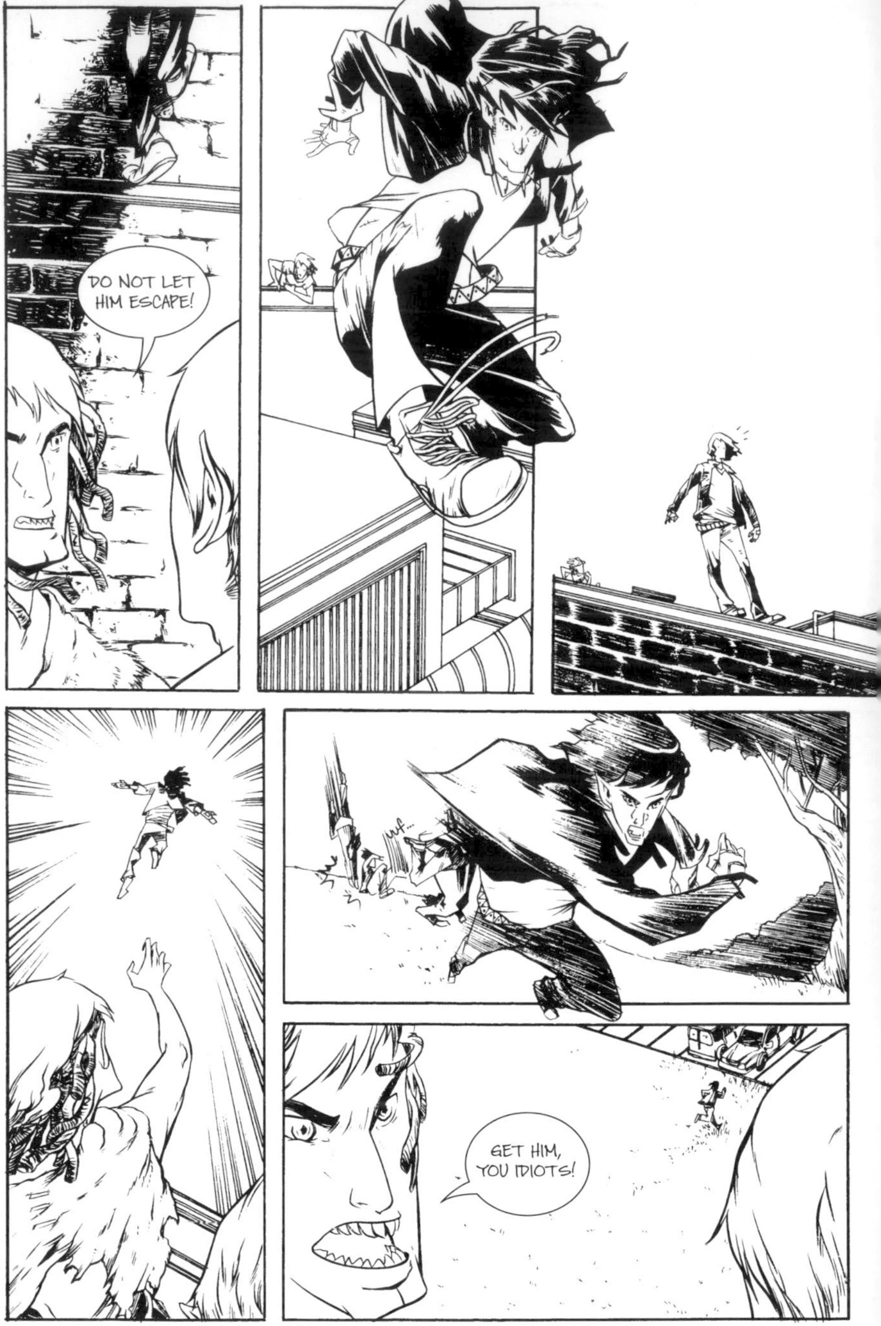
DO NOT LET HIM ESCAPE!
GET HIM, YOU IDIOTS!

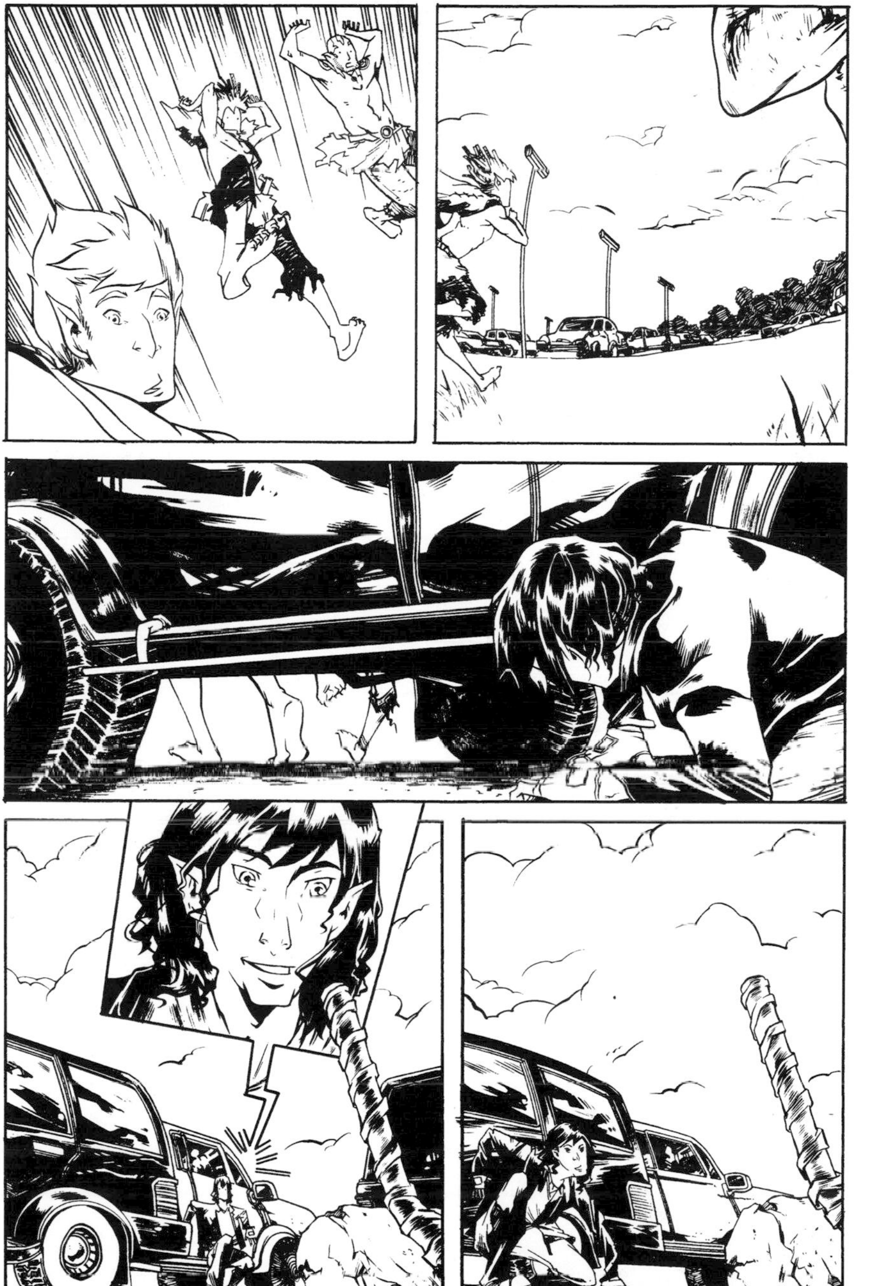

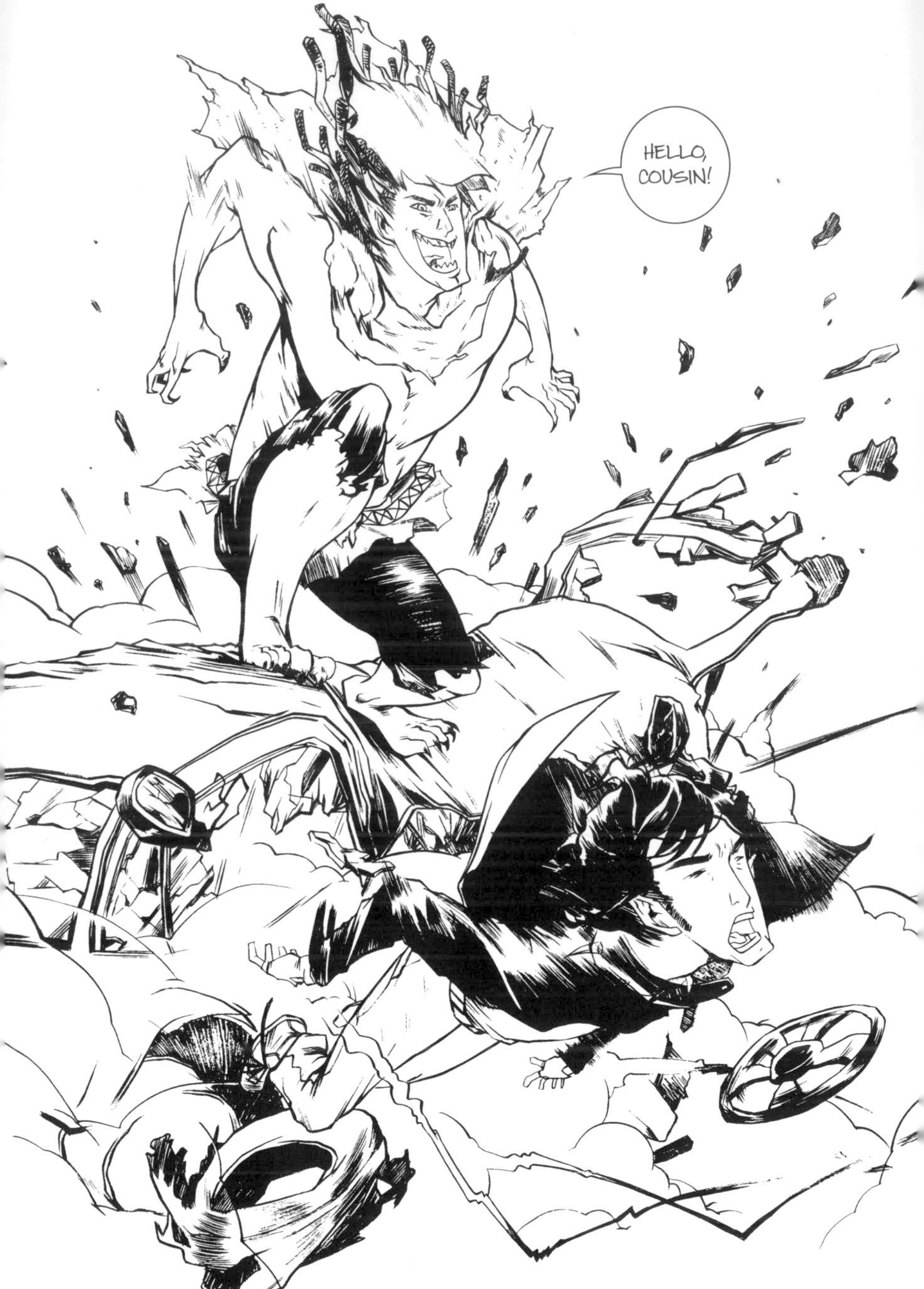
HELLO, COUSIN!

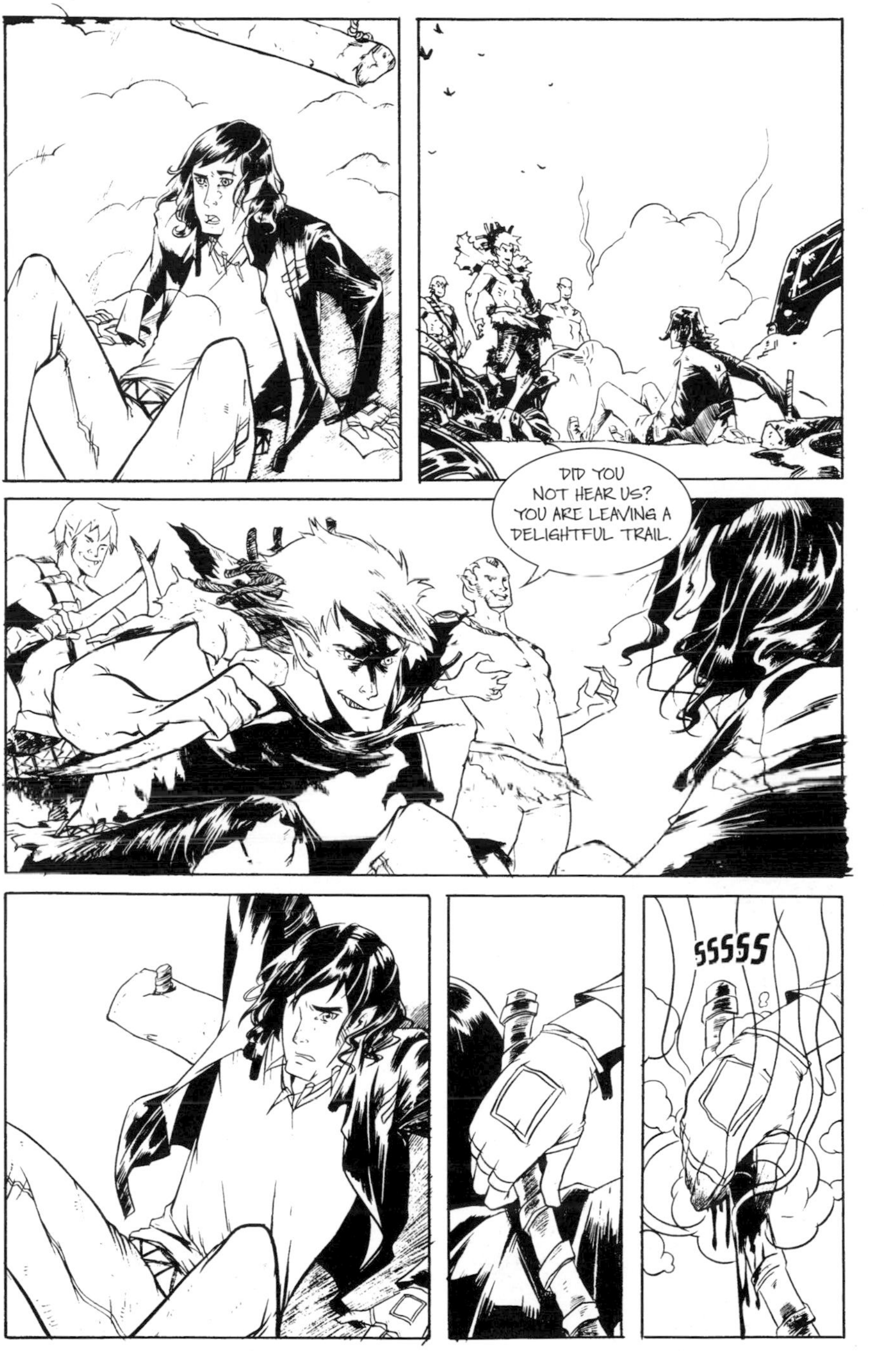
DID YOU NOT HEAR US? YOU ARE LEAVING A DELIGHTFUL TRAIL.
SSSSS

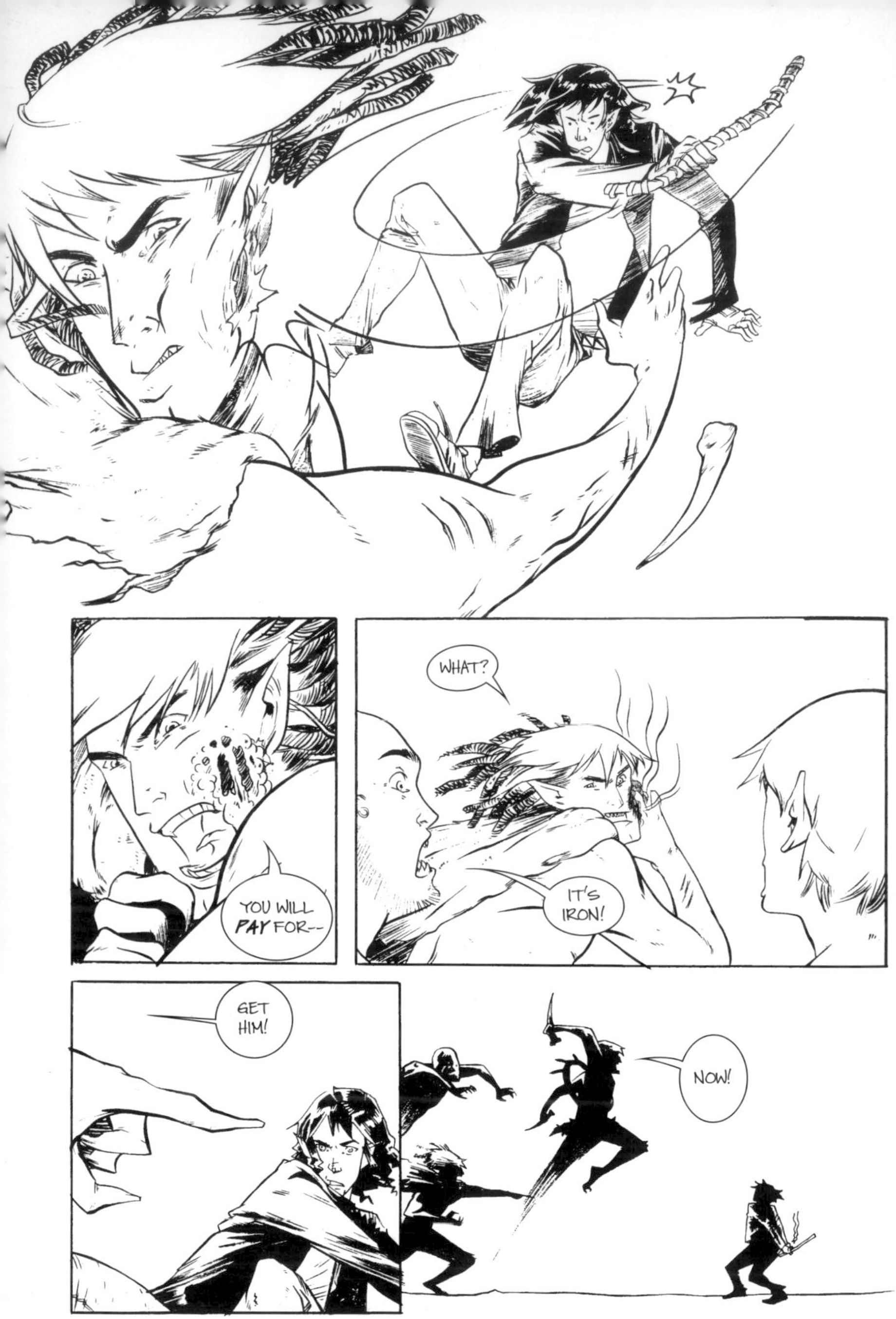
YOU WILL PAY FOR--
WHAT?
IT'S IRON!
GET HIM!
NOW!

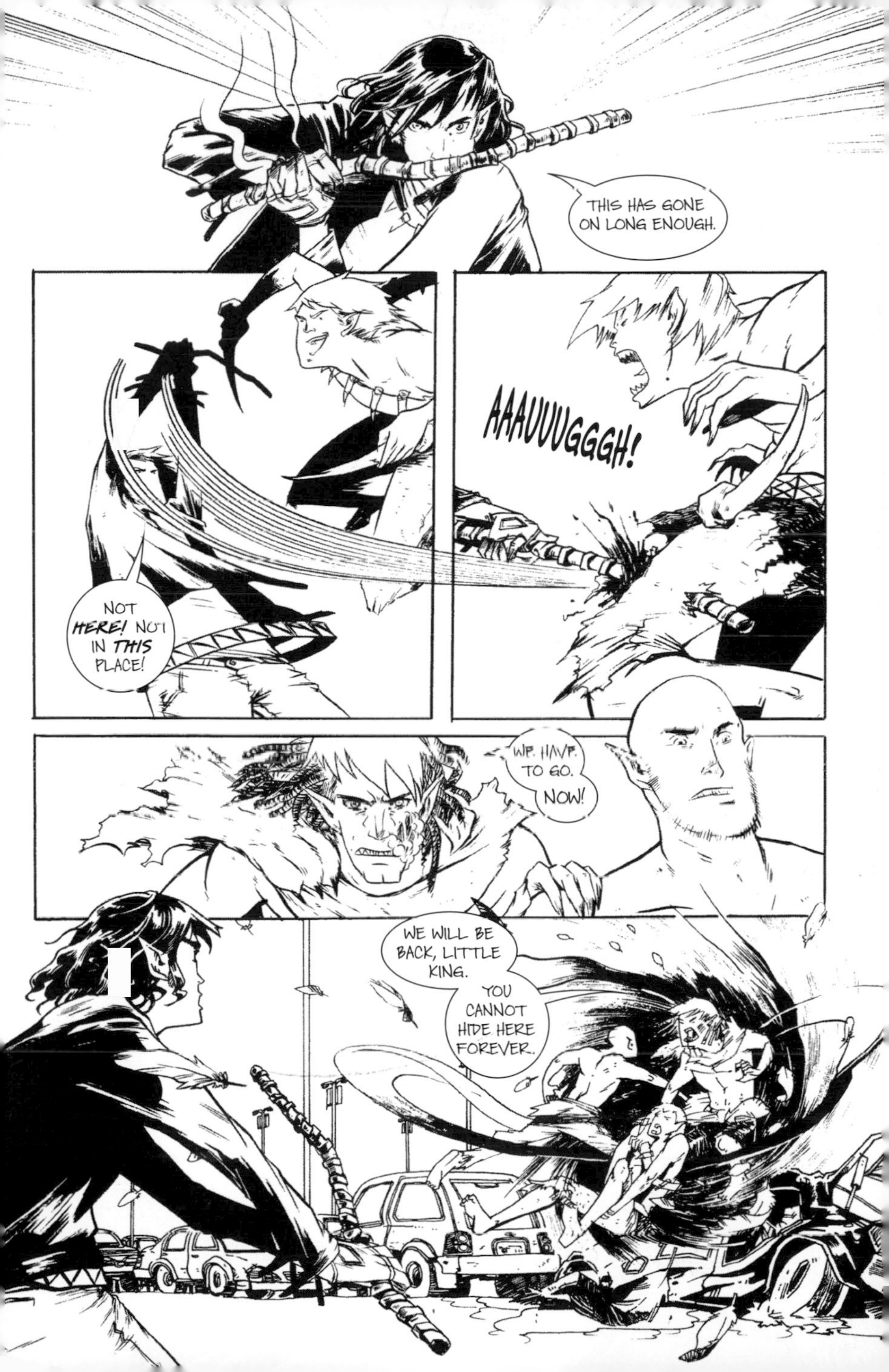
THIS HAS GONE ON LONG ENOUGH.
NOT HERE! NOT IN THIS PLACE!
AAAUUUGGGH!
WE HAVE TO GO. NOW!
WE WILL BE BACK, LITTLE KING.
YOU CANNOT HIDE HERE FOREVER.

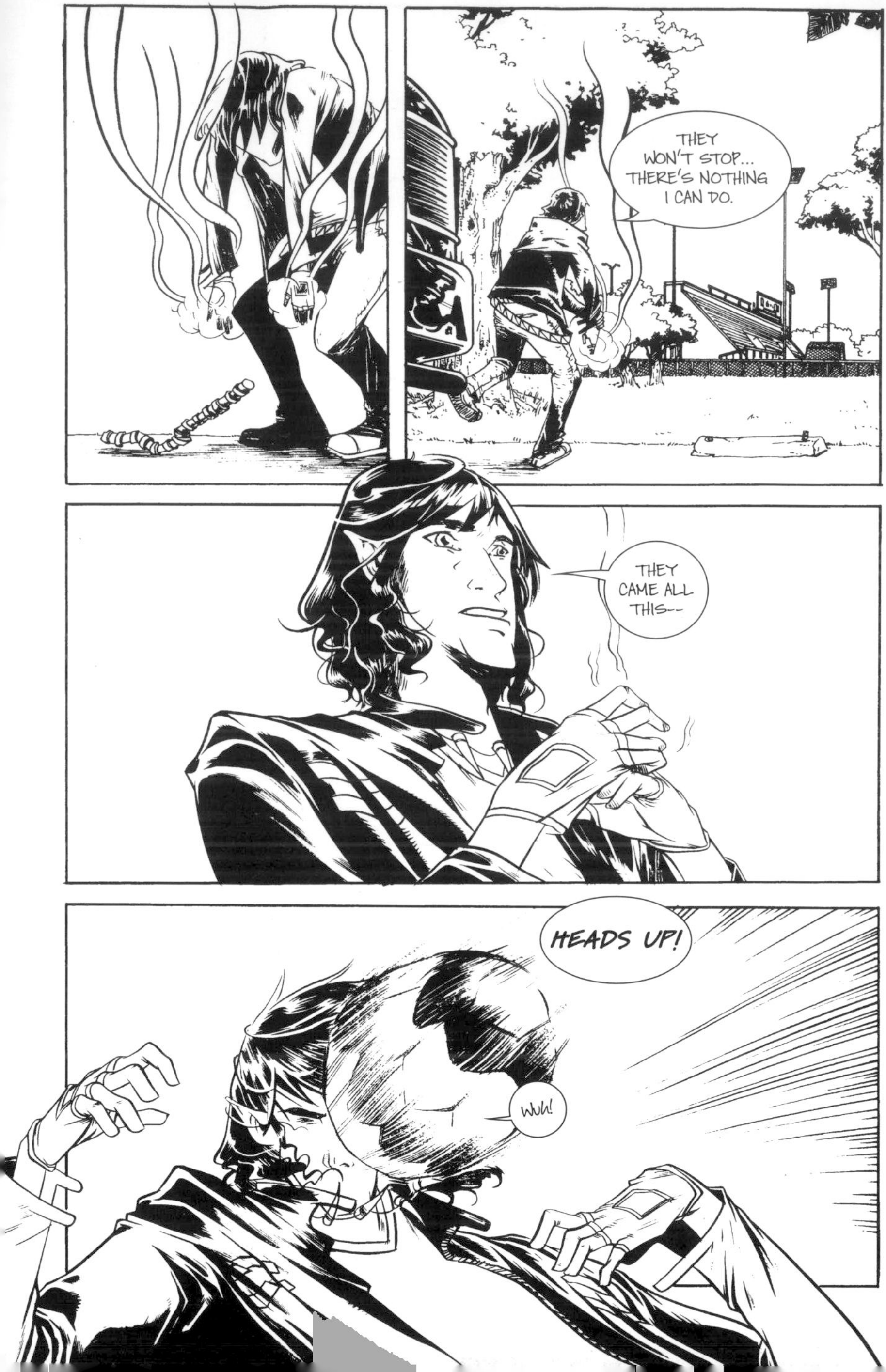
THEY WON'T STOP... THERE'S NOTHING I CAN DO.
THEY CAME ALL THIS--
HEADS UP!
WUH!

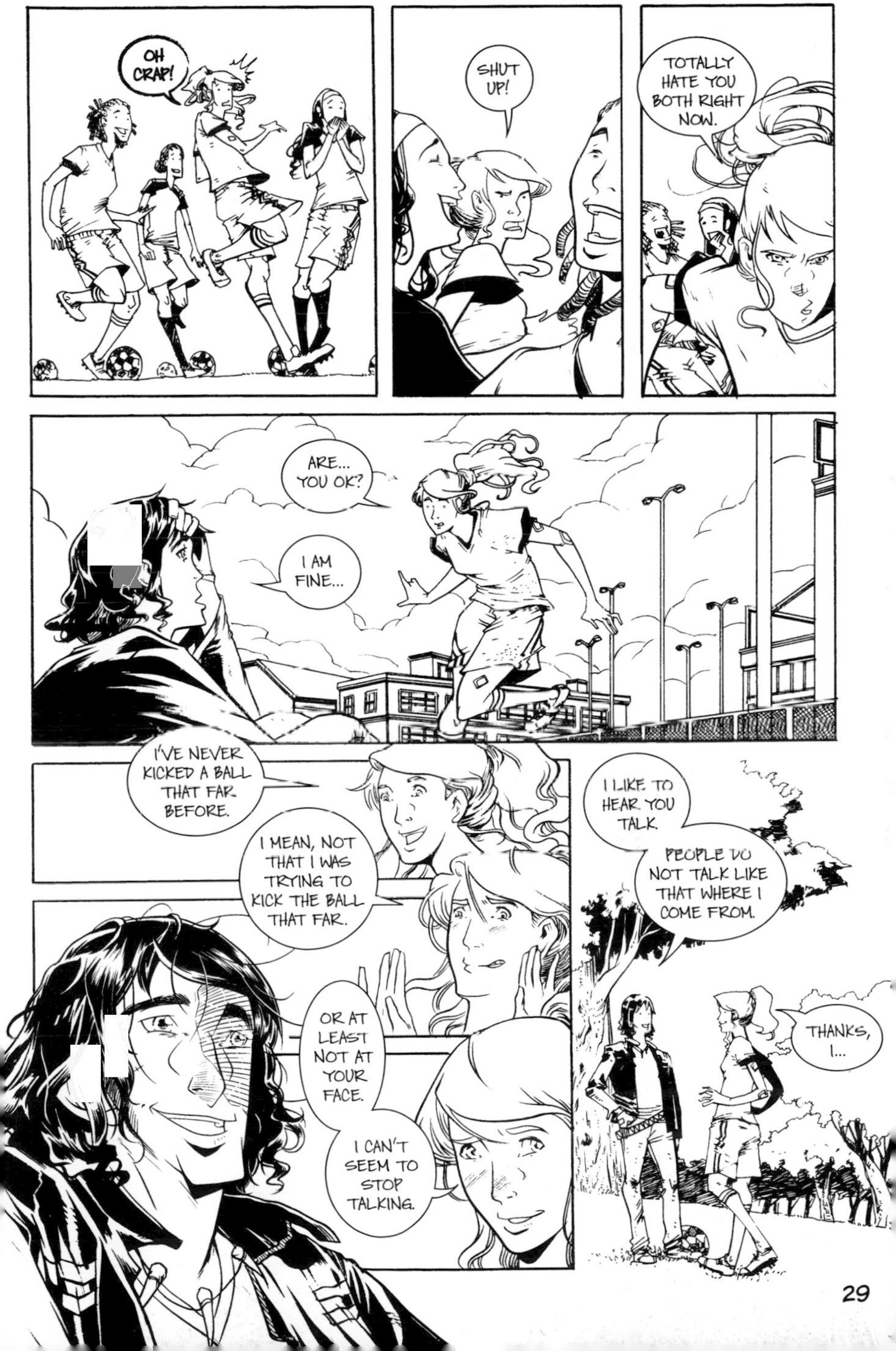
OH CRAP!
SHUT UP!
TOTALLY HATE YOU BOTH RIGHT NOW.
ARE... YOU OK?
I AM FINE...
I'VE NEVER KICKED A BALL THAT FAR BEFORE.
I MEAN, NOT THAT I WAS TRYING TO KICK THE BALL THAT FAR.
OR AT LEAST NOT AT YOUR FACE.
I CAN'T SEEM TO STOP TALKING.
I LIKE TO HEAR YOU TALK.
PEOPLE DO NOT TALK LIKE THAT WHERE I COME FROM.
THANKS, I...

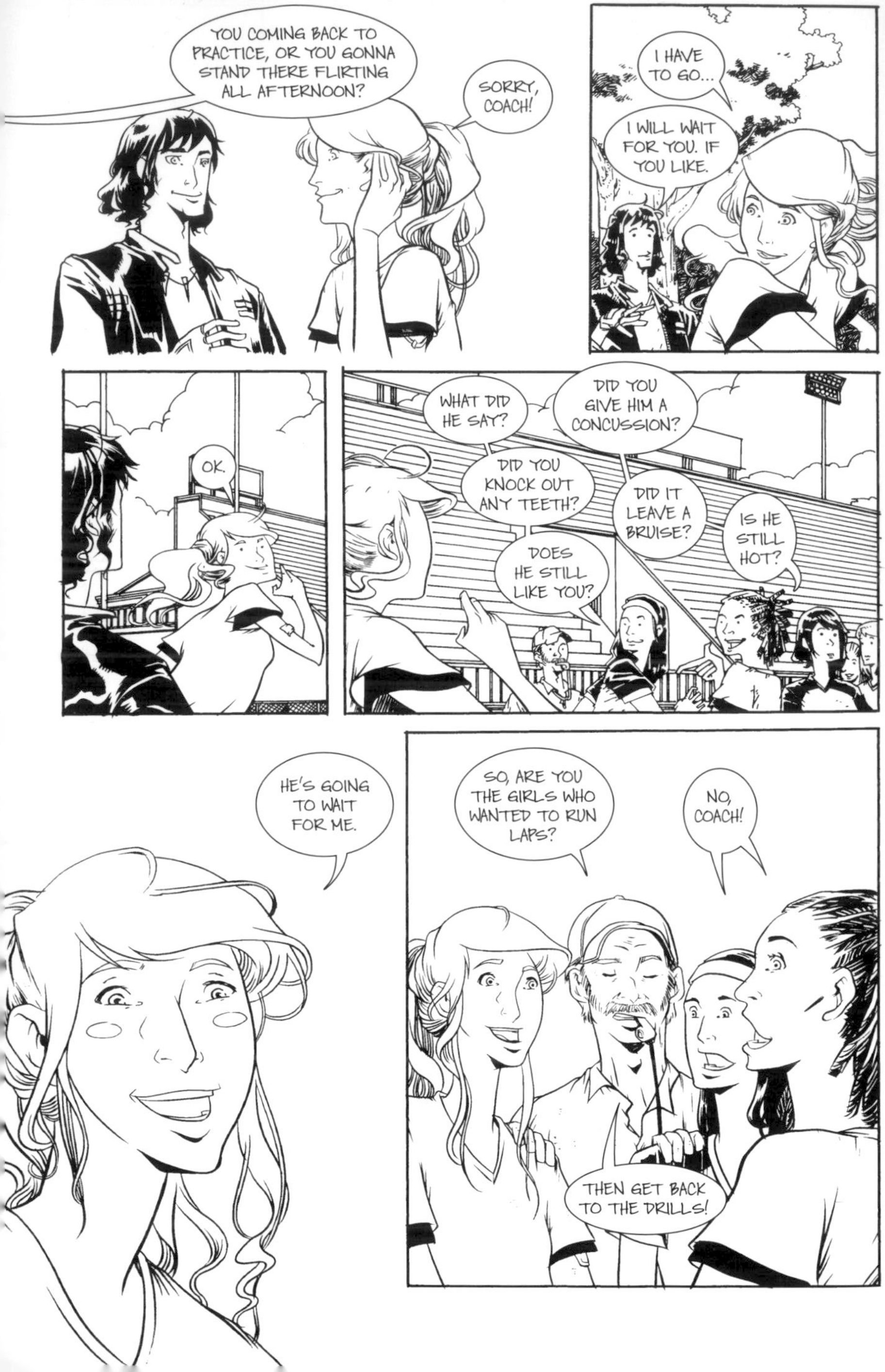
YOU COMING BACK TO PRACTICE, OR YOU GONNA STAND THERE FLIRTING ALL AFTERNOON?
SORRY, COACH!
I HAVE TO GO...
I WILL WAIT FOR YOU. IF YOU LIKE.
OK.
WHAT DID HE SAY?
DID YOU GIVE HIM A CONCUSSION?
DID YOU KNOCK OUT ANY TEETH?
DID IT LEAVE A BRUISE?
DOES HE STILL LIKE YOU?
IS HE STILL HOT?
HE'S GOING TO WAIT FOR ME.
SO, ARE YOU THE GIRLS WHO WANTED TO RUN LAPS?
NO, COACH!
THEN GET BACK TO THE DRILLS!

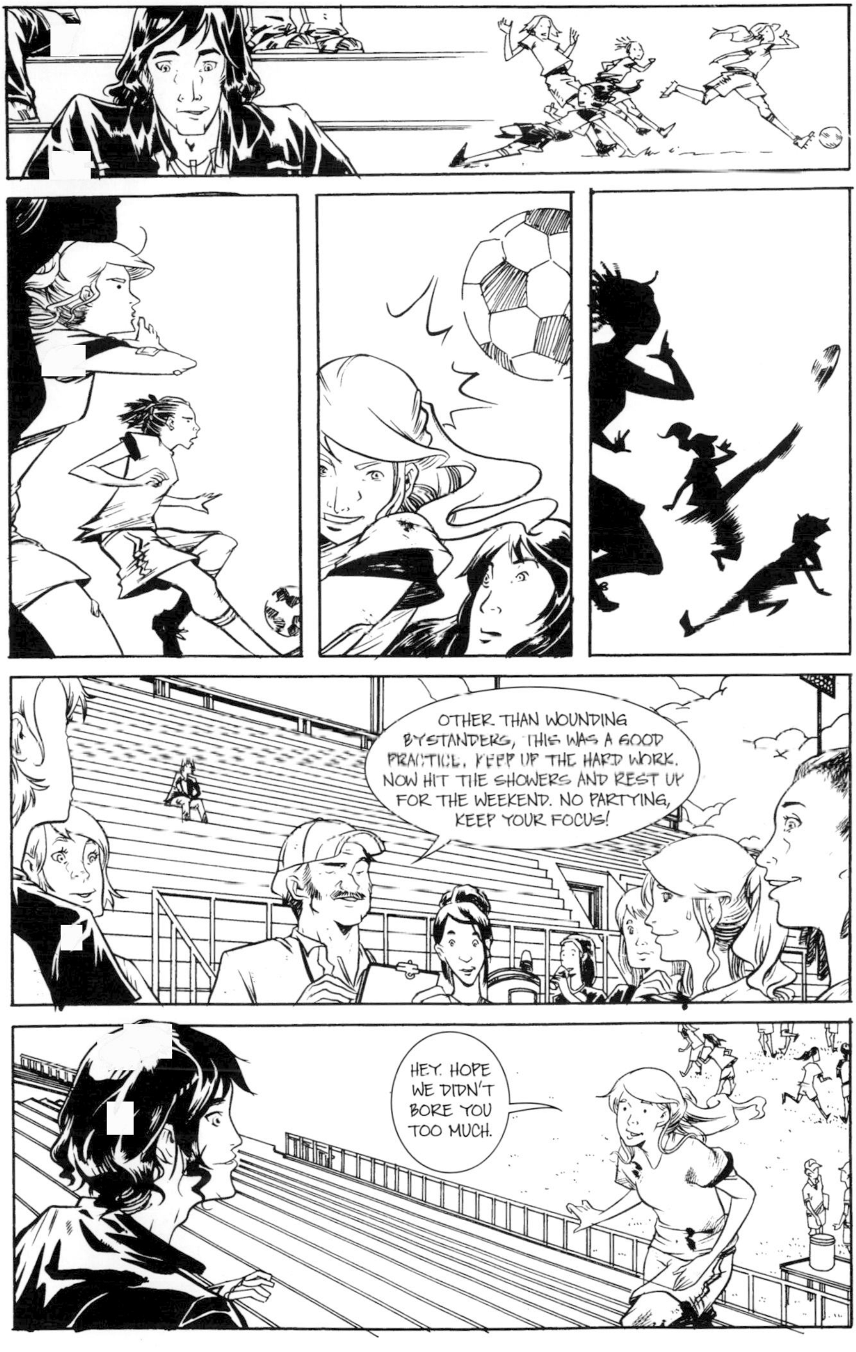
OTHER THAN WOUNDING BYSTANDERS, THIS WAS A GOOD PRACTICE. KEEP UP THE HARD WORK. NOW HIT THE SHOWERS AND REST UP FOR THE WEEKEND. NO PARTYING, KEEP YOUR FOCUS!
HEY. HOPE WE DIDN'T BORE YOU TOO MUCH.

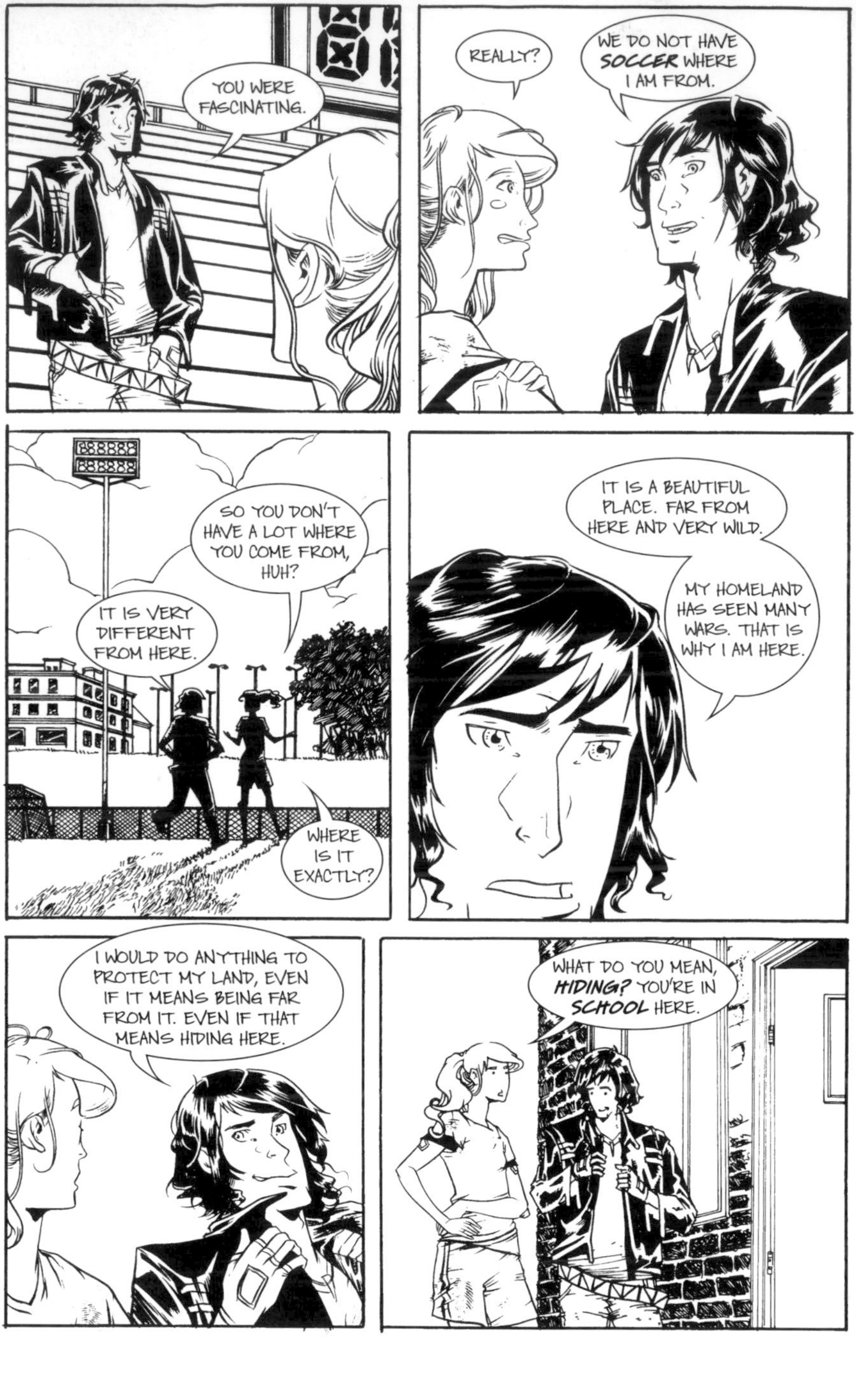

YOU WERE FASCINATING.
REALLY?
WE DO NOT HAVE SOCCER WHERE I AM FROM.
SO YOU DON'T HAVE A LOT WHERE YOU COME FROM, HUH?
IT IS VERY DIFFERENT FROM HERE.
WHERE IS IT EXACTLY?
IT IS A BEAUTIFUL PLACE. FAR FROM HERE AND VERY WILD.
MY HOMELAND HAS SEEN MANY WARS. THAT IS WHY I AM HERE.
I WOULD DO ANYTHING TO PROTECT MY LAND, EVEN IF IT MEANS BEING FAR FROM IT. EVEN IF THAT MEANS HIDING HERE.
WHAT DO YOU MEAN, HIDING? YOU'RE IN SCHOOL HERE.

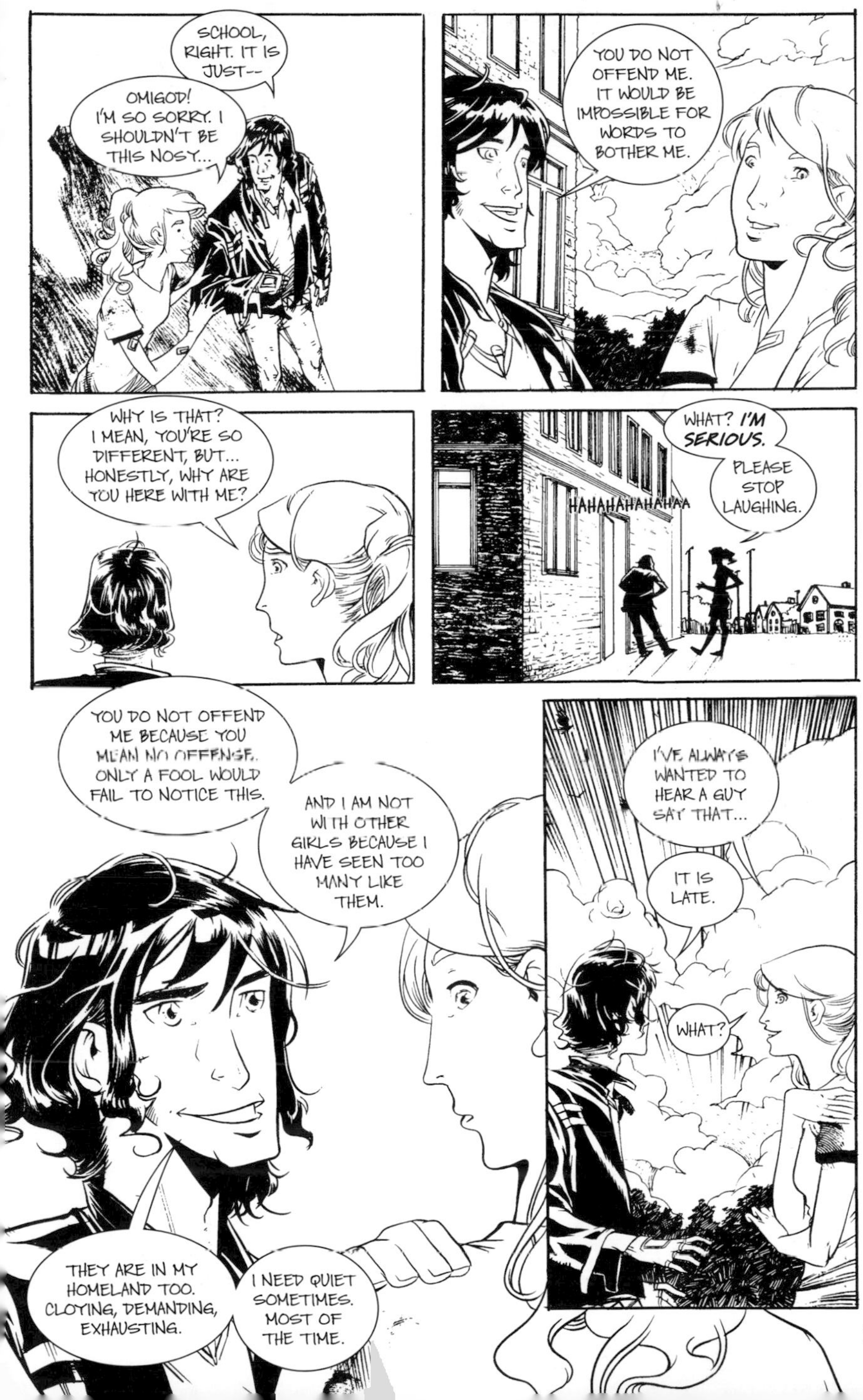
SCHOOL, RIGHT. IT IS JUST--
OMIGOD! I'M SO SORRY. I SHOULDN'T BE THIS NOSY...
YOU DO NOT OFFEND ME. IT WOULD BE IMPOSSIBLE FOR WORDS TO BOTHER ME.
WHY IS THAT? I MEAN, YOU'RE SO DIFFERENT, BUT... HONESTLY, WHY ARE YOU HERE WITH ME?
HAHAHAHAHAHAA
WHAT? I'M SERIOUS.
PLEASE STOP LAUGHING.
YOU DO NOT OFFEND ME BECAUSE YOU MEAN NO OFFENSE. ONLY A FOOL WOULD FAIL TO NOTICE THIS.
AND I AM NOT WITH OTHER GIRLS BECAUSE I HAVE SEEN TOO MANY LIKE THEM.
THEY ARE IN MY HOMELAND TOO. CLOYING, DEMANDING, EXHAUSTING.
I NEED QUIET SOMETIMES. MOST OF THE TIME.
I'VE ALWAYS WANTED TO HEAR A GUY SAY THAT...
IT IS LATE.
WHAT?

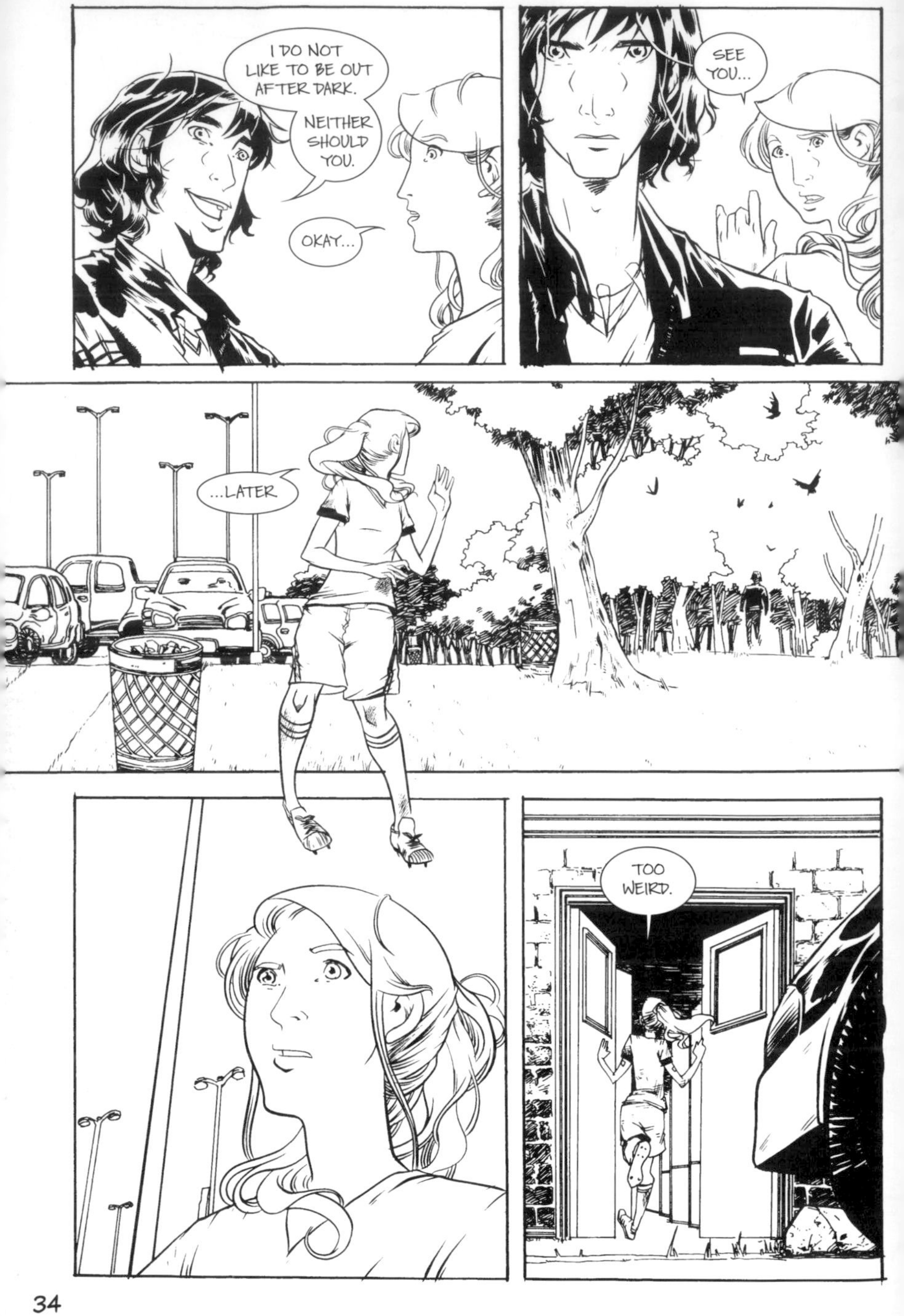
I DO NOT LIKE TO BE OUT AFTER DARK.
NEITHER SHOULD YOU.
OKAY...
SEE YOU...
...LATER
TOO WEIRD.

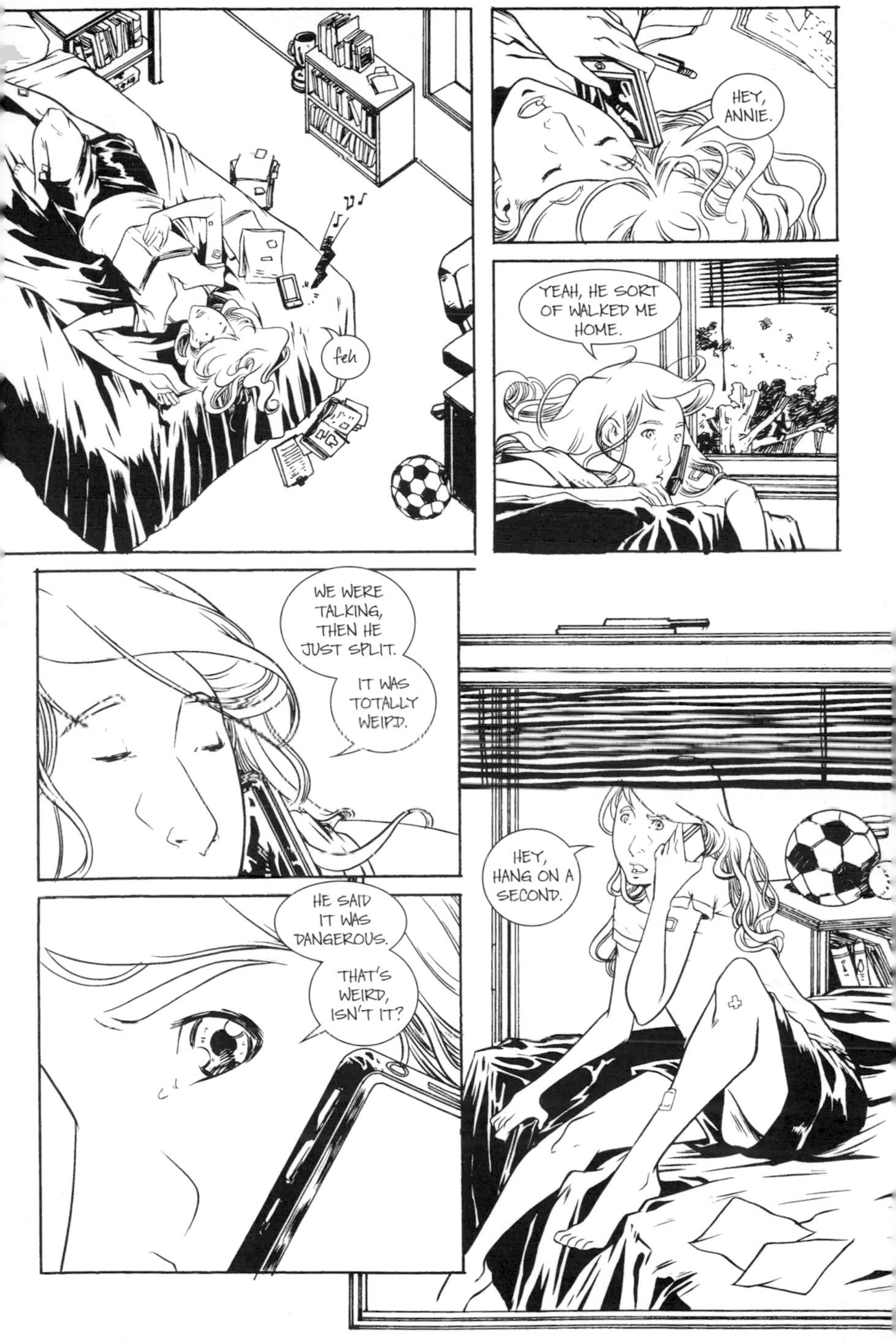
feh
HEY, ANNIE.
YEAH, HE SORT OF WALKED ME HOME.
WE WERE TALKING, THEN HE JUST SPLIT.
IT WAS TOTALLY WEIRD.
HE SAID IT WAS DANGEROUS.
THAT'S WEIRD, ISN'T IT?
HEY, HANG ON A SECOND.

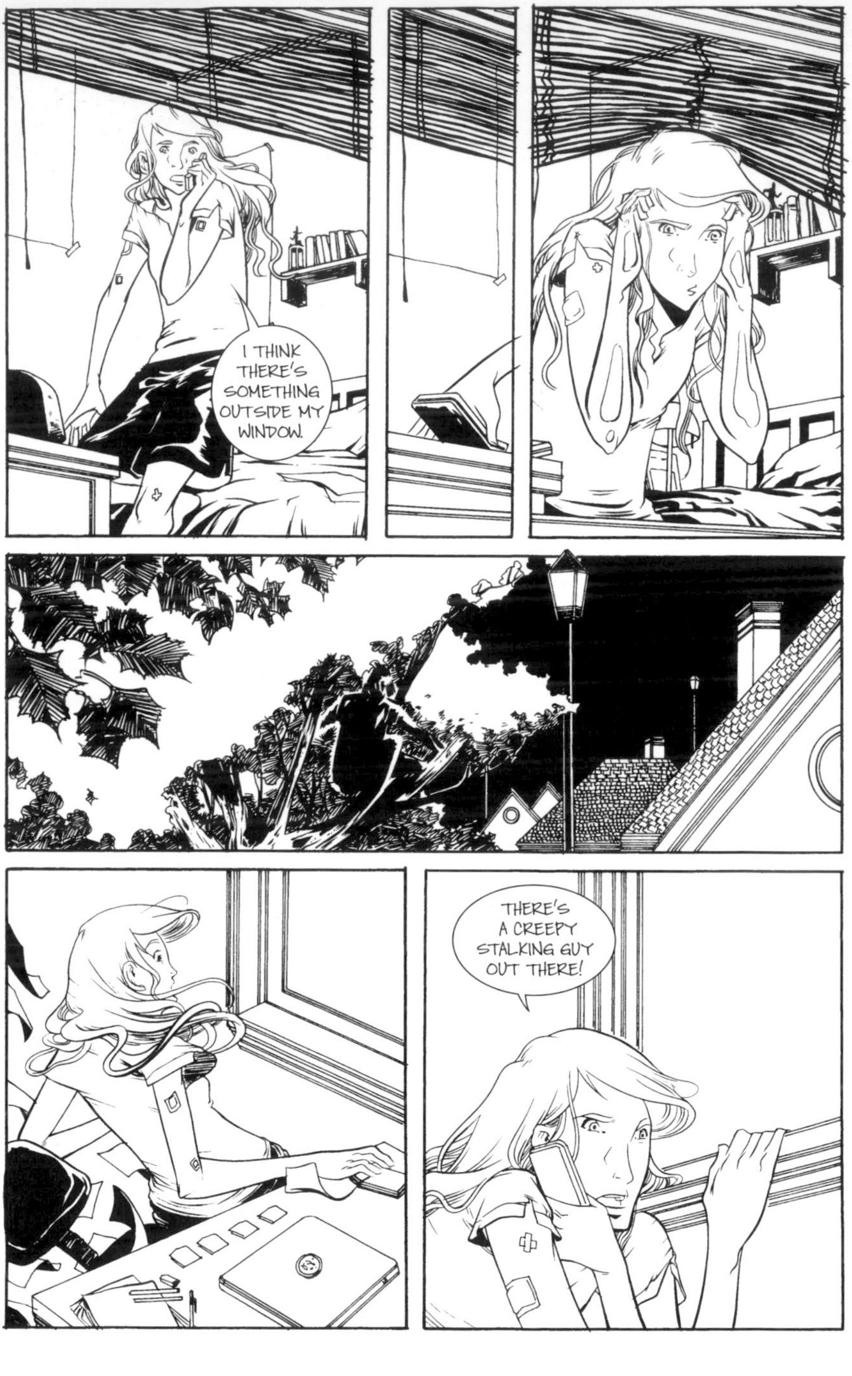
I THINK THERE'S SOMETHING OUTSIDE MY WINDOW.
THERE'S A CREEPY STALKING GUY OUT THERE!

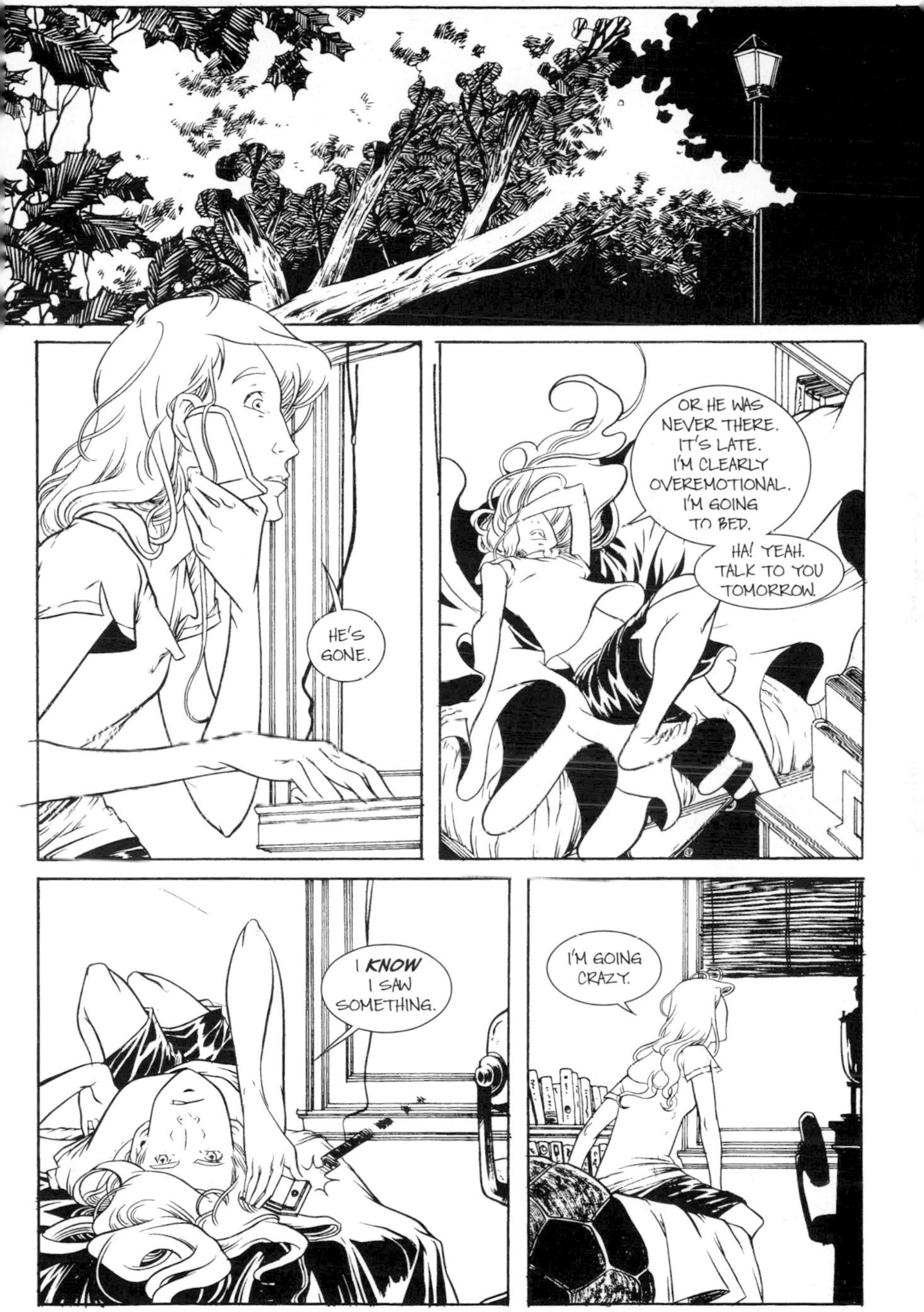
HE'S GONE.
OR HE WAS NEVER THERE. IT'S LATE. I'M CLEARLY OVEREMOTIONAL. I'M GOING TO BED.
HA! YEAH. TALK TO YOU TOMORROW.
I KNOW I SAW SOMETHING.
I'M GOING CRAZY.

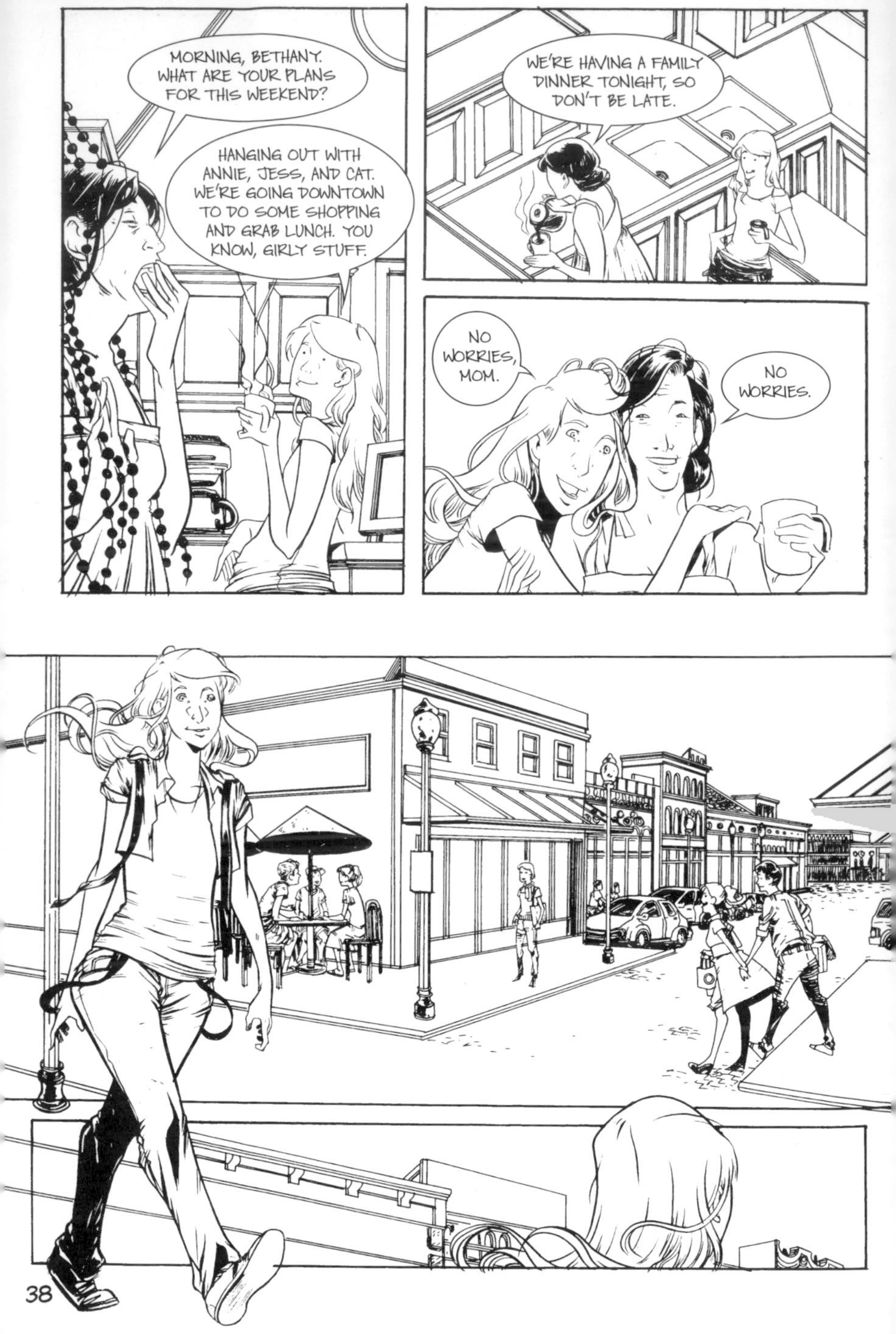
MORNING, BETHANY. WHAT ARE YOUR PLANS FOR THIS WEEKEND?
HANGING OUT WITH ANNIE, JESS, AND CAT. WE'RE GOING DOWNTOWN TO DO SOME SHOPPING AND GRAB LUNCH. YOU KNOW, GIRLY STUFF.
WE'RE HAVING A FAMILY DINNER TONIGHT, SO DON'T BE LATE.
NO WORRIES, MOM.
NO WORRIES.

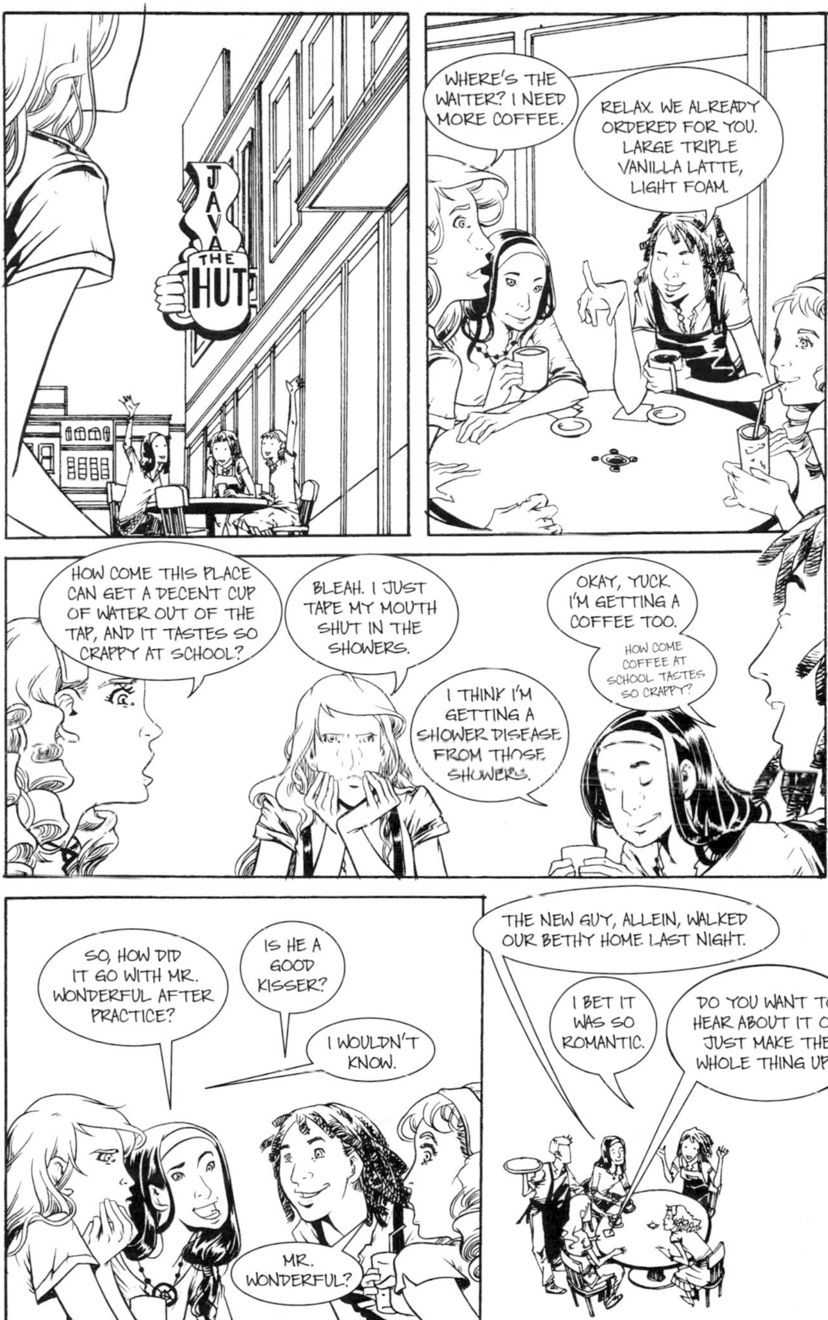
JAVA THE HUT
WHERE'S THE WAITER? I NEED MORE COFFEE.
RELAX. WE ALREADY ORDERED FOR YOU. LARGE TRIPLE VANILLA LATTE, LIGHT FOAM.
HOW COME THIS PLACE CAN GET A DECENT CUP OF WATER OUT OF THE TAP, AND IT TASTES SO CRAPPY AT SCHOOL?
BLEAH. I JUST TAPE MY MOUTH SHUT IN THE SHOWERS.
I THINK I'M GETTING A SHOWER DISEASE FROM THOSE SHOWERS.
OKAY, YUCK. I'M GETTING A COFFEE TOO.
HOW COME COFFEE AT SCHOOL TASTES SO CRAPPY?
SO, HOW DID IT GO WITH MR. WONDERFUL AFTER PRACTICE?
IS HE A GOOD KISSER?
I WOULDN'T KNOW.
MR. WONDERFUL?
THE NEW GUY, ALLEIN, WALKED OUR BETHY HOME LAST NIGHT.
I BET IT WAS SO ROMANTIC.
DO YOU WANT TO HEAR ABOUT IT OR JUST MAKE THE WHOLE THING UP?

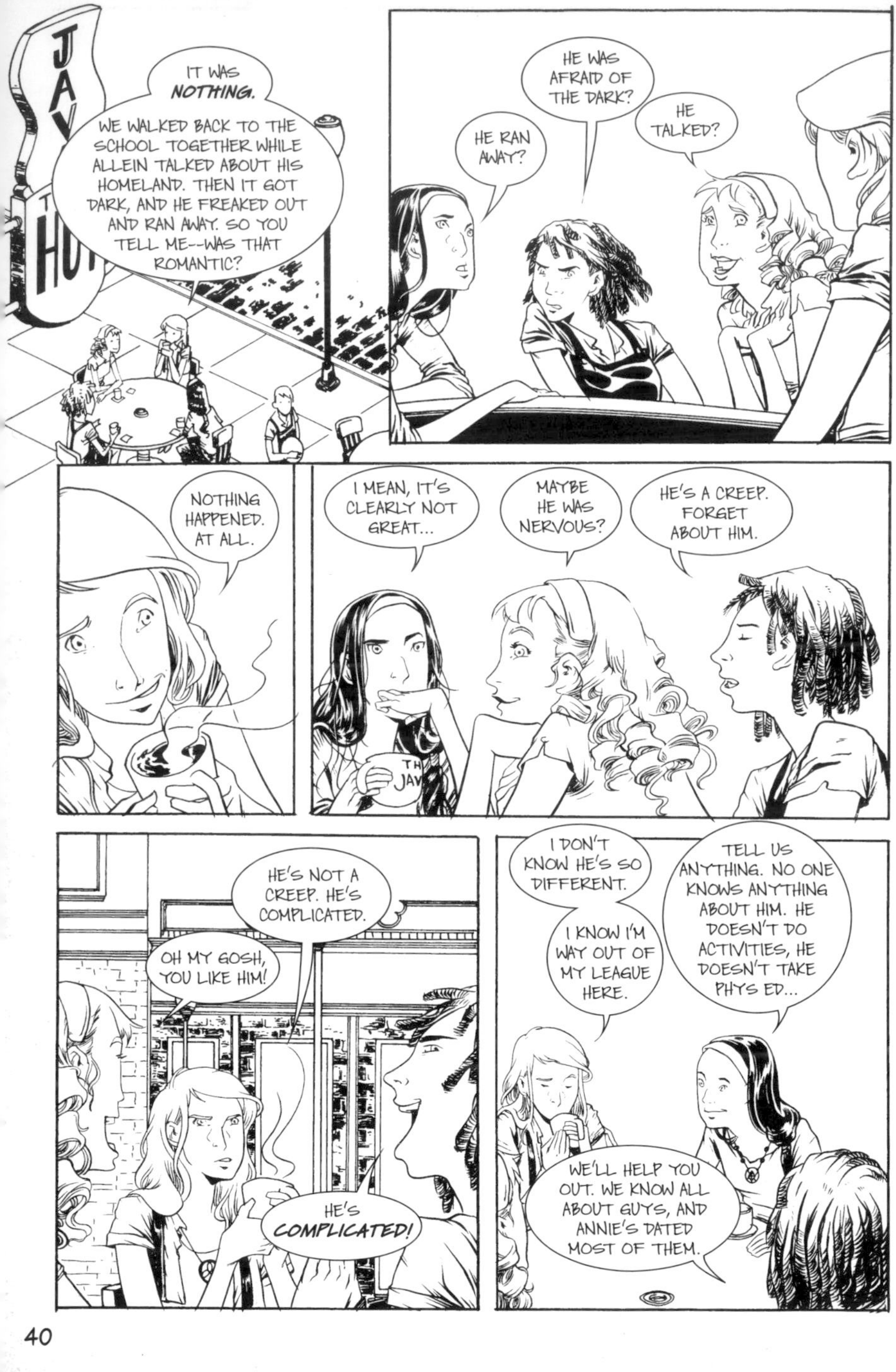
IT WAS *NOTHING.*
WE WALKED BACK TO THE SCHOOL TOGETHER WHILE ALLEIN TALKED ABOUT HIS HOMELAND. THEN IT GOT DARK, AND HE FREAKED OUT AND RAN AWAY. SO YOU TELL ME--WAS THAT ROMANTIC?
HE RAN AWAY?
HE WAS AFRAID OF THE DARK?
HE TALKED?
NOTHING HAPPENED. AT ALL.
I MEAN, IT'S CLEARLY NOT GREAT...
MAYBE HE WAS NERVOUS?
HE'S A CREEP. FORGET ABOUT HIM.
HE'S NOT A CREEP. HE'S COMPLICATED.
OH MY GOSH, YOU LIKE HIM!
HE'S *COMPLICATED!*
I DON'T KNOW HE'S SO DIFFERENT.
I KNOW I'M WAY OUT OF MY LEAGUE HERE.
TELL US ANYTHING. NO ONE KNOWS ANYTHING ABOUT HIM. HE DOESN'T DO ACTIVITIES, HE DOESN'T TAKE PHYS ED...
WE'LL HELP YOU OUT. WE KNOW ALL ABOUT GUYS, AND ANNIE'S DATED MOST OF THEM.

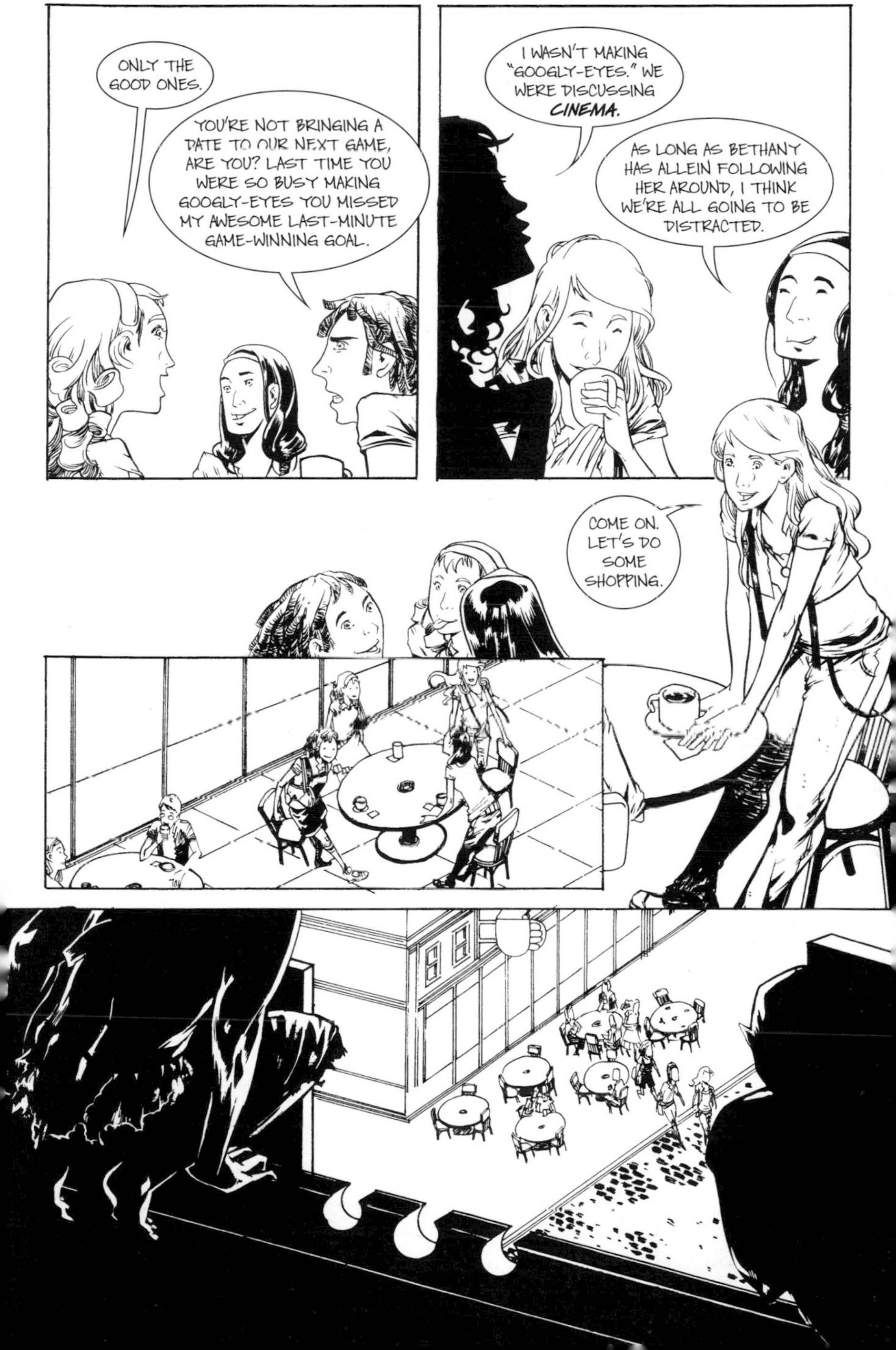
ONLY THE GOOD ONES.
YOU'RE NOT BRINGING A DATE TO OUR NEXT GAME, ARE YOU? LAST TIME YOU WERE SO BUSY MAKING GOOGLY-EYES YOU MISSED MY AWESOME LAST-MINUTE GAME-WINNING GOAL.
I WASN'T MAKING "GOOGLY-EYES." WE WERE DISCUSSING CINEMA.
AS LONG AS BETHANY HAS ALLEIN FOLLOWING HER AROUND, I THINK WE'RE ALL GOING TO BE DISTRACTED.
COME ON. LET'S DO SOME SHOPPING.

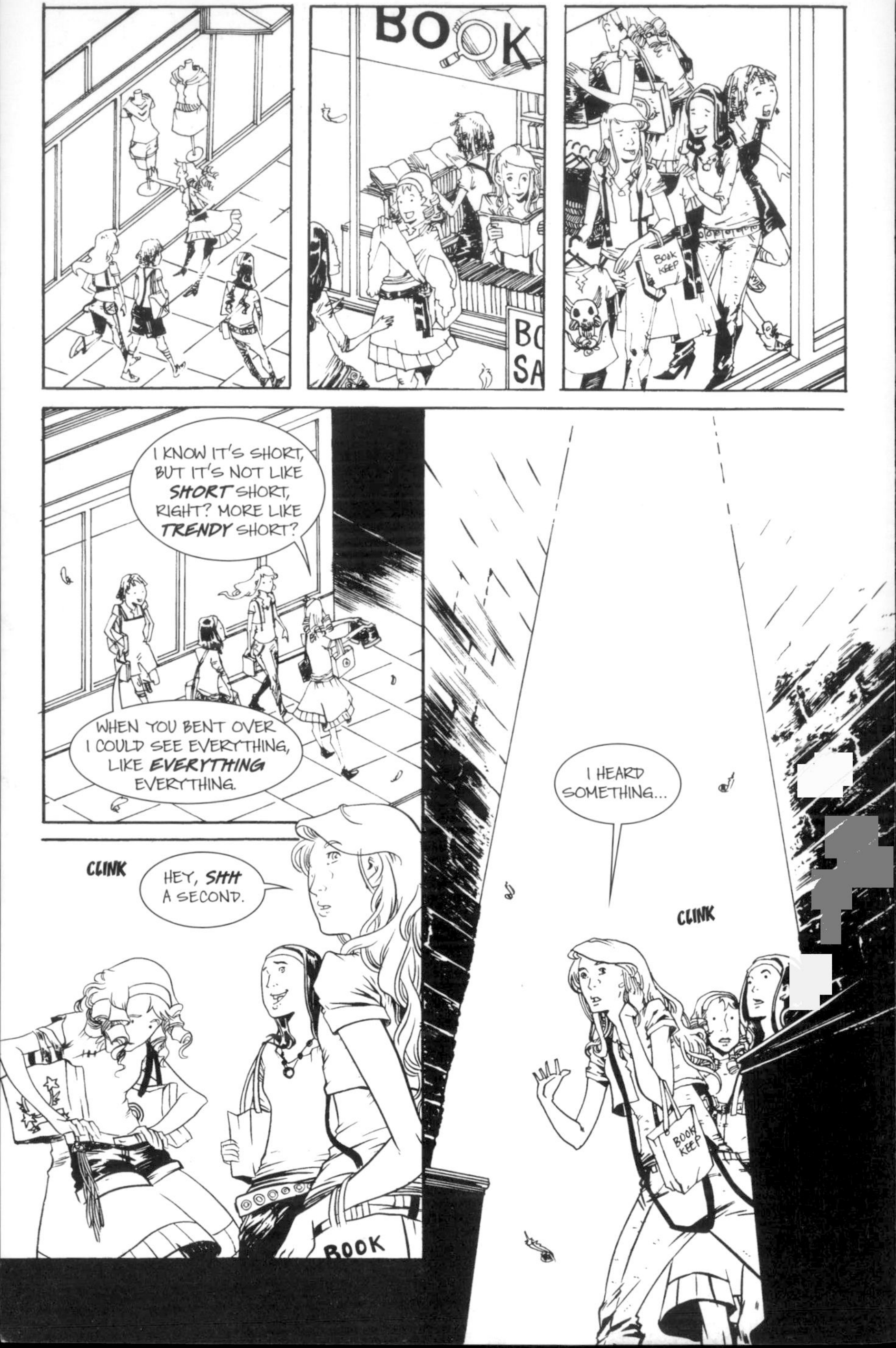
BOOK
BOOK KEEP
BO SA
I KNOW IT'S SHORT, BUT IT'S NOT LIKE SHORT SHORT, RIGHT? MORE LIKE TRENDY SHORT?
WHEN YOU BENT OVER I COULD SEE EVERYTHING, LIKE EVERYTHING EVERYTHING.
CLINK
HEY, SHH A SECOND.
BOOK
I HEARD SOMETHING...
CLINK
BOOK KEEP

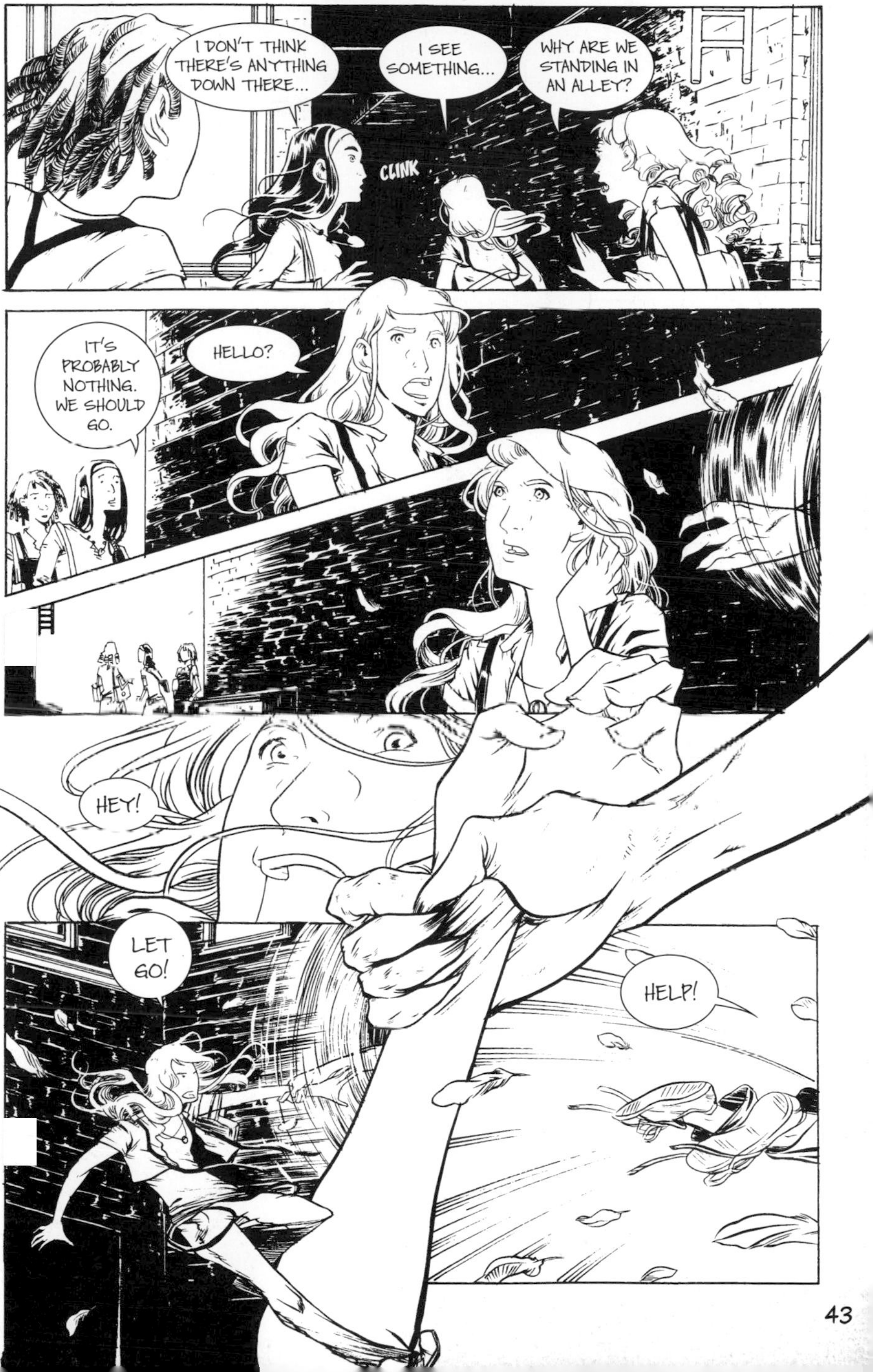
I DON'T THINK THERE'S ANYTHING DOWN THERE...
I SEE SOMETHING...
WHY ARE WE STANDING IN AN ALLEY?
CLINK
HELLO?
IT'S PROBABLY NOTHING. WE SHOULD GO.
HEY!
LET GO!
HELP!

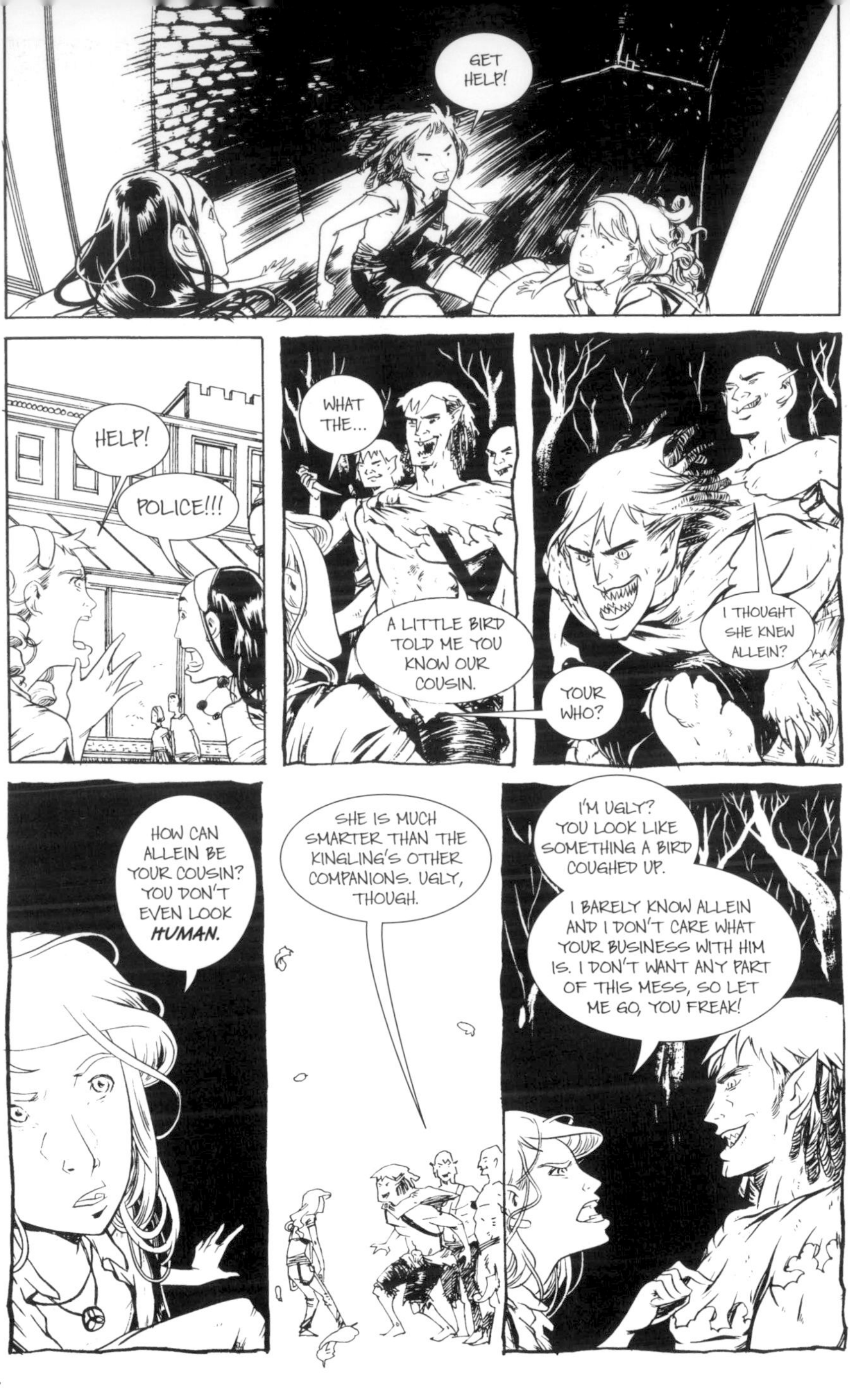
GET HELP!
HELP!
POLICE!!!
WHAT THE...
A LITTLE BIRD TOLD ME YOU KNOW OUR COUSIN.
YOUR WHO?
I THOUGHT SHE KNEW ALLEIN?
HOW CAN ALLEIN BE YOUR COUSIN? YOU DON'T EVEN LOOK **HUMAN.**
SHE IS MUCH SMARTER THAN THE KINGLING'S OTHER COMPANIONS. UGLY, THOUGH.
I'M UGLY? YOU LOOK LIKE SOMETHING A BIRD COUGHED UP.
I BARELY KNOW ALLEIN AND I DON'T CARE WHAT YOUR BUSINESS WITH HIM IS. I DON'T WANT ANY PART OF THIS MESS, SO LET ME GO, YOU FREAK!

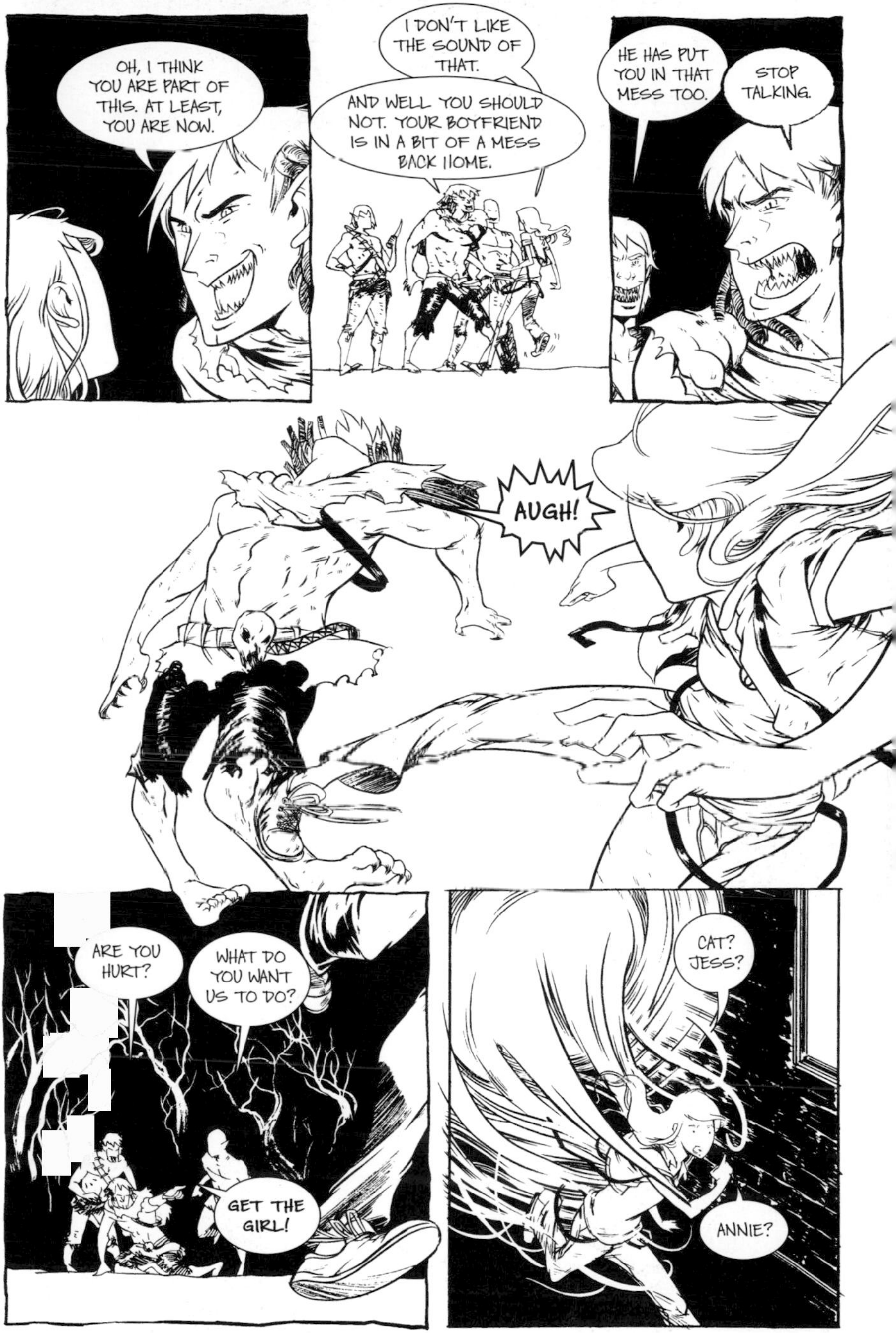
OH, I THINK YOU ARE PART OF THIS. AT LEAST, YOU ARE NOW.
I DON'T LIKE THE SOUND OF THAT.
AND WELL YOU SHOULD NOT. YOUR BOYFRIEND IS IN A BIT OF A MESS BACK HOME.
HE HAS PUT YOU IN THAT MESS TOO.
STOP TALKING.
AUGH!
ARE YOU HURT?
WHAT DO YOU WANT US TO DO?
GET THE GIRL!
CAT? JESS?
ANNIE?

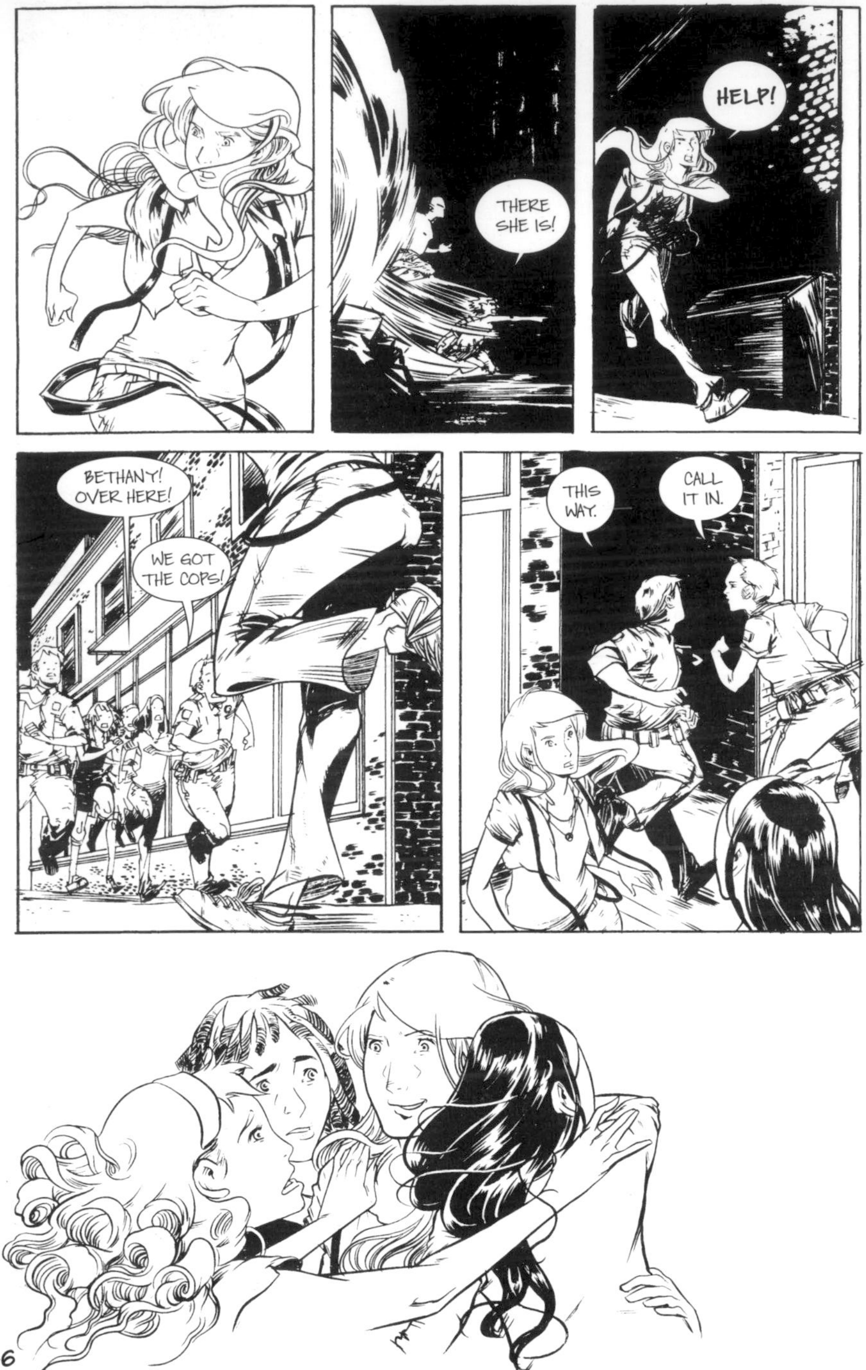
THERE SHE IS!
HELP!
BETHANY! OVER HERE!
WE GOT THE COPS!
THIS WAY.
CALL IT IN.

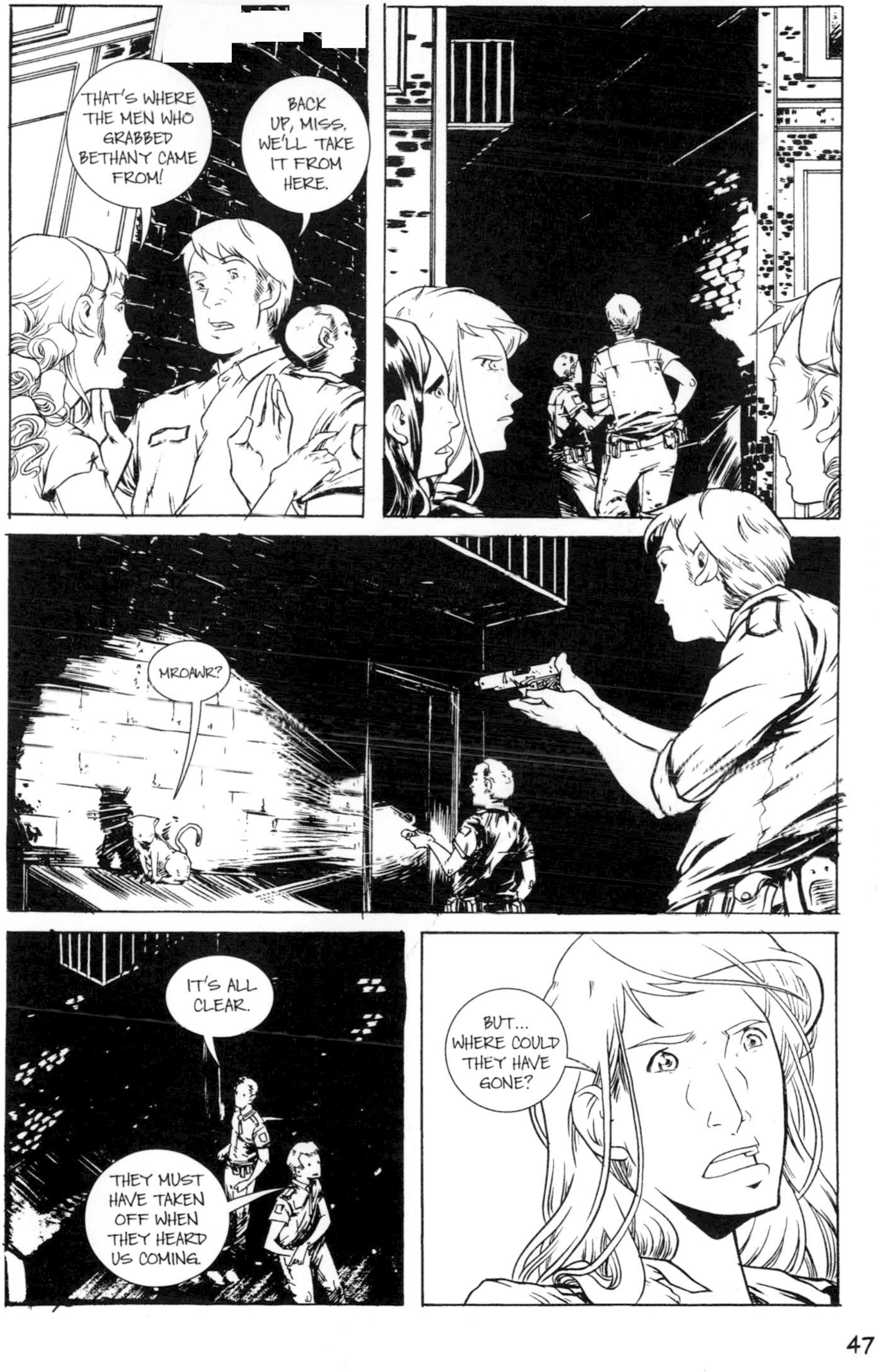
THAT'S WHERE THE MEN WHO GRABBED BETHANY CAME FROM!
BACK UP, MISS. WE'LL TAKE IT FROM HERE.
MROAWR?
IT'S ALL CLEAR.
THEY MUST HAVE TAKEN OFF WHEN THEY HEARD US COMING.
BUT... WHERE COULD THEY HAVE GONE?

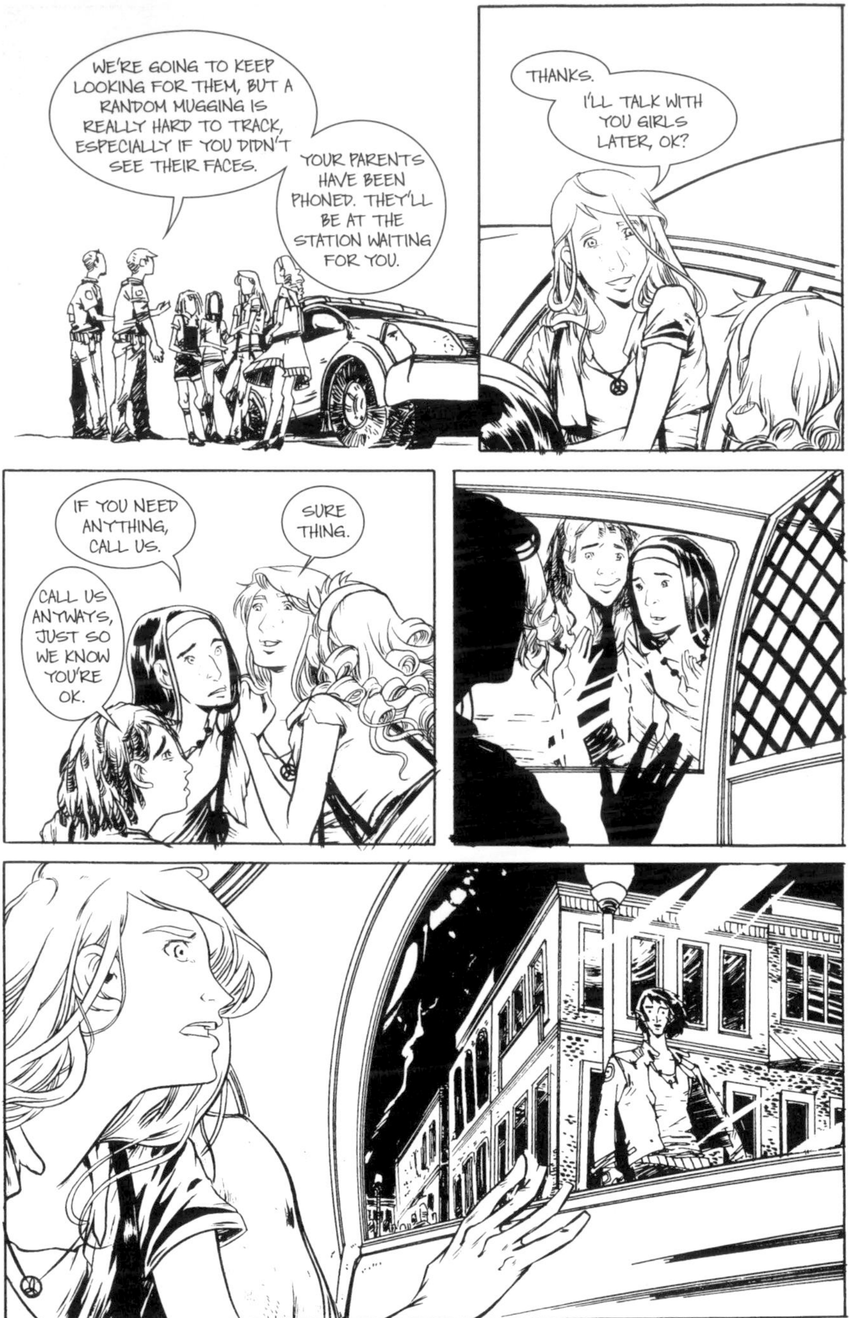
WE'RE GOING TO KEEP LOOKING FOR THEM, BUT A RANDOM MUGGING IS REALLY HARD TO TRACK, ESPECIALLY IF YOU DIDN'T SEE THEIR FACES.
YOUR PARENTS HAVE BEEN PHONED. THEY'LL BE AT THE STATION WAITING FOR YOU.
THANKS.
I'LL TALK WITH YOU GIRLS LATER, OK?
IF YOU NEED ANYTHING, CALL US.
SURE THING.
CALL US ANYWAYS, JUST SO WE KNOW YOU'RE OK.

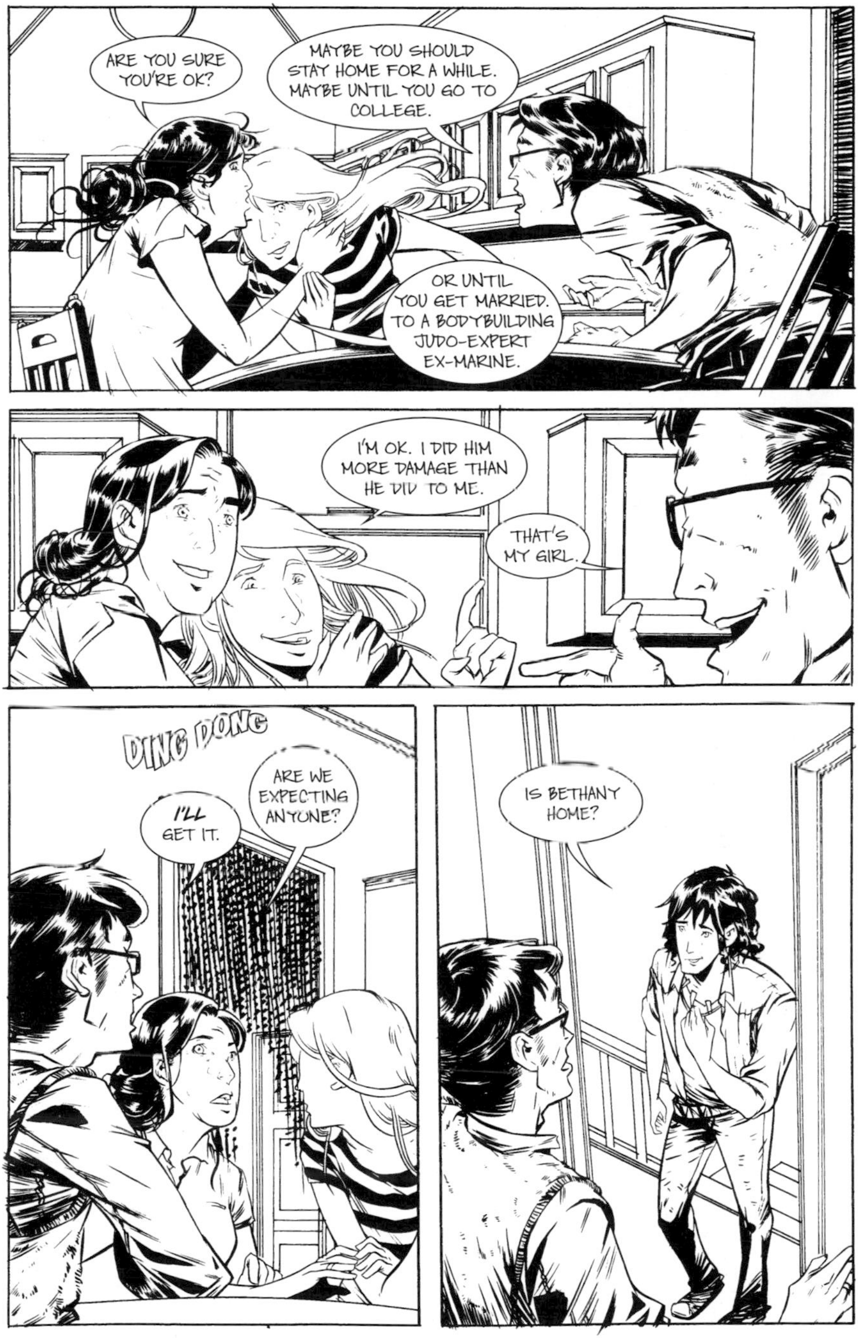
ARE YOU SURE YOU'RE OK?
MAYBE YOU SHOULD STAY HOME FOR A WHILE. MAYBE UNTIL YOU GO TO COLLEGE.
OR UNTIL YOU GET MARRIED. TO A BODYBUILDING JUDO-EXPERT EX-MARINE.
I'M OK. I DID HIM MORE DAMAGE THAN HE DID TO ME.
THAT'S MY GIRL.
DING DONG
I'LL GET IT.
ARE WE EXPECTING ANYONE?
IS BETHANY HOME?

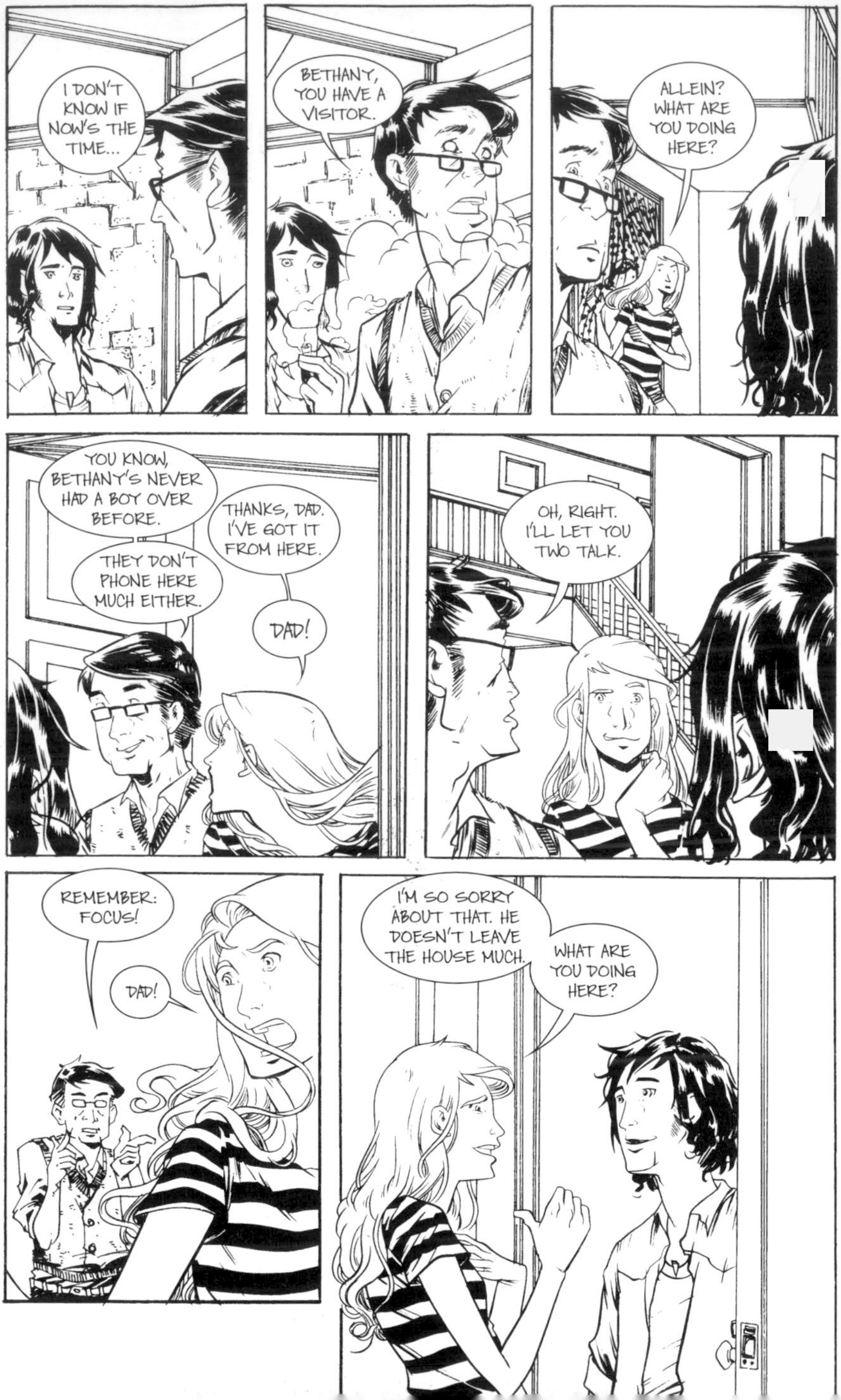

I DON'T KNOW IF NOW'S THE TIME...
BETHANY, YOU HAVE A VISITOR.
ALLEIN? WHAT ARE YOU DOING HERE?
YOU KNOW, BETHANY'S NEVER HAD A BOY OVER BEFORE.
THEY DON'T PHONE HERE MUCH EITHER.
THANKS, DAD. I'VE GOT IT FROM HERE.
DAD!
OH, RIGHT. I'LL LET YOU TWO TALK.
REMEMBER: FOCUS!
DAD!
I'M SO SORRY ABOUT THAT. HE DOESN'T LEAVE THE HOUSE MUCH.
WHAT ARE YOU DOING HERE?

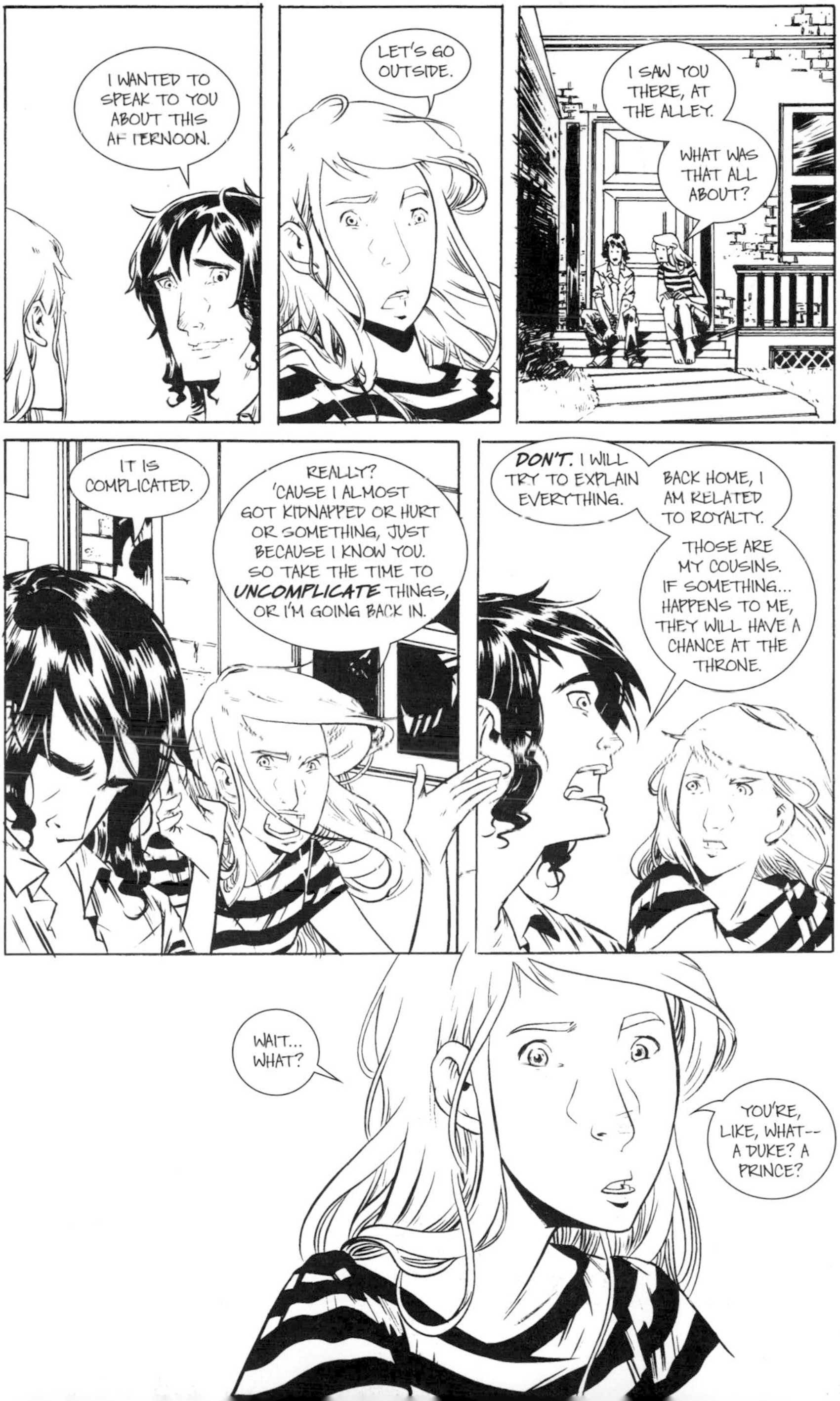
I WANTED TO SPEAK TO YOU ABOUT THIS AFTERNOON.
LET'S GO OUTSIDE.
I SAW YOU THERE, AT THE ALLEY.
WHAT WAS THAT ALL ABOUT?
IT IS COMPLICATED.
REALLY? 'CAUSE I ALMOST GOT KIDNAPPED OR HURT OR SOMETHING, JUST BECAUSE I KNOW YOU. SO TAKE THE TIME TO UNCOMPLICATE THINGS, OR I'M GOING BACK IN.
DON'T. I WILL TRY TO EXPLAIN EVERYTHING.
BACK HOME, I AM RELATED TO ROYALTY.
THOSE ARE MY COUSINS. IF SOMETHING... HAPPENS TO ME, THEY WILL HAVE A CHANCE AT THE THRONE.
WAIT... WHAT?
YOU'RE, LIKE, WHAT-- A DUKE? A PRINCE?

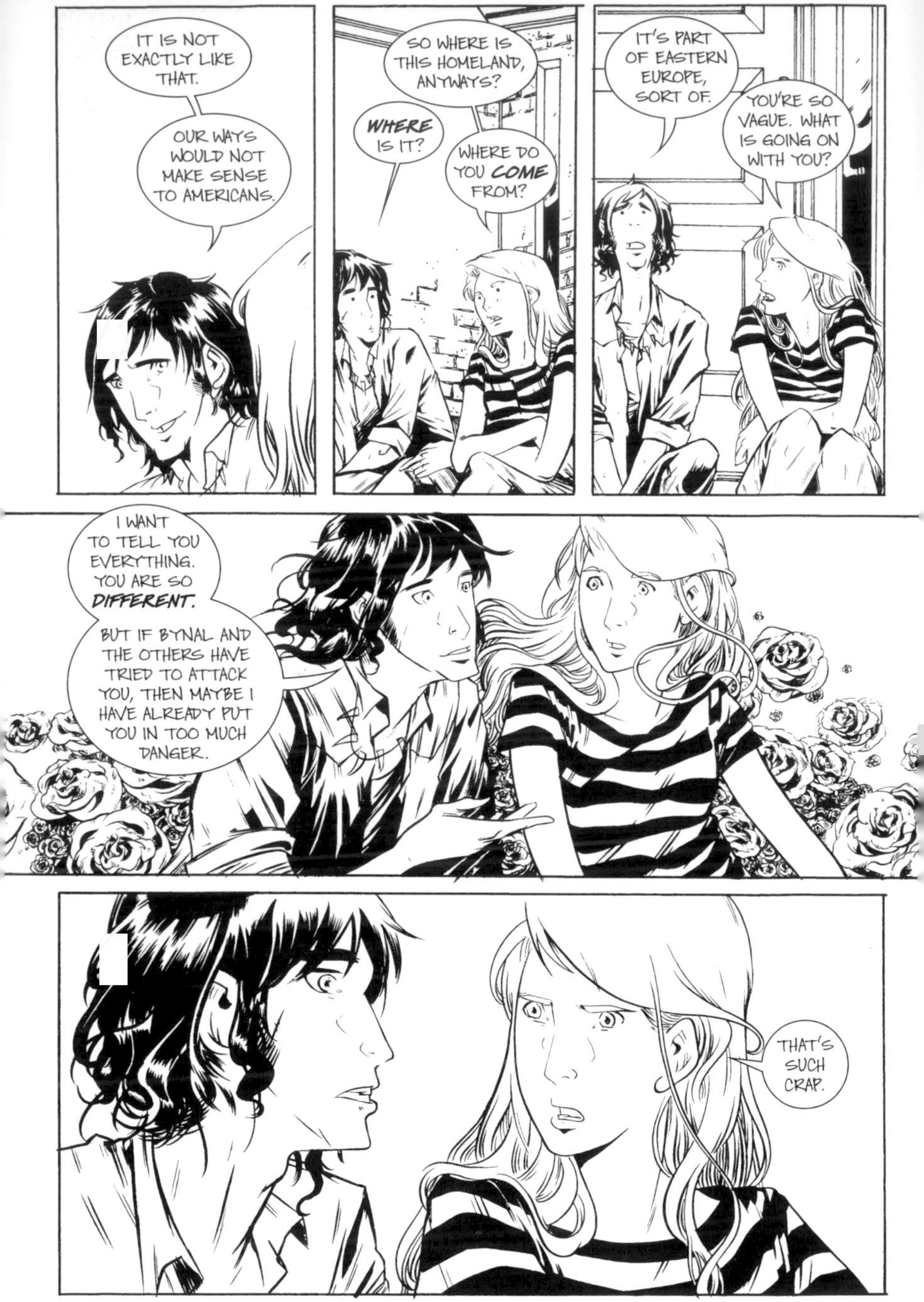
IT IS NOT EXACTLY LIKE THAT.
OUR WAYS WOULD NOT MAKE SENSE TO AMERICANS.
SO WHERE IS THIS HOMELAND, ANYWAYS?
WHERE IS IT?
WHERE DO YOU COME FROM?
IT'S PART OF EASTERN EUROPE, SORT OF.
YOU'RE SO VAGUE. WHAT IS GOING ON WITH YOU?
I WANT TO TELL YOU EVERYTHING. YOU ARE SO DIFFERENT.
BUT IF BYNAL AND THE OTHERS HAVE TRIED TO ATTACK YOU, THEN MAYBE I HAVE ALREADY PUT YOU IN TOO MUCH DANGER.
THAT'S SUCH CRAP.

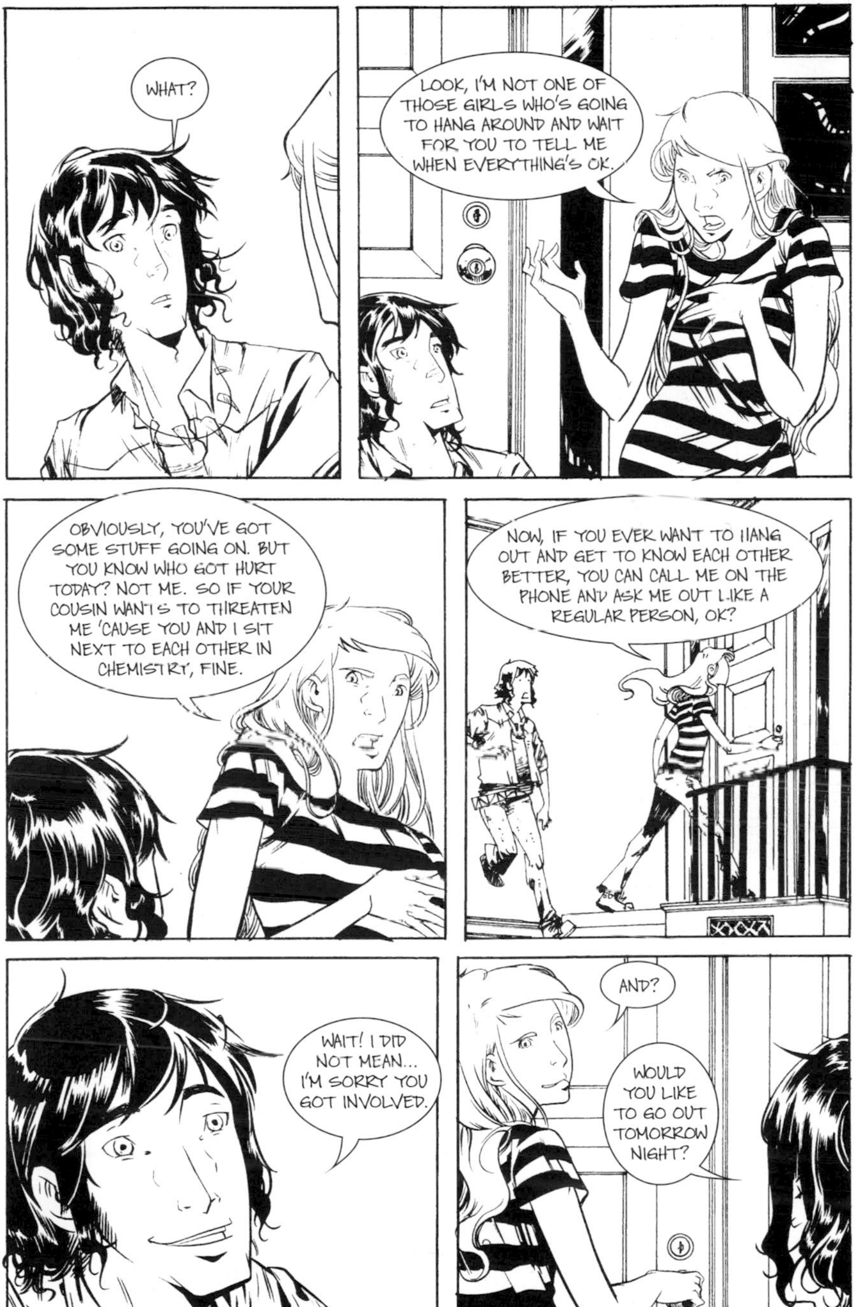
WHAT?
LOOK, I'M NOT ONE OF THOSE GIRLS WHO'S GOING TO HANG AROUND AND WAIT FOR YOU TO TELL ME WHEN EVERYTHING'S OK.
OBVIOUSLY, YOU'VE GOT SOME STUFF GOING ON. BUT YOU KNOW WHO GOT HURT TODAY? NOT ME. SO IF YOUR COUSIN WANTS TO THREATEN ME 'CAUSE YOU AND I SIT NEXT TO EACH OTHER IN CHEMISTRY, FINE.
NOW, IF YOU EVER WANT TO HANG OUT AND GET TO KNOW EACH OTHER BETTER, YOU CAN CALL ME ON THE PHONE AND ASK ME OUT LIKE A REGULAR PERSON, OK?
WAIT! I DID NOT MEAN... I'M SORRY YOU GOT INVOLVED.
AND?
WOULD YOU LIKE TO GO OUT TOMORROW NIGHT?

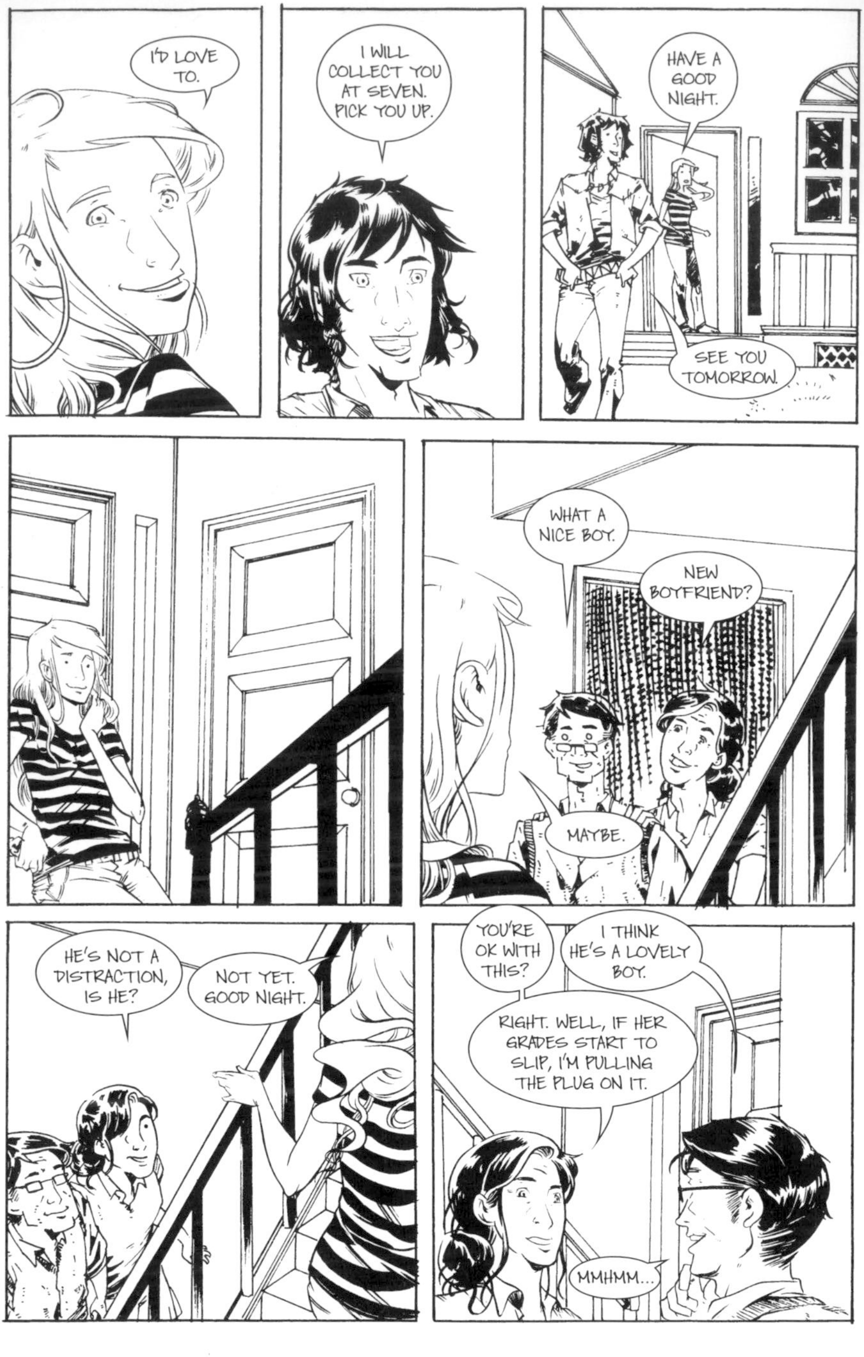
I'D LOVE TO.
I WILL COLLECT YOU AT SEVEN. PICK YOU UP.
HAVE A GOOD NIGHT.
SEE YOU TOMORROW.
WHAT A NICE BOY.
NEW BOYFRIEND?
MAYBE.
HE'S NOT A DISTRACTION, IS HE?
NOT YET. GOOD NIGHT.
YOU'RE OK WITH THIS?
I THINK HE'S A LOVELY BOY.
RIGHT. WELL, IF HER GRADES START TO SLIP, I'M PULLING THE PLUG ON IT.
MMHMM...

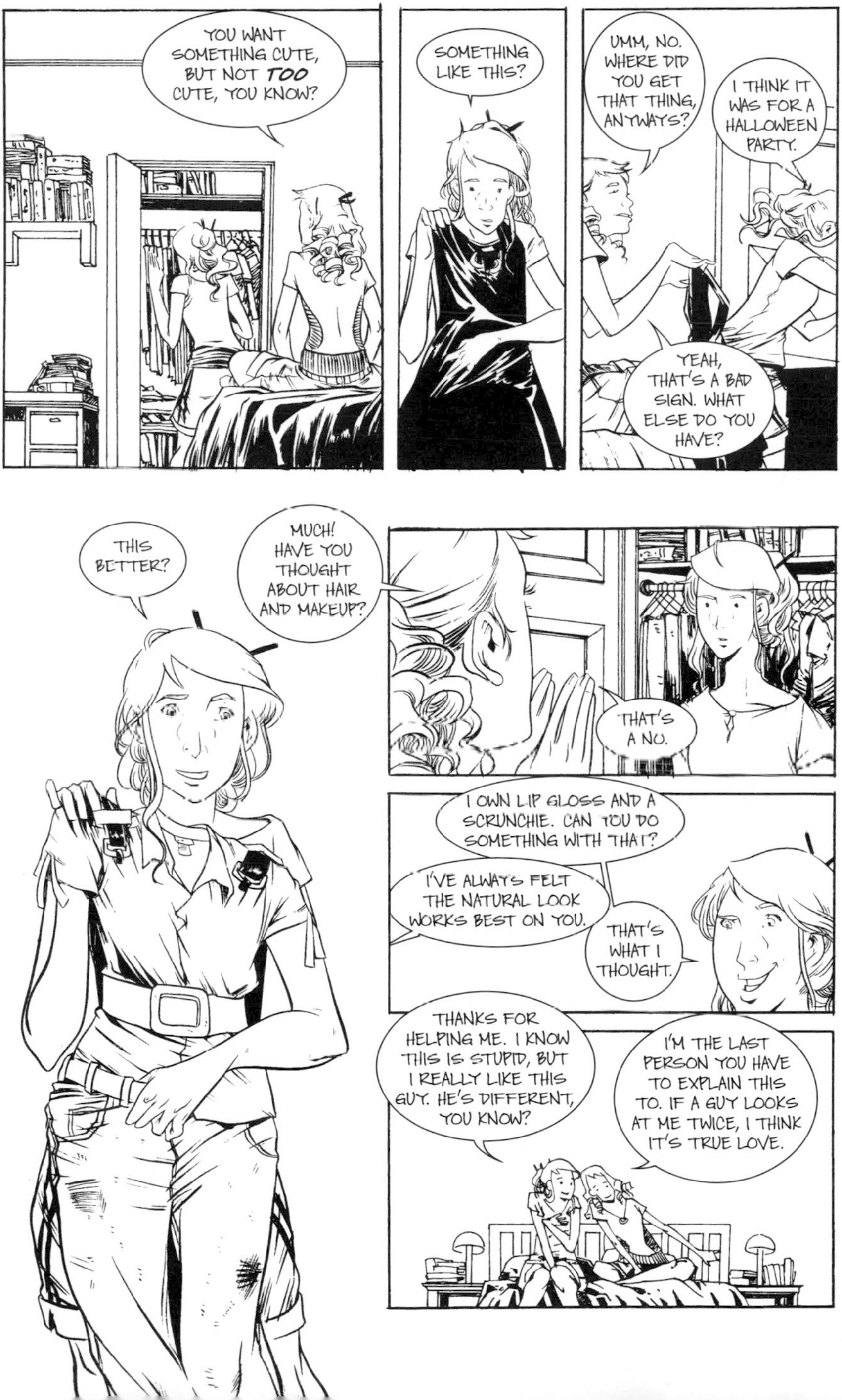
YOU WANT SOMETHING CUTE, BUT NOT TOO CUTE, YOU KNOW?
SOMETHING LIKE THIS?
UMM, NO. WHERE DID YOU GET THAT THING, ANYWAYS?
I THINK IT WAS FOR A HALLOWEEN PARTY.
YEAH, THAT'S A BAD SIGN. WHAT ELSE DO YOU HAVE?
THIS BETTER?
MUCH! HAVE YOU THOUGHT ABOUT HAIR AND MAKEUP?
THAT'S A NO.
I OWN LIP GLOSS AND A SCRUNCHIE. CAN YOU DO SOMETHING WITH THAT?
I'VE ALWAYS FELT THE NATURAL LOOK WORKS BEST ON YOU.
THAT'S WHAT I THOUGHT.
THANKS FOR HELPING ME. I KNOW THIS IS STUPID, BUT I REALLY LIKE THIS GUY. HE'S DIFFERENT, YOU KNOW?
I'M THE LAST PERSON YOU HAVE TO EXPLAIN THIS TO. IF A GUY LOOKS AT ME TWICE, I THINK IT'S TRUE LOVE.

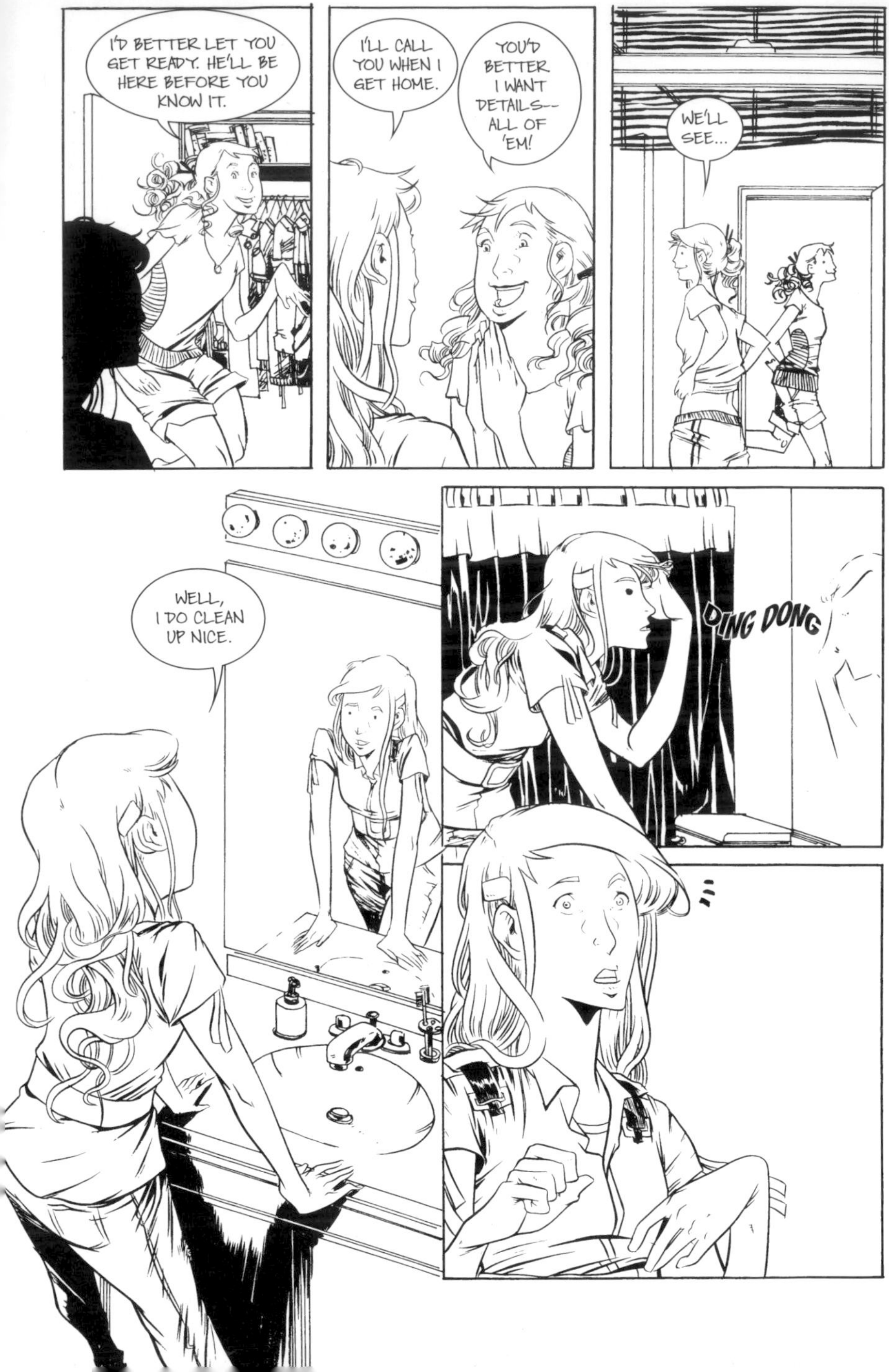
I'D BETTER LET YOU GET READY. HE'LL BE HERE BEFORE YOU KNOW IT.
I'LL CALL YOU WHEN I GET HOME.
YOU'D BETTER. I WANT DETAILS-- ALL OF 'EM!
WE'LL SEE...
WELL, I DO CLEAN UP NICE.
DING DONG

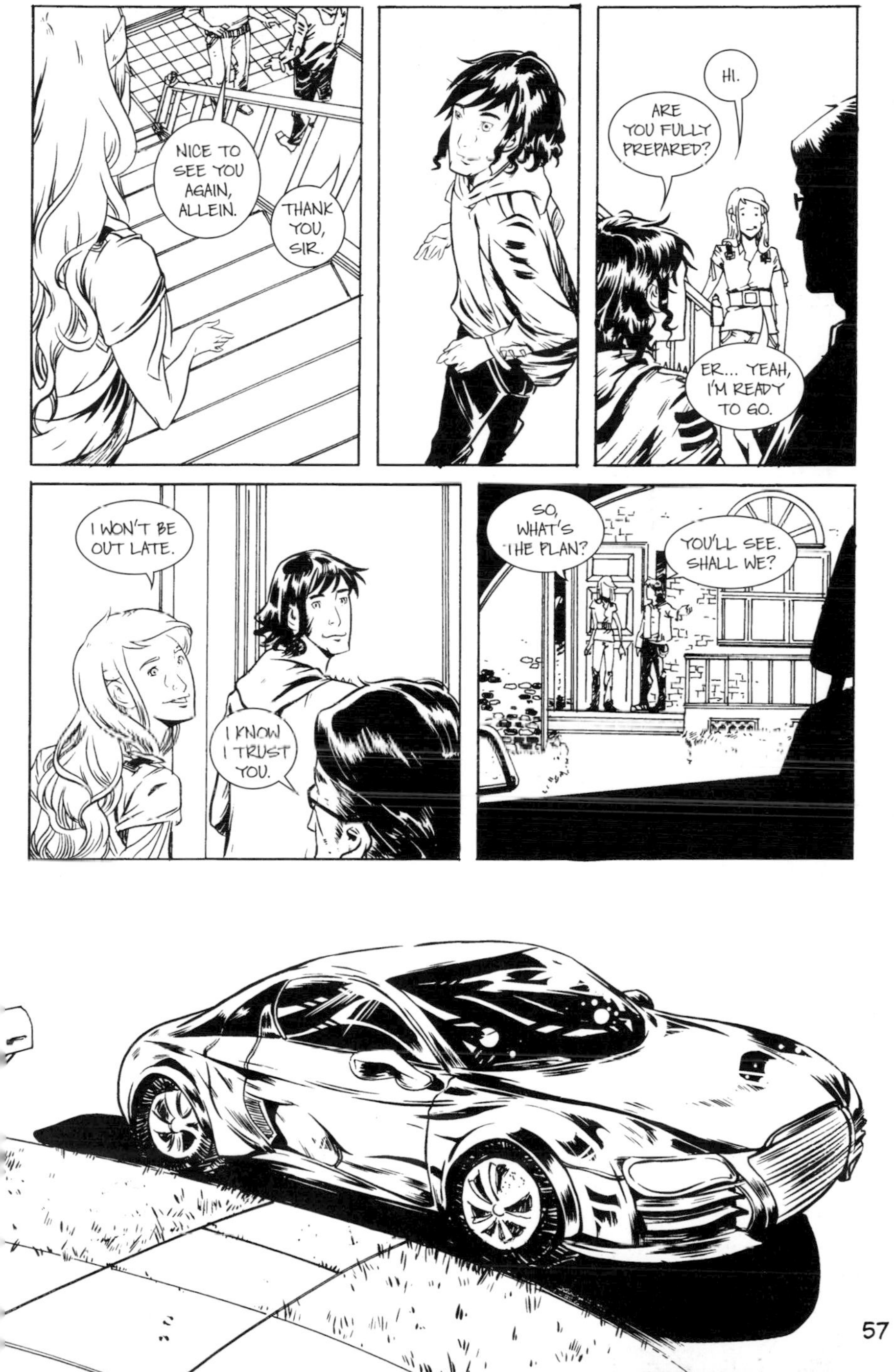
NICE TO SEE YOU AGAIN, ALLEIN.
THANK YOU, SIR.
HI.
ARE YOU FULLY PREPARED?
ER... YEAH, I'M READY TO GO.
I WON'T BE OUT LATE.
I KNOW I TRUST YOU.
SO, WHAT'S THE PLAN?
YOU'LL SEE. SHALL WE?

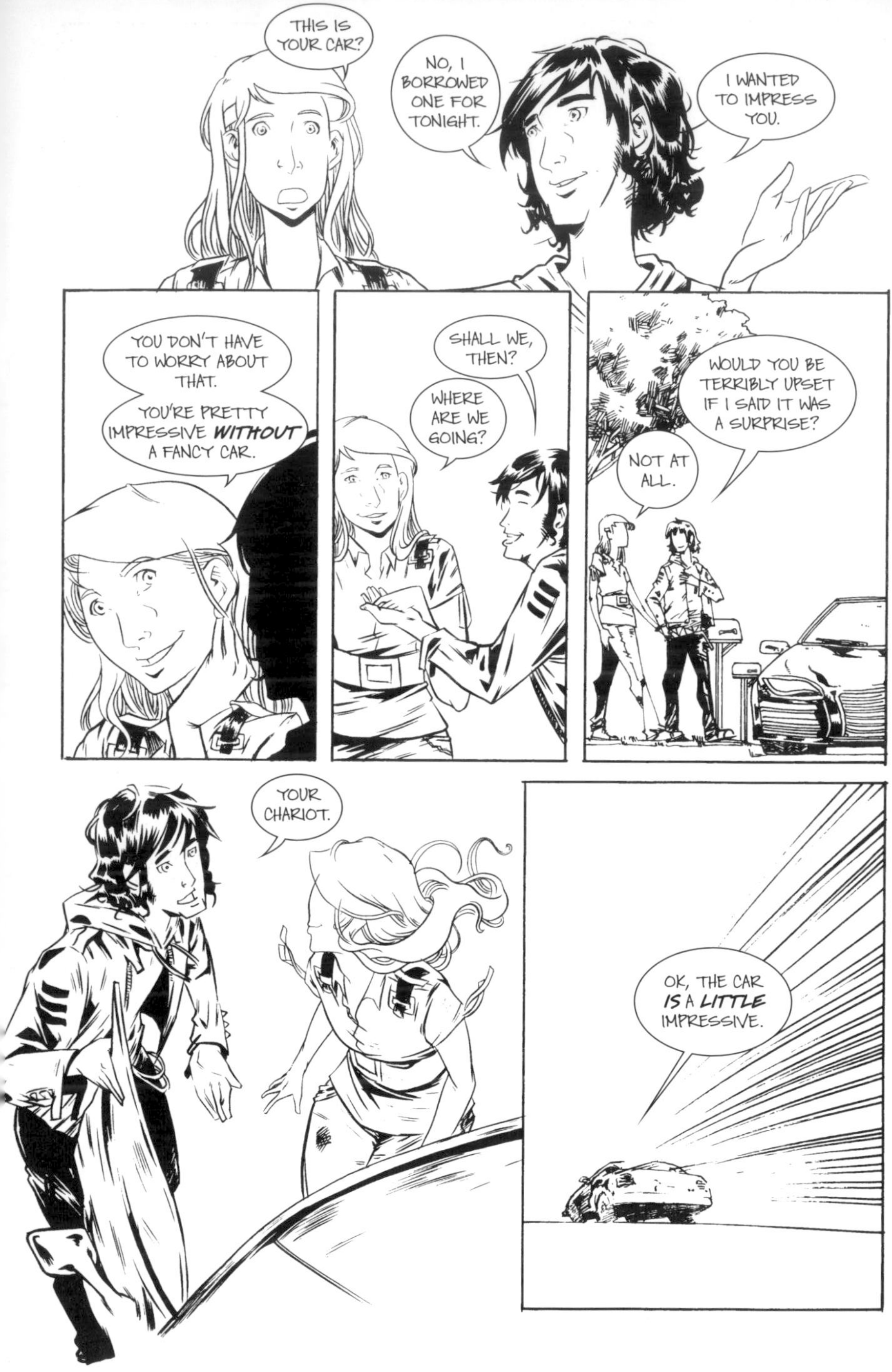
THIS IS YOUR CAR?
NO, I BORROWED ONE FOR TONIGHT.
I WANTED TO IMPRESS YOU.
YOU DON'T HAVE TO WORRY ABOUT THAT.
YOU'RE PRETTY IMPRESSIVE **WITHOUT** A FANCY CAR.
SHALL WE, THEN?
WHERE ARE WE GOING?
WOULD YOU BE TERRIBLY UPSET IF I SAID IT WAS A SURPRISE?
NOT AT ALL.
YOUR CHARIOT.
OK, THE CAR ***IS*** A ***LITTLE*** IMPRESSIVE.

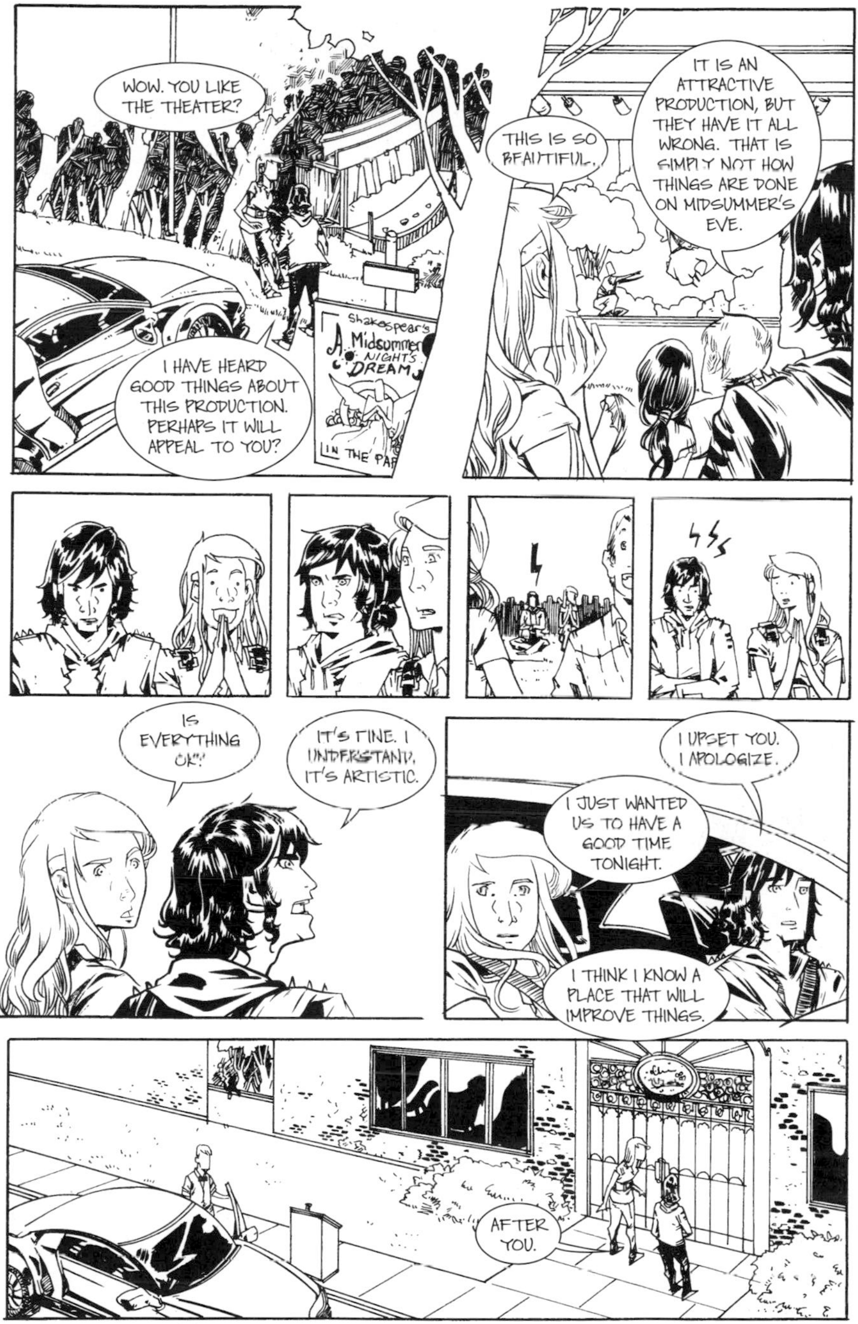
WOW. YOU LIKE THE THEATER?
I HAVE HEARD GOOD THINGS ABOUT THIS PRODUCTION. PERHAPS IT WILL APPEAL TO YOU?
Shakespear's A Midsummer NIGHT'S DREAM
IN THE PAR
THIS IS SO BEAUTIFUL.
IT IS AN ATTRACTIVE PRODUCTION, BUT THEY HAVE IT ALL WRONG. THAT IS SIMPLY NOT HOW THINGS ARE DONE ON MIDSUMMER'S EVE.
IS EVERYTHING OK?
IT'S FINE. I UNDERSTAND, IT'S ARTISTIC.
I UPSET YOU. I APOLOGIZE.
I JUST WANTED US TO HAVE A GOOD TIME TONIGHT.
I THINK I KNOW A PLACE THAT WILL IMPROVE THINGS.
AFTER YOU.

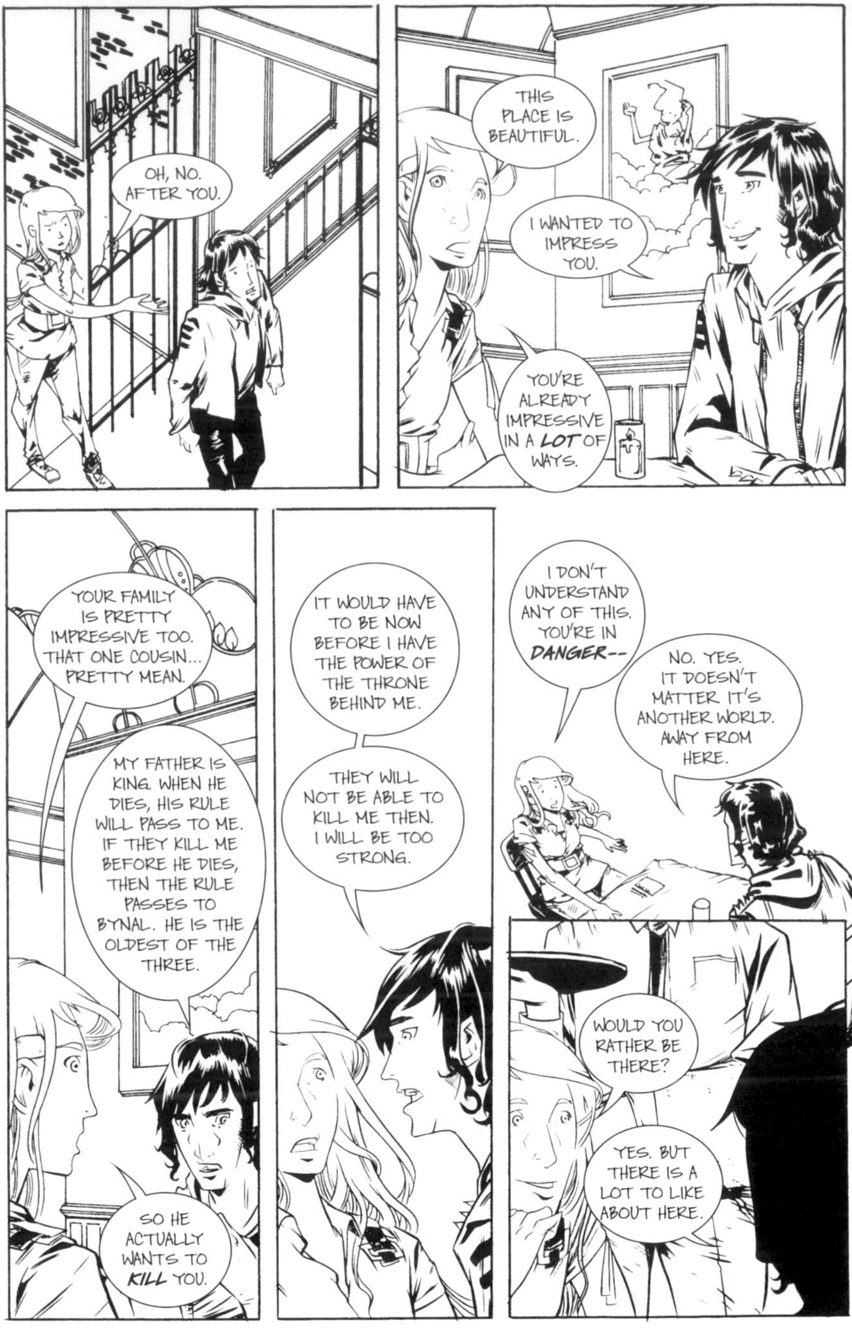
OH, NO. AFTER YOU.
THIS PLACE IS BEAUTIFUL.
I WANTED TO IMPRESS YOU.
YOU'RE ALREADY IMPRESSIVE IN A **LOT** OF WAYS.
YOUR FAMILY IS PRETTY IMPRESSIVE TOO. THAT ONE COUSIN... PRETTY MEAN.
MY FATHER IS KING. WHEN HE DIES, HIS RULE WILL PASS TO ME. IF THEY KILL ME BEFORE HE DIES, THEN THE RULE PASSES TO BYNAL. HE IS THE OLDEST OF THE THREE.
SO HE ACTUALLY WANTS TO **KILL** YOU.
IT WOULD HAVE TO BE NOW BEFORE I HAVE THE POWER OF THE THRONE BEHIND ME.
THEY WILL NOT BE ABLE TO KILL ME THEN. I WILL BE TOO STRONG.
I DON'T UNDERSTAND ANY OF THIS. YOU'RE IN **DANGER--**
NO. YES. IT DOESN'T MATTER IT'S ANOTHER WORLD. AWAY FROM HERE.
WOULD YOU RATHER BE THERE?
YES. BUT THERE IS A LOT TO LIKE ABOUT HERE.

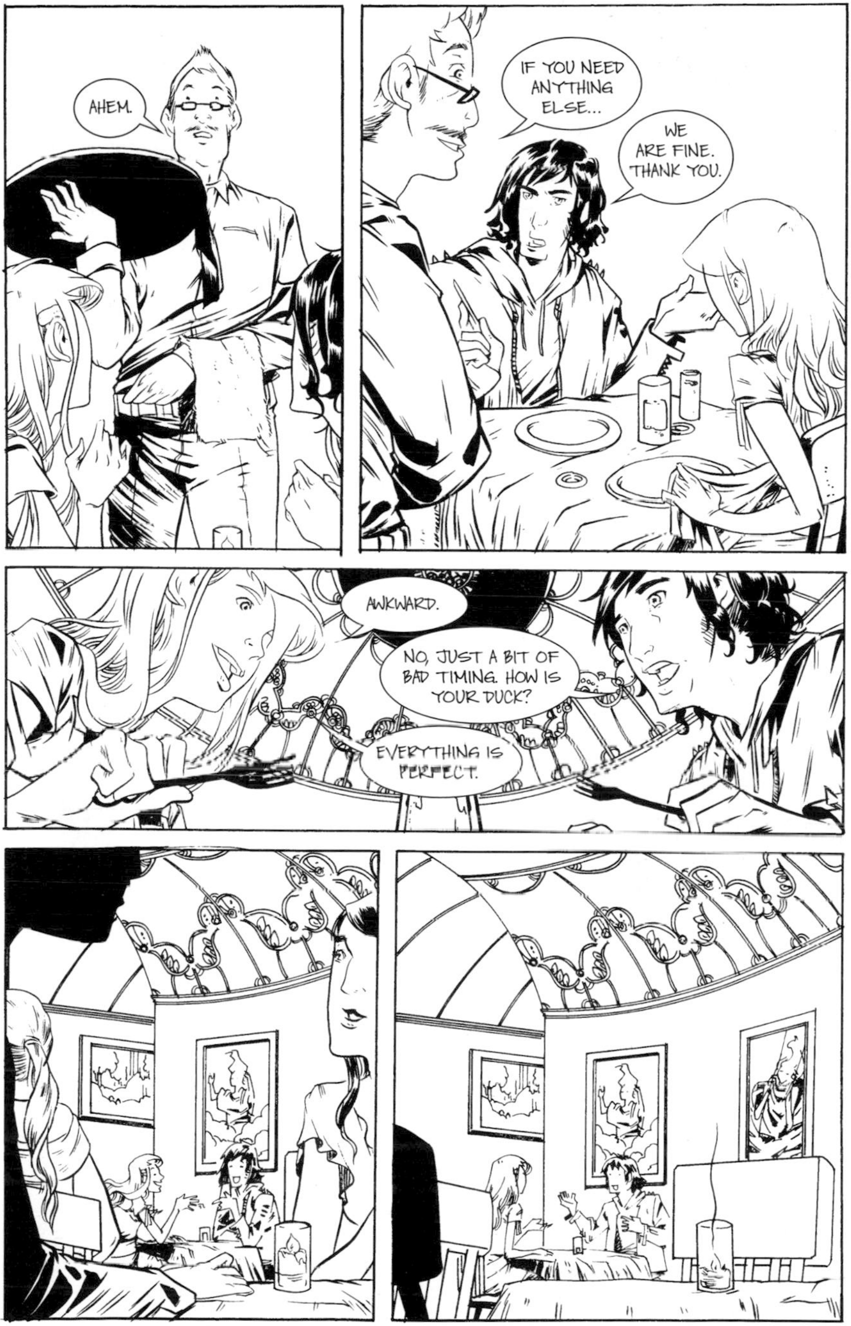
AHEM.
IF YOU NEED ANYTHING ELSE...
WE ARE FINE. THANK YOU.
AWKWARD.
NO, JUST A BIT OF BAD TIMING. HOW IS YOUR DUCK?
EVERYTHING IS PERFECT.

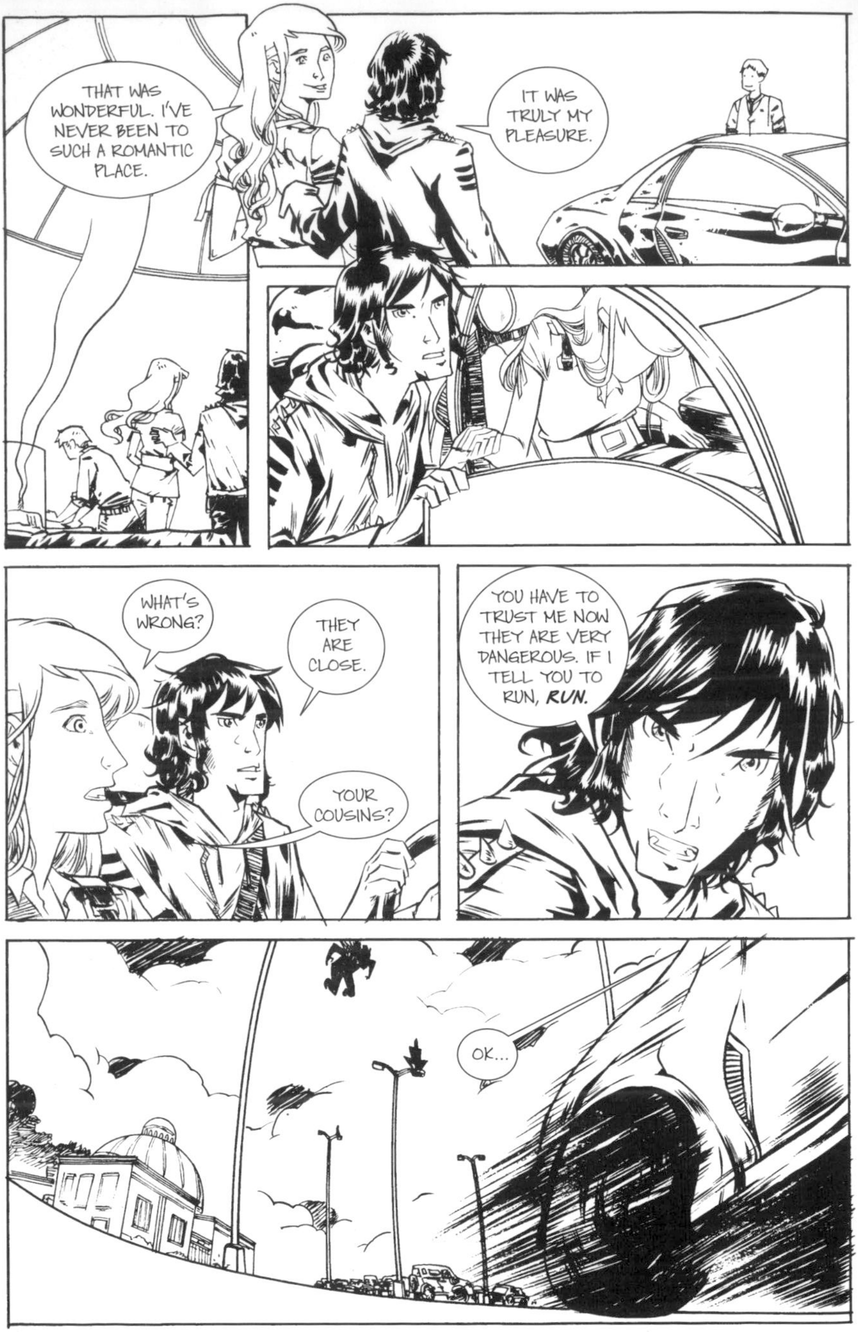

THAT WAS WONDERFUL. I'VE NEVER BEEN TO SUCH A ROMANTIC PLACE.
IT WAS TRULY MY PLEASURE.
WHAT'S WRONG?
THEY ARE CLOSE.
YOUR COUSINS?
YOU HAVE TO TRUST ME NOW THEY ARE VERY DANGEROUS. IF I TELL YOU TO RUN, ***RUN.***
OK...

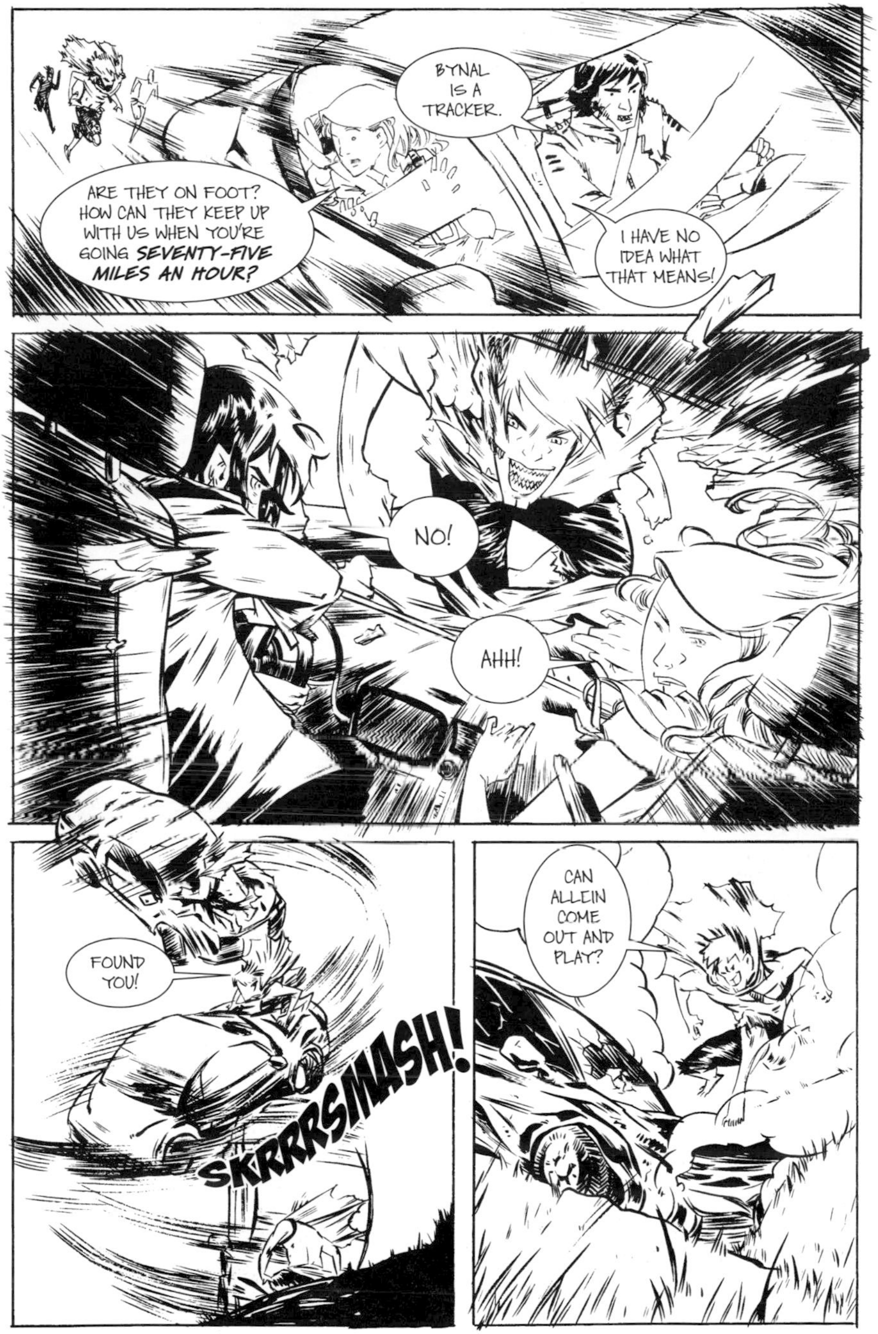
BYNAL IS A TRACKER.
ARE THEY ON FOOT? HOW CAN THEY KEEP UP WITH US WHEN YOU'RE GOING SEVENTY-FIVE MILES AN HOUR?
I HAVE NO IDEA WHAT THAT MEANS!
NO!
AHH!
FOUND YOU!
SKRRRSMASH!
CAN ALLEIN COME OUT AND PLAY?

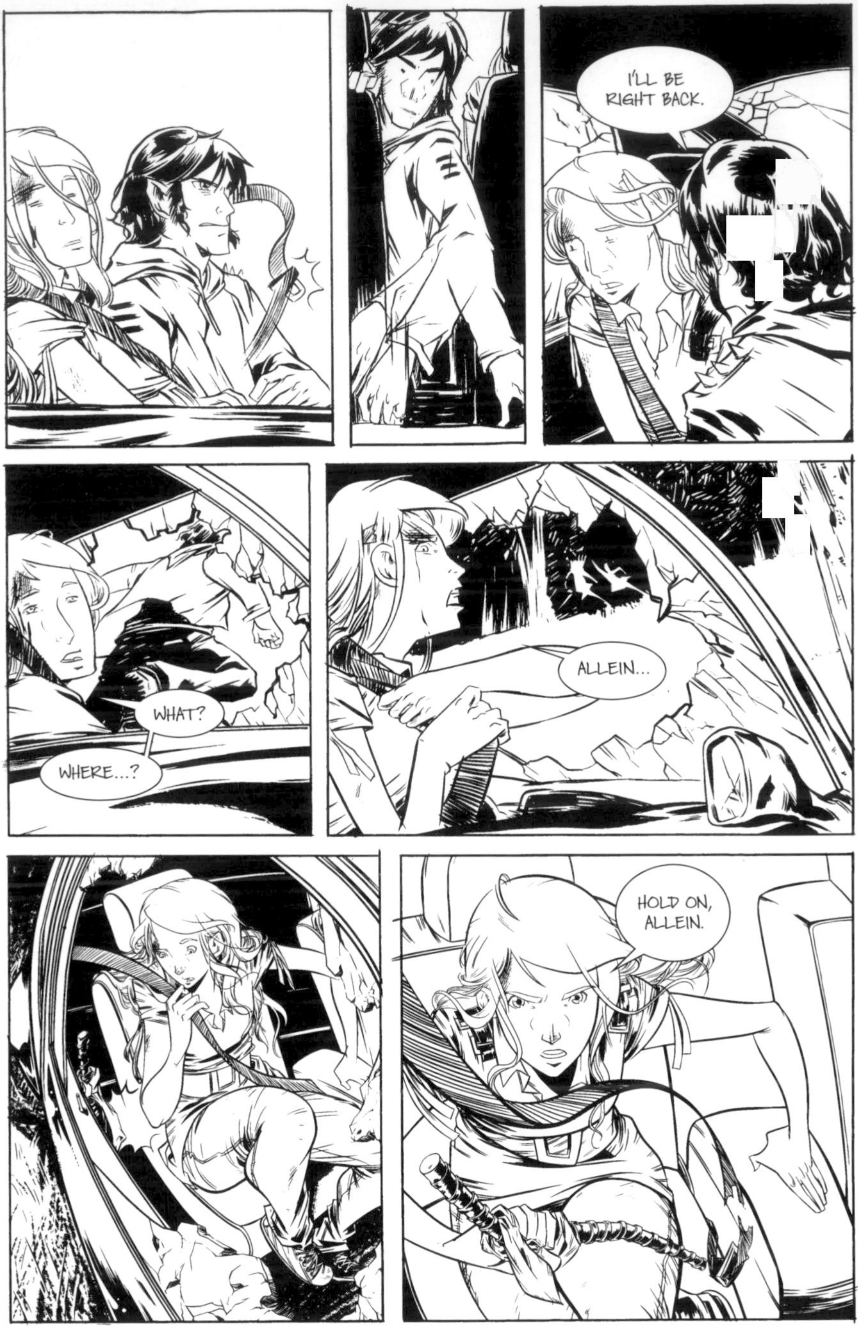
I'LL BE RIGHT BACK.
WHAT?
WHERE...?
ALLEIN...
HOLD ON, ALLEIN.

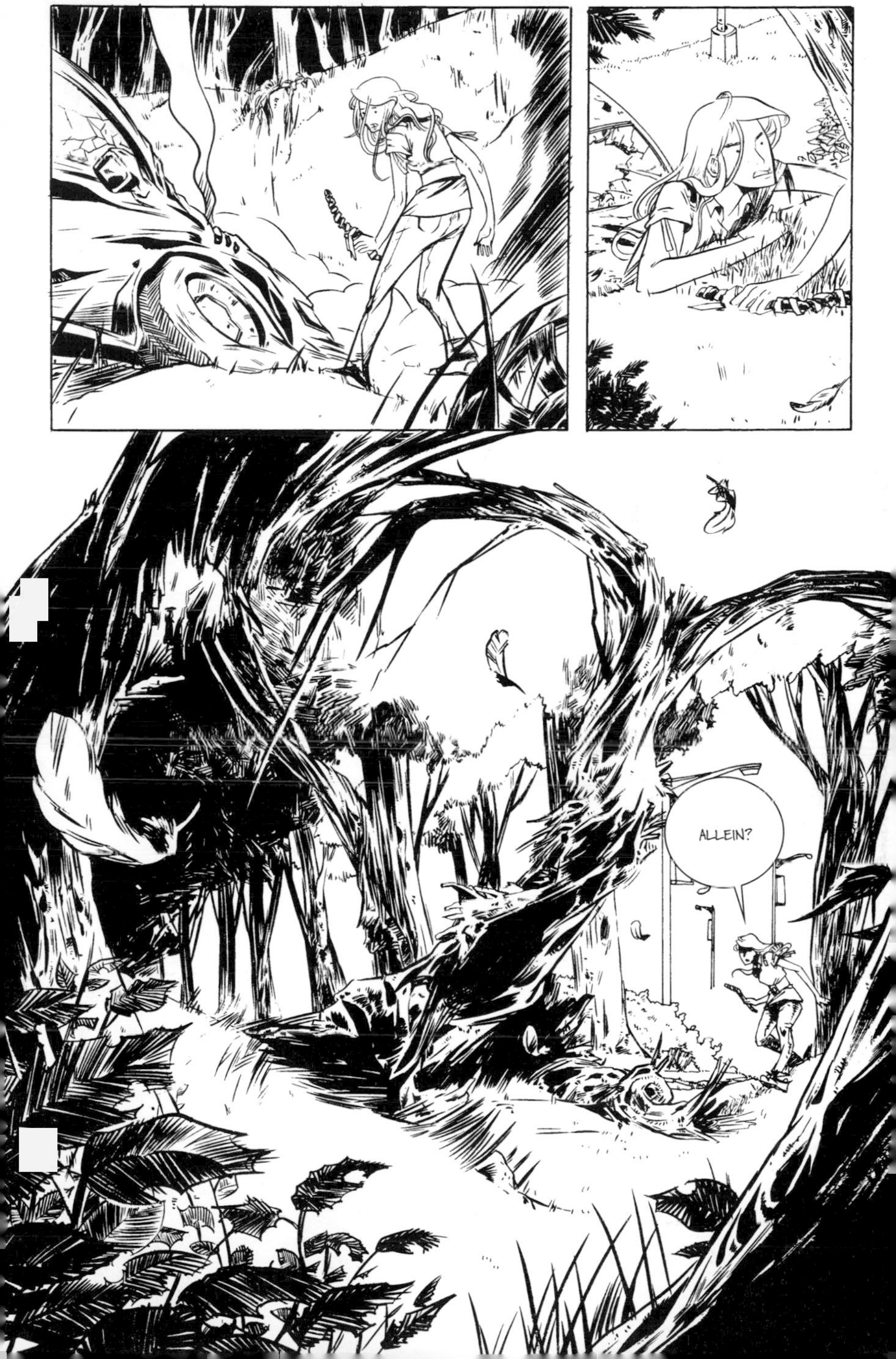
ALLEIN?

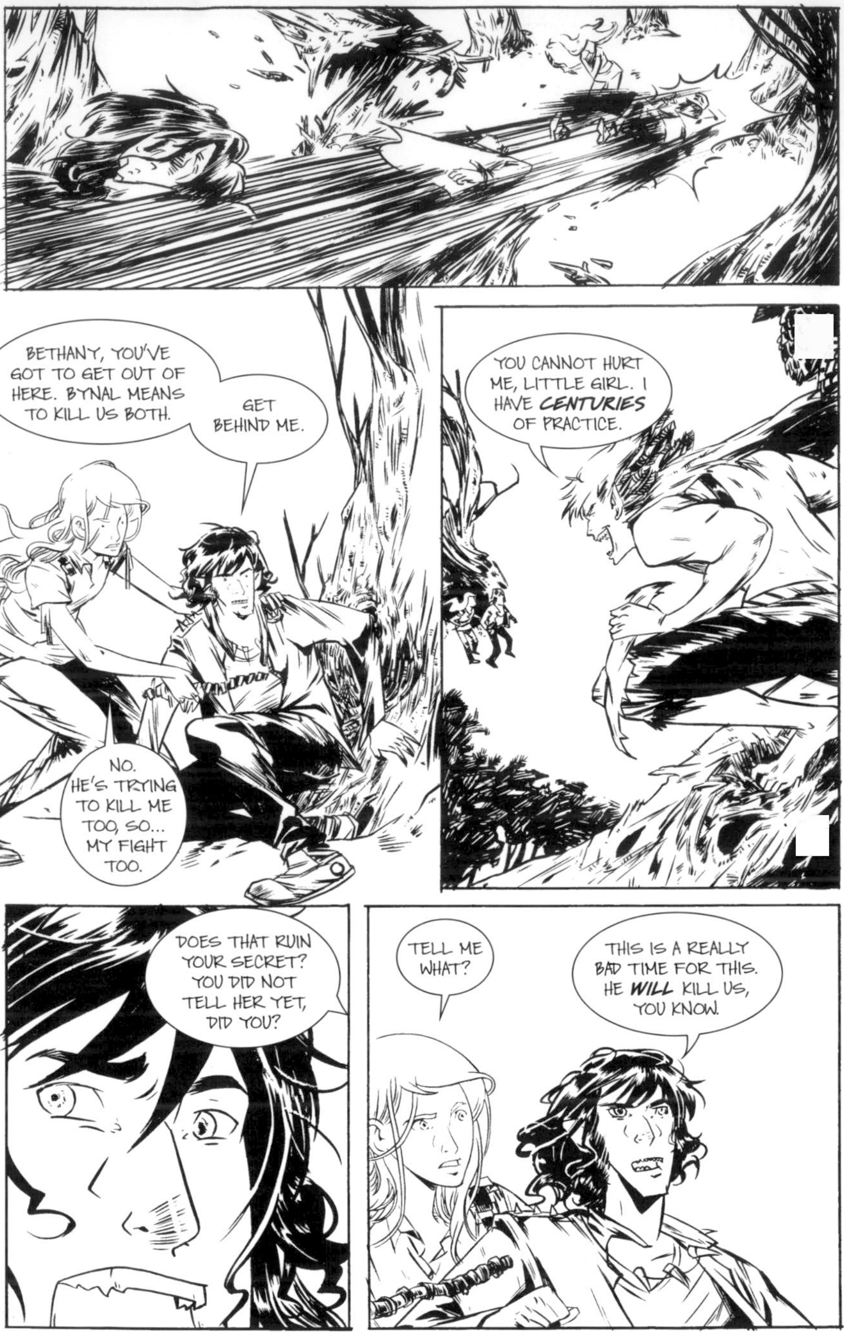
BETHANY, YOU'VE GOT TO GET OUT OF HERE. BYNAL MEANS TO KILL US BOTH.
GET BEHIND ME.
NO. HE'S TRYING TO KILL ME TOO, SO... MY FIGHT TOO.
YOU CANNOT HURT ME, LITTLE GIRL. I HAVE CENTURIES OF PRACTICE.
DOES THAT RUIN YOUR SECRET? YOU DID NOT TELL HER YET, DID YOU?
TELL ME WHAT?
THIS IS A REALLY BAD TIME FOR THIS. HE WILL KILL US, YOU KNOW.

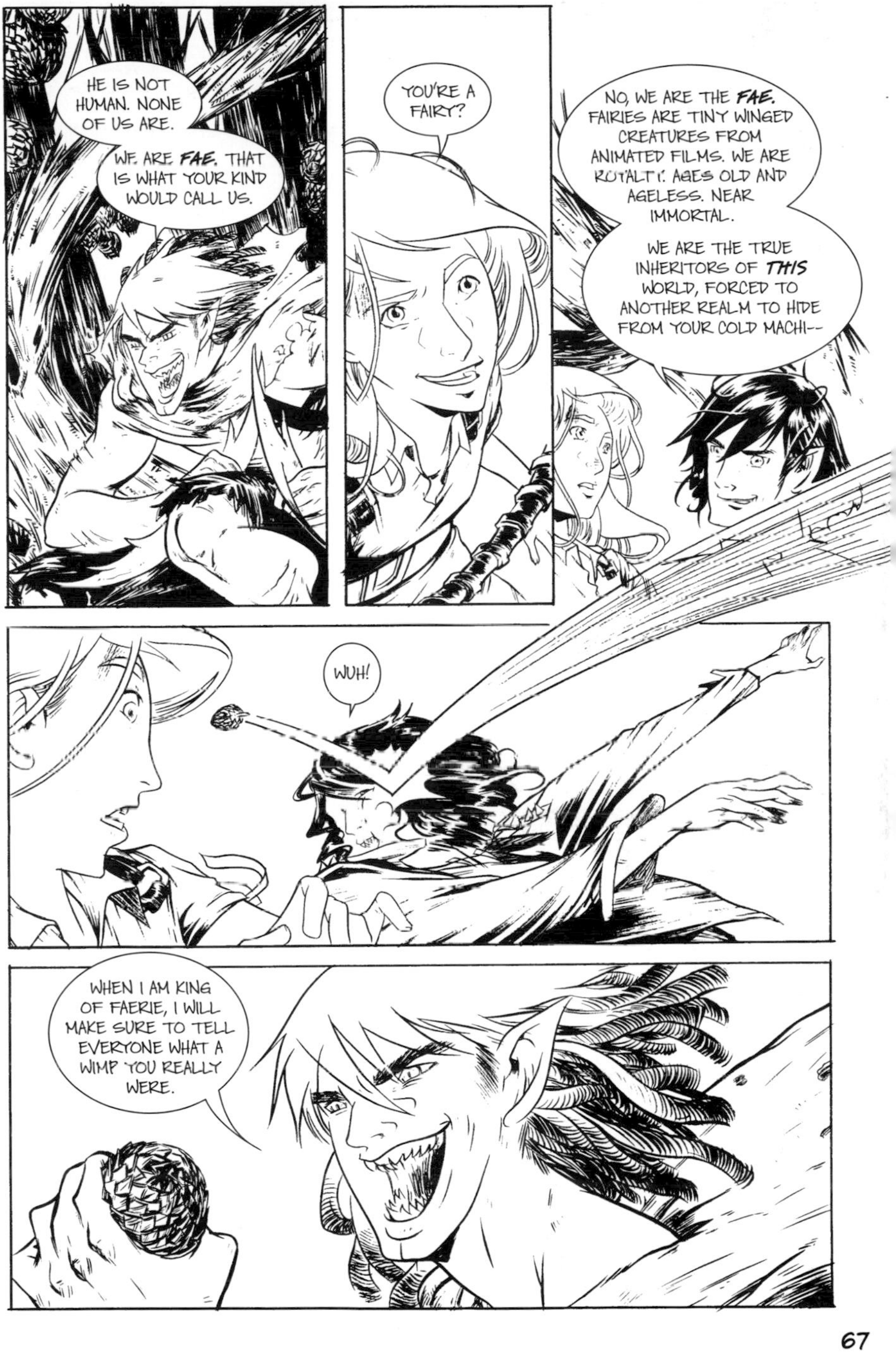

HE IS NOT HUMAN. NONE OF US ARE.
WE ARE FAE. THAT IS WHAT YOUR KIND WOULD CALL US.
YOU'RE A FAIRY?
NO, WE ARE THE FAE. FAIRIES ARE TINY WINGED CREATURES FROM ANIMATED FILMS. WE ARE ROYALTY. AGES OLD AND AGELESS. NEAR IMMORTAL.
WE ARE THE TRUE INHERITORS OF THIS WORLD, FORCED TO ANOTHER REALM TO HIDE FROM YOUR COLD MACHI--
WUH!
WHEN I AM KING OF FAERIE, I WILL MAKE SURE TO TELL EVERYONE WHAT A WIMP YOU REALLY WERE.

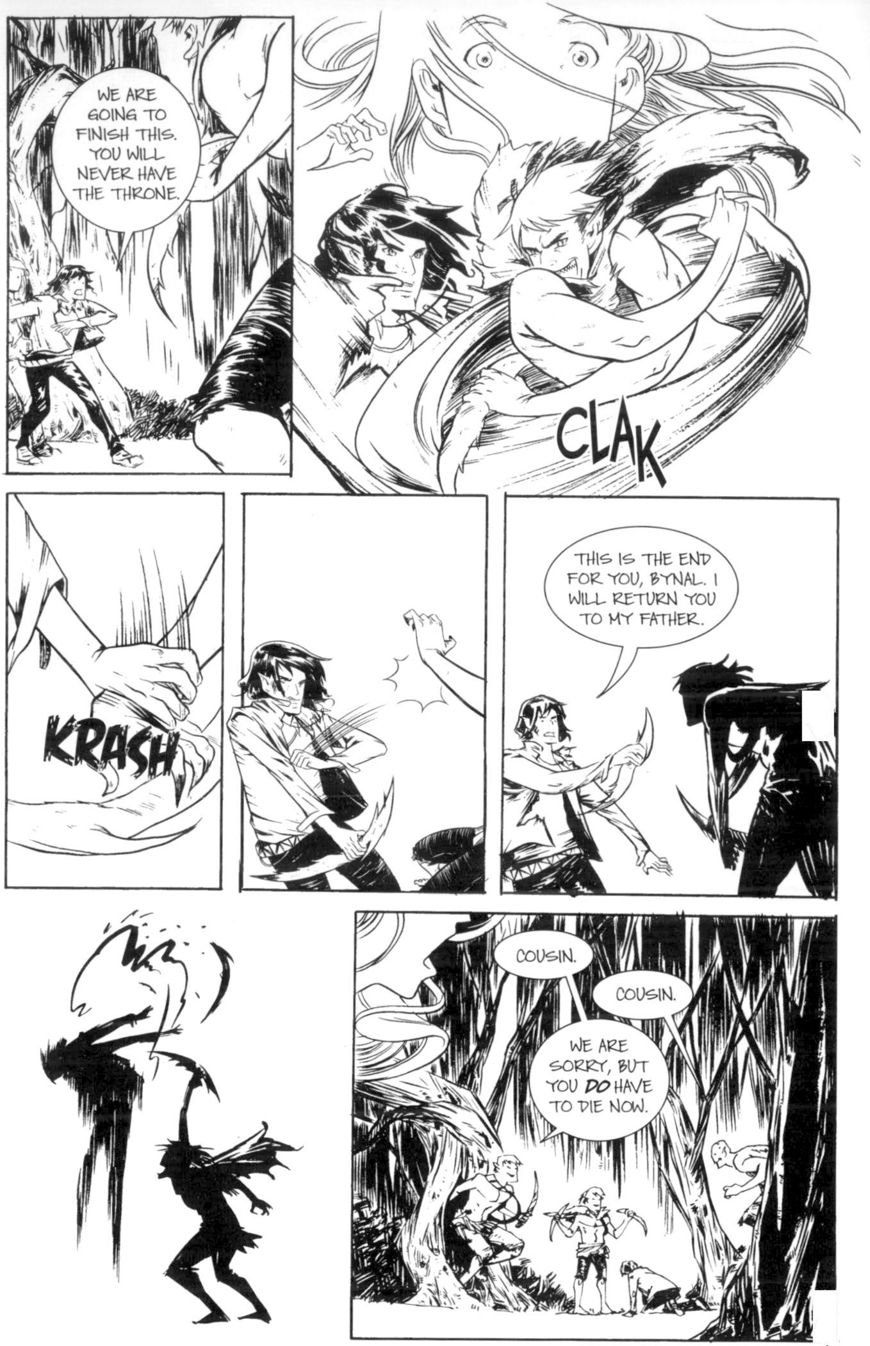
WE ARE GOING TO FINISH THIS. YOU WILL NEVER HAVE THE THRONE.
CLAK
KRASH
THIS IS THE END FOR YOU, BYNAL. I WILL RETURN YOU TO MY FATHER.
COUSIN.
COUSIN.
WE ARE SORRY, BUT YOU **DO** HAVE TO DIE NOW.

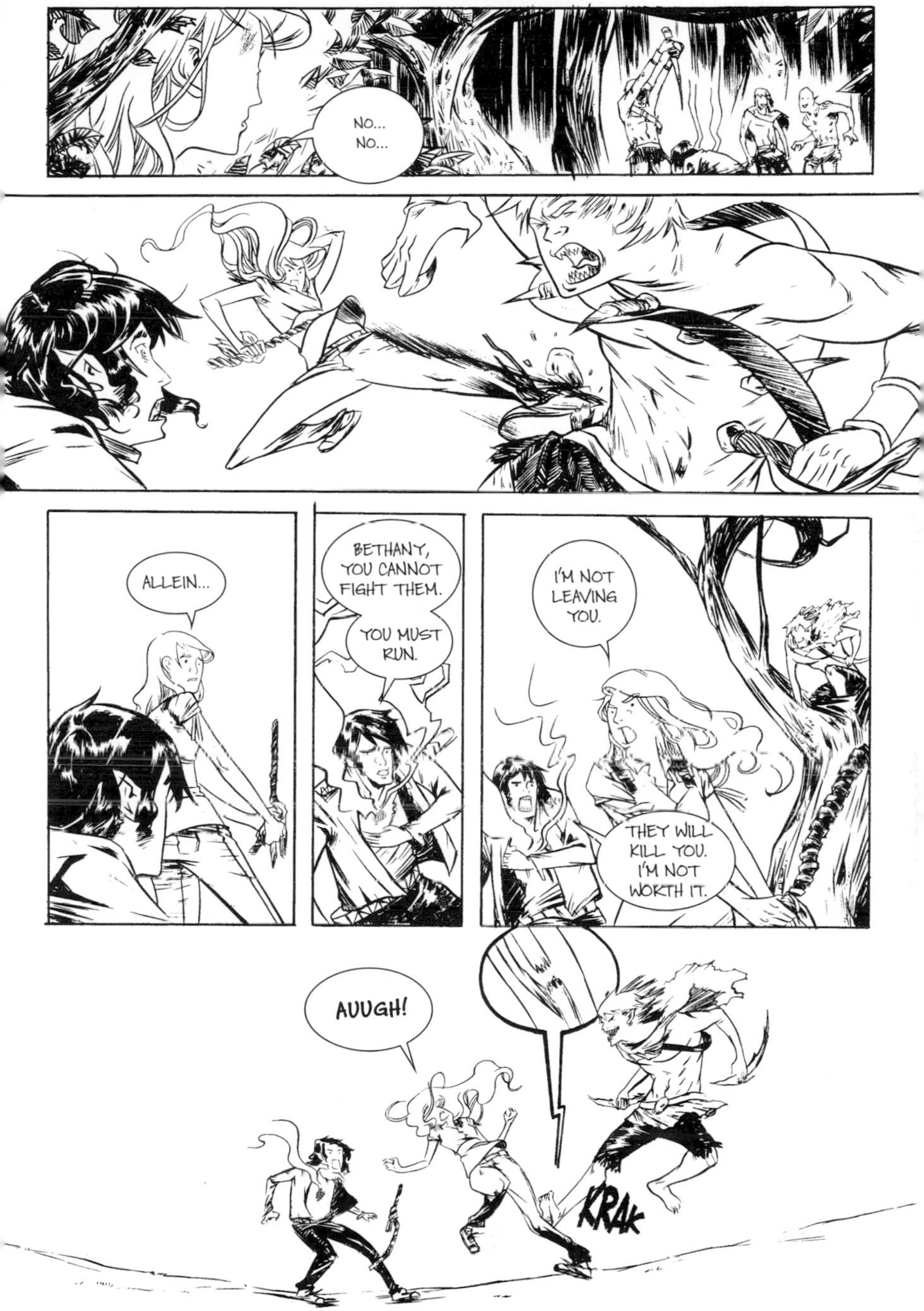
NO... NO...
ALLEIN...
BETHANY, YOU CANNOT FIGHT THEM.
YOU MUST RUN.
I'M NOT LEAVING YOU.
THEY WILL KILL YOU. I'M NOT WORTH IT.
AUUGH!
KRAK

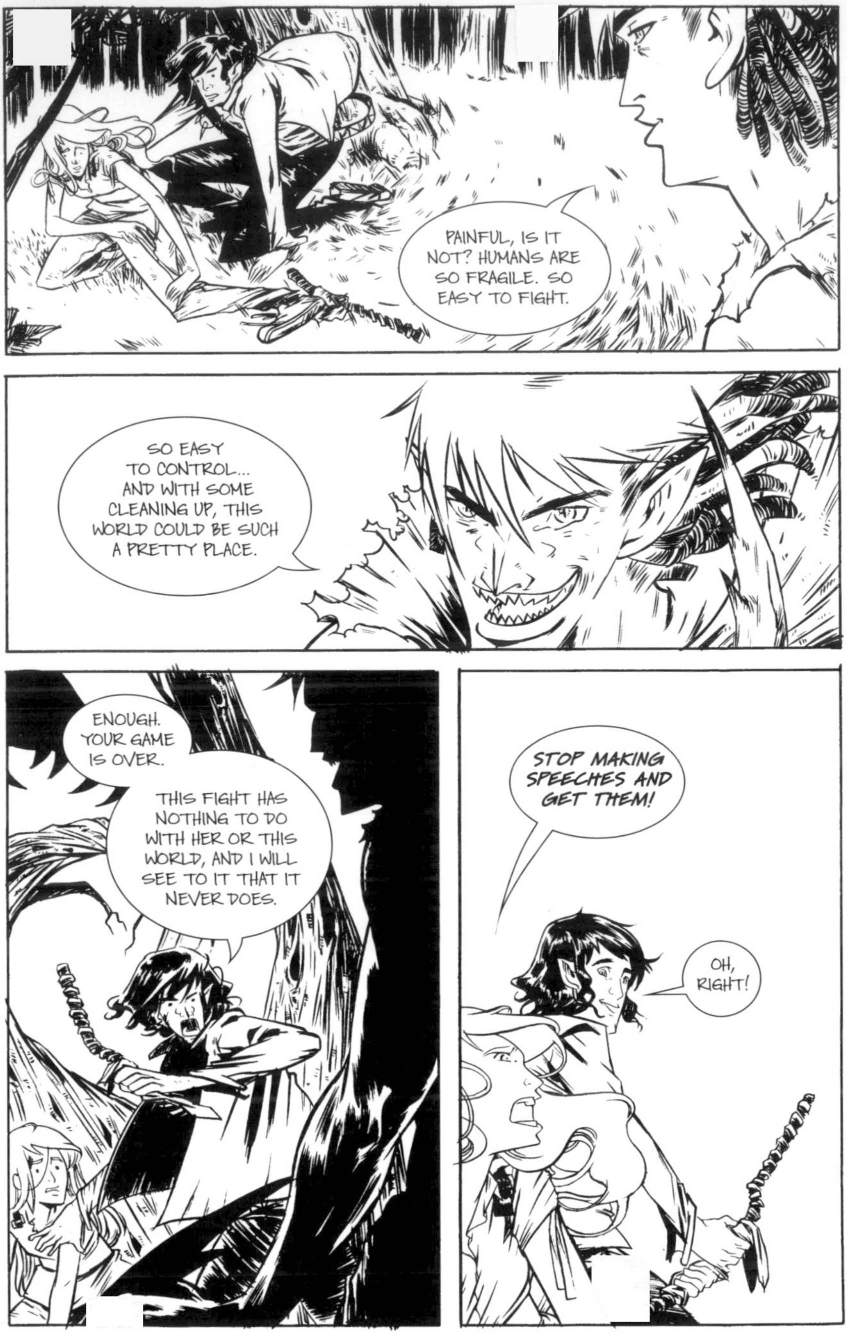
PAINFUL, IS IT NOT? HUMANS ARE SO FRAGILE. SO EASY TO FIGHT.
SO EASY TO CONTROL... AND WITH SOME CLEANING UP, THIS WORLD COULD BE SUCH A PRETTY PLACE.
ENOUGH. YOUR GAME IS OVER.
THIS FIGHT HAS NOTHING TO DO WITH HER OR THIS WORLD, AND I WILL SEE TO IT THAT IT NEVER DOES.
STOP MAKING SPEECHES AND GET THEM!
OH, RIGHT!

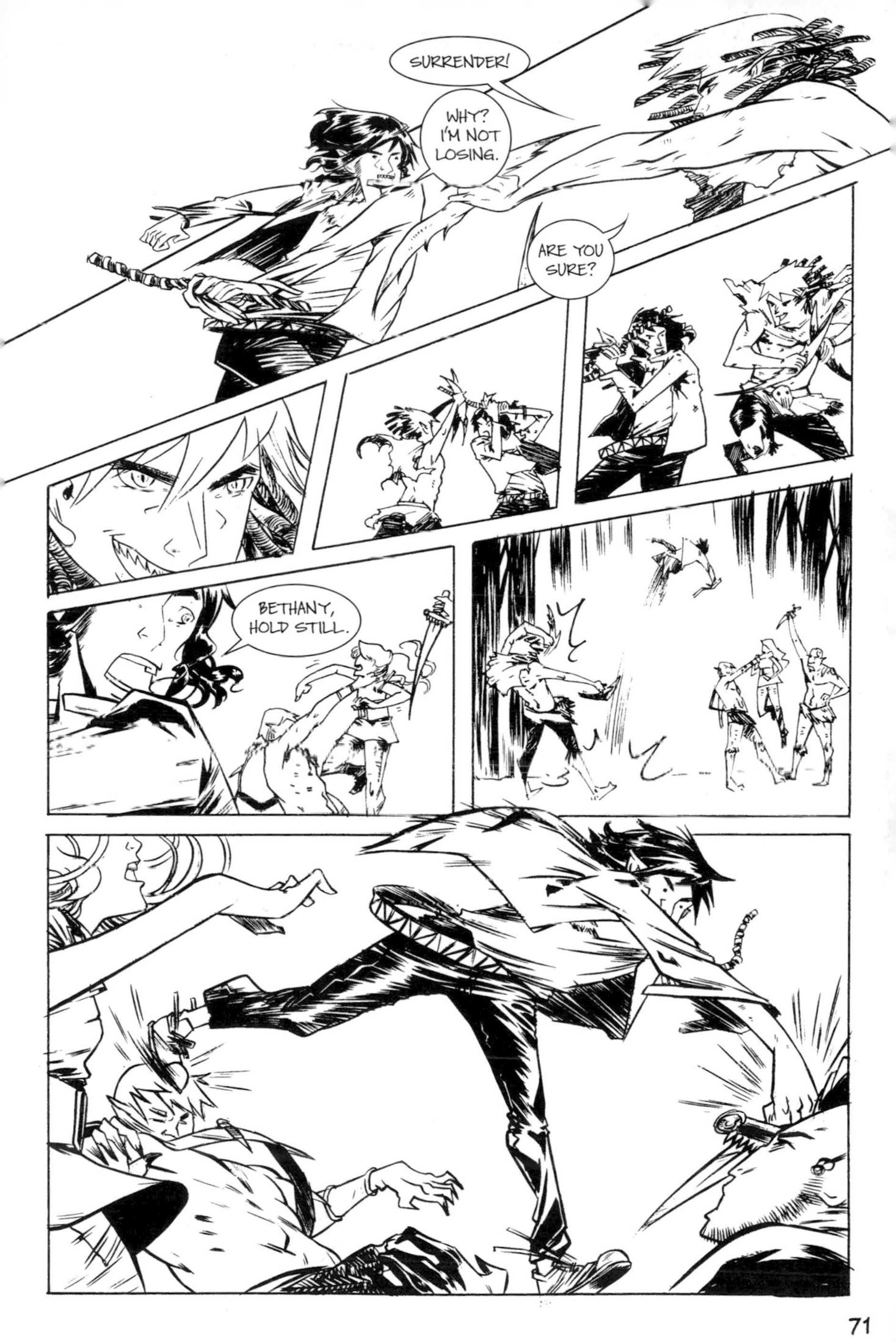
SURRENDER!
WHY? I'M NOT LOSING.
ARE YOU SURE?
BETHANY, HOLD STILL.

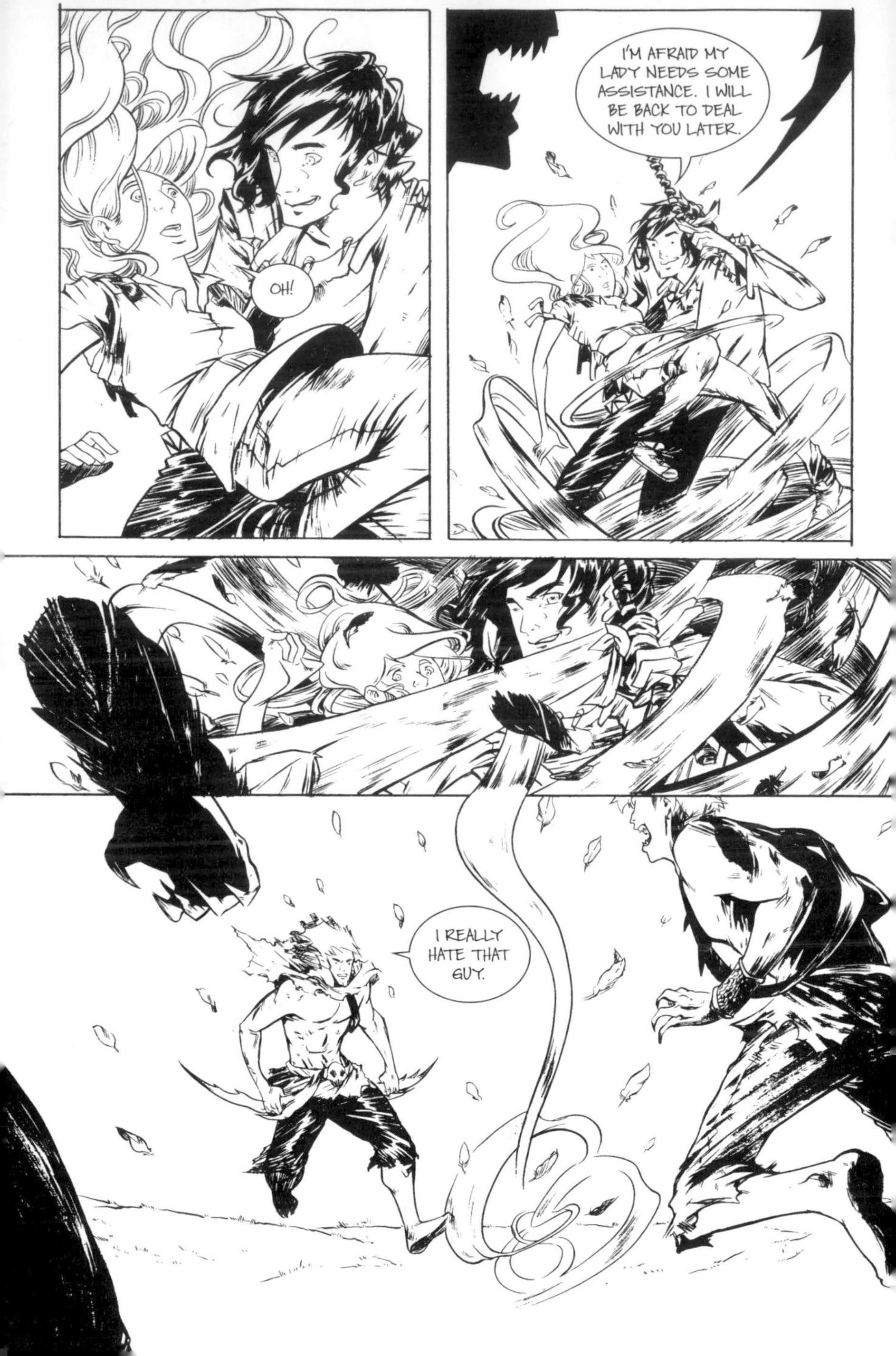
OH!
I'M AFRAID MY LADY NEEDS SOME ASSISTANCE. I WILL BE BACK TO DEAL WITH YOU LATER.
I REALLY HATE THAT GUY.

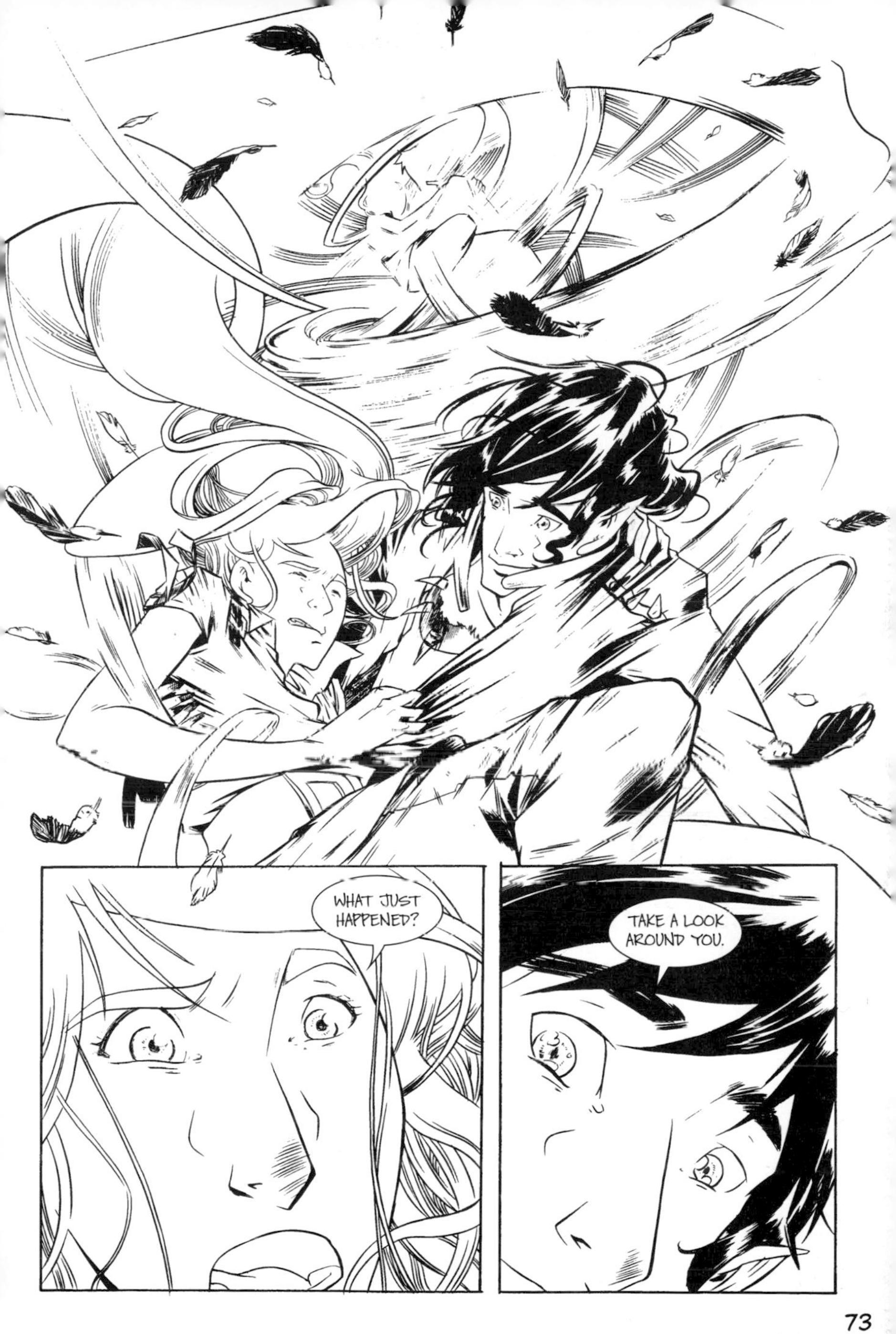
WHAT JUST HAPPENED?
TAKE A LOOK AROUND YOU.

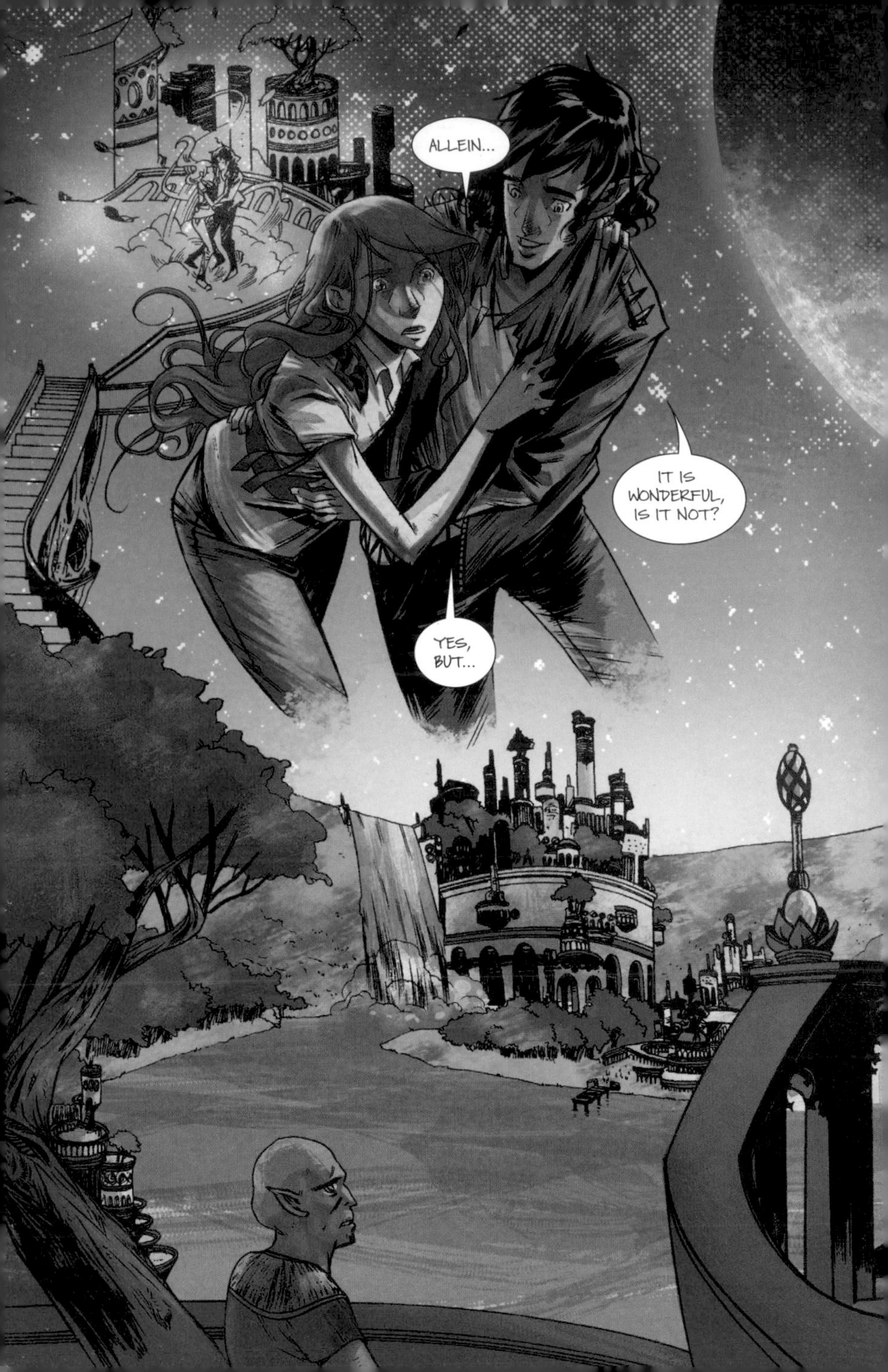
ALLEIN...
IT IS WONDERFUL, IS IT NOT?
YES, BUT...

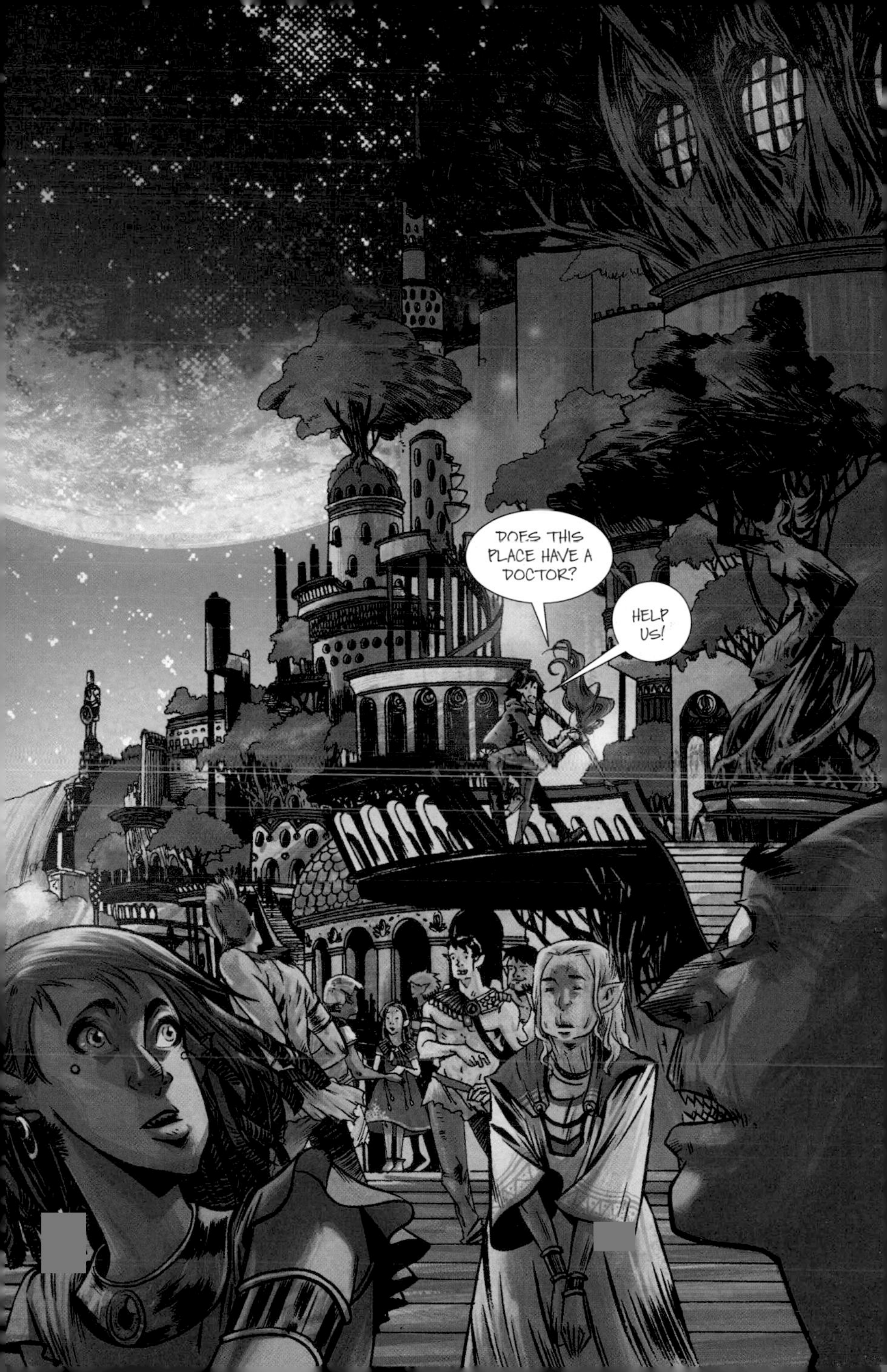
DOES THIS PLACE HAVE A DOCTOR?
HELP US!

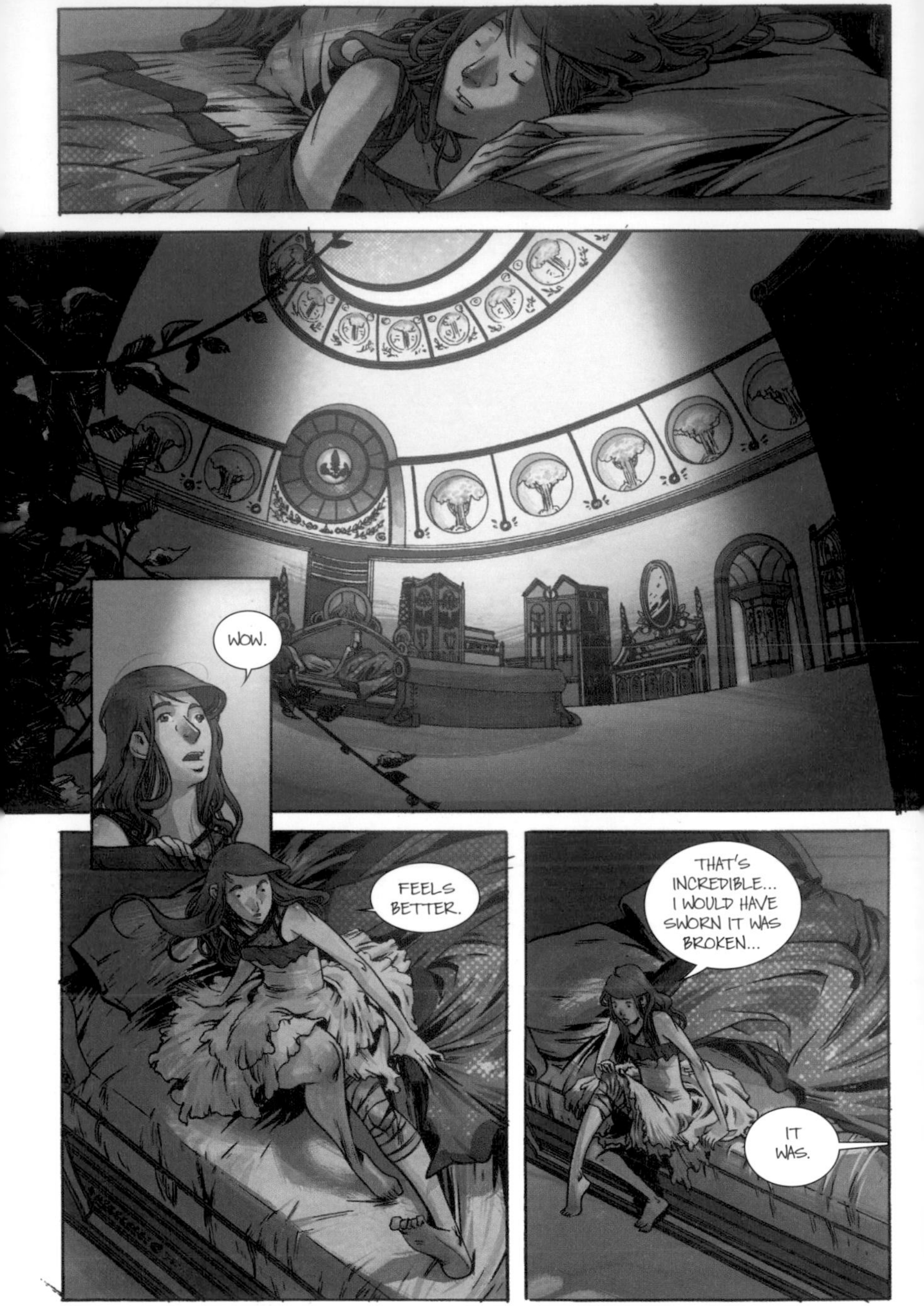
WOW.
FEELS BETTER.
THAT'S INCREDIBLE... I WOULD HAVE SWORN IT WAS BROKEN...
IT WAS.

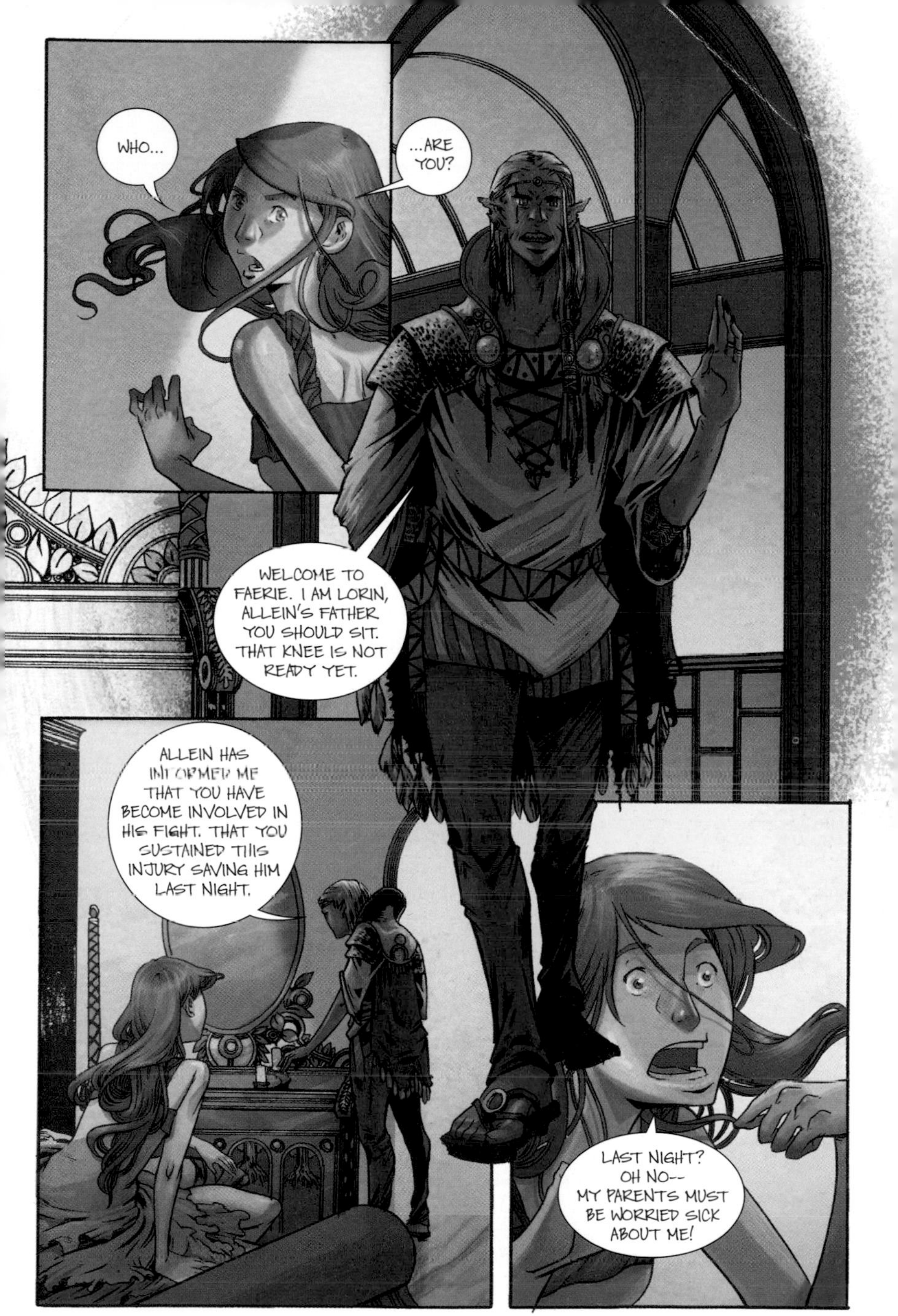
WHO...
...ARE YOU?
WELCOME TO FAERIE. I AM LORIN, ALLEIN'S FATHER YOU SHOULD SIT. THAT KNEE IS NOT READY YET.
ALLEIN HAS INFORMED ME THAT YOU HAVE BECOME INVOLVED IN HIS FIGHT. THAT YOU SUSTAINED THIS INJURY SAVING HIM LAST NIGHT.
LAST NIGHT? OH NO-- MY PARENTS MUST BE WORRIED SICK ABOUT ME!

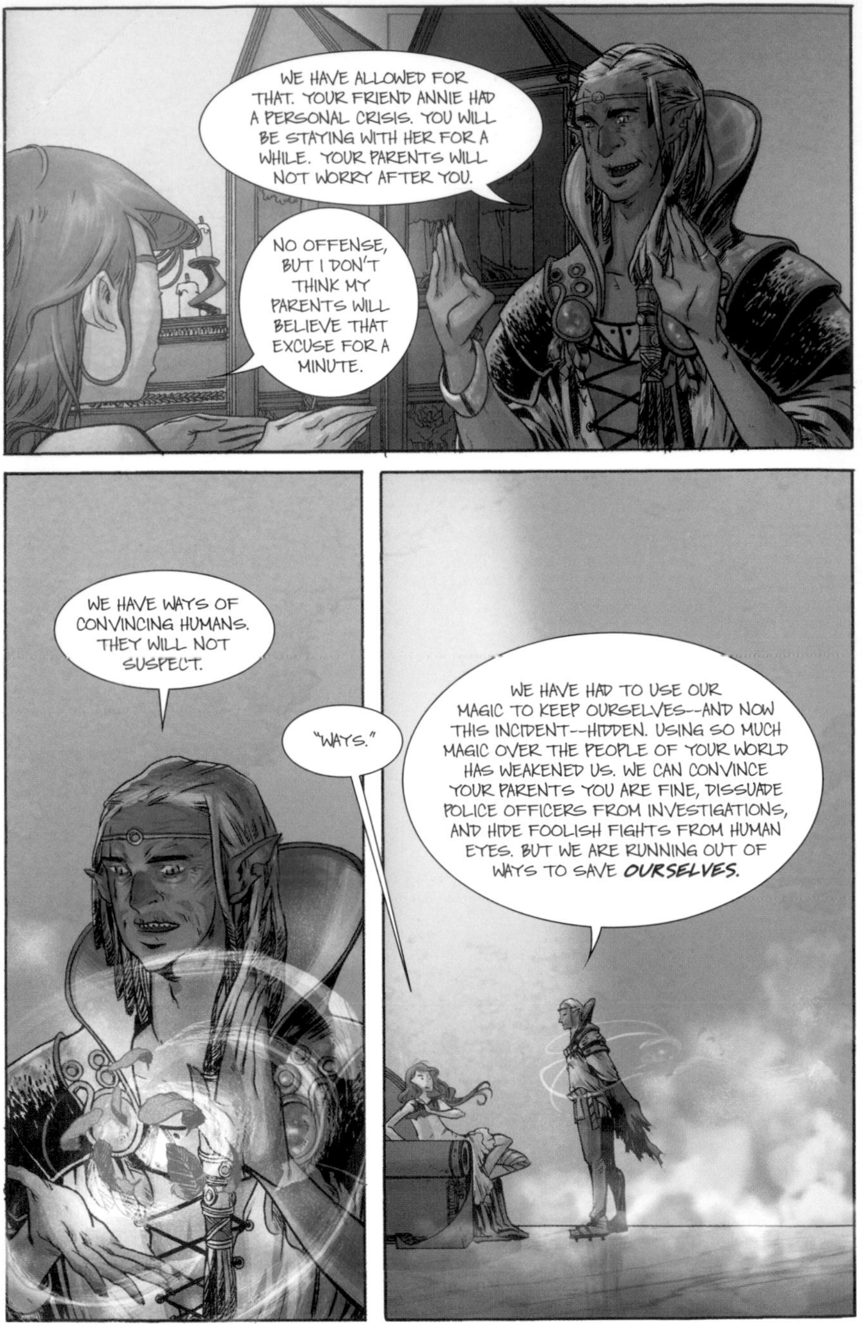
WE HAVE ALLOWED FOR THAT. YOUR FRIEND ANNIE HAD A PERSONAL CRISIS. YOU WILL BE STAYING WITH HER FOR A WHILE. YOUR PARENTS WILL NOT WORRY AFTER YOU.
NO OFFENSE, BUT I DON'T THINK MY PARENTS WILL BELIEVE THAT EXCUSE FOR A MINUTE.
WE HAVE WAYS OF CONVINCING HUMANS. THEY WILL NOT SUSPECT.
"WAYS."
WE HAVE HAD TO USE OUR MAGIC TO KEEP OURSELVES--AND NOW THIS INCIDENT--HIDDEN. USING SO MUCH MAGIC OVER THE PEOPLE OF YOUR WORLD HAS WEAKENED US. WE CAN CONVINCE YOUR PARENTS YOU ARE FINE, DISSUADE POLICE OFFICERS FROM INVESTIGATIONS, AND HIDE FOOLISH FIGHTS FROM HUMAN EYES. BUT WE ARE RUNNING OUT OF WAYS TO SAVE ***OURSELVES.***

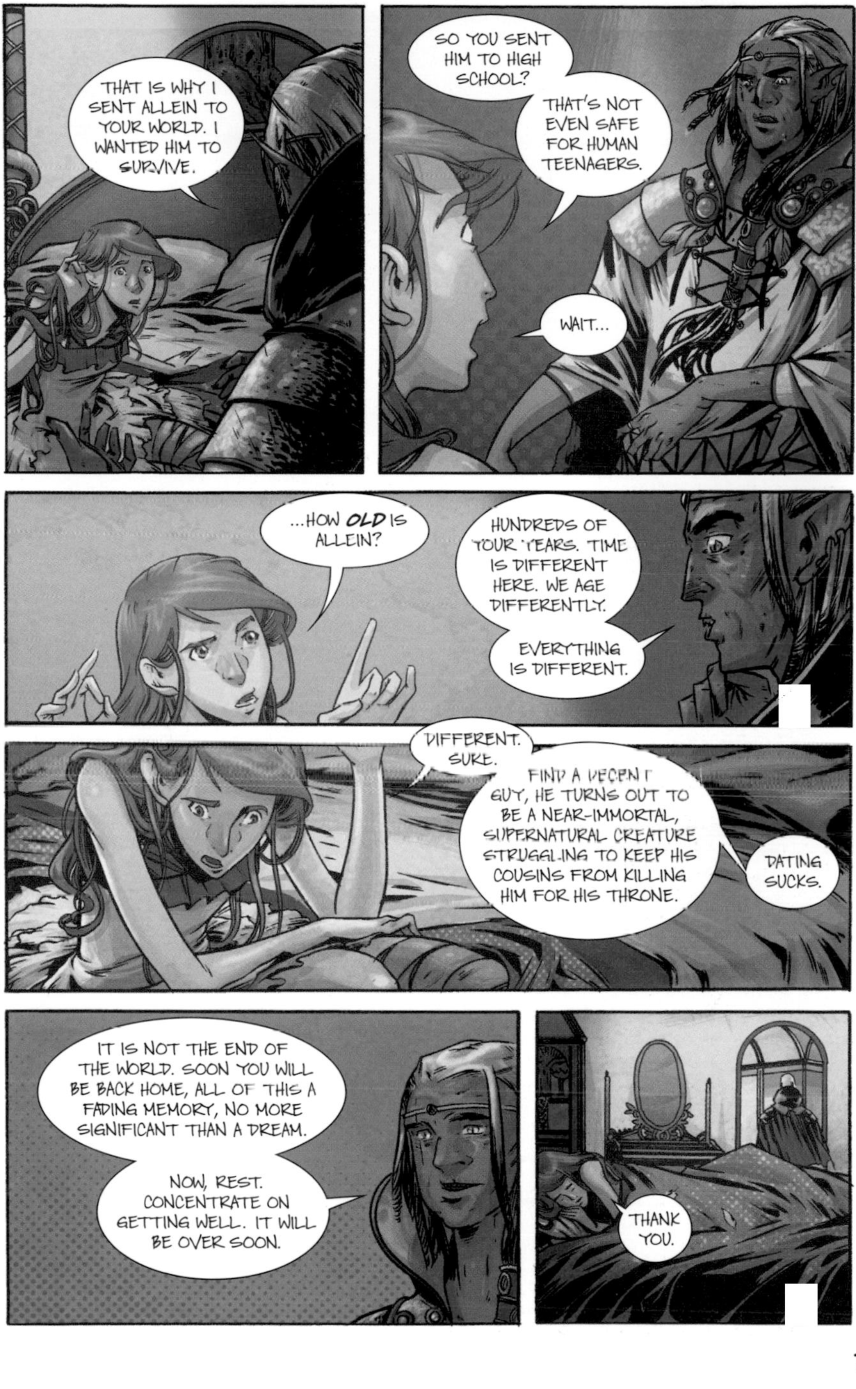
THAT IS WHY I SENT ALLEIN TO YOUR WORLD. I WANTED HIM TO SURVIVE.
SO YOU SENT HIM TO HIGH SCHOOL?
THAT'S NOT EVEN SAFE FOR HUMAN TEENAGERS.
WAIT...
...HOW OLD IS ALLEIN?
HUNDREDS OF YOUR YEARS. TIME IS DIFFERENT HERE. WE AGE DIFFERENTLY.
EVERYTHING IS DIFFERENT.
DIFFERENT. SURE.
FIND A DECENT GUY, HE TURNS OUT TO BE A NEAR-IMMORTAL, SUPERNATURAL CREATURE STRUGGLING TO KEEP HIS COUSINS FROM KILLING HIM FOR HIS THRONE.
DATING SUCKS.
IT IS NOT THE END OF THE WORLD. SOON YOU WILL BE BACK HOME, ALL OF THIS A FADING MEMORY, NO MORE SIGNIFICANT THAN A DREAM.
NOW, REST. CONCENTRATE ON GETTING WELL. IT WILL BE OVER SOON.
THANK YOU.

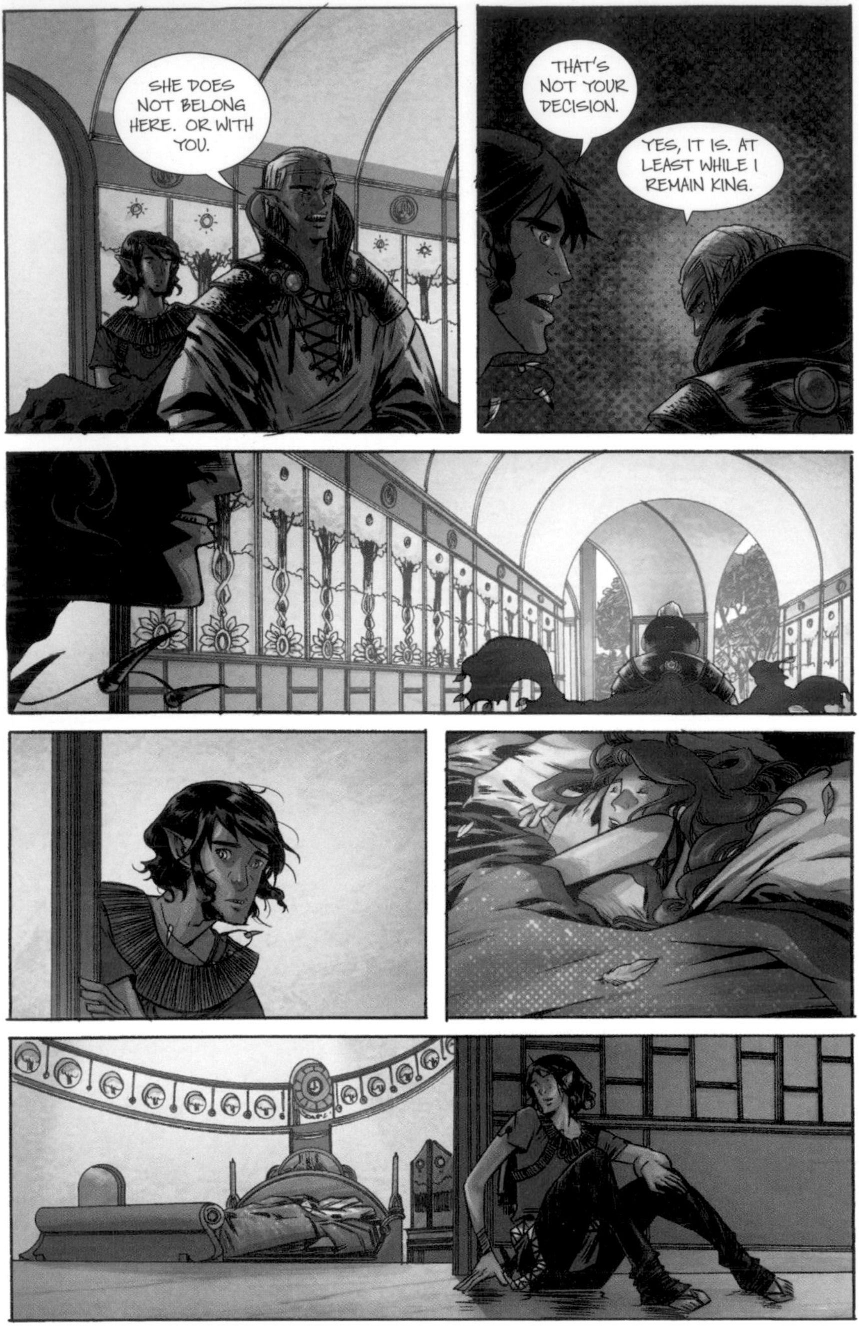
SHE DOES NOT BELONG HERE. OR WITH YOU.
THAT'S NOT YOUR DECISION.
YES, IT IS. AT LEAST WHILE I REMAIN KING.

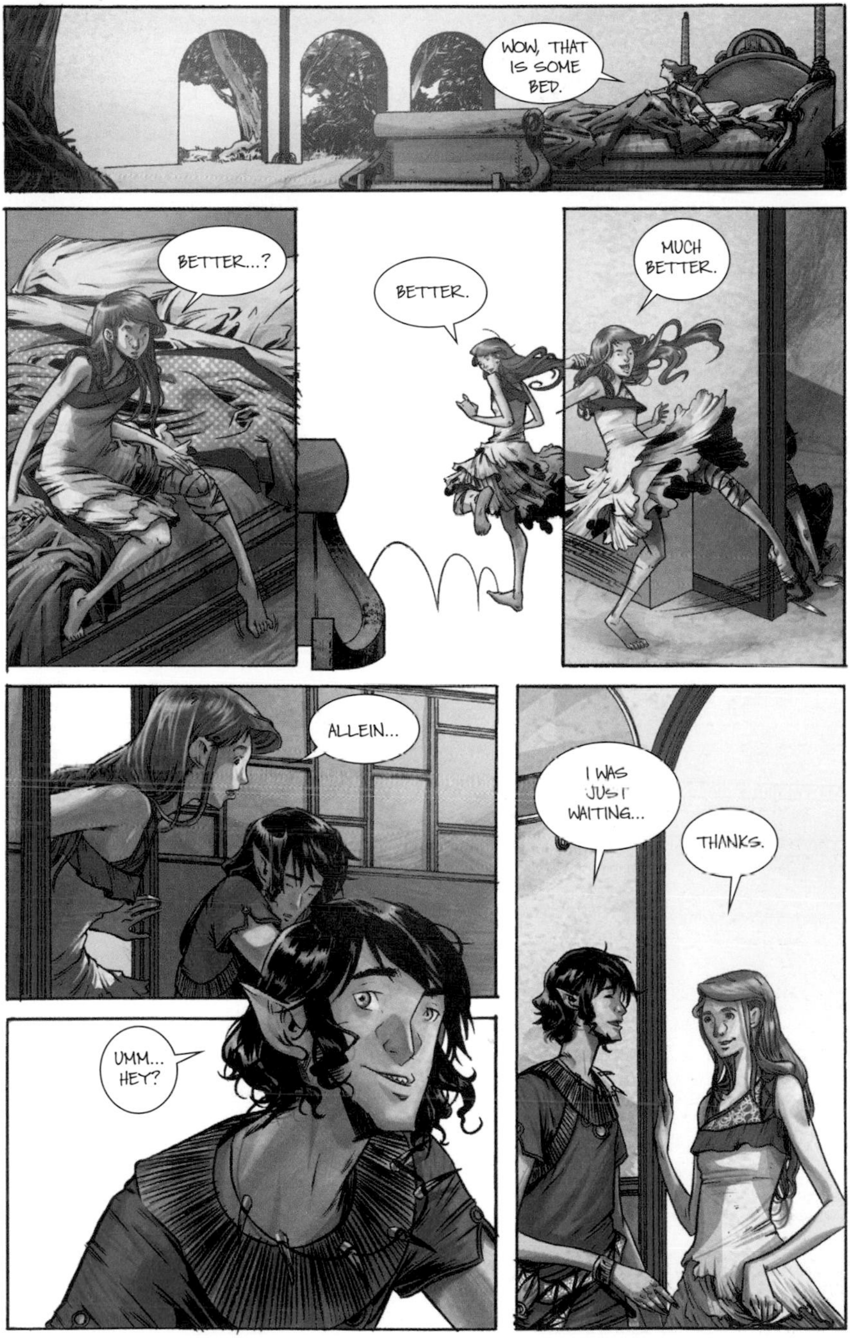
WOW, THAT IS SOME BED.
BETTER...?
BETTER.
MUCH BETTER.
ALLEIN...
UMM... HEY?
I WAS JUST WAITING...
THANKS.

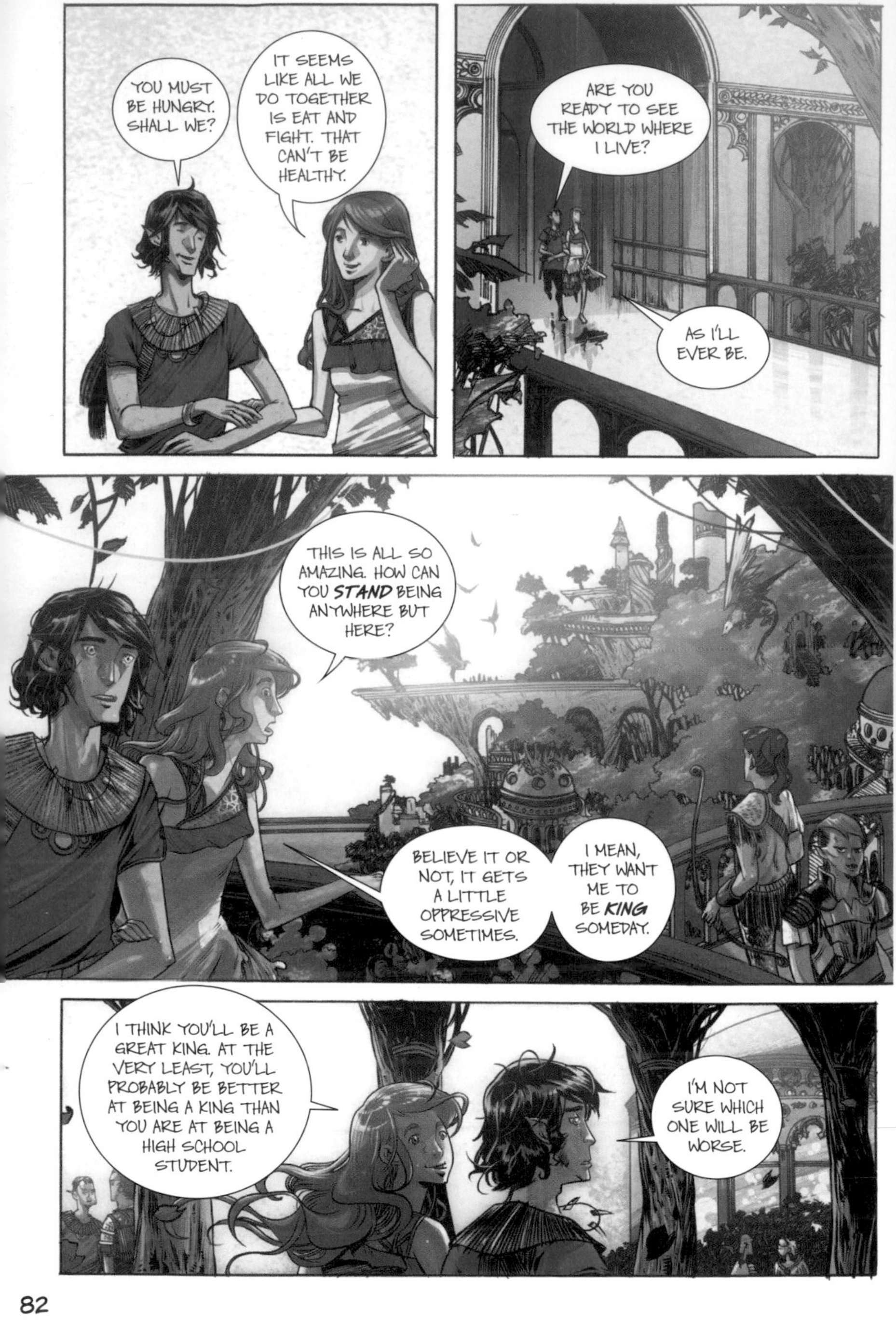
YOU MUST BE HUNGRY. SHALL WE?
IT SEEMS LIKE ALL WE DO TOGETHER IS EAT AND FIGHT. THAT CAN'T BE HEALTHY.
ARE YOU READY TO SEE THE WORLD WHERE I LIVE?
AS I'LL EVER BE.
THIS IS ALL SO AMAZING. HOW CAN YOU **STAND** BEING ANYWHERE BUT HERE?
BELIEVE IT OR NOT, IT GETS A LITTLE OPPRESSIVE SOMETIMES.
I MEAN, THEY WANT ME TO BE **KING** SOMEDAY.
I THINK YOU'LL BE A GREAT KING. AT THE VERY LEAST, YOU'LL PROBABLY BE BETTER AT BEING A KING THAN YOU ARE AT BEING A HIGH SCHOOL STUDENT.
I'M NOT SURE WHICH ONE WILL BE WORSE.

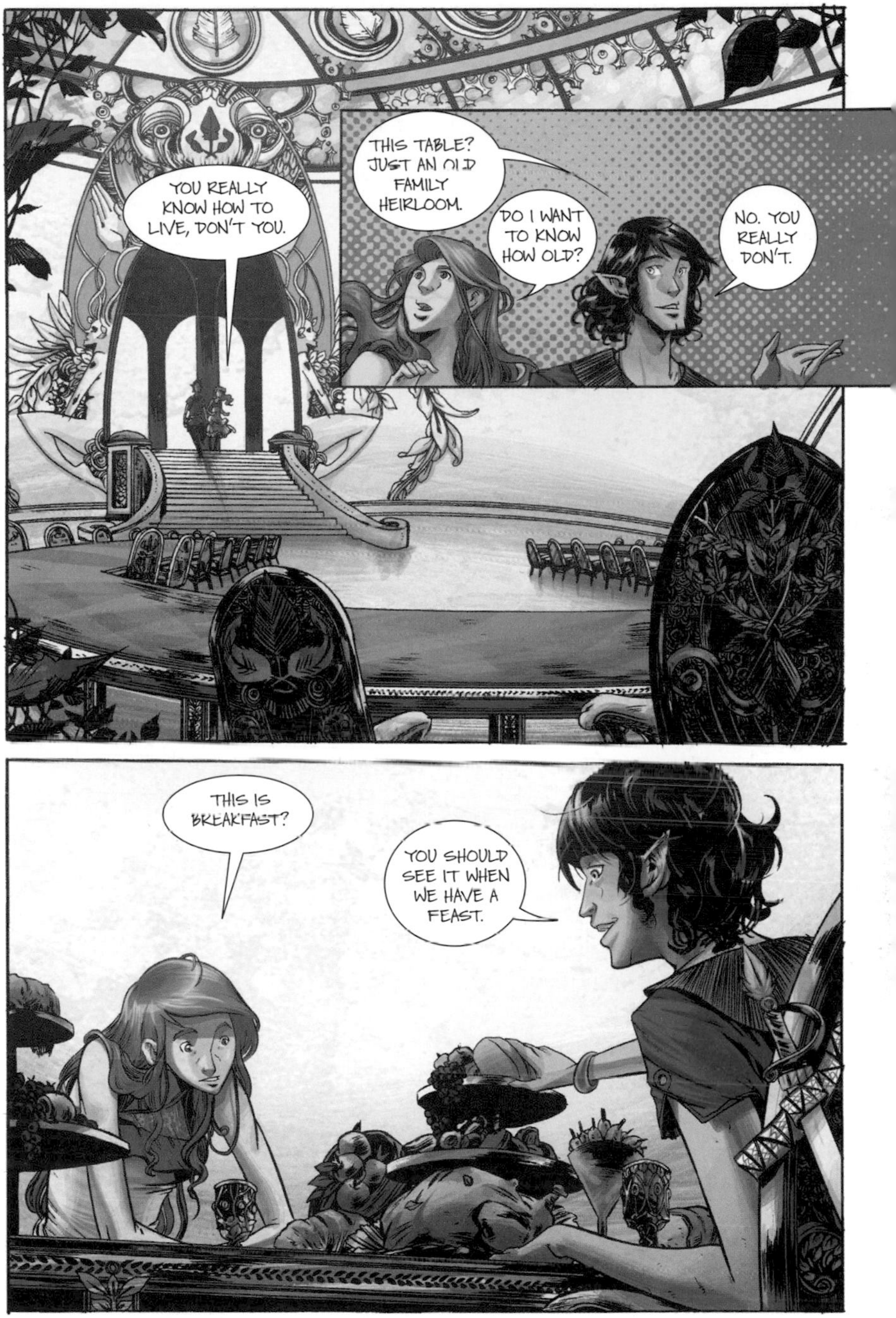
YOU REALLY KNOW HOW TO LIVE, DON'T YOU.
THIS TABLE? JUST AN OLD FAMILY HEIRLOOM.
DO I WANT TO KNOW HOW OLD?
NO. YOU REALLY DON'T.
THIS IS BREAKFAST?
YOU SHOULD SEE IT WHEN WE HAVE A FEAST.

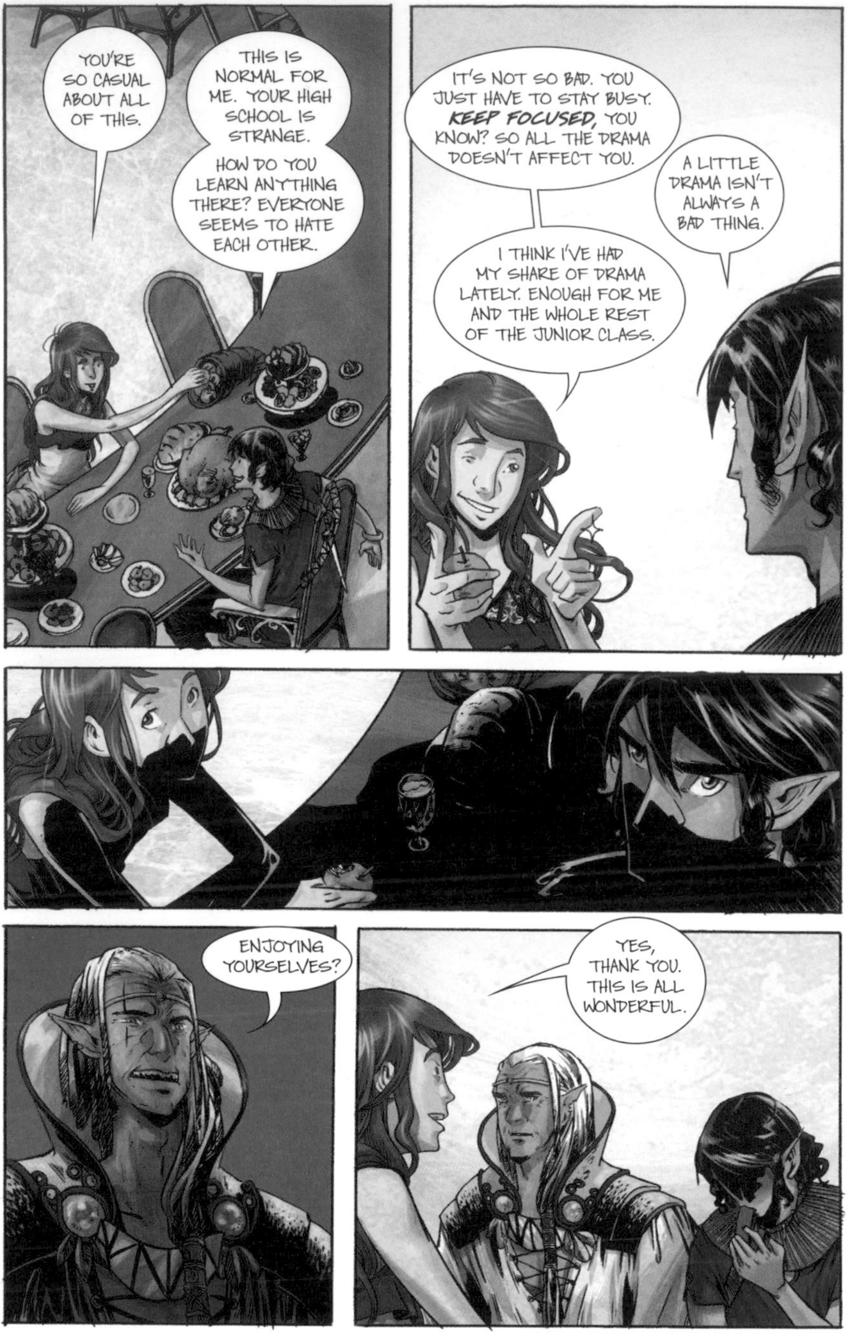
YOU'RE SO CASUAL ABOUT ALL OF THIS.
THIS IS NORMAL FOR ME. YOUR HIGH SCHOOL IS STRANGE.
HOW DO YOU LEARN ANYTHING THERE? EVERYONE SEEMS TO HATE EACH OTHER.
IT'S NOT SO BAD. YOU JUST HAVE TO STAY BUSY. **KEEP FOCUSED,** YOU KNOW? SO ALL THE DRAMA DOESN'T AFFECT YOU.
A LITTLE DRAMA ISN'T ALWAYS A BAD THING.
I THINK I'VE HAD MY SHARE OF DRAMA LATELY. ENOUGH FOR ME AND THE WHOLE REST OF THE JUNIOR CLASS.
ENJOYING YOURSELVES?
YES, THANK YOU. THIS IS ALL WONDERFUL.

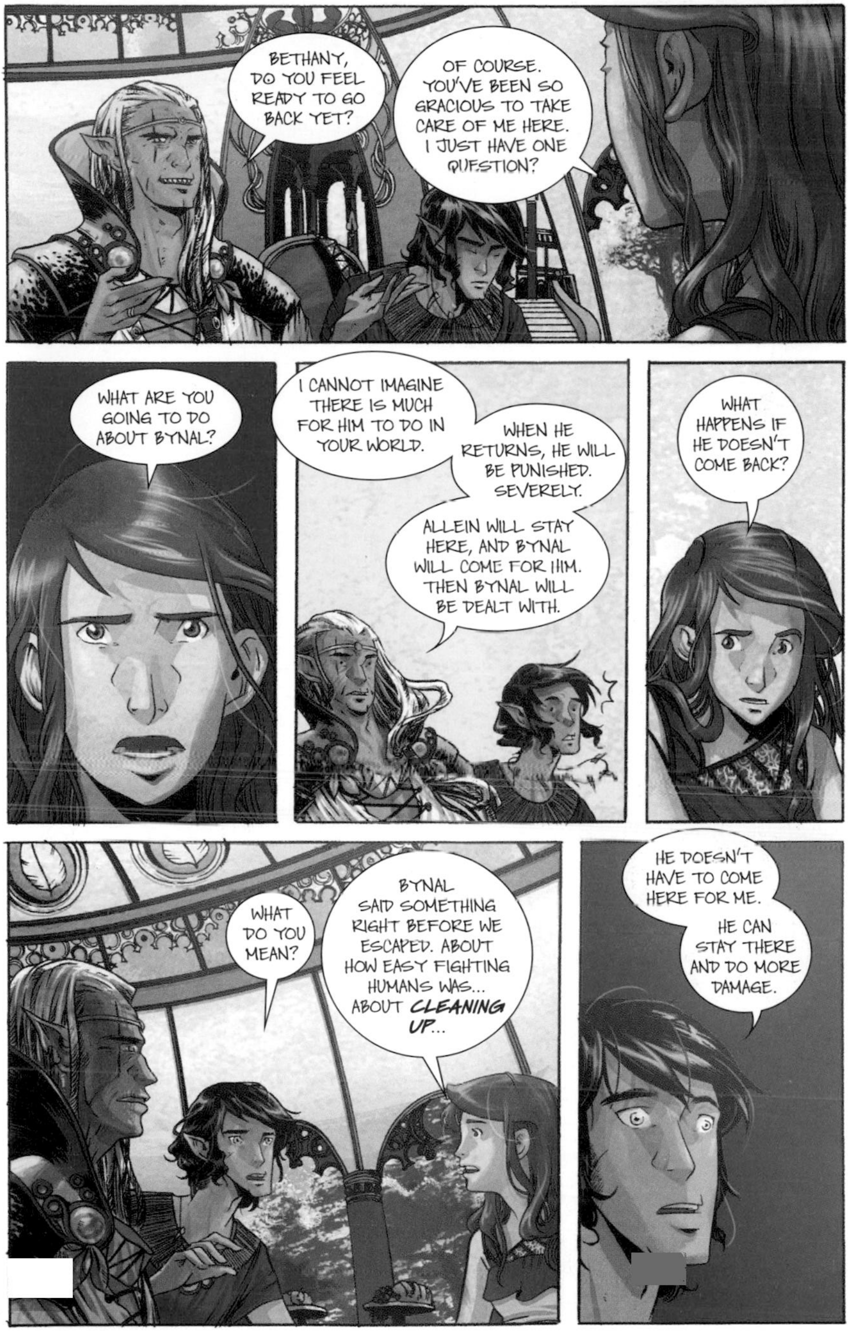
BETHANY, DO YOU FEEL READY TO GO BACK YET?
OF COURSE. YOU'VE BEEN SO GRACIOUS TO TAKE CARE OF ME HERE. I JUST HAVE ONE QUESTION?
WHAT ARE YOU GOING TO DO ABOUT BYNAL?
I CANNOT IMAGINE THERE IS MUCH FOR HIM TO DO IN YOUR WORLD.
WHEN HE RETURNS, HE WILL BE PUNISHED. SEVERELY.
ALLEIN WILL STAY HERE, AND BYNAL WILL COME FOR HIM. THEN BYNAL WILL BE DEALT WITH.
WHAT HAPPENS IF HE DOESN'T COME BACK?
WHAT DO YOU MEAN?
BYNAL SAID SOMETHING RIGHT BEFORE WE ESCAPED. ABOUT HOW EASY FIGHTING HUMANS WAS... ABOUT ***CLEANING UP***...
HE DOESN'T HAVE TO COME HERE FOR ME.
HE CAN STAY THERE AND DO MORE DAMAGE.

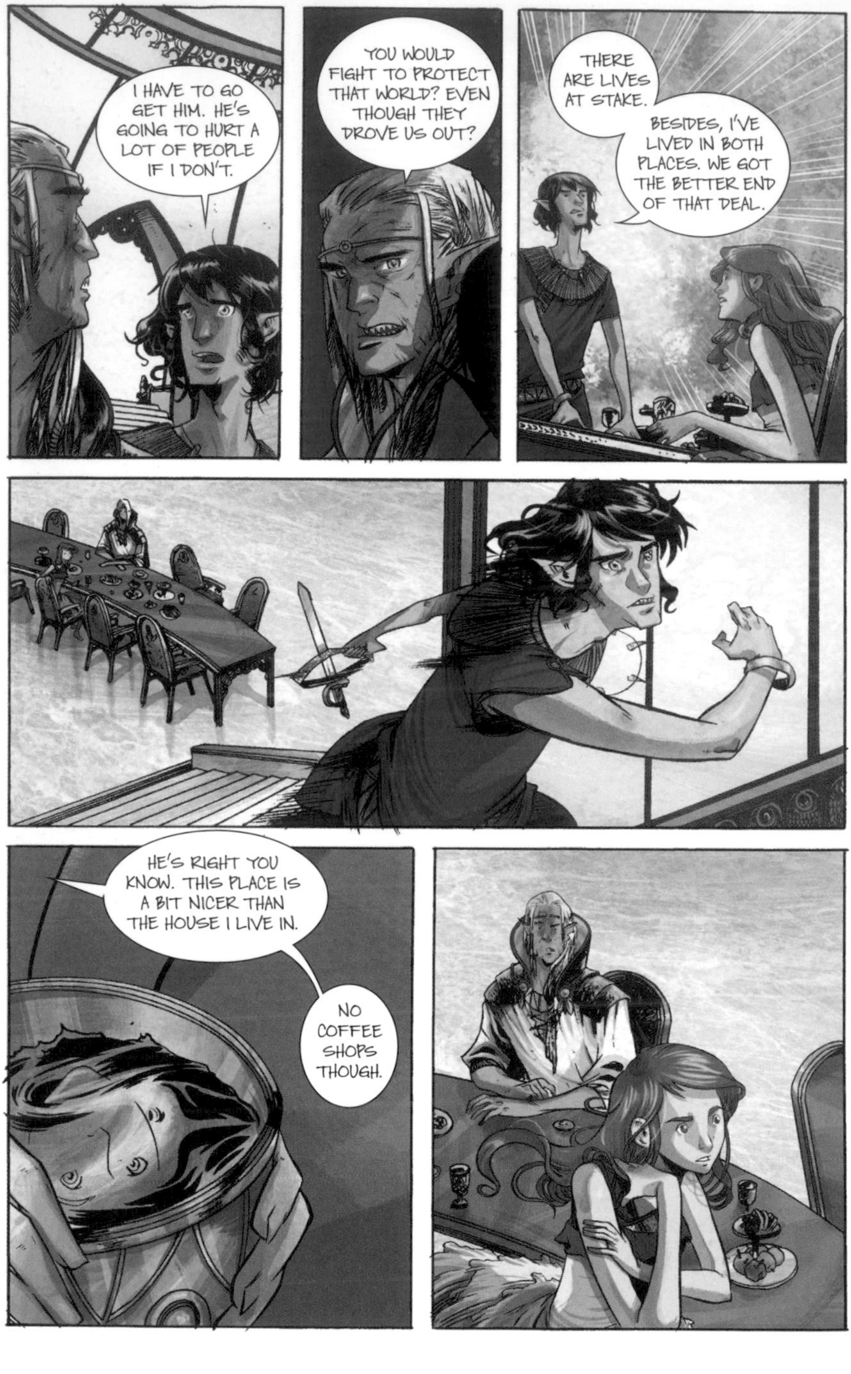
I HAVE TO GO GET HIM. HE'S GOING TO HURT A LOT OF PEOPLE IF I DON'T.
YOU WOULD FIGHT TO PROTECT THAT WORLD? EVEN THOUGH THEY DROVE US OUT?
THERE ARE LIVES AT STAKE.
BESIDES, I'VE LIVED IN BOTH PLACES. WE GOT THE BETTER END OF THAT DEAL.
HE'S RIGHT YOU KNOW. THIS PLACE IS A BIT NICER THAN THE HOUSE I LIVE IN.
NO COFFEE SHOPS THOUGH.

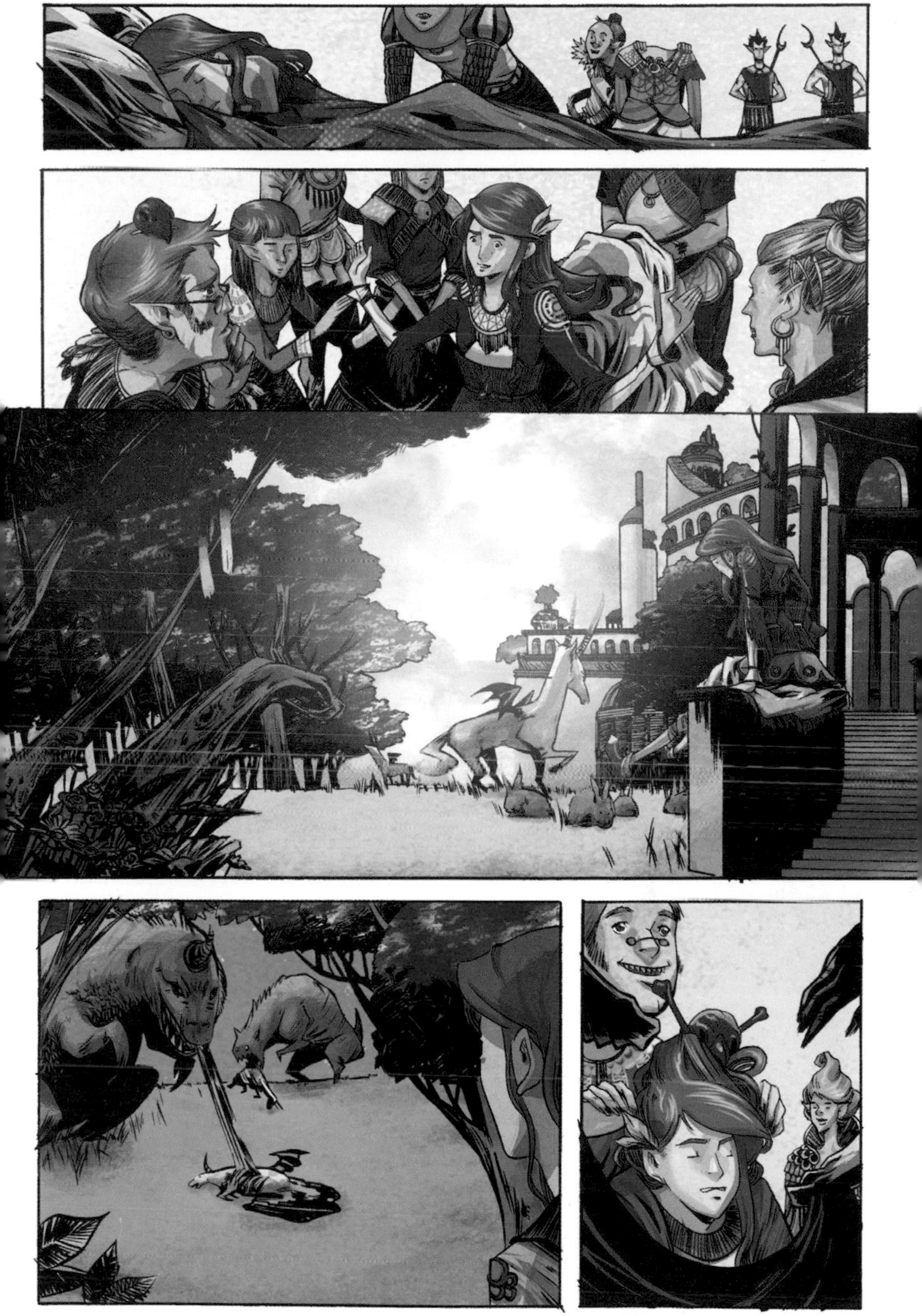

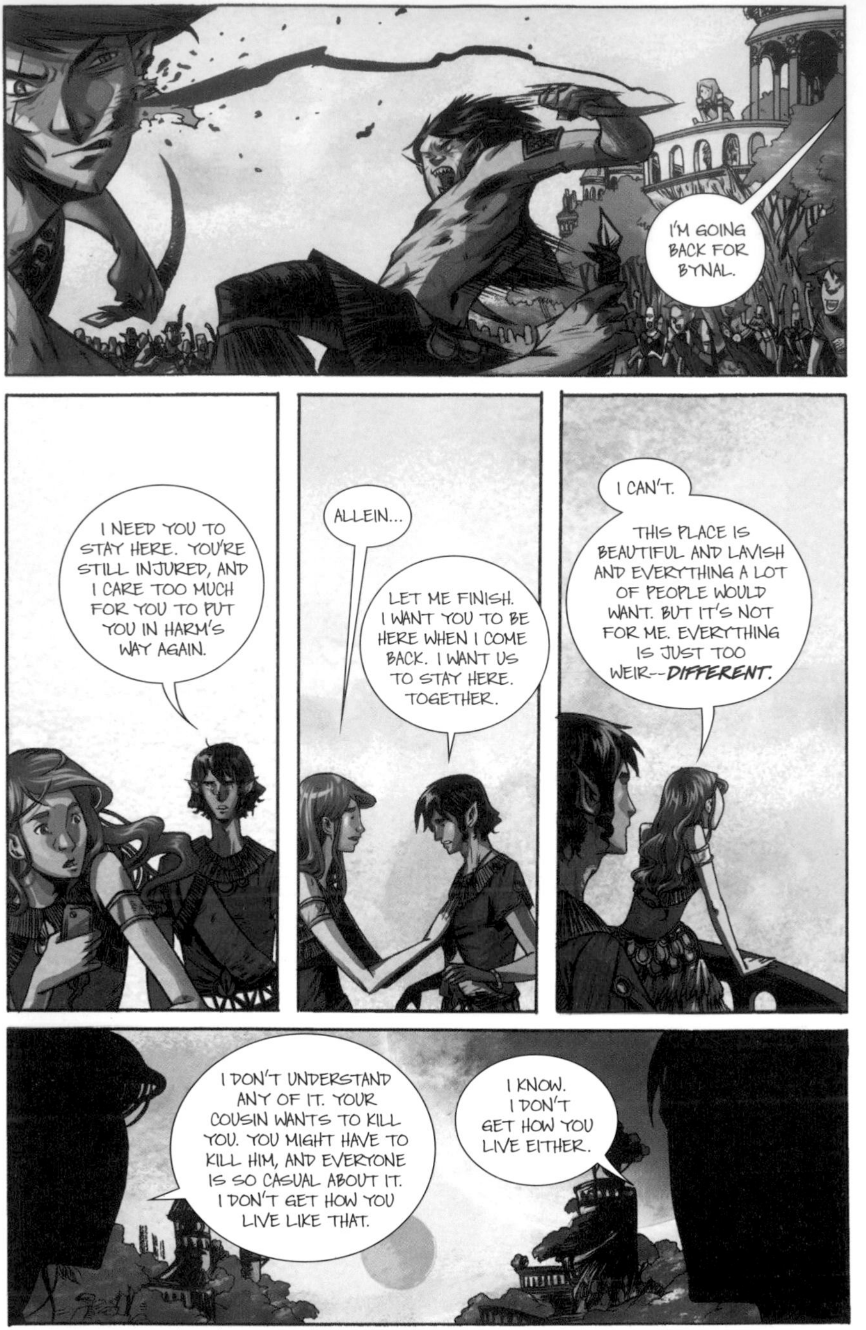
I'M GOING BACK FOR BYNAL.
I NEED YOU TO STAY HERE. YOU'RE STILL INJURED, AND I CARE TOO MUCH FOR YOU TO PUT YOU IN HARM'S WAY AGAIN.
ALLEIN...
LET ME FINISH. I WANT YOU TO BE HERE WHEN I COME BACK. I WANT US TO STAY HERE. TOGETHER.
I CAN'T.
THIS PLACE IS BEAUTIFUL AND LAVISH AND EVERYTHING A LOT OF PEOPLE WOULD WANT. BUT IT'S NOT FOR ME. EVERYTHING IS JUST TOO WEIR--*DIFFERENT.*
I DON'T UNDERSTAND ANY OF IT. YOUR COUSIN WANTS TO KILL YOU. YOU MIGHT HAVE TO KILL HIM, AND EVERYONE IS SO CASUAL ABOUT IT. I DON'T GET HOW YOU LIVE LIKE THAT.
I KNOW. I DON'T GET HOW YOU LIVE EITHER.

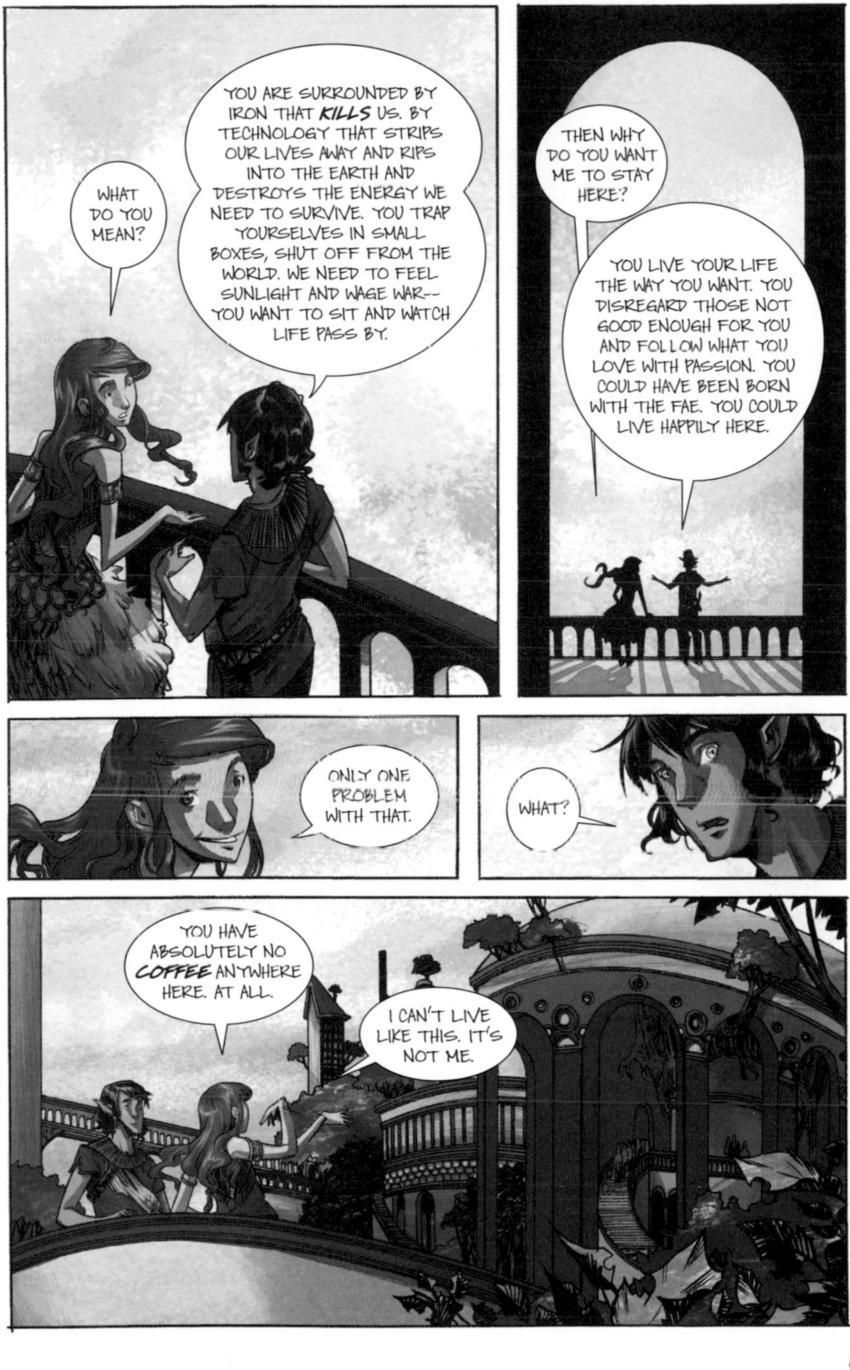
WHAT DO YOU MEAN?
YOU ARE SURROUNDED BY IRON THAT KILLS US. BY TECHNOLOGY THAT STRIPS OUR LIVES AWAY AND RIPS INTO THE EARTH AND DESTROYS THE ENERGY WE NEED TO SURVIVE. YOU TRAP YOURSELVES IN SMALL BOXES, SHUT OFF FROM THE WORLD. WE NEED TO FEEL SUNLIGHT AND WAGE WAR-- YOU WANT TO SIT AND WATCH LIFE PASS BY.
THEN WHY DO YOU WANT ME TO STAY HERE?
YOU LIVE YOUR LIFE THE WAY YOU WANT. YOU DISREGARD THOSE NOT GOOD ENOUGH FOR YOU AND FOLLOW WHAT YOU LOVE WITH PASSION. YOU COULD HAVE BEEN BORN WITH THE FAE. YOU COULD LIVE HAPPILY HERE.
ONLY ONE PROBLEM WITH THAT.
WHAT?
YOU HAVE ABSOLUTELY NO COFFEE ANYWHERE HERE. AT ALL.
I CAN'T LIVE LIKE THIS. IT'S NOT ME.

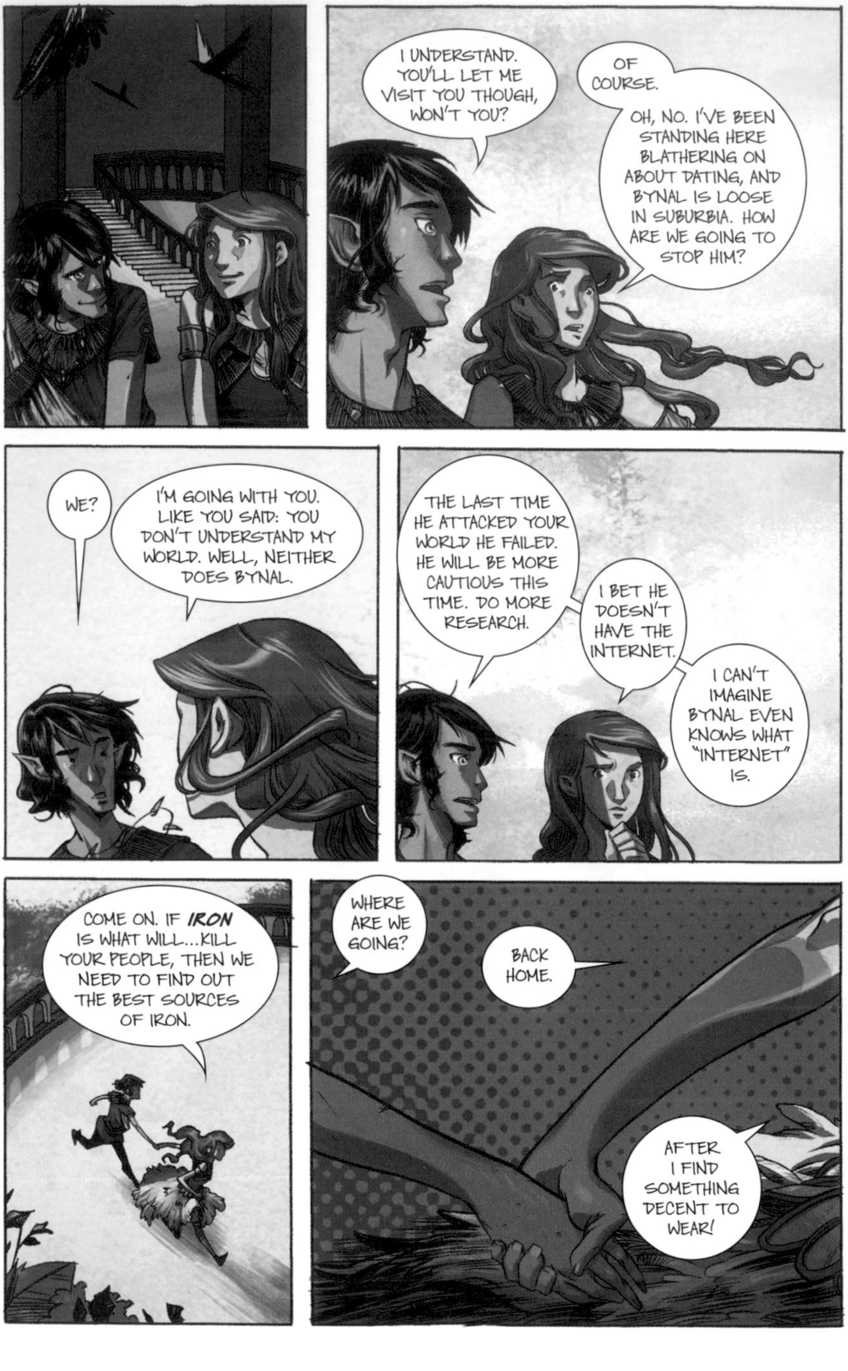
I UNDERSTAND. YOU'LL LET ME VISIT YOU THOUGH, WON'T YOU?
OF COURSE.
OH, NO. I'VE BEEN STANDING HERE BLATHERING ON ABOUT DATING, AND BYNAL IS LOOSE IN SUBURBIA. HOW ARE WE GOING TO STOP HIM?
WE?
I'M GOING WITH YOU. LIKE YOU SAID: YOU DON'T UNDERSTAND MY WORLD. WELL, NEITHER DOES BYNAL.
THE LAST TIME HE ATTACKED YOUR WORLD HE FAILED. HE WILL BE MORE CAUTIOUS THIS TIME. DO MORE RESEARCH.
I BET HE DOESN'T HAVE THE INTERNET.
I CAN'T IMAGINE BYNAL EVEN KNOWS WHAT "INTERNET" IS.
COME ON. IF *IRON* IS WHAT WILL...KILL YOUR PEOPLE, THEN WE NEED TO FIND OUT THE BEST SOURCES OF IRON.
WHERE ARE WE GOING?
BACK HOME.
AFTER I FIND SOMETHING DECENT TO WEAR!

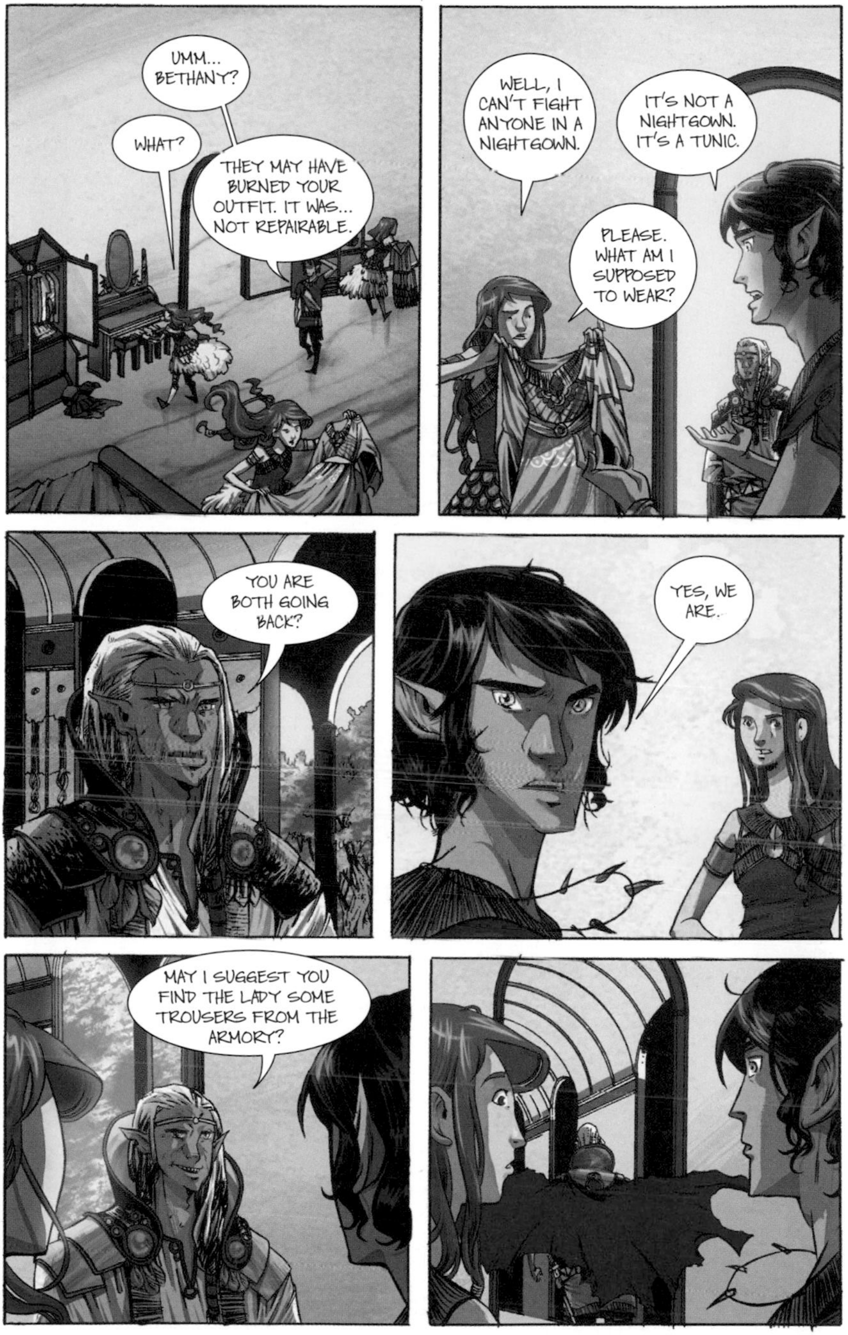
UMM... BETHANY?
WHAT?
THEY MAY HAVE BURNED YOUR OUTFIT. IT WAS... NOT REPAIRABLE.
WELL, I CAN'T FIGHT ANYONE IN A NIGHTGOWN.
IT'S NOT A NIGHTGOWN. IT'S A TUNIC.
PLEASE. WHAT AM I SUPPOSED TO WEAR?
YOU ARE BOTH GOING BACK?
YES, WE ARE.
MAY I SUGGEST YOU FIND THE LADY SOME TROUSERS FROM THE ARMORY?

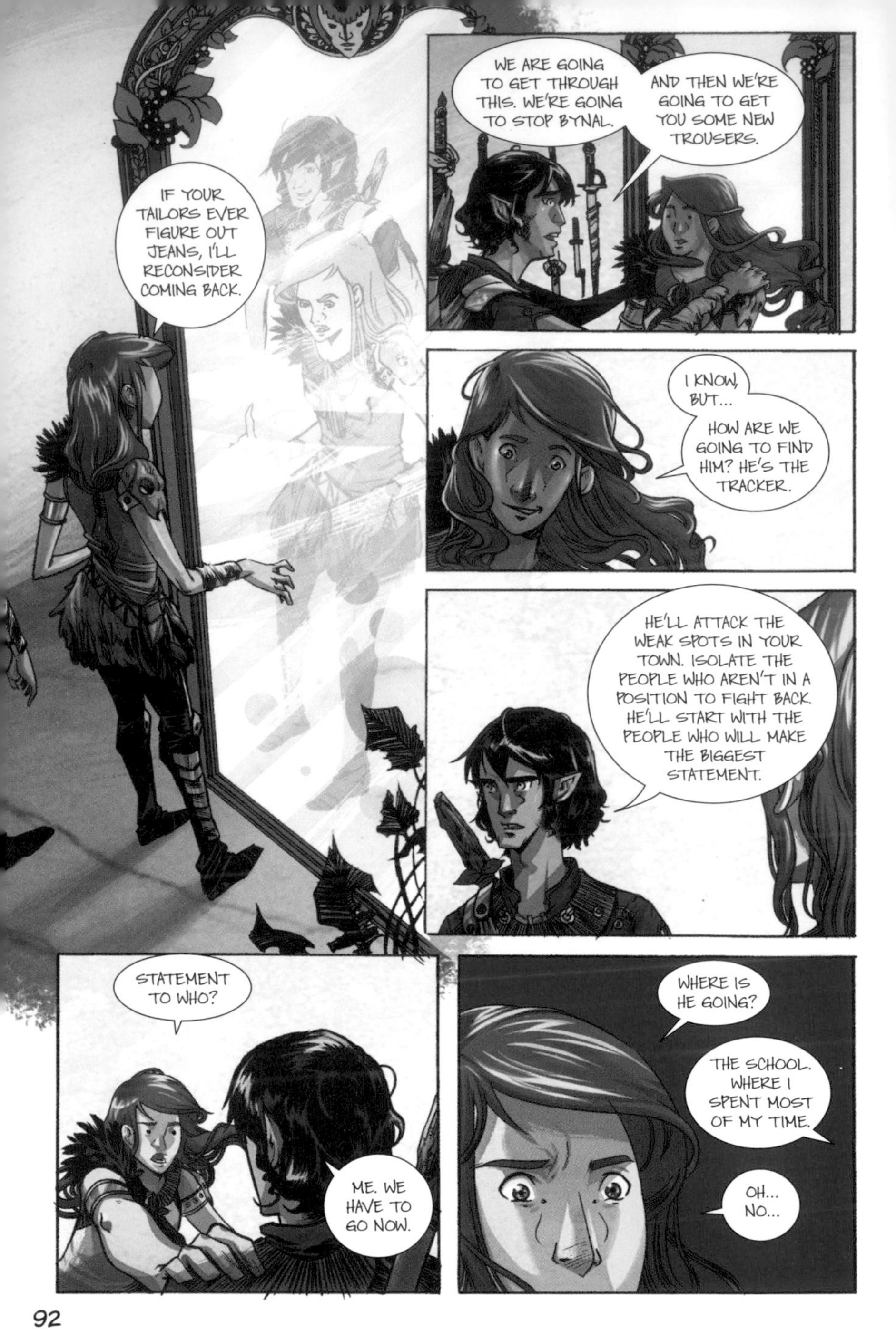
WE ARE GOING TO GET THROUGH THIS. WE'RE GOING TO STOP BYNAL.
AND THEN WE'RE GOING TO GET YOU SOME NEW TROUSERS.
IF YOUR TAILORS EVER FIGURE OUT JEANS, I'LL RECONSIDER COMING BACK.
I KNOW, BUT...
HOW ARE WE GOING TO FIND HIM? HE'S THE TRACKER.
HE'LL ATTACK THE WEAK SPOTS IN YOUR TOWN. ISOLATE THE PEOPLE WHO AREN'T IN A POSITION TO FIGHT BACK. HE'LL START WITH THE PEOPLE WHO WILL MAKE THE BIGGEST STATEMENT.
STATEMENT TO WHO?
ME. WE HAVE TO GO NOW.
WHERE IS HE GOING?
THE SCHOOL. WHERE I SPENT MOST OF MY TIME.
OH... NO...

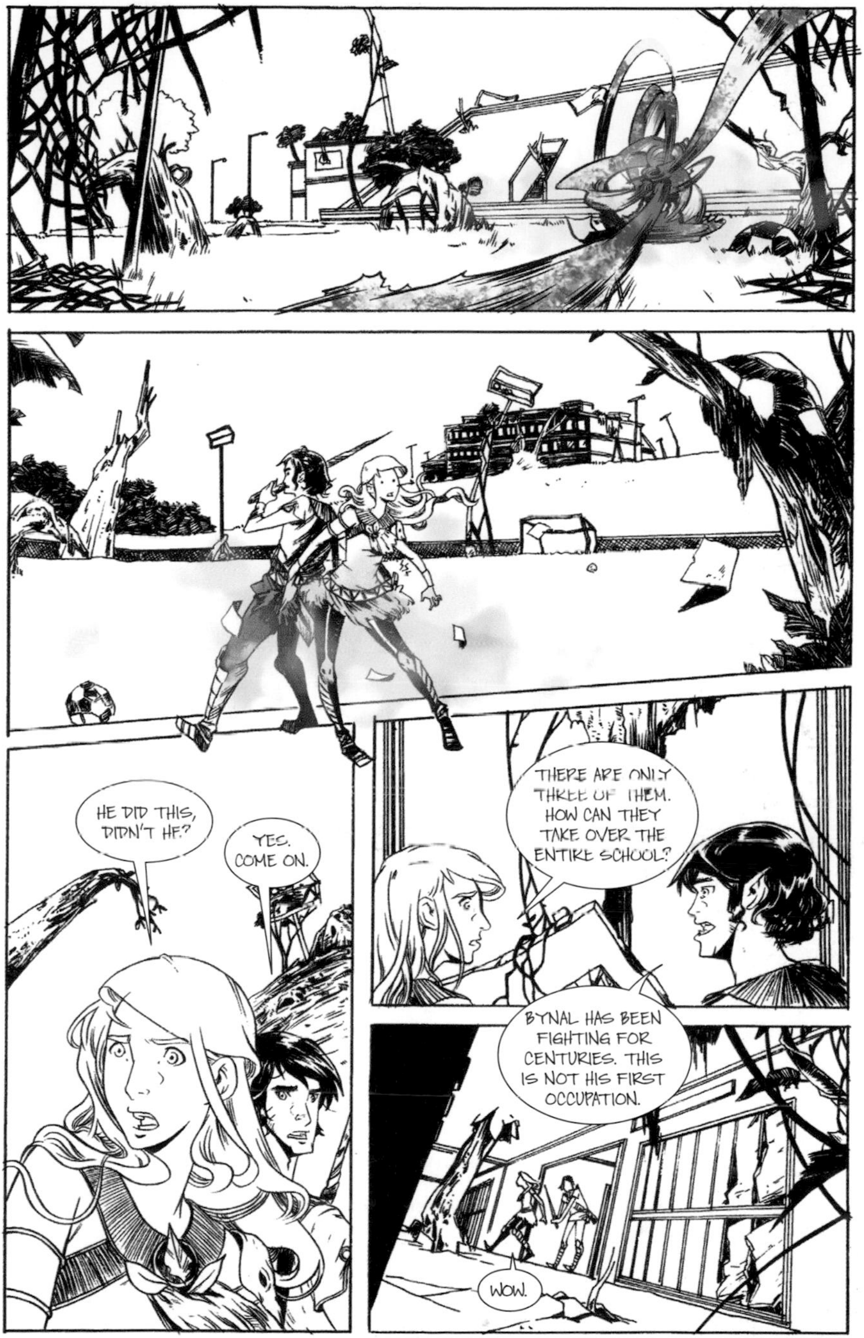
HE DID THIS, DIDN'T HE?
YES. COME ON.
THERE ARE ONLY THREE OF THEM. HOW CAN THEY TAKE OVER THE ENTIRE SCHOOL?
BYNAL HAS BEEN FIGHTING FOR CENTURIES. THIS IS NOT HIS FIRST OCCUPATION.
WOW.

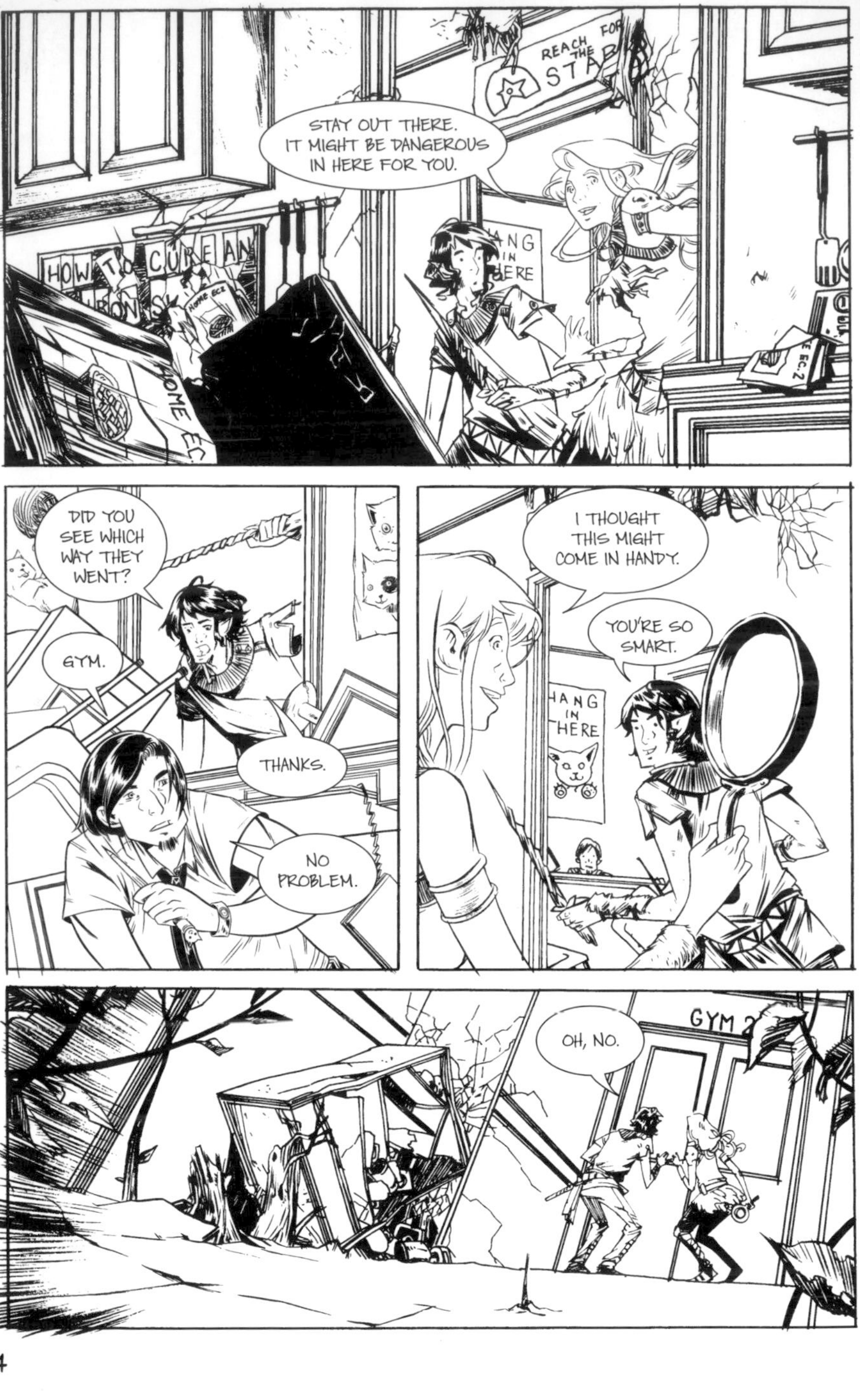
STAY OUT THERE. IT MIGHT BE DANGEROUS IN HERE FOR YOU.
DID YOU SEE WHICH WAY THEY WENT?
GYM.
THANKS.
NO PROBLEM.
I THOUGHT THIS MIGHT COME IN HANDY.
YOU'RE SO SMART.
HANG IN THERE
GYM 2
OH, NO.

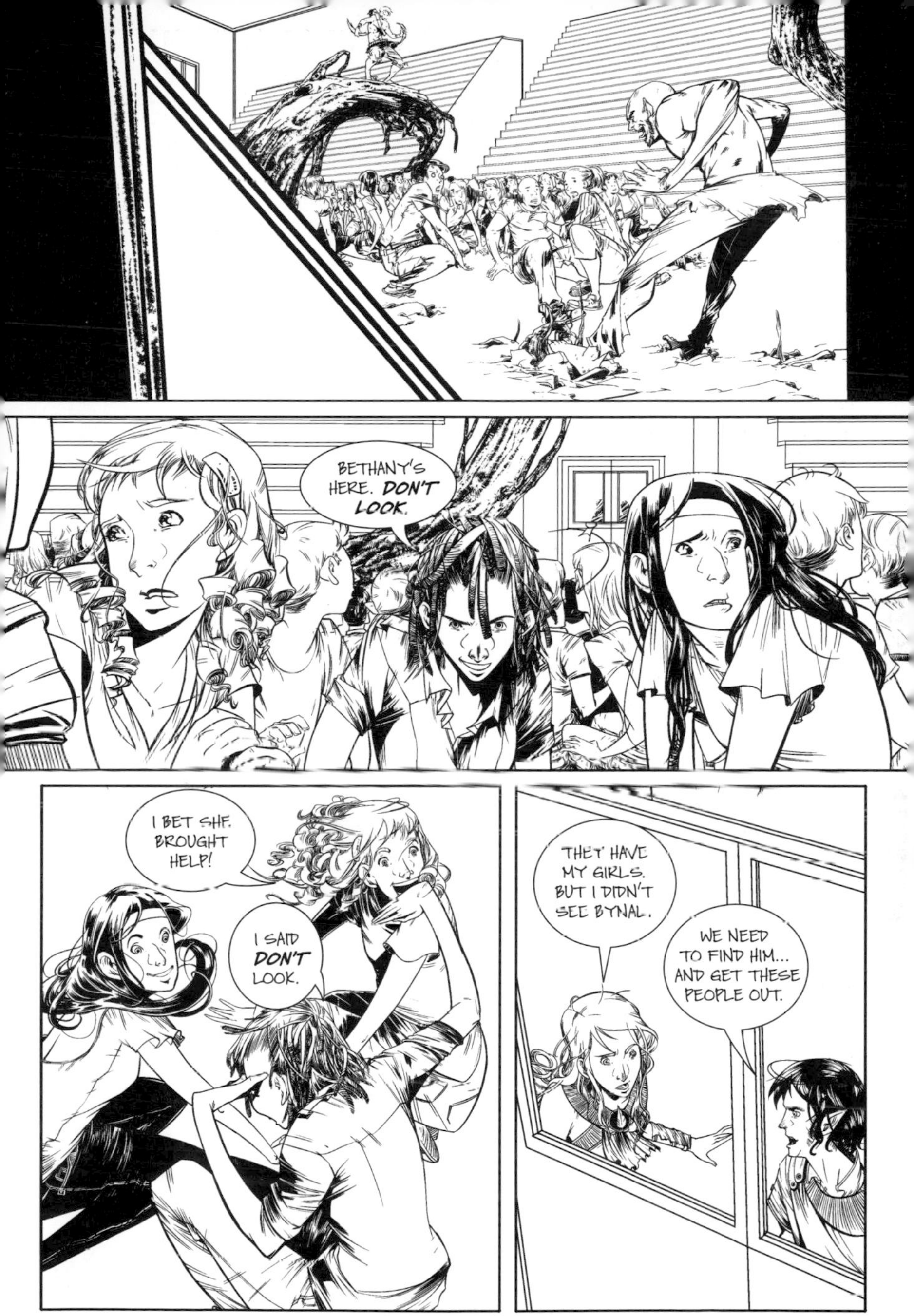
BETHANY'S HERE. **DON'T LOOK.**
I BET SHE BROUGHT HELP!
I SAID **DON'T** LOOK.
THEY HAVE MY GIRLS. BUT I DIDN'T SEE BYNAL.
WE NEED TO FIND HIM... AND GET THESE PEOPLE OUT.

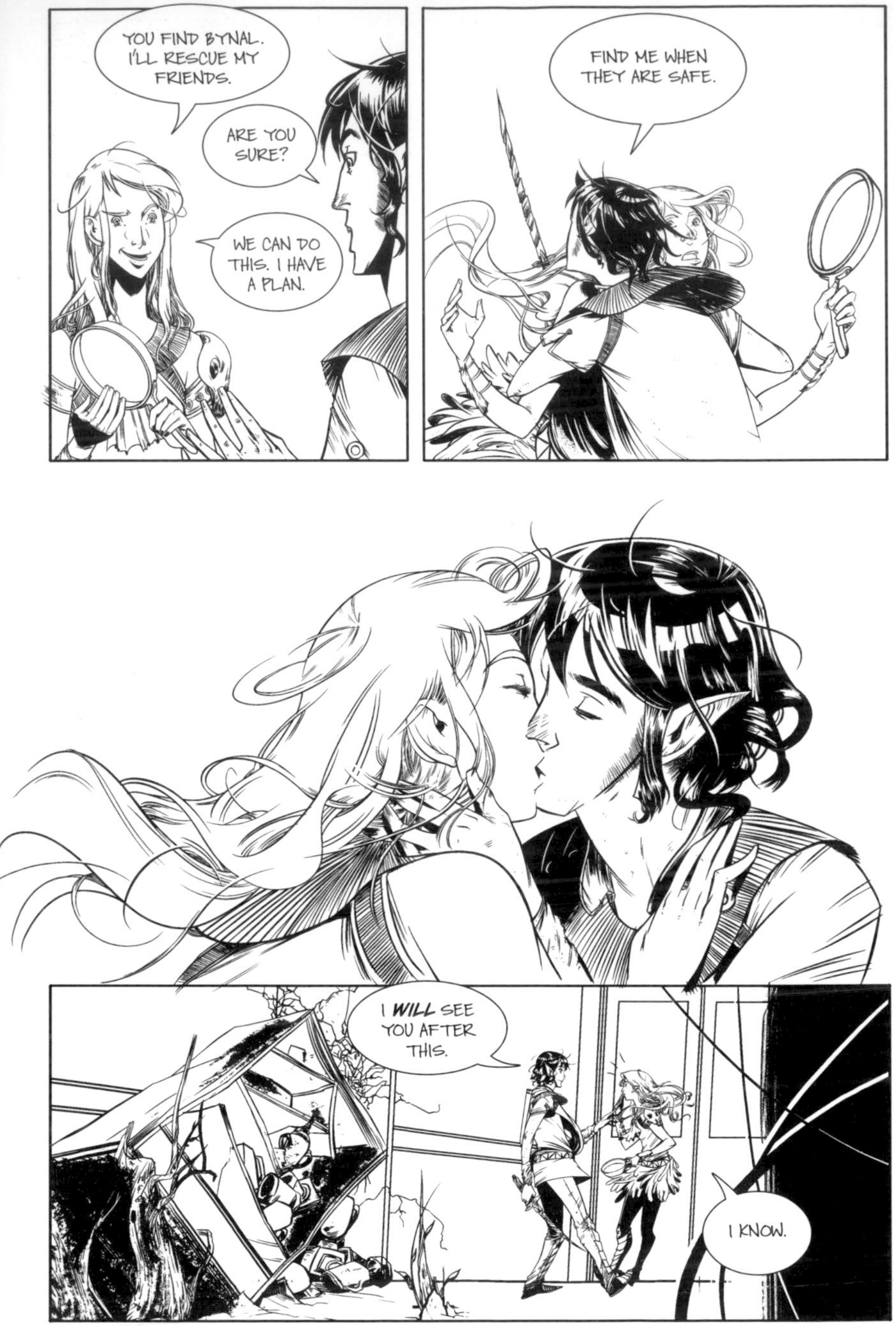
YOU FIND BYNAL. I'LL RESCUE MY FRIENDS.
ARE YOU SURE?
WE CAN DO THIS. I HAVE A PLAN.
FIND ME WHEN THEY ARE SAFE.
I **WILL** SEE YOU AFTER THIS.
I KNOW.

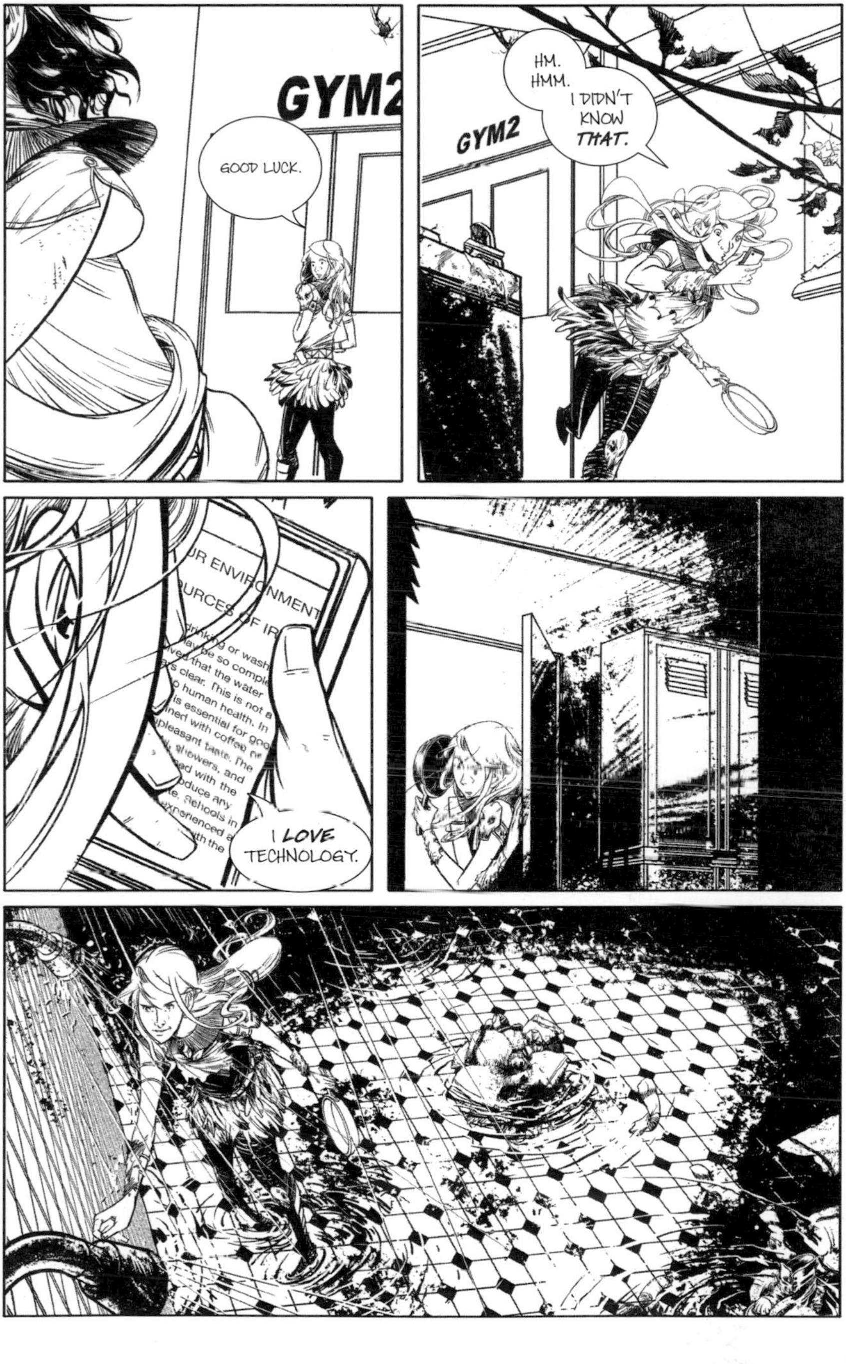
GYM2
GOOD LUCK.
GYM2
HM. HMM. I DIDN'T KNOW THAT.
I LOVE TECHNOLOGY.

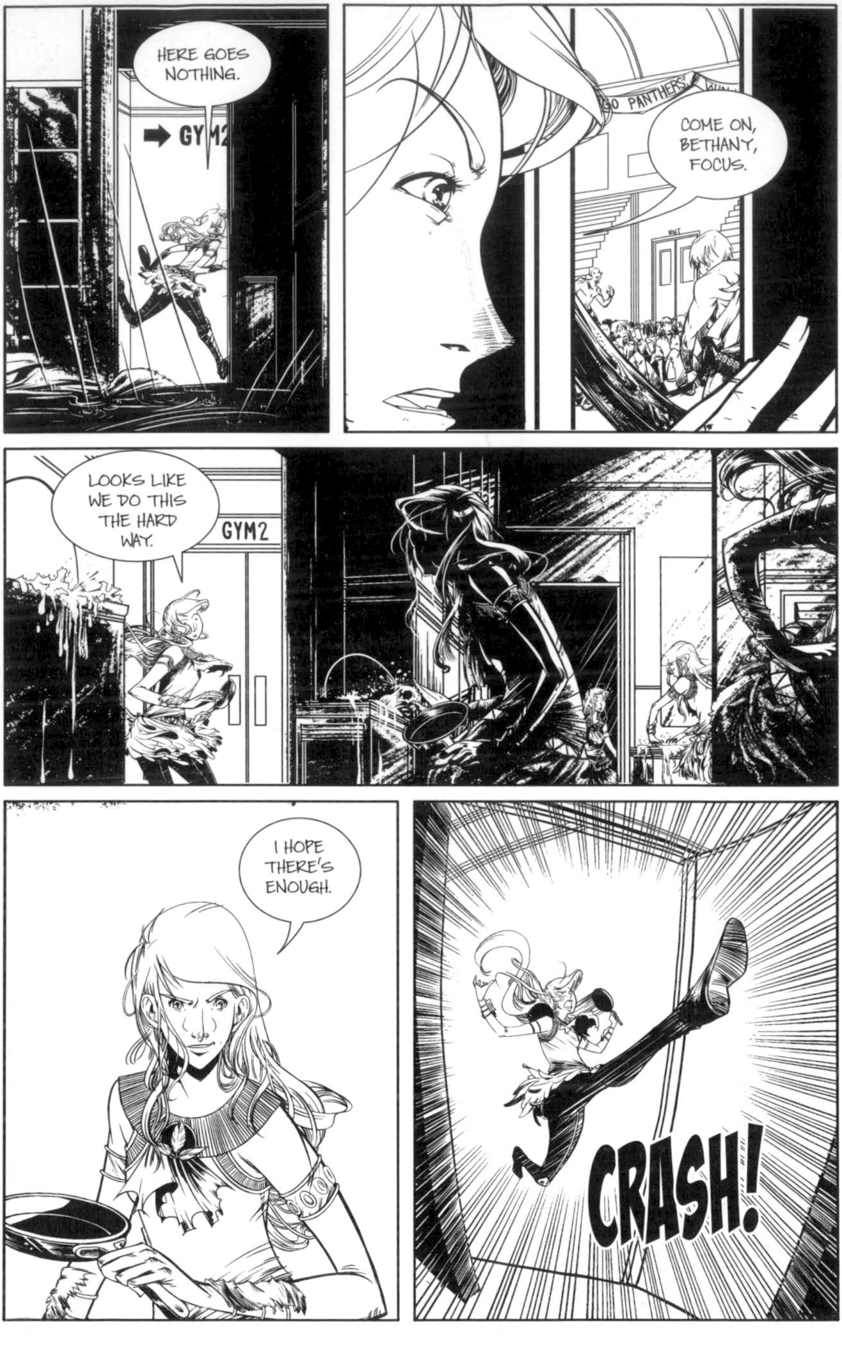
HERE GOES NOTHING.
GYM2
GO PANTHERS
COME ON, BETHANY, FOCUS.
LOOKS LIKE WE DO THIS THE HARD WAY.
GYM2
I HOPE THERE'S ENOUGH.
CRASH!

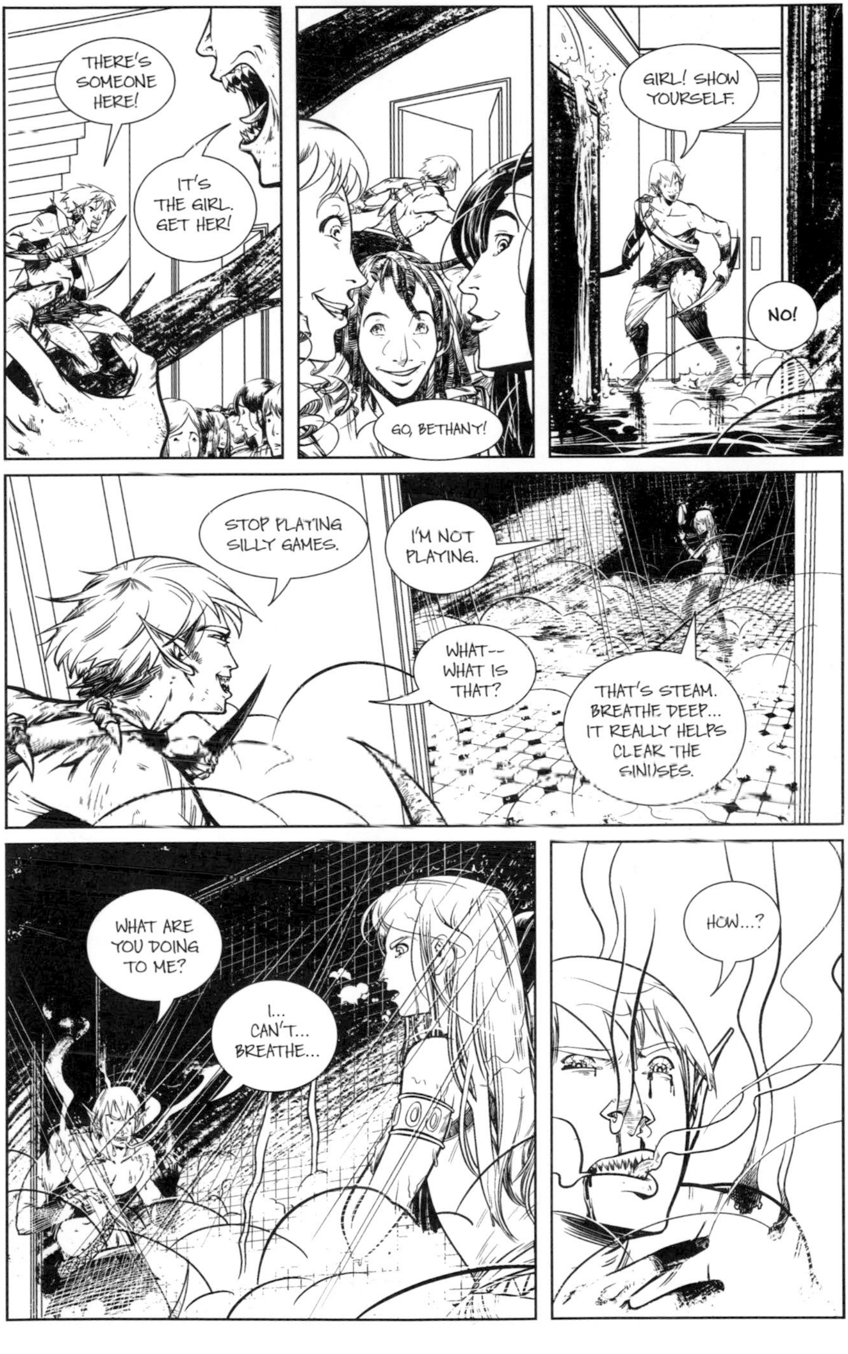
THERE'S SOMEONE HERE!
IT'S THE GIRL. GET HER!
GO, BETHANY!
GIRL! SHOW YOURSELF.
NO!
STOP PLAYING SILLY GAMES.
I'M NOT PLAYING.
WHAT-- WHAT IS THAT?
THAT'S STEAM. BREATHE DEEP... IT REALLY HELPS CLEAR THE SINUSES.
WHAT ARE YOU DOING TO ME?
I... CAN'T... BREATHE...
HOW...?

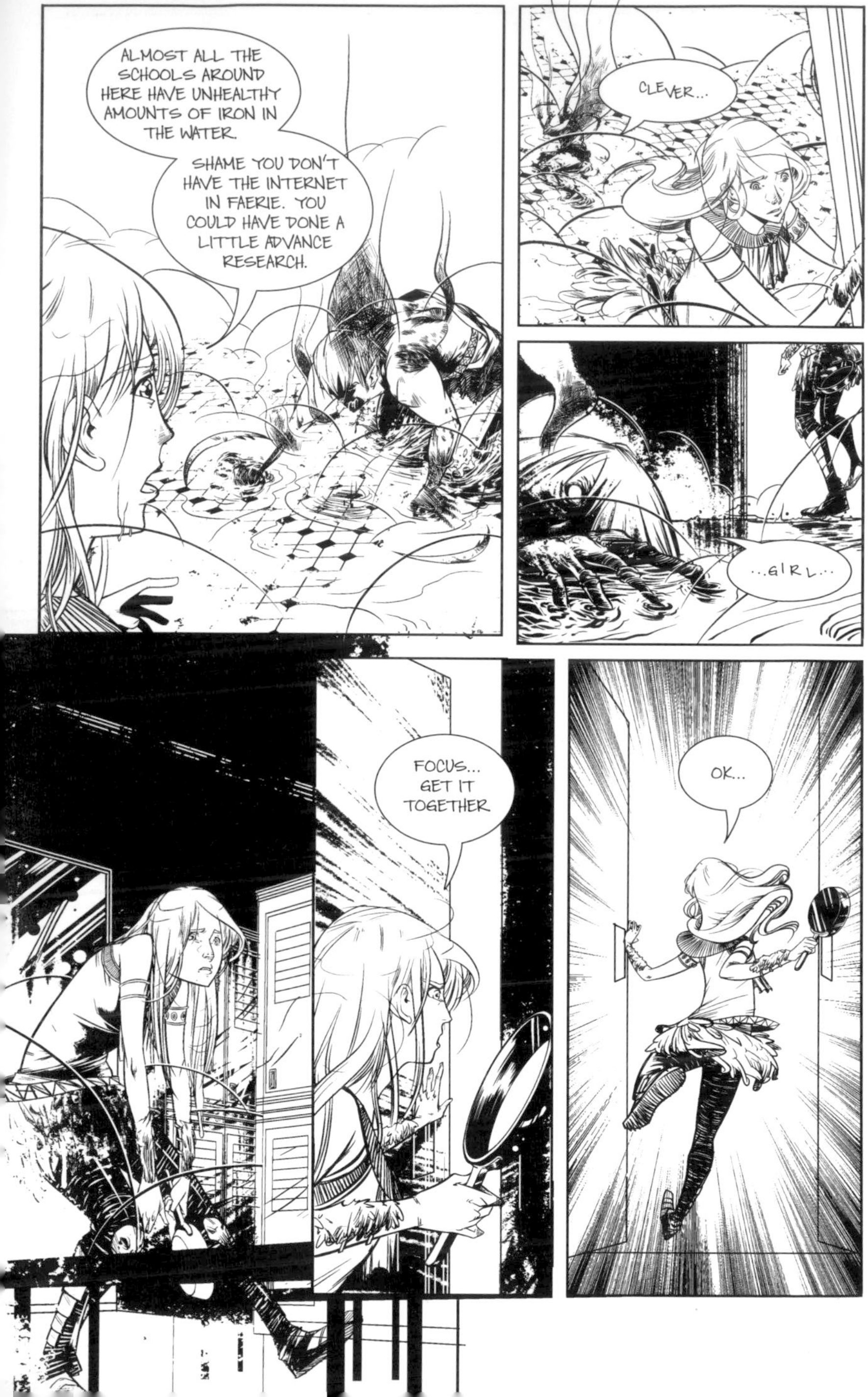
ALMOST ALL THE SCHOOLS AROUND HERE HAVE UNHEALTHY AMOUNTS OF IRON IN THE WATER.
SHAME YOU DON'T HAVE THE INTERNET IN FAERIE. YOU COULD HAVE DONE A LITTLE ADVANCE RESEARCH.
CLEVER...
...GIRL...
FOCUS... GET IT TOGETHER
OK...

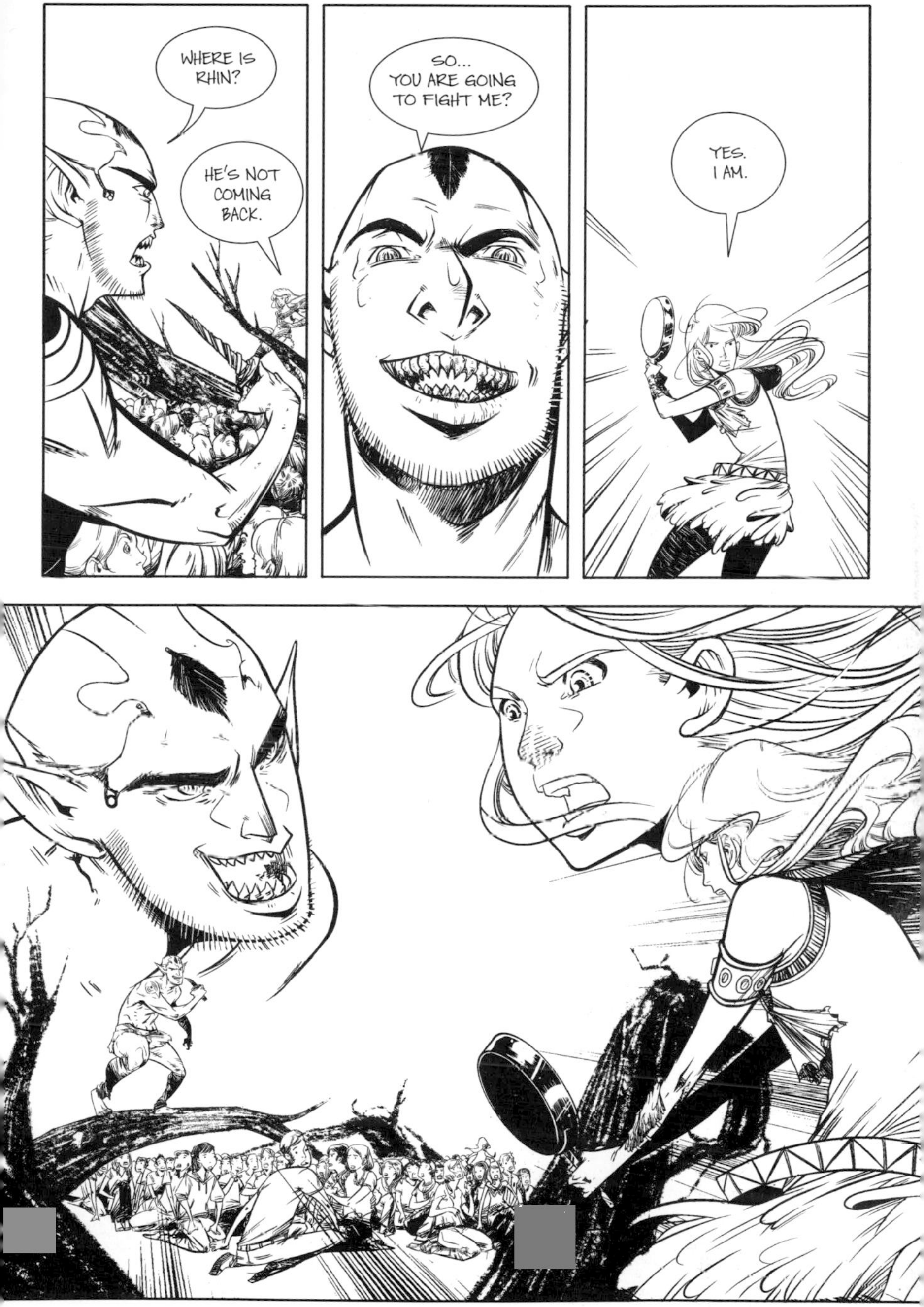
WHERE IS RHIN?
HE'S NOT COMING BACK.
SO... YOU ARE GOING TO FIGHT ME?
YES. I AM.

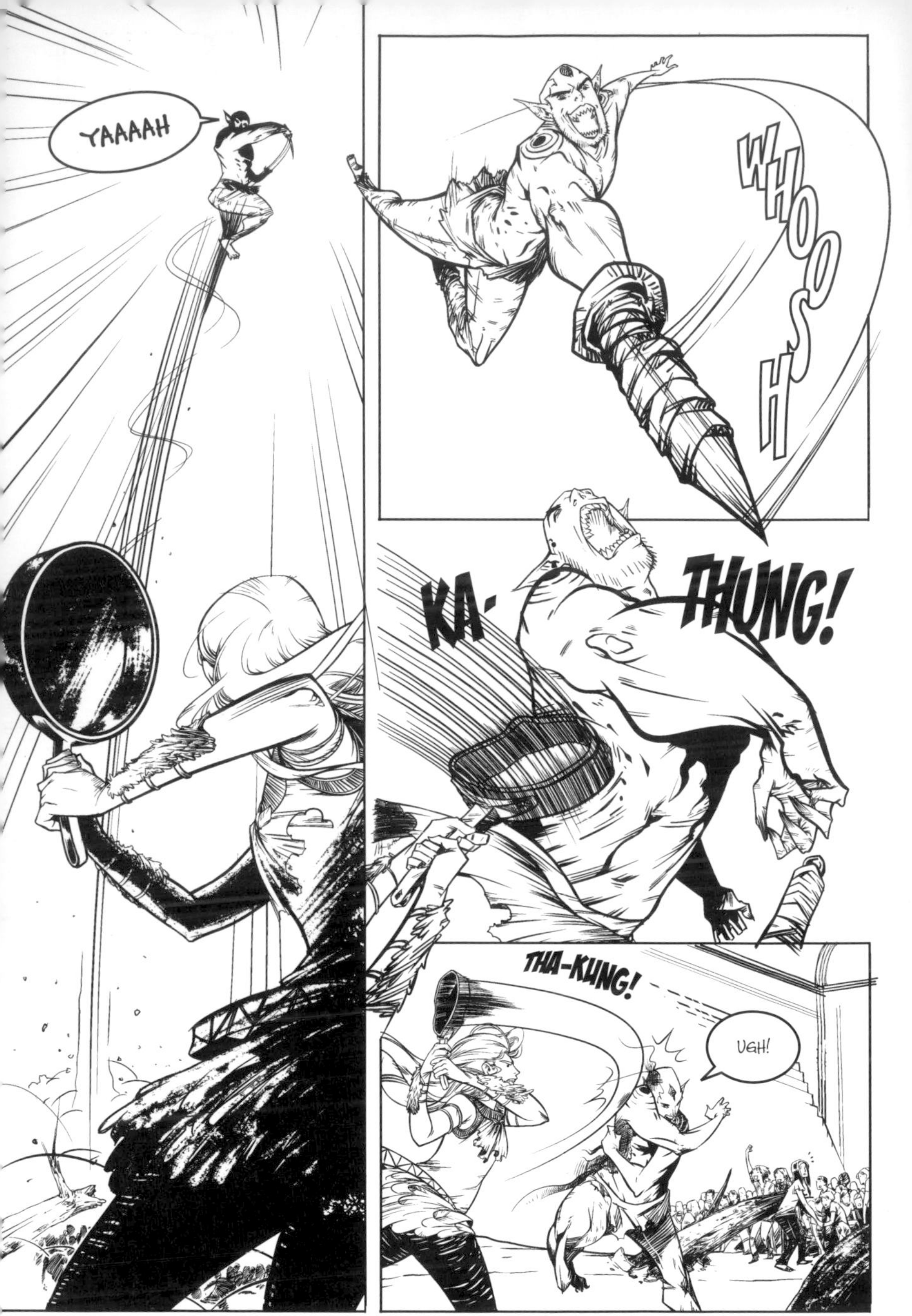
YAAAAH
WHOOOSH
KA-THUNG!
THA-KUNG!
UGH!

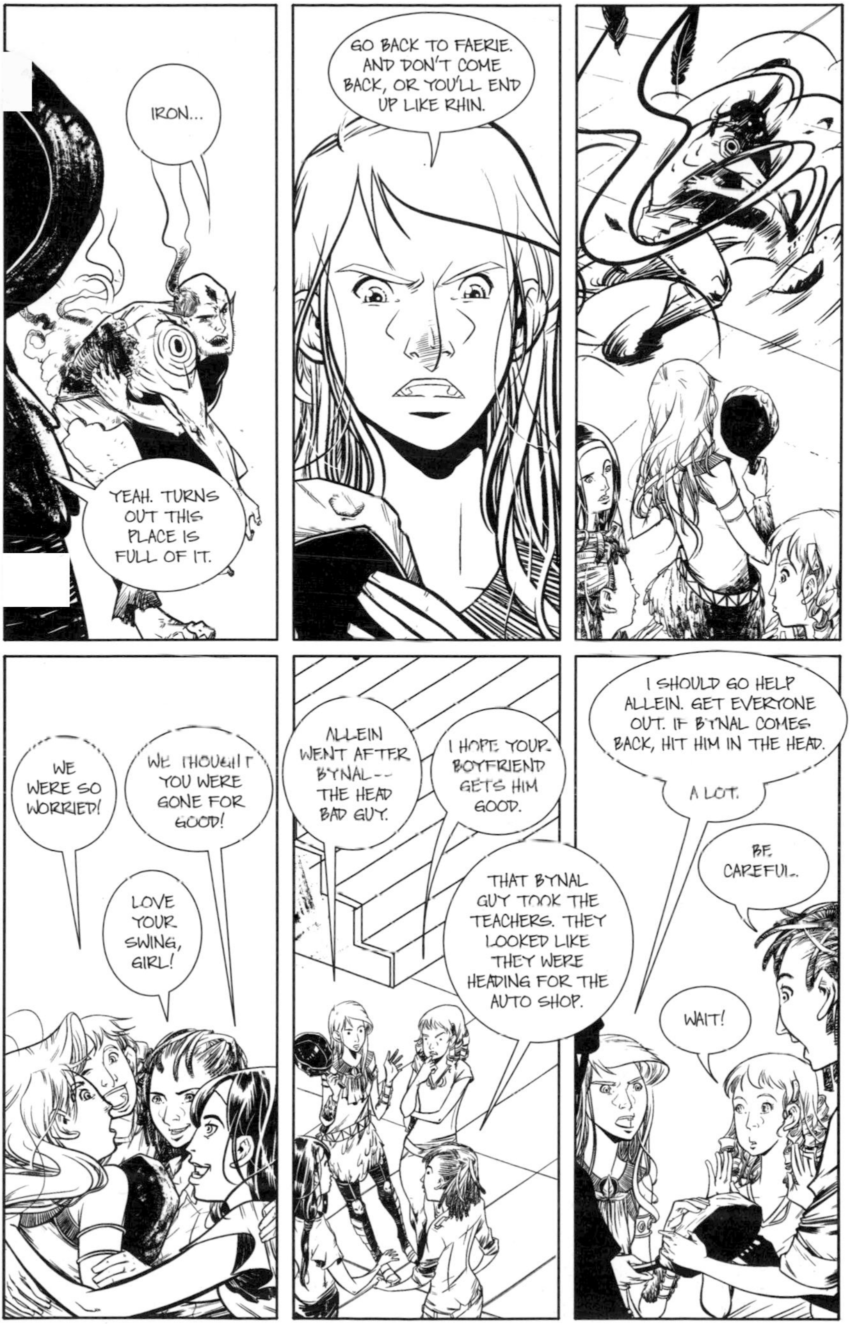
IRON...
YEAH. TURNS OUT THIS PLACE IS FULL OF IT.
GO BACK TO FAERIE. AND DON'T COME BACK, OR YOU'LL END UP LIKE RHIN.
WE WERE SO WORRIED!
WE THOUGHT YOU WERE GONE FOR GOOD!
LOVE YOUR SWING, GIRL!
ALLEIN WENT AFTER BYNAL-- THE HEAD BAD GUY.
I HOPE YOUR BOYFRIEND GETS HIM GOOD.
THAT BYNAL GUY TOOK THE TEACHERS. THEY LOOKED LIKE THEY WERE HEADING FOR THE AUTO SHOP.
I SHOULD GO HELP ALLEIN. GET EVERYONE OUT. IF BYNAL COMES BACK, HIT HIM IN THE HEAD.
A LOT.
BE CAREFUL.
WAIT!

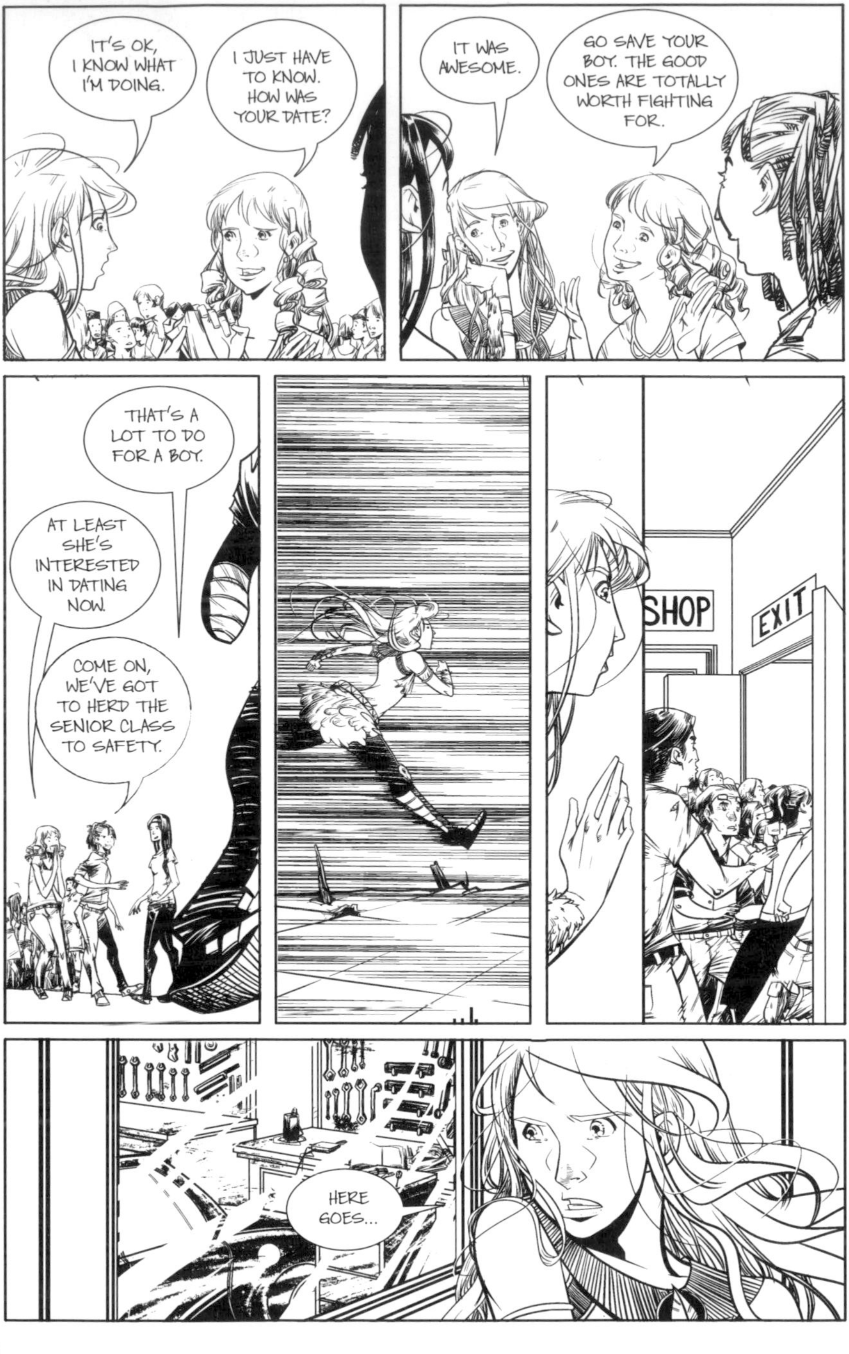
IT'S OK, I KNOW WHAT I'M DOING.
I JUST HAVE TO KNOW. HOW WAS YOUR DATE?
IT WAS AWESOME.
GO SAVE YOUR BOY. THE GOOD ONES ARE TOTALLY WORTH FIGHTING FOR.
THAT'S A LOT TO DO FOR A BOY.
AT LEAST SHE'S INTERESTED IN DATING NOW.
COME ON, WE'VE GOT TO HERD THE SENIOR CLASS TO SAFETY.
SHOP
EXIT
HERE GOES...

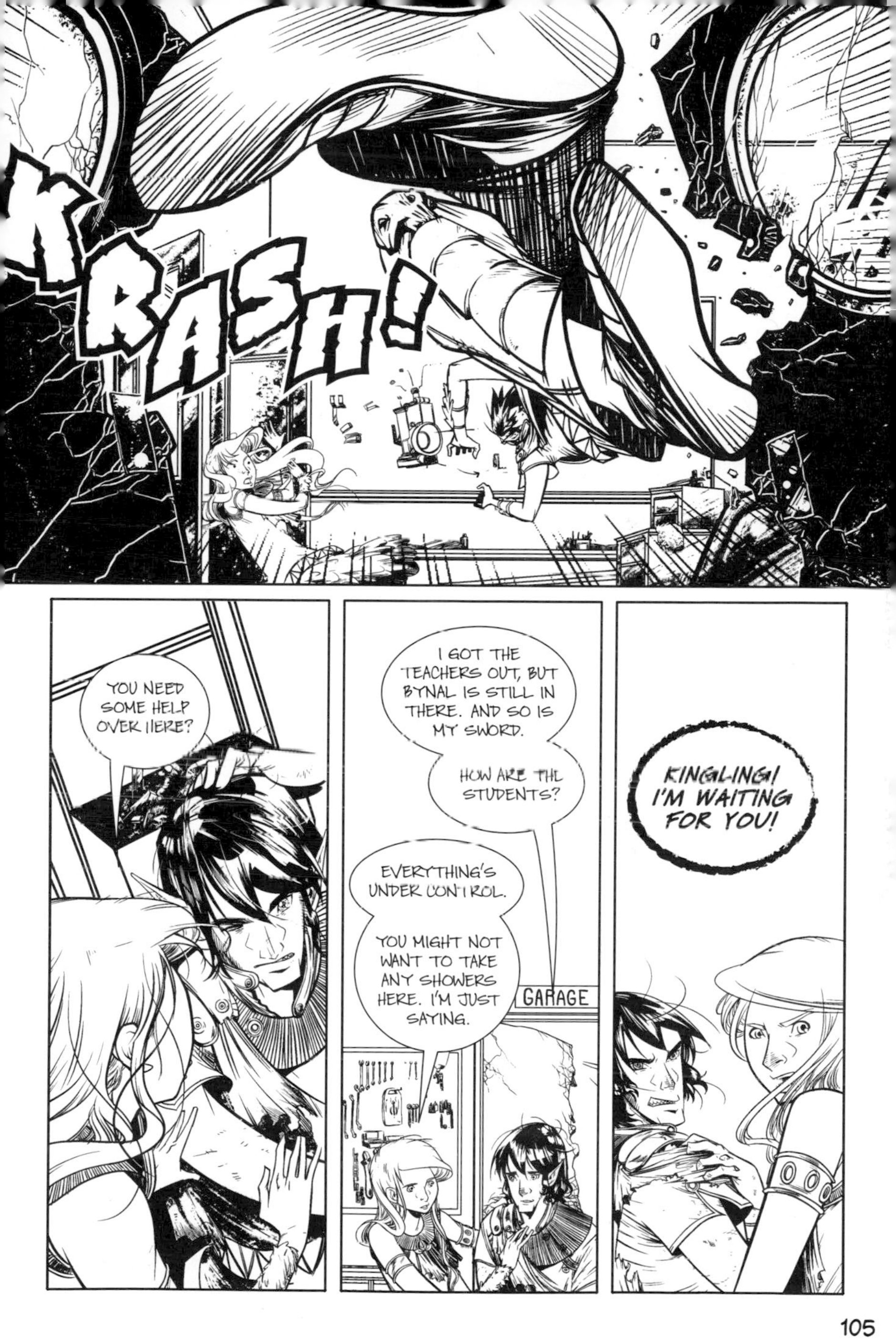
KRASH!
YOU NEED SOME HELP OVER HERE?
I GOT THE TEACHERS OUT, BUT BYNAL IS STILL IN THERE. AND SO IS MY SWORD.
HOW ARE THE STUDENTS?
EVERYTHING'S UNDER CONTROL.
YOU MIGHT NOT WANT TO TAKE ANY SHOWERS HERE. I'M JUST SAYING.
GARAGE
KINGLING! I'M WAITING FOR YOU!

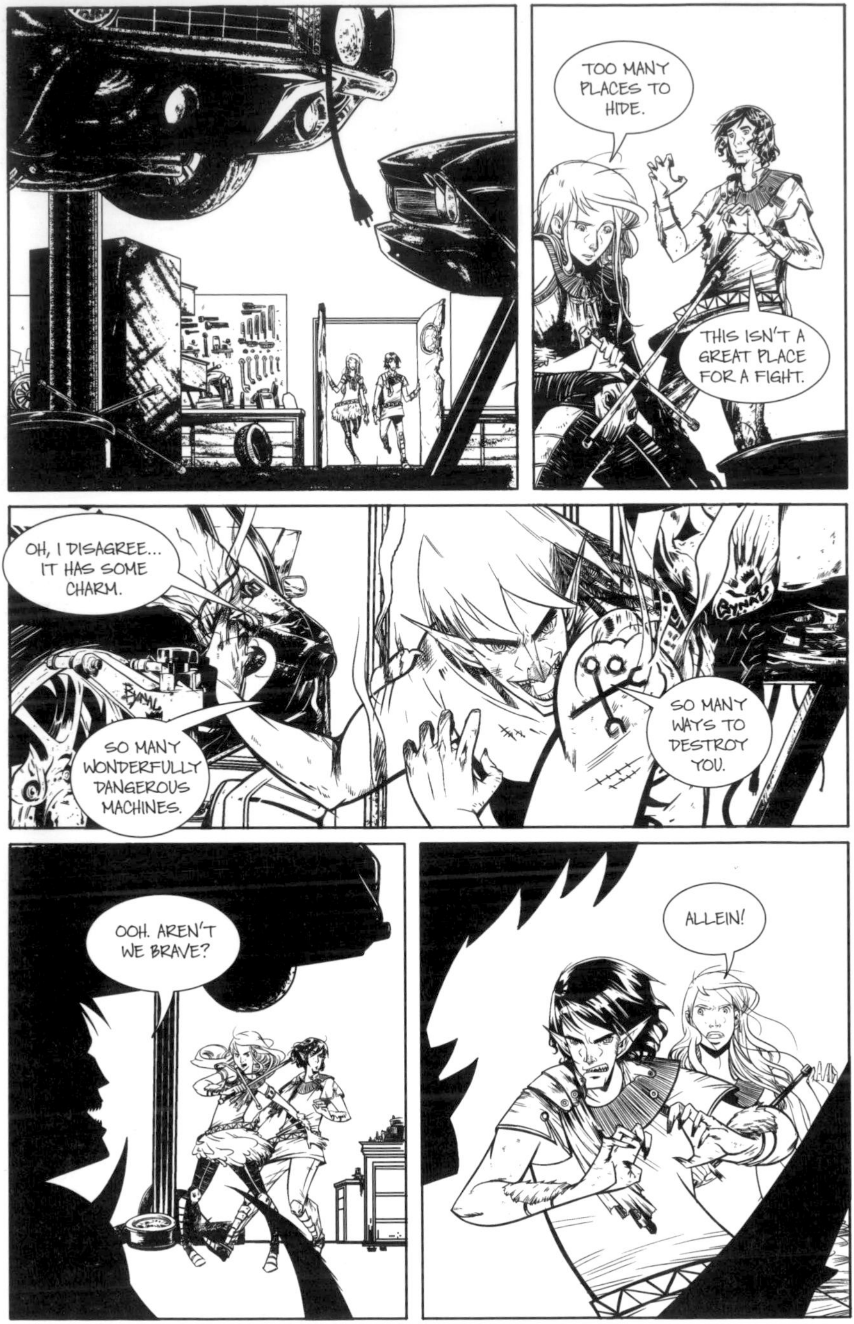
TOO MANY PLACES TO HIDE.
THIS ISN'T A GREAT PLACE FOR A FIGHT.
OH, I DISAGREE... IT HAS SOME CHARM.
SO MANY WONDERFULLY DANGEROUS MACHINES.
SO MANY WAYS TO DESTROY YOU.
OOH. AREN'T WE BRAVE?
ALLEIN!

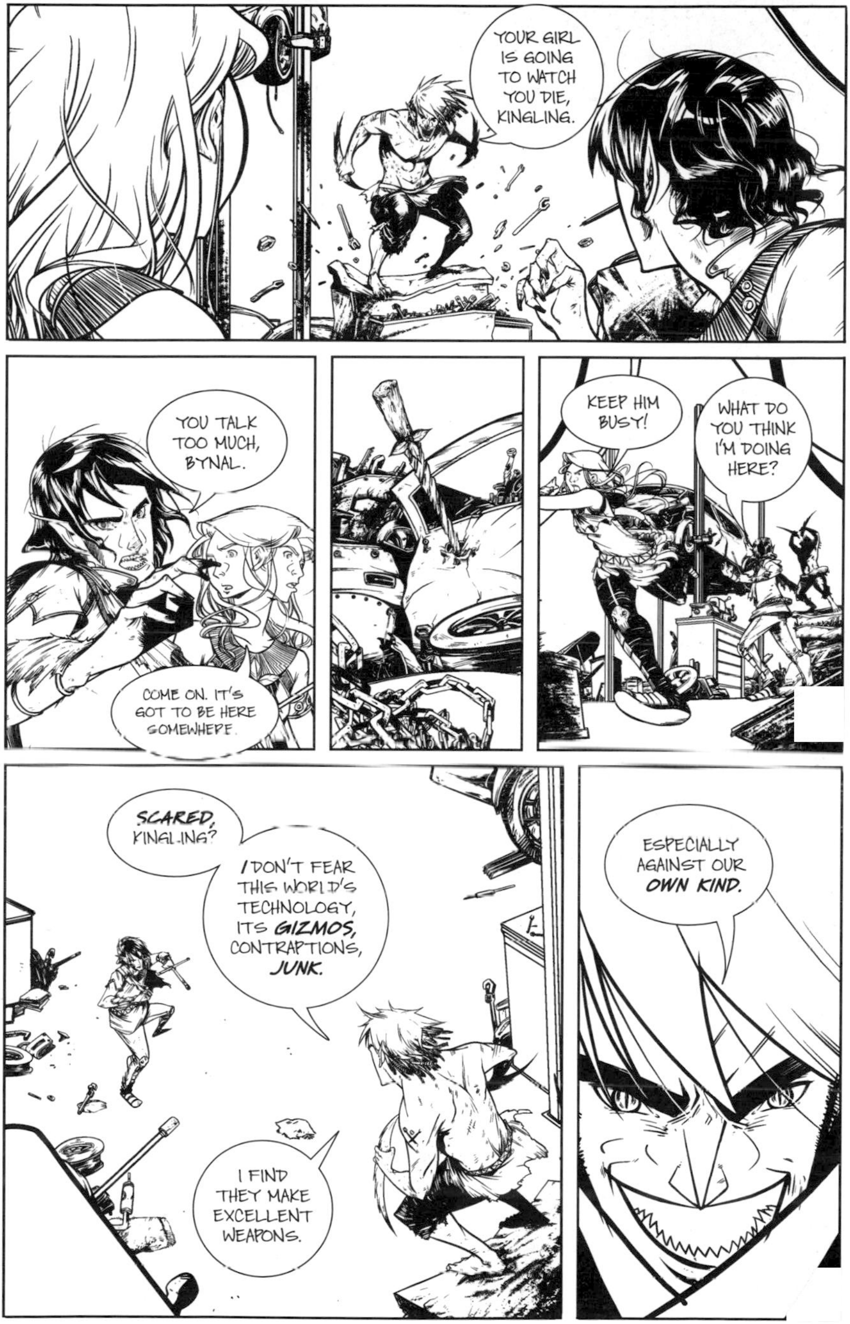
YOUR GIRL IS GOING TO WATCH YOU DIE, KINGLING.
YOU TALK TOO MUCH, BYNAL.
COME ON. IT'S GOT TO BE HERE SOMEWHERE.
KEEP HIM BUSY!
WHAT DO YOU THINK I'M DOING HERE?
SCARED, KINGLING?
I DON'T FEAR THIS WORLD'S TECHNOLOGY, ITS GIZMOS, CONTRAPTIONS, JUNK.
I FIND THEY MAKE EXCELLENT WEAPONS.
ESPECIALLY AGAINST OUR OWN KIND.

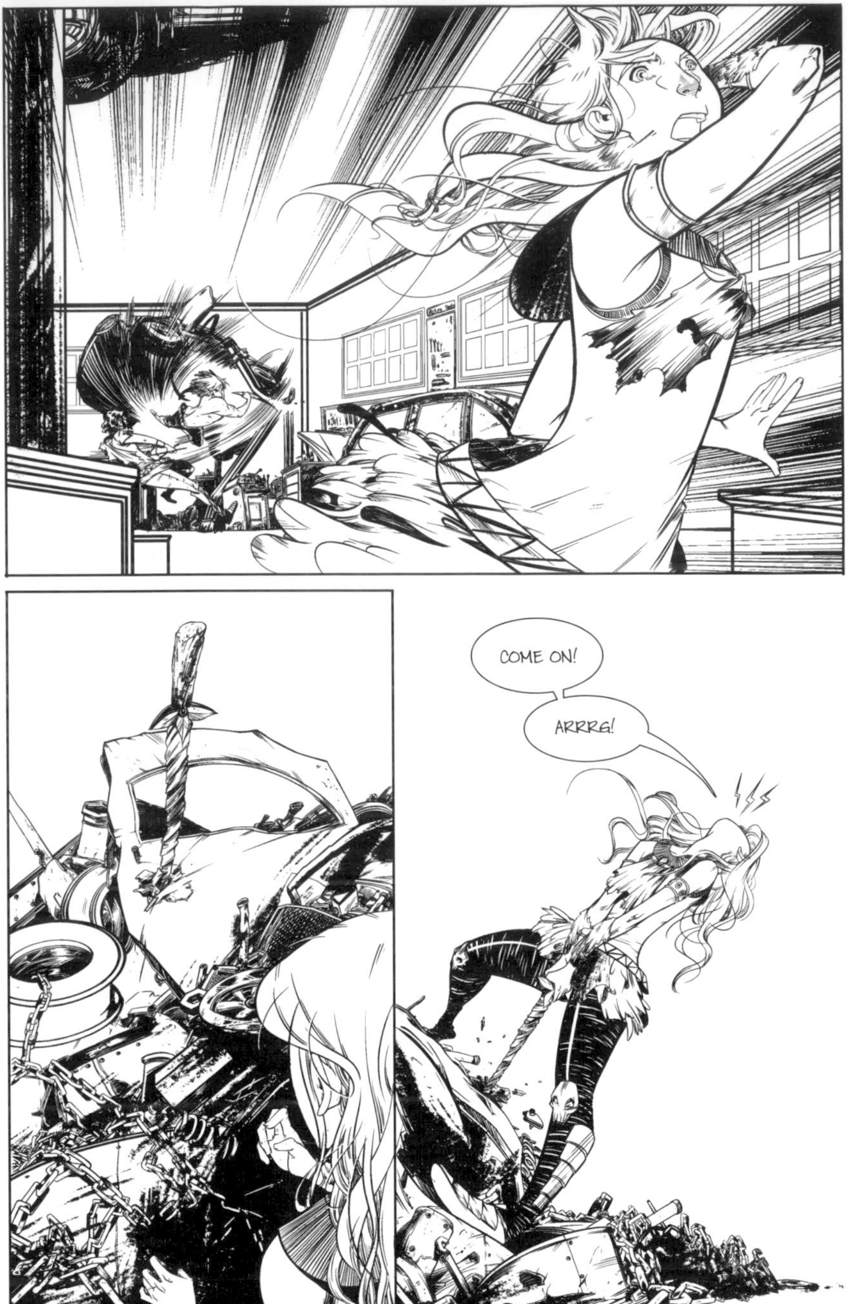
COME ON!
ARRRG!

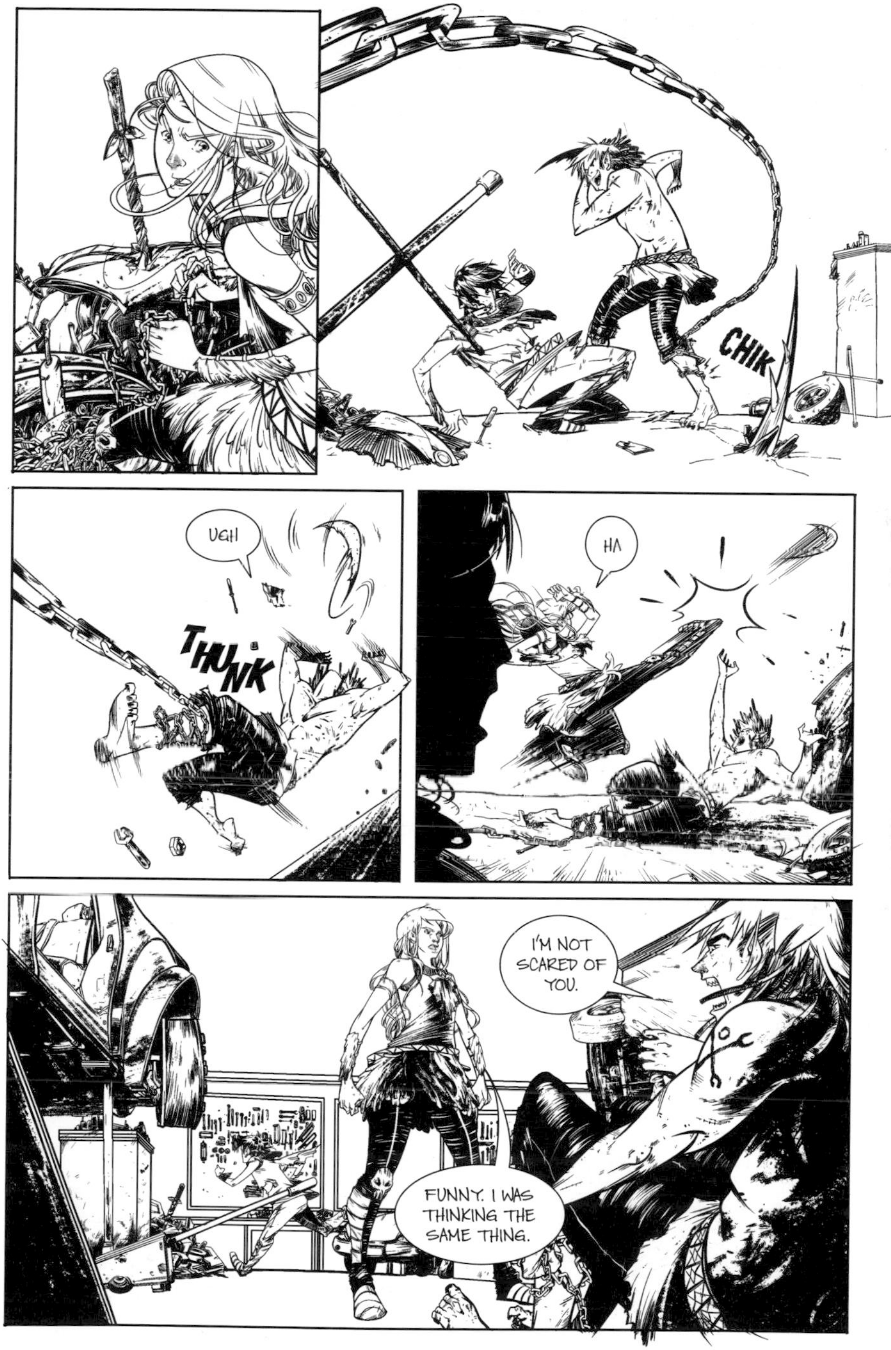
CHIK
UGH
THUNK
HA
I'M NOT SCARED OF YOU.
FUNNY. I WAS THINKING THE SAME THING.

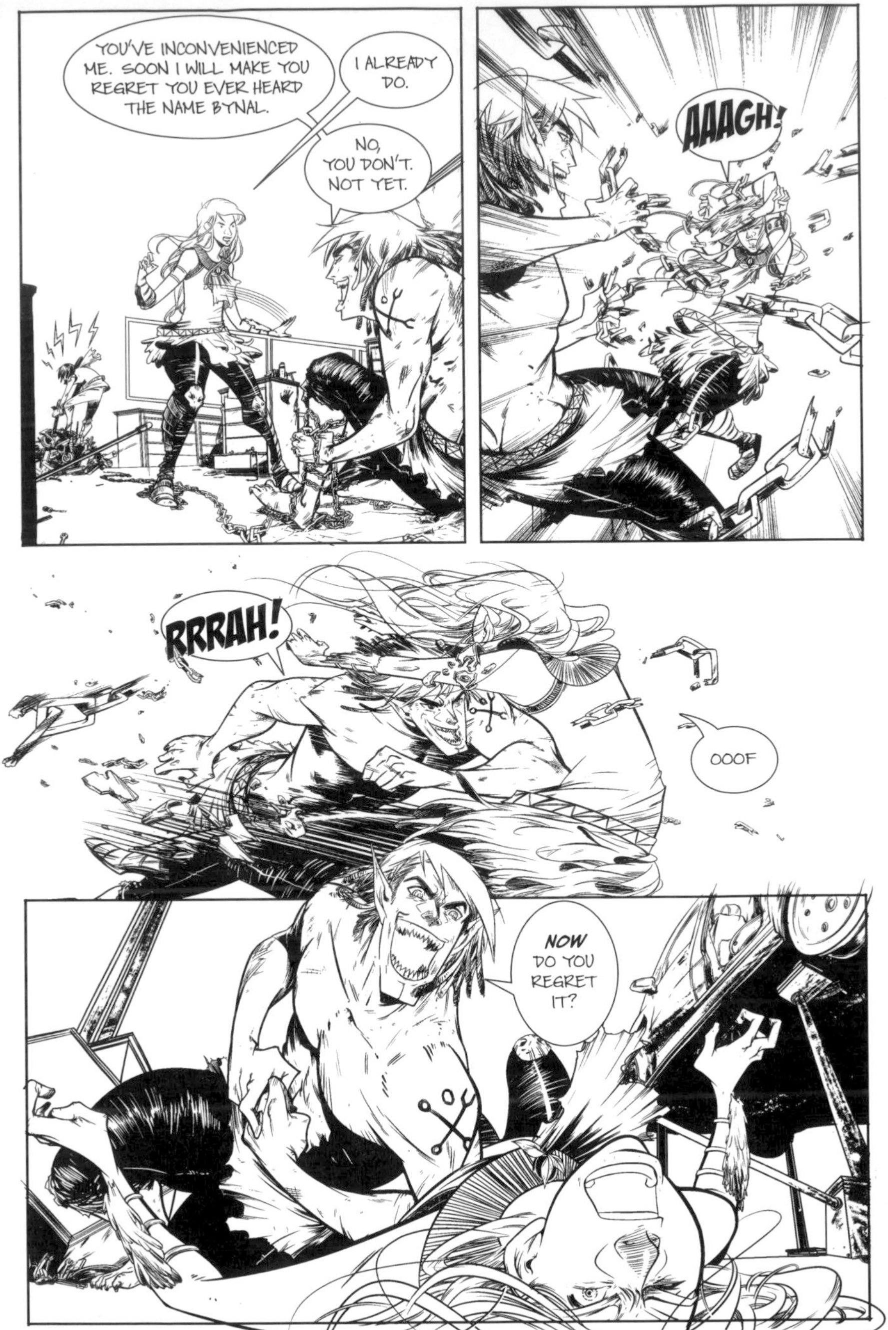
YOU'VE INCONVENIENCED ME. SOON I WILL MAKE YOU REGRET YOU EVER HEARD THE NAME BYNAL.
I ALREADY DO.
NO, YOU DON'T. NOT YET.
AAAGH!
RRRAH!
OOOF
NOW DO YOU REGRET IT?

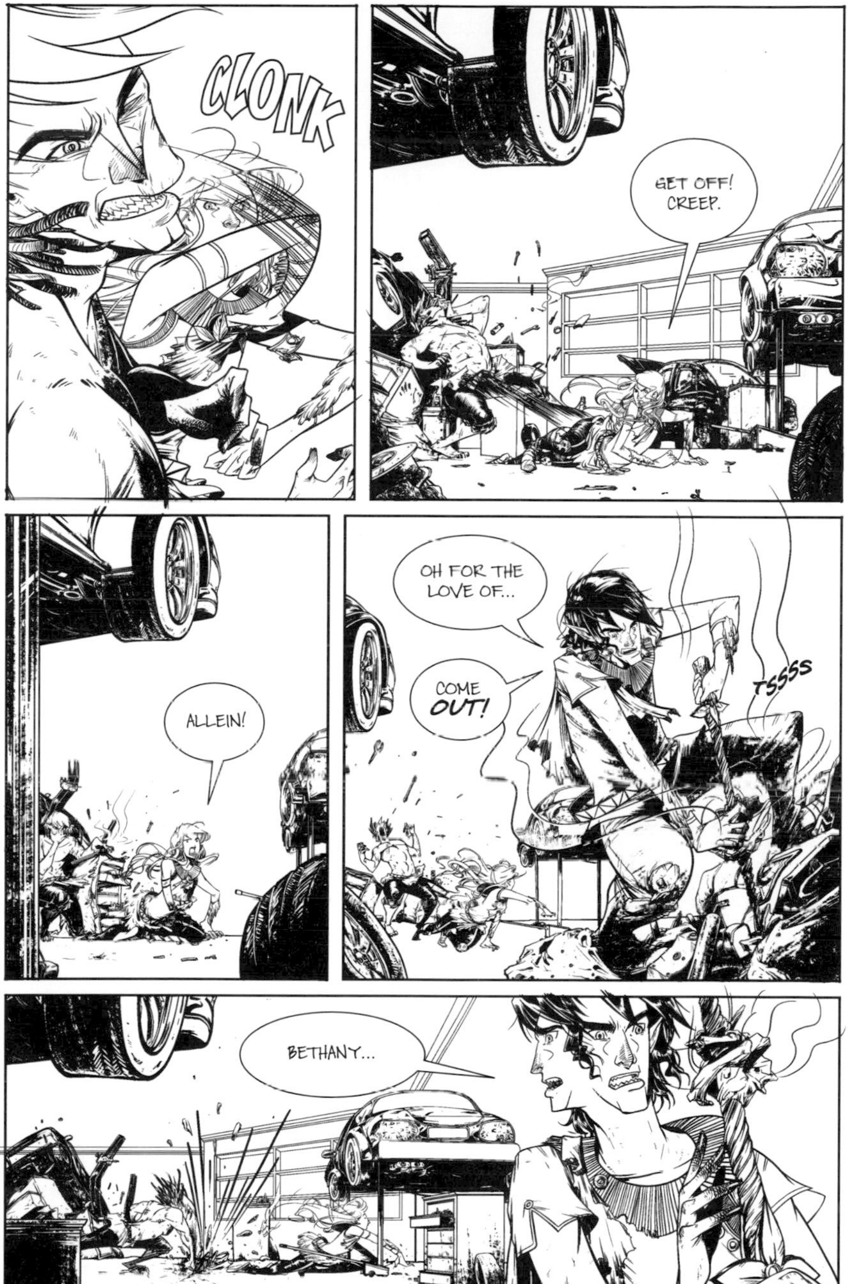
CLONK
GET OFF! CREEP.
ALLEIN!
OH FOR THE LOVE OF...
COME OUT!
TSSSS
BETHANY...

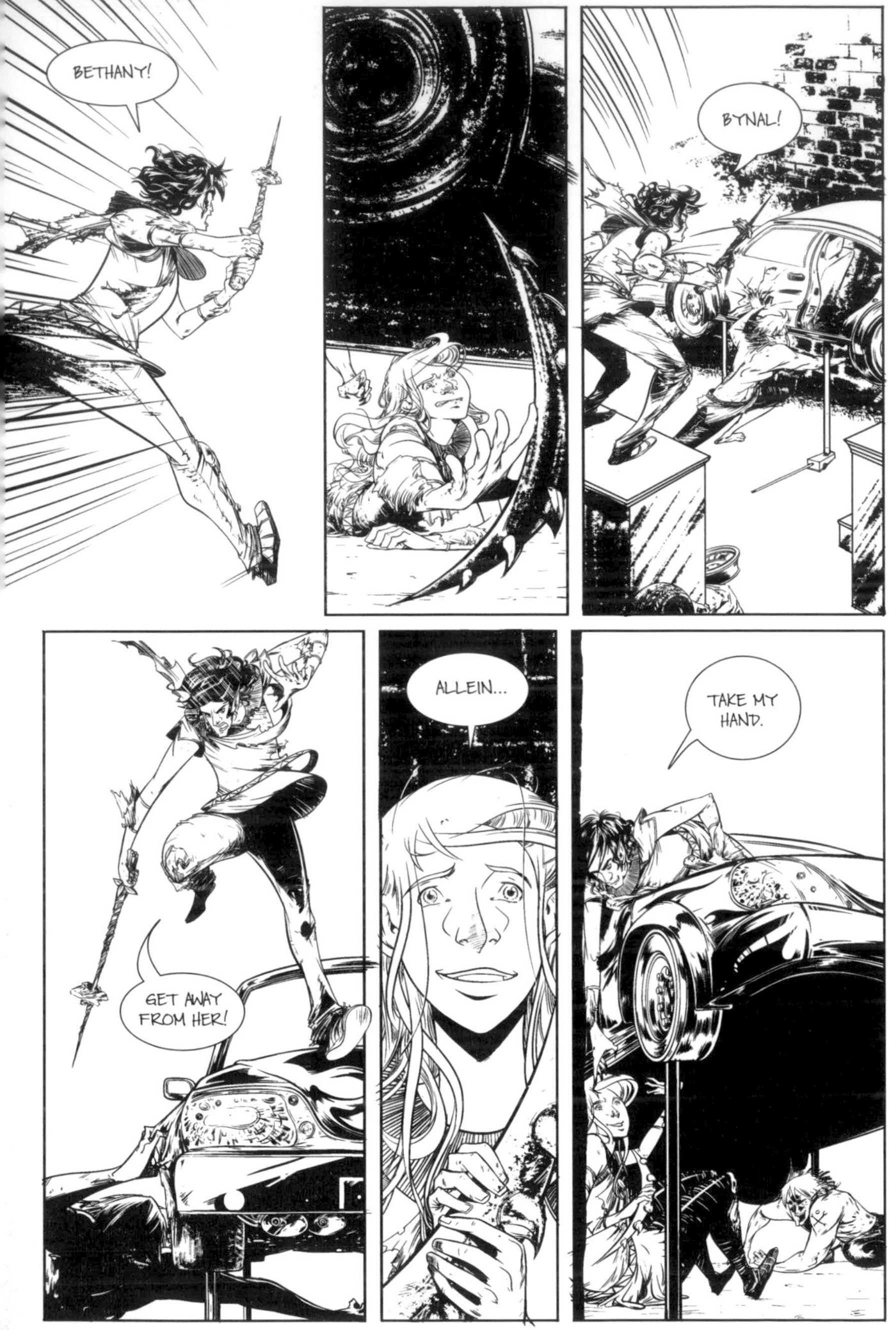
BETHANY!
BYNAL!
GET AWAY FROM HER!
ALLEIN...
TAKE MY HAND.

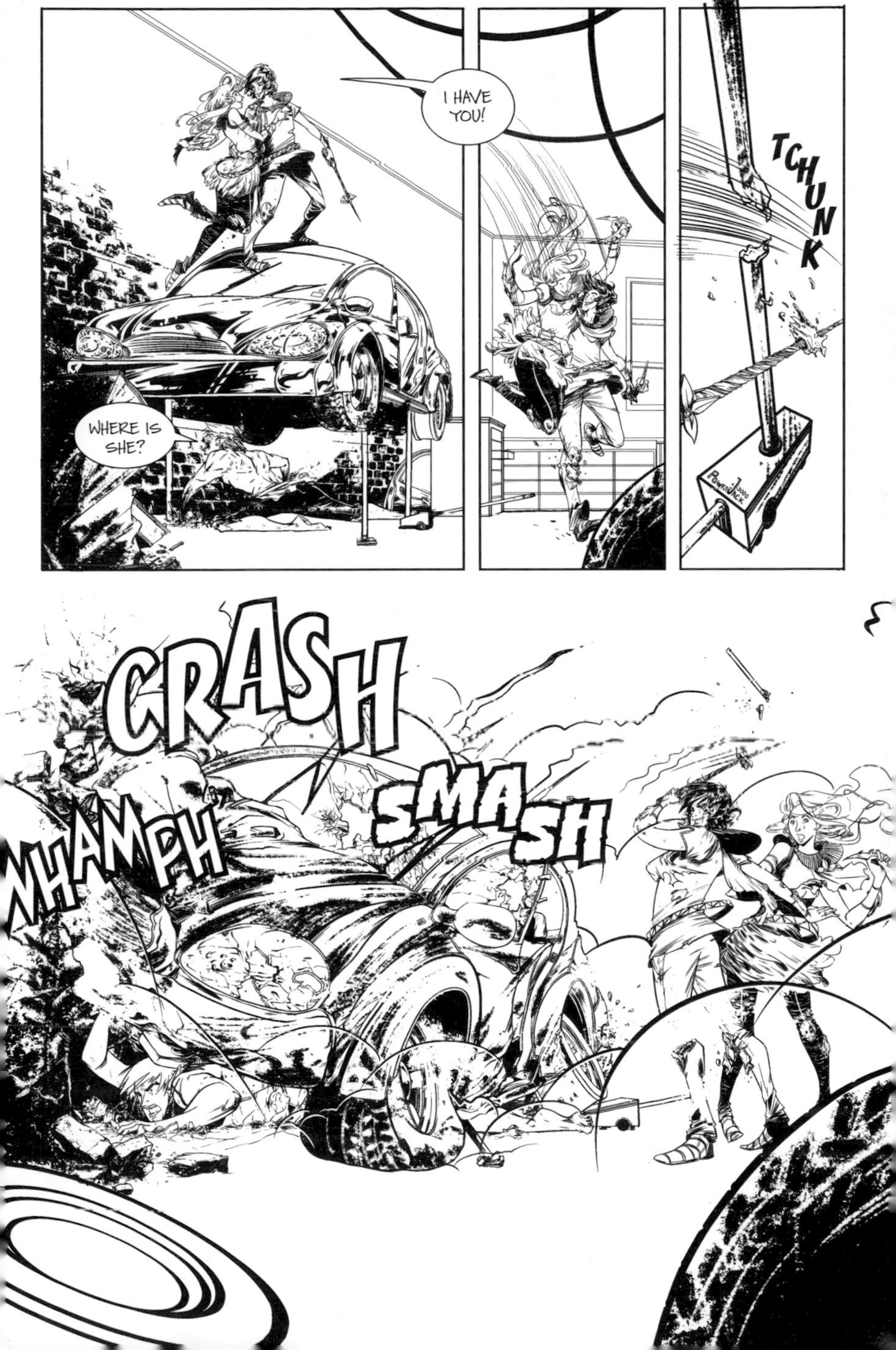
WHERE IS SHE?
I HAVE YOU!
TCHUNK
POWERJACK 3000
CRASH
WHAMPH
SMASH

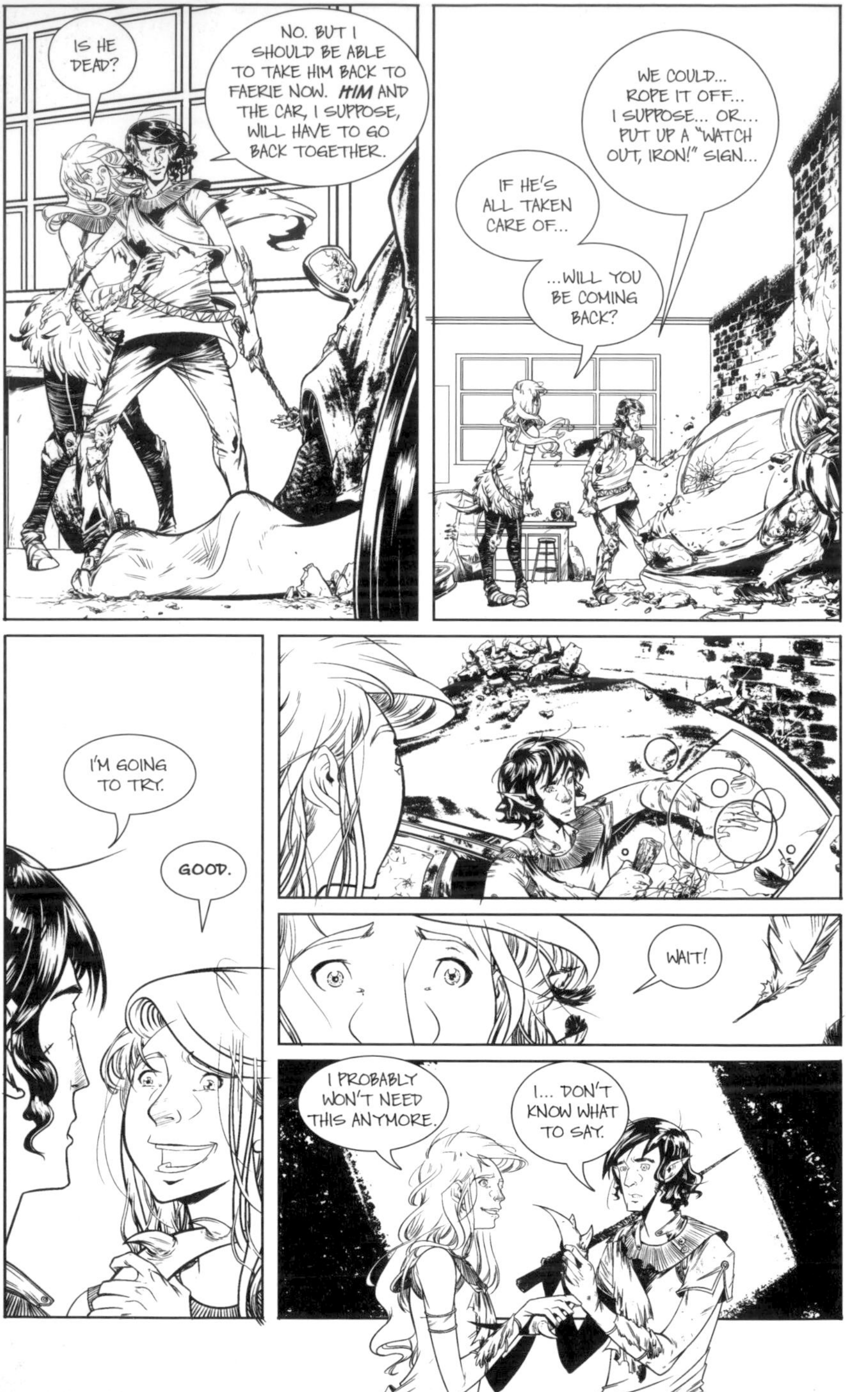
IS HE DEAD?
NO. BUT I SHOULD BE ABLE TO TAKE HIM BACK TO FAERIE NOW. ***HIM*** AND THE CAR, I SUPPOSE, WILL HAVE TO GO BACK TOGETHER.
WE COULD... ROPE IT OFF... I SUPPOSE... OR... PUT UP A "WATCH OUT, IRON!" SIGN...
IF HE'S ALL TAKEN CARE OF...
...WILL YOU BE COMING BACK?
I'M GOING TO TRY.
GOOD.
WAIT!
I PROBABLY WON'T NEED THIS ANYMORE.
I... DON'T KNOW WHAT TO SAY.

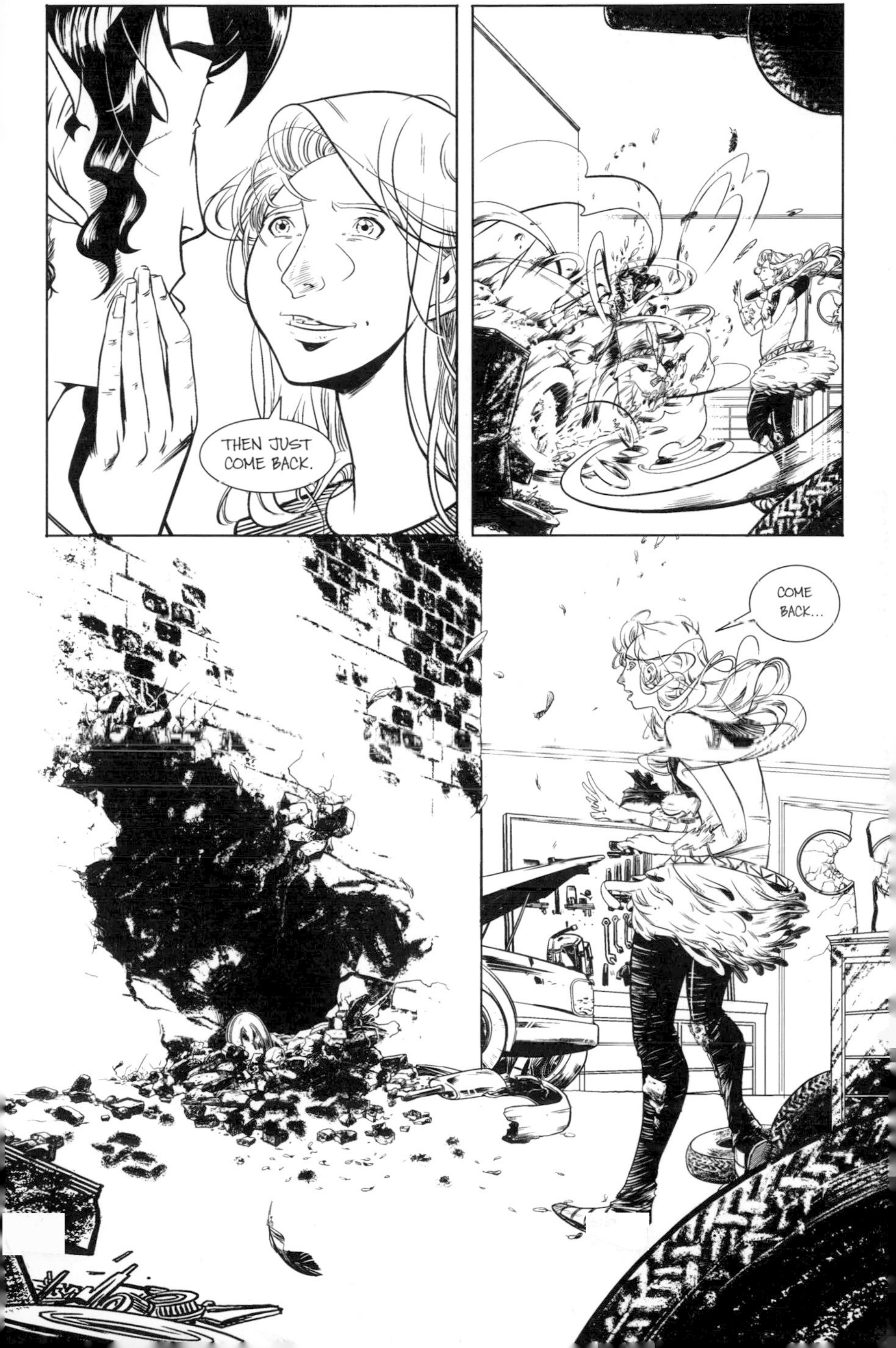
THEN JUST COME BACK.
COME BACK...

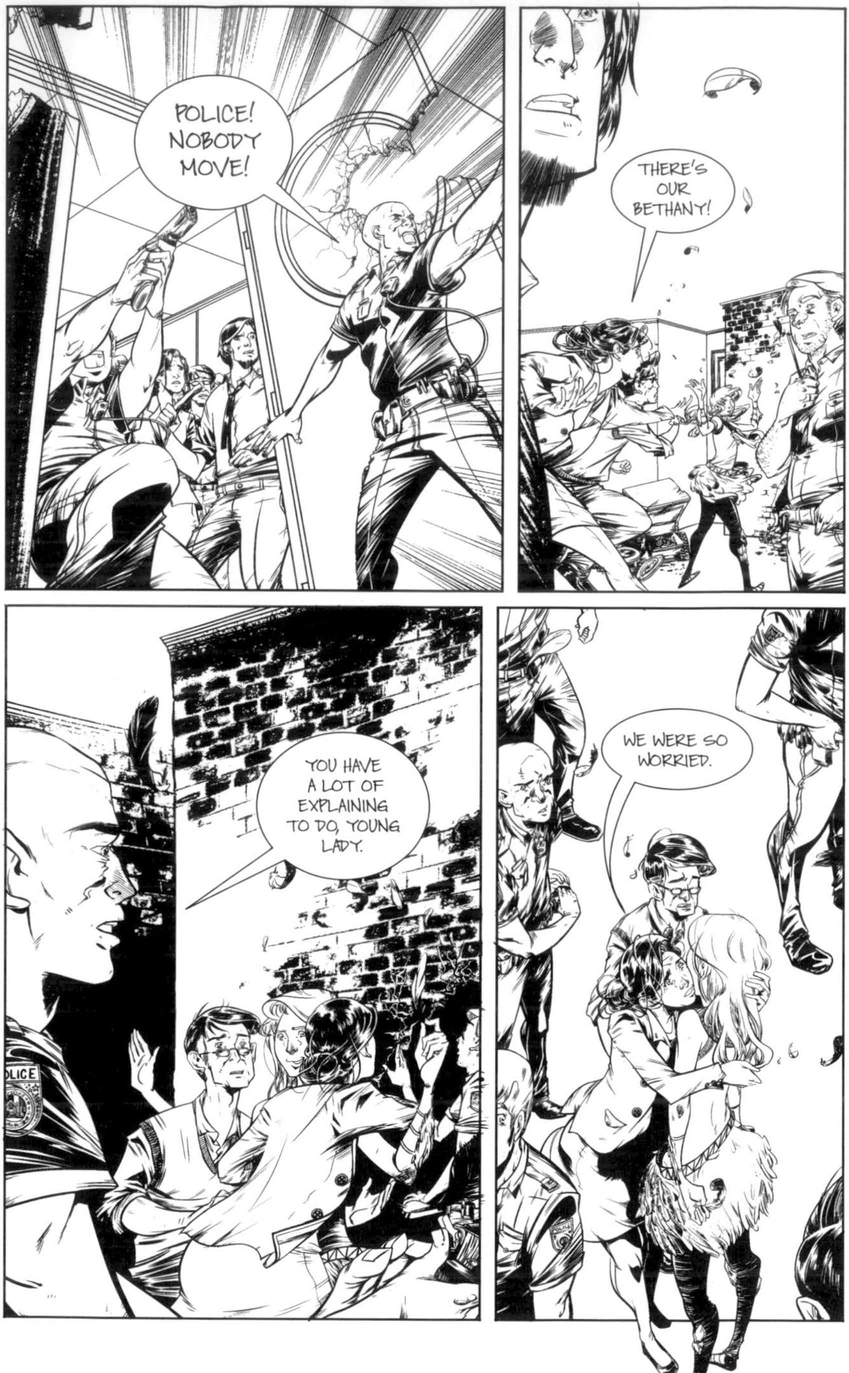
POLICE! NOBODY MOVE!
THERE'S OUR BETHANY!
YOU HAVE A LOT OF EXPLAINING TO DO, YOUNG LADY.
WE WERE SO WORRIED.

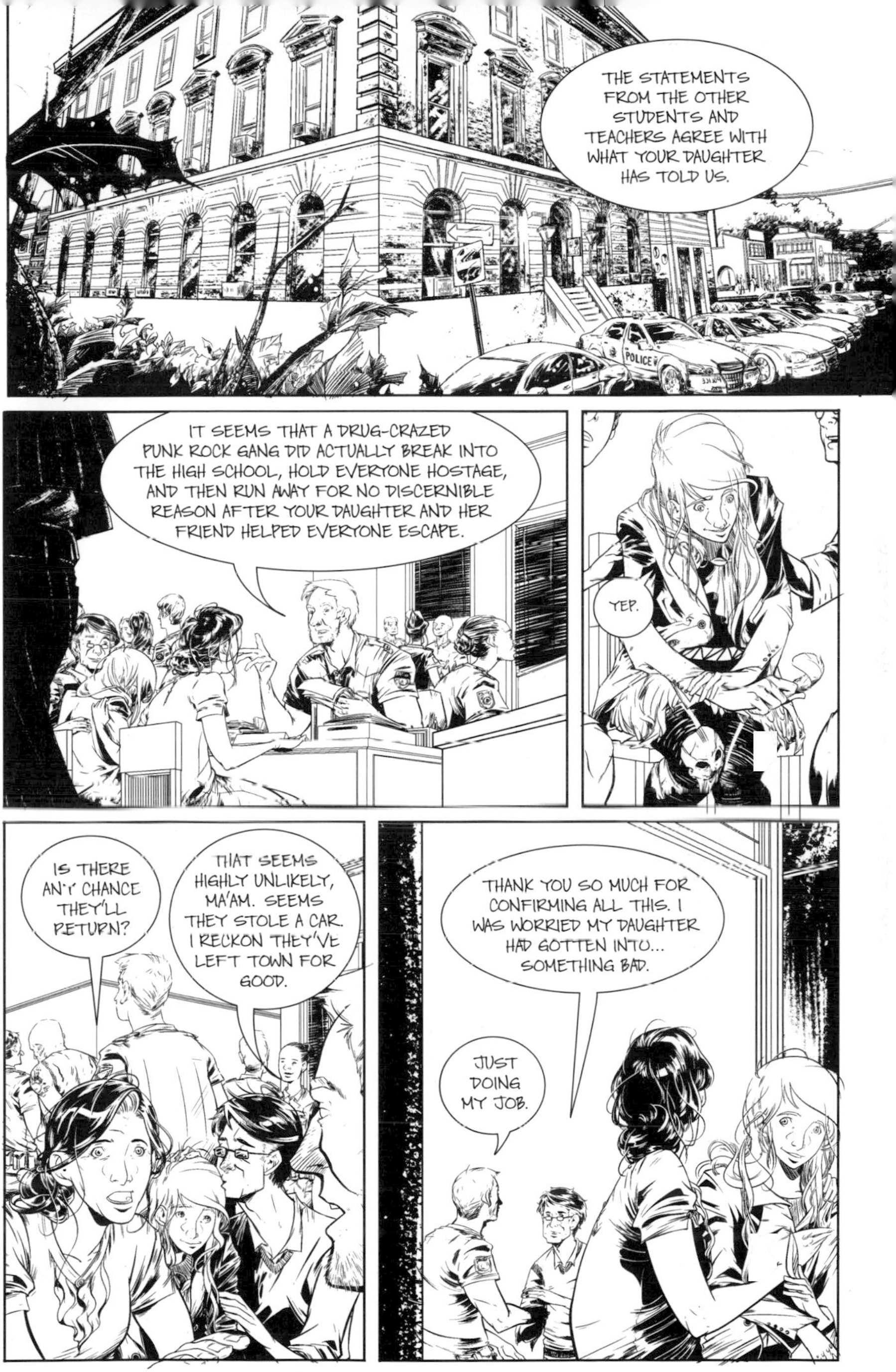
THE STATEMENTS FROM THE OTHER STUDENTS AND TEACHERS AGREE WITH WHAT YOUR DAUGHTER HAS TOLD US.
POLICE
IT SEEMS THAT A DRUG-CRAZED PUNK ROCK GANG DID ACTUALLY BREAK INTO THE HIGH SCHOOL, HOLD EVERYONE HOSTAGE, AND THEN RUN AWAY FOR NO DISCERNIBLE REASON AFTER YOUR DAUGHTER AND HER FRIEND HELPED EVERYONE ESCAPE.
YEP.
IS THERE ANY CHANCE THEY'LL RETURN?
THAT SEEMS HIGHLY UNLIKELY, MA'AM. SEEMS THEY STOLE A CAR. I RECKON THEY'VE LEFT TOWN FOR GOOD.
THANK YOU SO MUCH FOR CONFIRMING ALL THIS. I WAS WORRIED MY DAUGHTER HAD GOTTEN INTO... SOMETHING BAD.
JUST DOING MY JOB.

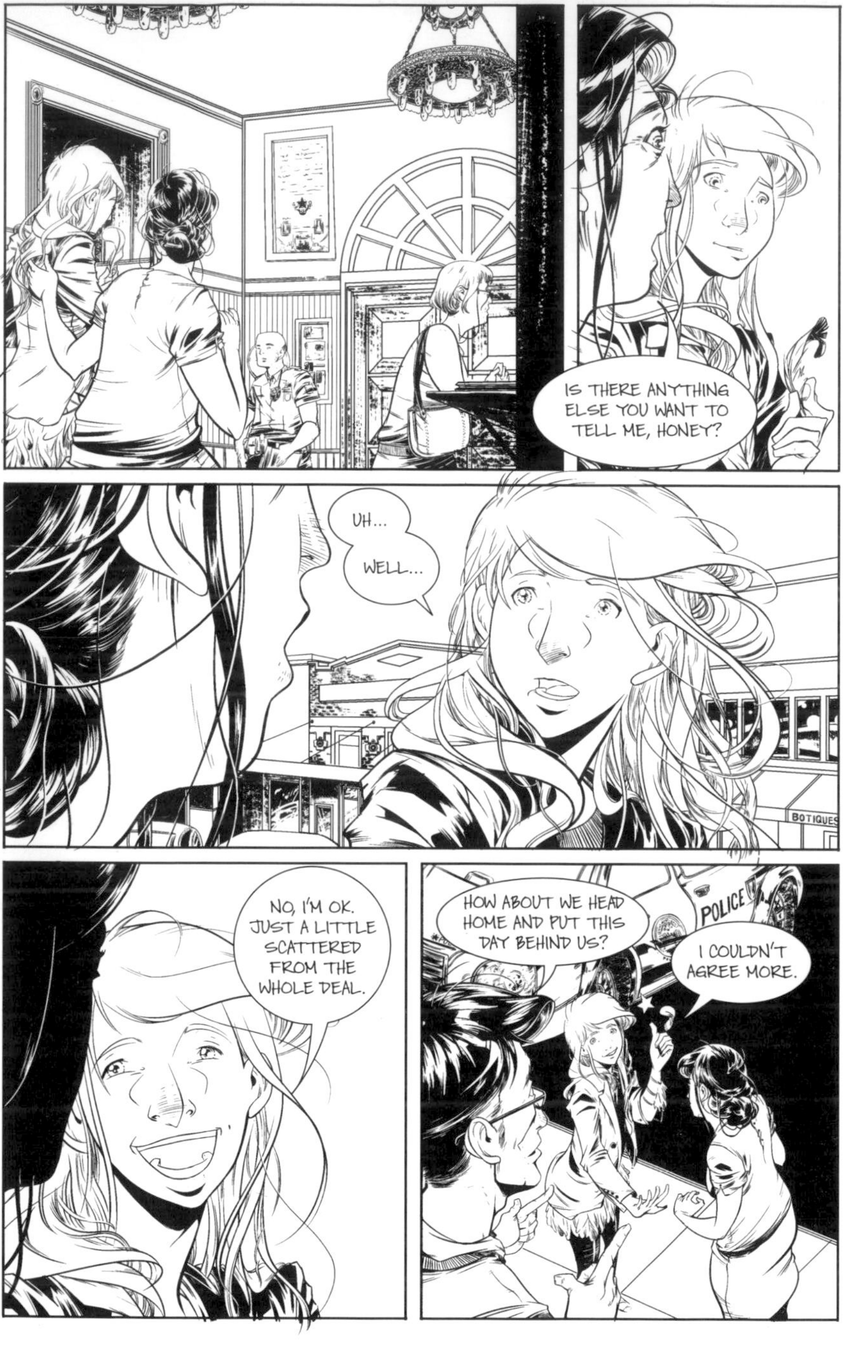

IS THERE ANYTHING ELSE YOU WANT TO TELL ME, HONEY?
UH...
WELL...
BOTIQUES
NO, I'M OK. JUST A LITTLE SCATTERED FROM THE WHOLE DEAL.
HOW ABOUT WE HEAD HOME AND PUT THIS DAY BEHIND US?
POLICE
I COULDN'T AGREE MORE.

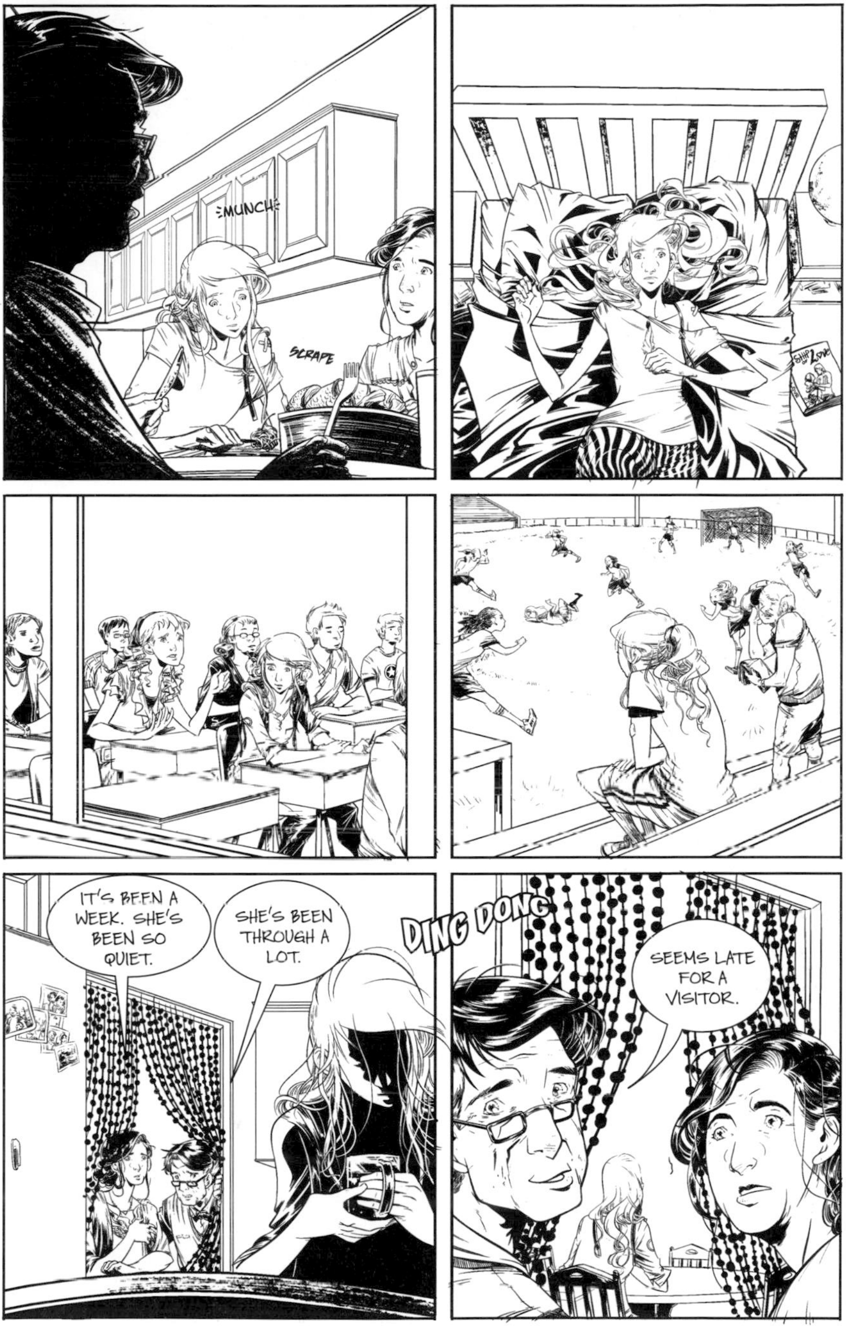
MUNCH
SCRAPE
IT'S BEEN A WEEK. SHE'S BEEN SO QUIET.
SHE'S BEEN THROUGH A LOT.
DING DONG
SEEMS LATE FOR A VISITOR.

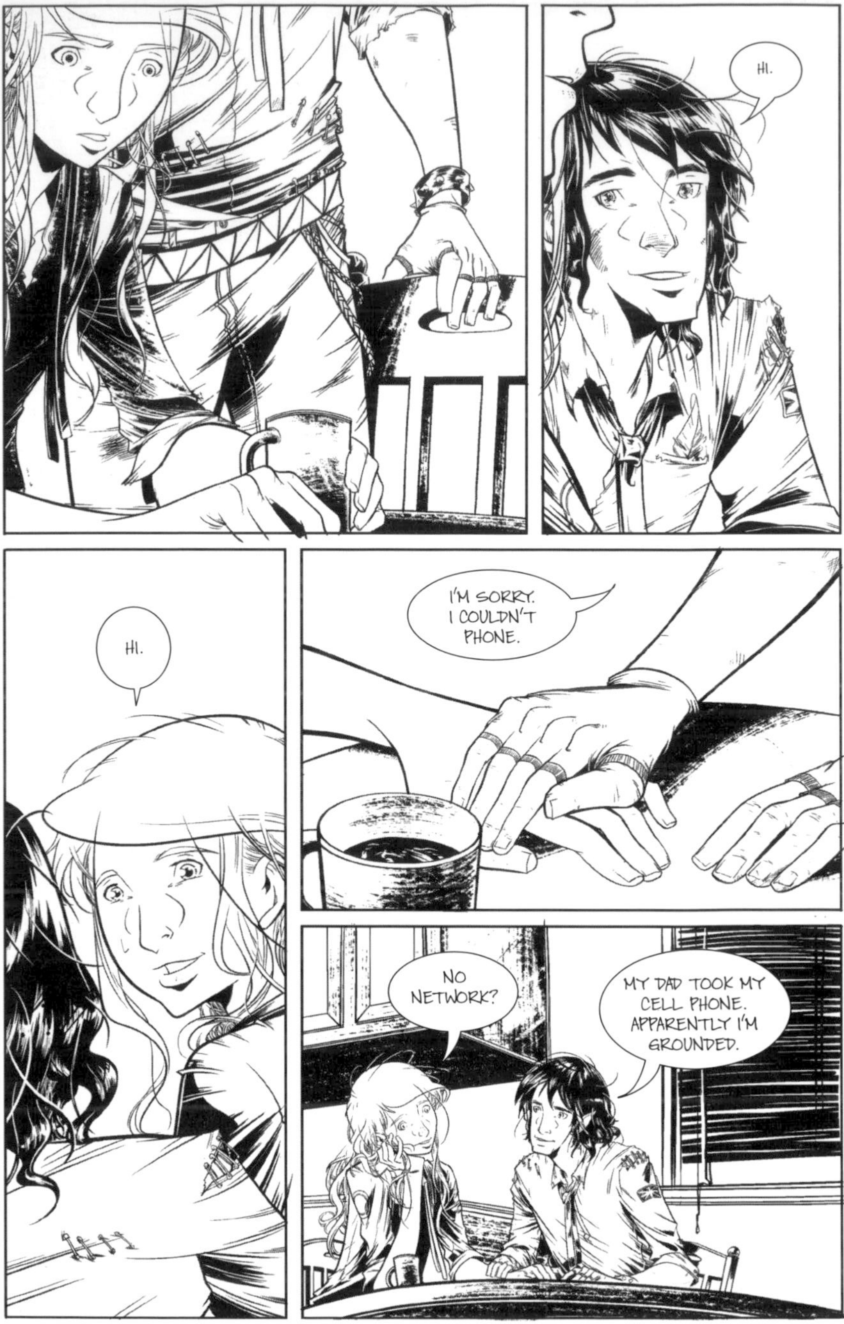
HI.
HI.
I'M SORRY. I COULDN'T PHONE.
NO NETWORK?
MY DAD TOOK MY CELL PHONE. APPARENTLY I'M GROUNDED.

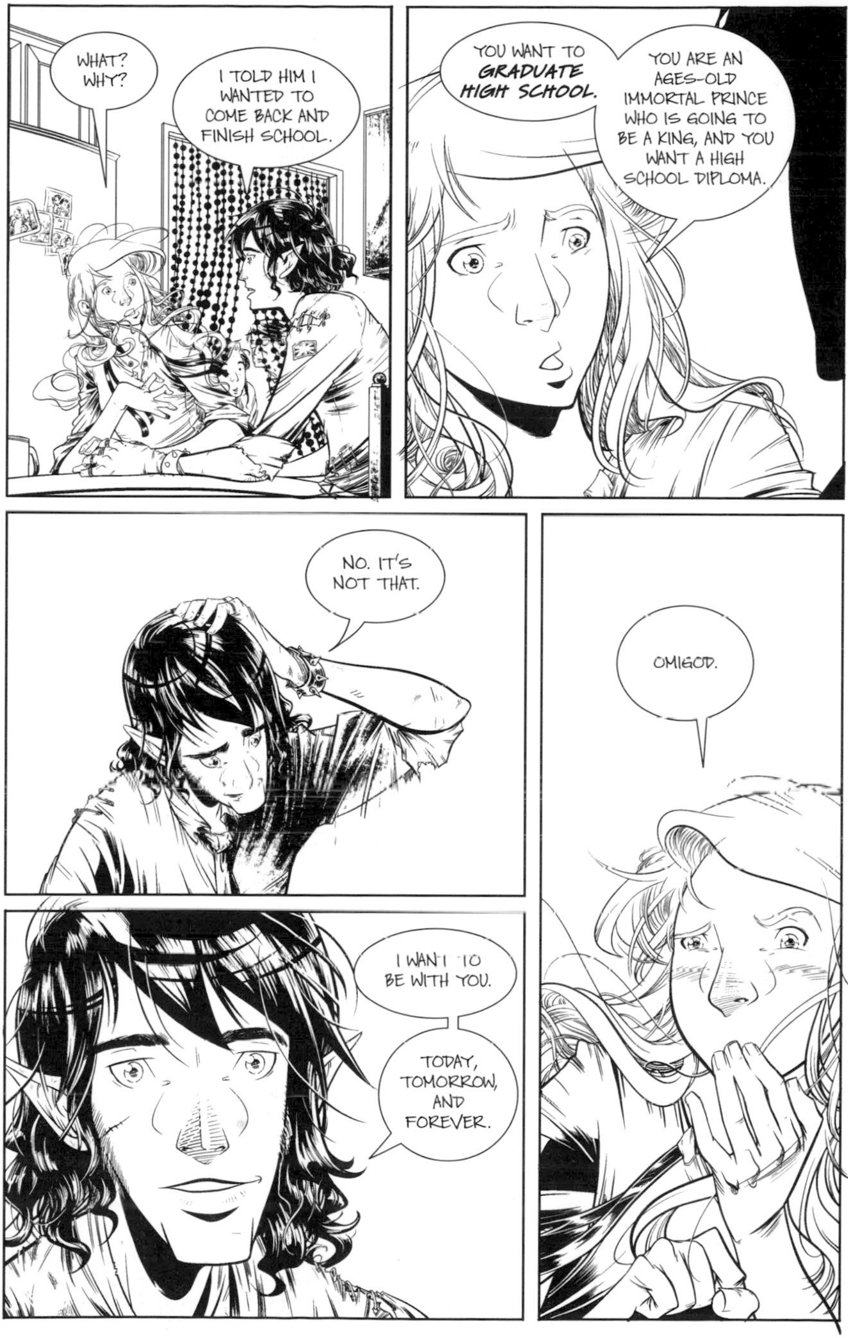
WHAT? WHY?
I TOLD HIM I WANTED TO COME BACK AND FINISH SCHOOL.
YOU WANT TO **GRADUATE HIGH SCHOOL.**
YOU ARE AN AGES-OLD IMMORTAL PRINCE WHO IS GOING TO BE A KING, AND YOU WANT A HIGH SCHOOL DIPLOMA.
NO. IT'S NOT THAT.
I WANT TO BE WITH YOU.
TODAY, TOMORROW, AND FOREVER.
OMIGOD.

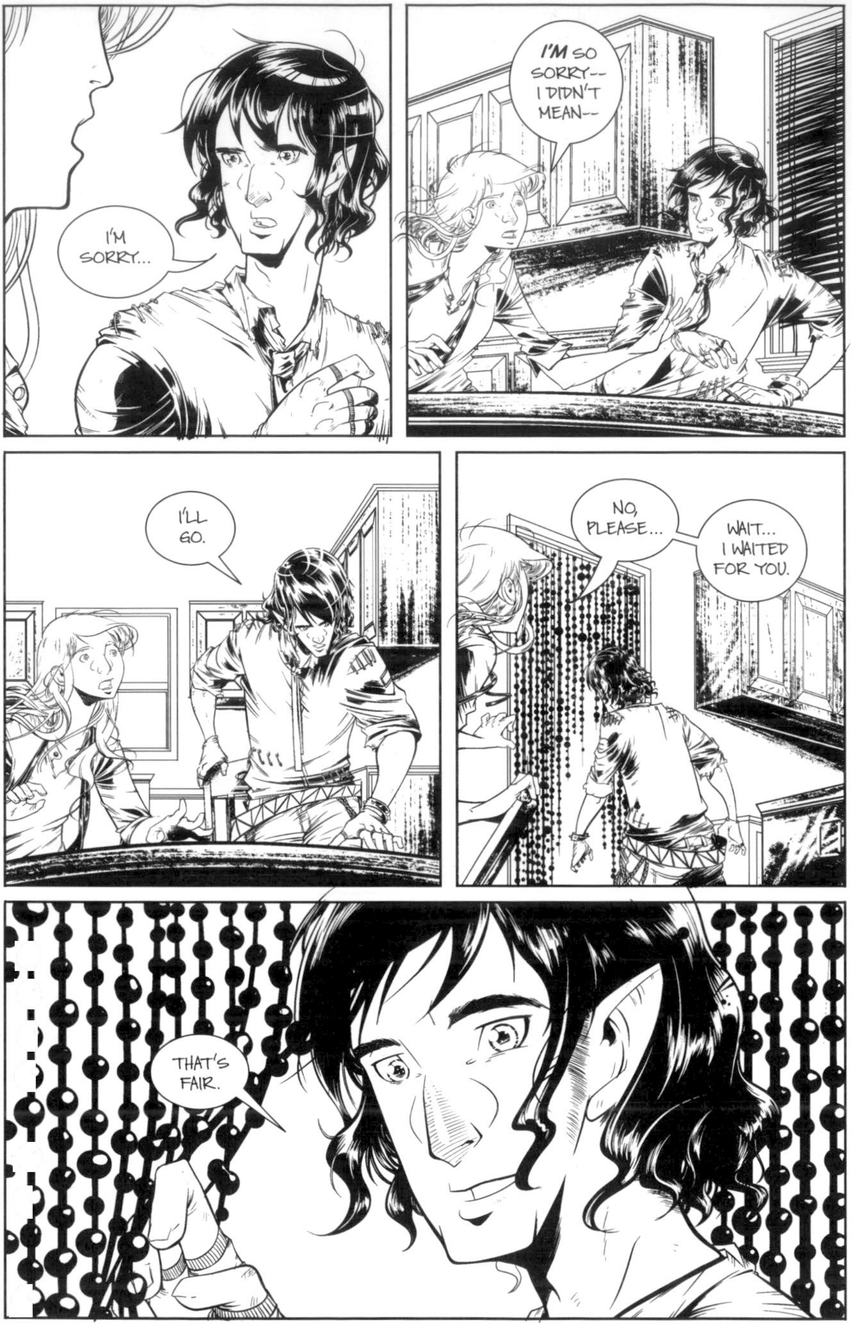

I'M SORRY...
I'M SO SORRY-- I DIDN'T MEAN--
I'LL GO.
NO, PLEASE...
WAIT... I WAITED FOR YOU.
THAT'S FAIR.

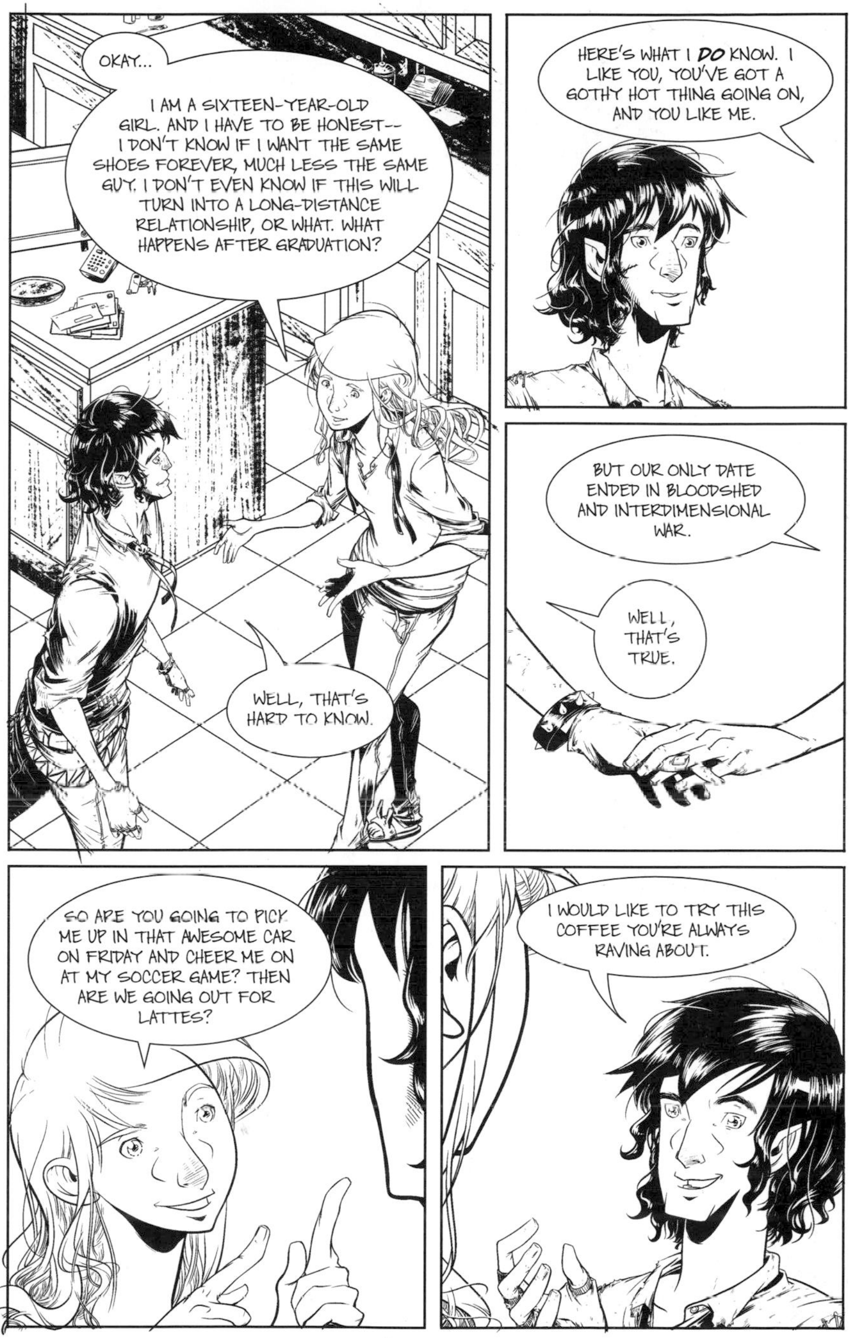
OKAY...
I AM A SIXTEEN-YEAR-OLD GIRL. AND I HAVE TO BE HONEST-- I DON'T KNOW IF I WANT THE SAME SHOES FOREVER, MUCH LESS THE SAME GUY. I DON'T EVEN KNOW IF THIS WILL TURN INTO A LONG-DISTANCE RELATIONSHIP, OR WHAT. WHAT HAPPENS AFTER GRADUATION?
WELL, THAT'S HARD TO KNOW.
HERE'S WHAT I **DO** KNOW. I LIKE YOU, YOU'VE GOT A GOTHY HOT THING GOING ON, AND YOU LIKE ME.
BUT OUR ONLY DATE ENDED IN BLOODSHED AND INTERDIMENSIONAL WAR.
WELL, THAT'S TRUE.
SO ARE YOU GOING TO PICK ME UP IN THAT AWESOME CAR ON FRIDAY AND CHEER ME ON AT MY SOCCER GAME? THEN ARE WE GOING OUT FOR LATTES?
I WOULD LIKE TO TRY THIS COFFEE YOU'RE ALWAYS RAVING ABOUT.

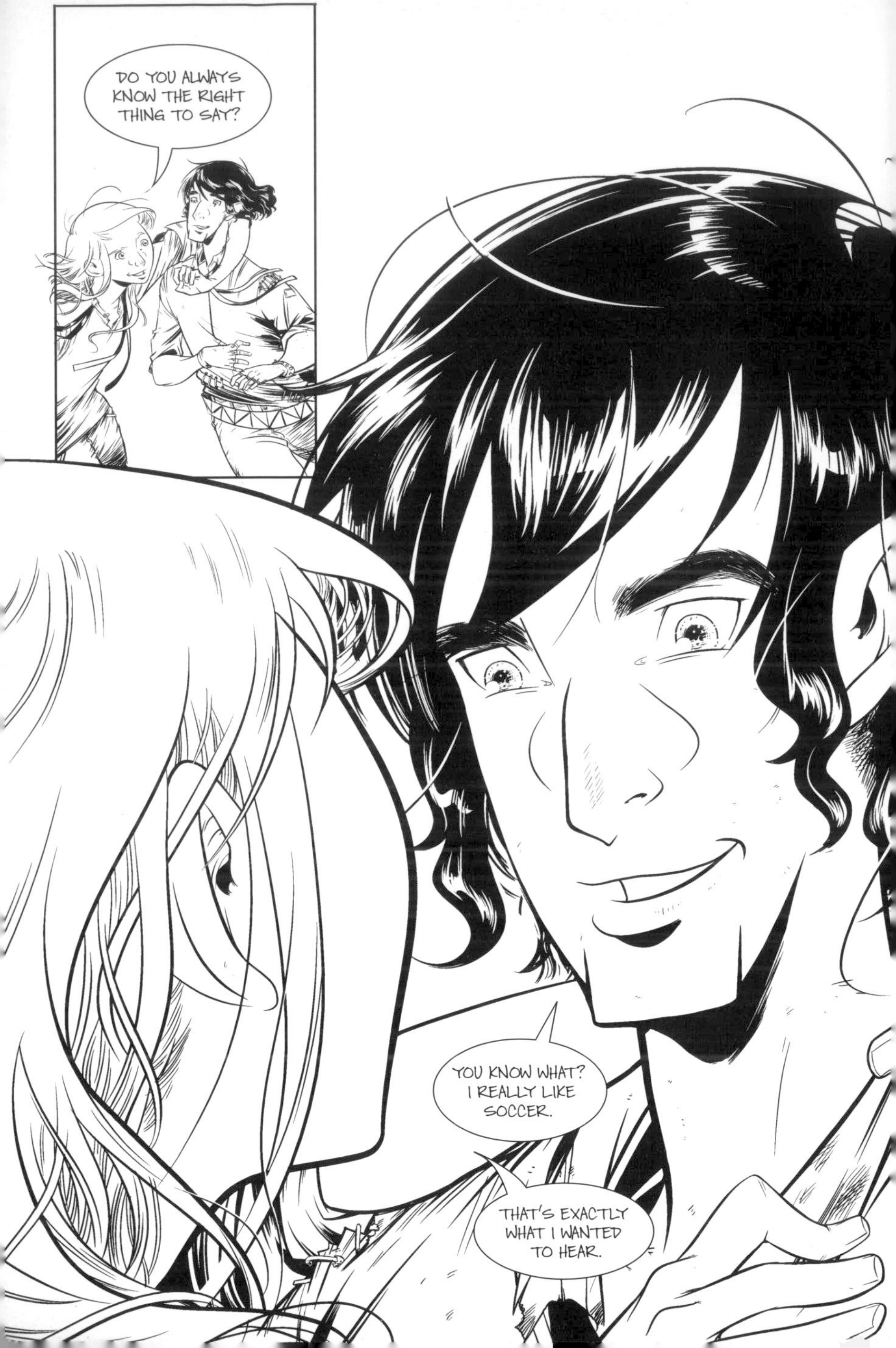
DO YOU ALWAYS KNOW THE RIGHT THING TO SAY?
YOU KNOW WHAT? I REALLY LIKE SOCCER.
THAT'S EXACTLY WHAT I WANTED TO HEAR.

Property of Bethany Farmer HANDS OFF!!!

~~FAIRIES~~ the fae

ORIGINS

Fairies (also known as faeries, fay, fae, and the Fair Folk) are magical beings that appear in the stories of many peoples, though they are most commonly based on the pre-Christian folklore of the British Isles. The root of the word *fairy* comes from the Latin *fata,* which referred to the three Fates of Greek and Roman mythology. From *fata* the Old French word *fae* is derived, meaning "a state of enchantment."

The fairies who inhabited Ireland before the coming of the Gaels were described as beautiful and ageless beings, tall and noble, called "gods and not gods" but something in between—nothing at all like the tiny sprites with delicate gossamer wings that are popular in more modern stories. Small, winged fairies did not appear in folktales until the 1800s. The fairies were forced into hiding during the invasion of Ireland by humans and took refuge in underground mounds. These mounds still dot the landscape of Ireland, and legends say ill fortune will befall anyone who dares to disturb them.

The fairies of Celtic folklore can either help or harm. In Scotland, friendly fairies are members of the Seelie Court (or "the blessed court"). These gentle beings are known to help humans. However, they are not above creating mischief for sport or taking revenge when they are wronged. Members of the Unseelie Court are dangerous and often monstrous. They appeared after dark, riding the night sky in search of helpless travelers to kidnap or lead astray. According to legend, members of the Unseelie Court once belonged to the Seelie Court but then fell from grace. In years past, wars were fought between the two courts, and innocent humans often found themselves caught in their battles.

SOUND FAMILIAR?

So that's why Allein is afraid of the dark?!

COLD IRON

Cautious humans avoid fairies whenever possible. Even speaking the word "fairy" can be dangerous should a fairy hear you—they cherish their privacy, and a human who admits to seeing a fairy might face dramatic punishment . . . even having one's eyes poked out. During the Middle Ages in the British Isles, people rarely spoke of fairies. When they did, they gave them flattering names such as the Fair Folk or the Good Neighbors.

Humans are sometimes transported to the fairies' homeland, usually against their will. Fairies live in an otherworld that may be underground, underwater, on an island, in a realm parallel to our own . . . but almost always

BINGO!

OOPS

invisible to humans. Should you find yourself in the fairy realm, consume neither food nor drink. Dining at a fairy feast may trap you in their land forever. ← *I guess they didn't like my company*

If you do encounter a fairy, there are ways to protect yourself. Fairies have a natural aversion to iron, because of the iron weapons that drove them into hiding. Legends suggest they have a similar aversion to salt, bells, and bread. But in rare cases, you might win a fairy's favor. Fairies appreciate generosity and will often reward it in kind. You may be able to win their favor by setting a gift of fresh water, butter, or cheese outside your doorstep at night. Keeping a tidy house may also impress them. *They must love my mom*

Should you ever speak to a fairy, be polite and honest—lying to a fairy is a dangerous endeavor. Should a fairy give you a boon, keep it secret. Bragging about a fairy gift will often result in it disappearing. More than once a braggart found that a gift of gold coins turned to yellow autumn leaves.

Maybe if Bynal and his henchmen had bothered being polite first

Keep these tips in mind, and with luck, your next fairy encounter will have a happy ending!

Allein and I are working on it!

ABOUT THE AUTHOR
AND THE ARTIST

MARIE P. CROALL lives in Cary, North Carolina. She has written for Marvel, DC Comics, Moonstone Books, Devils Due, and Harris Comics, and has completed a self-published graphic novel and a short film. Marie has spent much of her life reading fables and legends, and enjoys discovering new things about different cultures. She is also the author of *Marwe: Into the Land of the Dead* from the Graphic Myths and Legends series.

HYEONDO PARK was born in South Korea and moved to Dallas, Texas, when he was ten. He earned a BFA in cartooning/illustration from the School of Visual Arts in New York City. Hyeondo has illustrated manga adaptations of *The Adventures of Huckleberry Finn* and Shakespeare's *Julius Caesar,* and illustrates *Sam & Lilah* for the acclaimed webcomic site ACT-I-VATE. More of his work can be read on his website at hanaroda.net.